ONE KISS
MORE

Books by Mandy Baxter

One Kiss More

One Night More

Published by Kensington Publishing Corporation

ONE KISS
MORE

Mandy Baxter

ZEBRA BOOKS
KENSINGTON PUBLISHING CORP.
http://www.kensingtonbooks.com

ZEBRA BOOKS are published by

Kensington Publishing Corp.
119 West 40th Street
New York, NY 10018

All Kensington titles, imprints and distributed lines are available at
special quantity discounts for bulk purchases for sales promotion,
premiums, fund-raising, educational or institutional use.

Special book excerpts or customized printings can also be created
to fit specific needs. For details, write or phone the office of the
Kensington Sales Manager. Attn.: Sales Department. Kensington
Publishing Corp., 119 West 40th Street, New York, NY 10018.
Phone: 1-800-221-2647.

Zebra and the Z logo Reg. U.S. Pat. & TM Off.

First Printing: March 2015
ISBN-13: 978-1-4201-3481-0
ISBN-10: 1-4201-3481-7

First Electronic Edition: March 2015
eISBN-13: 978-1-4201-3482-7
eISBN-10: 1-4201-3482-5

10 9 8 7 6 5 4 3 2 1

Printed in the United States of America

Chapter One

Landon McCabe could think of a thousand things he'd rather be doing right now. Skydiving, BASE jumping, climbing to the top of Mount Hood would be nice. When did the running of the bulls begin, anyway? Law enforcement was supposed to be an exciting, adrenaline-infused career. Maybe he should have applied for the Marshals' elite Special Operations Group when he had the chance. Of course, knowing his luck, he'd get an assignment like his friend Galen Kelly had snagged: babysitter to some foreign dignitary for a year. Prestigious? Maybe. But Landon wasn't interested in recognition or prestige. He was in it for the action. Which was why, as he pulled up to the swanky Aspira building in downtown Seattle, he wished he were jumping out of a plane, thousands of feet from the ground. He hadn't felt an exhilarating rush of any kind for a long goddamned time. And like any addict, he was itching for a fix.

He pulled his phone out of his pocket and dialed. After a few rings, Galen answered and the fucker had the nerve to sound upbeat. "Hey, man. Did you see me on *Anderson Cooper* last night?"

Galen had recently come off a case that had landed him not only in the media spotlight, but in bed with the woman he'd been assigned to protect. Lucky bastard. "Yeah. And you know what? It's true what they say about the camera adding ten pounds. You might want to think about hitting the gym."

"Jealous much?"

"Please," Landon scoffed. "I've got nothing to be jealous about. You go ahead and be the poster boy for the Marshals Service while the rest of us go out and get shit done."

Galen's laughter rumbled through the receiver. Playful hostility was what Landon appreciated most about their friendship. Galen deserved his accolades, though. He was damn good at his job. "Have you questioned Ruiz's daughter yet?"

The consummate professional, Galen would forgo the banter for work talk any day of the week, and as always, Landon was on the same page. "On my way up to her condo now," he said as he flashed his badge to the parking attendant at the underground garage. The Aspira had top-of-the-line security, which might make it tough to sneak a fugitive in. On the other hand . . . it might also be the perfect place to hide someone from prying eyes. Landon pulled the phone away from his ear long enough to get directions to the public parking and pulled through the levered gate. "I doubt she's going to be cooperative, though."

"Who's your contact there?"

Technically, the Ruiz case was in the Oregon district's jurisdiction, but since Ruiz's daughter lived in Seattle, the investigation had become an interregional effort. "Ethan Morgan," Landon replied as he hit the key fob with his thumb and locked his black Chevy Tahoe. He pivoted on a heel as he searched out the elevators and found a bank of silver doors on the far left wall. "I'm meeting him at the office later, but I thought I'd get a jump on Emma first."

Galen was silent for a moment, and Landon could almost picture the shit-eating grin on his face. "Get a jump on her, huh?"

"Unlike you, I'm a professional," Landon remarked, as he stepped inside the elevator and hit the button for the twenty-first floor.

"Touché," Galen replied.

"Dude, the French," Landon said with a snort. "So not manly. Later."

Galen's answering laughter was the last thing Landon heard as he ended the call. For the past few days, he'd been staking out Emma Ruiz's building and tracking her every move in the hopes that she'd lead them to her father. But the only thing he'd learned so far in his time on this assignment was that the more things changed, the more they stayed the same. Emma was still a hard-core party girl. She still hung out with pro athletes and rich playboys and lived her life as publicly as she dared, as though she invited the media attention and gossipmongers while simultaneously not giving a shit about any of it.

The Ruiz case had been high profile six years ago when they'd conducted their investigation into the federal judge's dealings with Mendelson Corp. Once one of the country's shrewdest and most successful attorneys, later, the consummate legal hero who defended the little guy, Javier Ruiz had landed a federal judgeship in Oregon after retiring from a firm that dealt primarily in environmental safety and wrongful death suits. His judgeship had taken a nosedive when his dealings with Mendelson had been scrutinized. The U.S. Marshals had gotten involved after he'd dismissed what should have been an open-and-shut FTC trade violation case against the multinational corporation. Through an anonymous tip, the feds had been alerted that Ruiz was extorting money from Mendelson, and the CEO had admitted to paying the judge in exchange for a favorable ruling in their case.

And for the last six years, Emma had been a staunch supporter of her father, declaring his innocence on several national news programs as well as on *E! News* and in the pages of *US Weekly*. A first-class celebutante, Emma was often categorized as famous for being famous, or whatever it was the gossip rags said about overprivileged daddy's girls like her. She had often been whispered about in the Portland office when they'd investigated Javier. At eighteen, she had already been on the road to stop-your-heart gorgeous and had a reputation for playing fast and loose with several pro athletes. She had a mouth on her, not to mention a penchant for fucking with anyone who fucked with her dad. During the course of the Marshals Service's investigation, she'd made it her life's ambition to cause any deputy involved in bringing dear old daddy down a world of hurt. Landon's team had been on the receiving end of several of her malicious pranks including the old potato-in-the-tailpipe routine. That shit wasn't urban legend, and the blowback from the exhaust had damned near asphyxiated him. Not the best experience for a rookie on his first case.

Watching her over the past couple of weeks had stirred up all sorts of memories. One of those being the euphoric rush he experienced every time he laid eyes on her. Landon couldn't explain it. He wasn't usually the sort of guy who got twisted up at the sight of a pretty girl. But Emma was different. Her presence triggered something primal in his subconscious. And that instant, gut-clenching reaction bothered the shit out of him. So, yeah, he wasn't exactly enthused about paying a visit to the now-twenty-four-year-old Emma, and grilling her about daddy's whereabouts while he tried not to fall under her spell yet again. Landon was certain that no matter what, Emma was going to give him a run for his money. Paybacks were a bitch.

Emma Ruiz hung up the phone, her heart racing like a thoroughbred, and stared off into space as she tried to collect her thoughts. One of the benefits of living in a building with the best security money could buy was getting a heads-up from the front desk that a deputy U.S. marshal was about to pay her a visit. Not that she hadn't been expecting it, though the timing could have been better.

She cast a furtive glance toward her closed bedroom door as a riot of butterflies took flight in her stomach and fluttered toward her throat. Everything was happening so fast and she needed to play her A-game right now. The key to a good defense was a strong offense. Any sports fan worth her salt realized that. And Emma knew that if she wanted the ball to be in her court with the Marshals Service, she needed to make sure they were *off* their game. She looked down the length of her purple cami top, black yoga pants, and bare feet. Not exactly an outfit that screamed *I'm in charge!* And while she'd hoped never to go toe-to-toe with those self-righteous do-gooders again, she guessed she had no choice but to suck it up and face the music. At least the next few weeks wouldn't be boring.

When the doorbell rang a few minutes later, Emma took a deep breath and held it in her lungs before expelling it all in a rush. The cops weren't as scary as they liked to come off. Emma wasn't easily intimidated, and besides, she'd done this dance with them six years ago. If she could handle their pushy bullshit then, she could certainly handle it now. She could do this.

A round of obnoxious knocks followed on the heels of the bell and Emma rolled her eyes as she walked to the door. God forbid she keep the U.S. Marshals waiting. After all, they had a dangerous criminal to find and apprehend. She snorted. They were all a bunch of idiots if they thought that Javier Ruiz was a criminal mastermind. So ready to believe he'd orchestrated the perfect escape and itching to get one up on him. And of course, none of them knew how far off base they really were.

Emma curved her lips into what she hoped was a pleasant smile to mask the apprehension creeping up her spine and swung open the door. The smile melted right off of her face and her stomach did a twisting backflip that kicked out at her lungs on the dismount, leaving her breathless and a little stunned. *Great.* They would send the guy who'd arrested her dad in the first place, wouldn't they? The one guy who'd get under her skin. Emma clenched her fists at her sides as she wondered how much jail time she'd get for socking a U.S. marshal in the jaw.

"Deputy McCabe," she said, infusing her voice with innocence. "What a surprise. By all means, *don't* come in."

The bastard had the nerve to smirk.

"Obviously you know why I'm here," McCabe said. "So tell me where Javier is and I'll be on my way."

Emma relaxed against the doorknob, shifting her weight so that her braced arm supported her. It took a lot of effort to look so calm while her knuckles turned white as her fingers clenched the knob in a death grip. Coming face-to-face with Landon McCabe again was like stepping back in time. He was technically the enemy, but even after all this time Emma couldn't deny his appeal. His voice tumbled over her like a cascade of warm water, relaxing the tight knot that had settled in her chest. His blond hair was almost too short, but Emma was willing to bet she could still tangle her fingers in its length. And his eyes . . . keen and bright blue running with veins of gold. A warm spark that, when focused on her, ignited something low in her stomach. Her brow puckered as she realized his presence had become even more commanding, his face even more handsome with the passage of years. Totally not fair.

"Why ask me?" She made sure her voice was devoid of any emotion. If she sounded even a little nervous, McCabe would pick up on it. "When Dad was remanded into the *care* of the U.S. government, I was sort of under the impression that you'd be keeping an eye on him. It's not my fault you guys suck at your jobs."

"Come on, Emma. I'm not in the mood to play games."

Emma saw an opportunity not only to intercept McCabe's innuendo, but to deflect his questioning with her own distraction while she ran in for the touchdown. "That's too bad, Deputy. I love to play. Maybe later? You can be shirts and I'll be skins."

McCabe's jaw tensed, and it gave Emma a perverse sense of satisfaction to have rattled the cocky deputy's chain. The quicker she could get him out of there, the better.

"Mind if I come in? Take a look around?"

What part of *don't come in* did he not understand? "Do you have a warrant?"

His tawny brows pulled down tight over his eyes. "No."

"Then yes, I do mind." Emma's pulse rushed in her ears, nearly drowning out the sound of her own voice. The last thing she needed right now was to have him nosing around her apartment. She fought the urge to glance back at the closed door of her bedroom. No, she *definitely* didn't need to direct his attention there.

"Don't say I didn't try to make this easy on you." His voice hardened and lowered an octave, causing a pleasant chill to trickle from the top of Emma's head down the length of her body. "You'd better clear your schedule for the rest of the day, *Miss* Ruiz. A pair of deputies will be along in an hour or so to escort you to the federal courthouse for questioning."

Yeah, well, Emma could be hard, too. "What's

the matter, McCabe? Not man enough to cuff me yourself?"

He took a step back from her doorway as though resisting the urge to do just that. He looked down the length of her body, and though she assumed it was meant to be disdainful, a thrill rushed through Emma's veins. "Just be ready to cooperate," he said. "Otherwise, I won't hesitate to issue a warrant for your arrest."

Without allowing her to respond, McCabe turned on a heel and sauntered down the hallway toward the elevator. Emma couldn't help it—she leaned out of the doorway to watch him leave, appreciative of the way his designer jeans hugged his ass. Boy was tight. His shoulders rolled as he walked, the precision and grace of every placed step a thing of beauty. Deputy U.S. Marshal Landon McCabe was still the enemy. He was the one who'd arrested her father and the man who was looking to do it again. But, damn, was he ever something to look at.

"That wasn't so hard, was it?"

Emma bristled at the sound of the voice behind her. An icy chill that was nothing like what she felt in Landon's presence chased over her skin, and she rubbed at her arms to banish the goose bumps that rose up there. "I told you, you have nothing to worry about."

"Oh, I know, *chica*. I only wanted to be sure you could play your part. Now that I know you can, I'll leave you alone. For now."

Emma tried to slow the racing of her heart with a few deep breaths. All of this was her fault. If she'd stayed out of trouble like her dad had asked her to, he'd be okay and getting the care he needed right now. "I know what's expected of me," Emma said, still refusing to turn and face the man speaking to her. She just wanted him to get the hell out of her condo.

"Good. That's good." His low voice snaked around her, dark and dangerous. "I'll be in touch."

Emma closed her eyes as he walked past her through the door. His body brushed against hers and she cringed as she inched away. She waited until the sounds of his footsteps disappeared down the hallway before she closed the door with shaking hands and turned the dead bolt into place. Her mind raced as adrenaline seeped into her bloodstream, making it difficult to focus. Landon McCabe's appearance in Seattle was going to be a problem. And she hoped that his interference in her life wouldn't get him killed.

Chapter Two

Landon sat in a bland, undecorated cubicle in the Seattle field office staring at a computer screen with Emma Ruiz's face plastered all over it. The website was dedicated to local Seattle gossip, and the images depicted a ruffled-looking Emma being escorted into a nightclub under the arm of Tyson Kennedy, the starting sweeper for the Seattle Sounders. People here were crazy for soccer; it rivaled the fanaticism seen in the European leagues. Emma might as well have been hanging on the arm of a king as far as the fans were concerned. One of Tyson's hands jutted out at the camera, as if to shield her from the gawkers while his other hand was wrapped protectively around her shoulder. And why did that image make Landon want to sock Tyson in the jaw?

"I take it your visit didn't go well?"

Landon turned his chair around to face Ethan Morgan. As the liaison for the Ruiz investigation, the Seattle-based deputy had been assigned to keep an eye on Emma's comings and goings as well as monitor her landline and computer usage. A judge had approved the warrant within hours of Ruiz's escape, but so far, their monitoring of his daughter had failed to turn up any clues as to the former judge's whereabouts.

"About as well as a dive off a three-hundred-foot cliff without a parachute," Landon replied. "It's not like I expected her to cooperate, I just hoped that maybe the son of a bitch would be sitting in her living room or some shit."

Ethan laughed. "It'd be nice if it worked out that way. But I have a feeling Ruiz is long gone. Probably halfway to Mexico or South America by now."

Manhunts, like missing-person investigations, focused on the critical first forty-eight hours. It rankled that they'd hit dead end after dead end those initial two days. It was like the son of a bitch had simply vanished into thin air. And while the smart move would have been to hightail it out of the country, Landon doubted that would have been Ruiz's move.

"Nah. He and Emma are tight. Plus, the man has cancer. It's a wonder he escaped at all. He's got to be in the city somewhere."

"Maybe the old man is already out of the country and Emma's waiting for the heat to die down so she can fly out and meet him," Ethan suggested.

"No." Landon couldn't explain it, but his intuition told him that fleeing the country wasn't the plan. "Emma knows where he is and he's close. We just have to get her to come clean."

Ethan gave a disbelieving chuckle. "Good luck

with that. She makes stubborn look downright accommodating."

"That's one way to put it," Landon laughed.

"She's agreed to come in for an interview, though, right?"

Landon hadn't exactly asked, but she didn't have a choice. It was either come in or be arrested. The eighteen-year-old Emma probably would have opted for the arrest, but would the older, hopefully wiser Emma be more cooperative? *Shit*. Maybe he should have cuffed her and brought her in himself. "I wouldn't waste any time in picking her up. The sooner, the better."

Ethan smiled. "I'll take Courtney and go now. What are the chances of getting the rest of the case files on Ruiz by this afternoon? I'd like to take a closer look so I'm better acquainted with the history."

"The hard copies of the case files should be here no later than three," Landon said. "What we have on the case has been archived so it took a little effort to drag it all out again. Six years." He shook his head. "Why, after so long, would Ruiz attempt an escape?"

"It's not an attempt," Ethan replied. "The bastard did it. Sick, no less."

"It doesn't make sense," Landon said. "He wasn't in a supermax. We're talking Club Fed. All the amenities a white-collar criminal could ask for, including top-of-the-line medical care. Dude was getting the taxpayers' money's worth in that facility. So why bounce?"

"Emma?" Ethan suggested. "Maybe he figured he

didn't have much time left and he wanted to get square with her before he checked out."

"No. I went through the visitor logs. She saw him once a week. And the drive from Seattle to Sheridan isn't exactly a short one. They weren't estranged so it can't be Emma. But I don't doubt for a second that she knows not only where he is, but why he planned an escape."

"Once a week seems like a pretty frequent number of visits, even for a doting daughter. Do you think she was in on it?"

"I hope not." As it was, she'd be in hot water if she was harboring a fugitive. If she engaged in conspiracy by helping her father to escape . . . well, the gossip rags would certainly have a field day with the story and Emma would have thrown her life away to help a dying man escape from prison.

"At any rate, we'll try to get something out of her. Anything I need to know about the illustrious Miss Ruiz before I pick her up?"

Landon chuckled, "Yeah. Don't let her fuck with your car."

Ethan quirked a brow. "I have a feeling there's a story behind that, and I want it when I get back."

"Sorry, man. That one's in the vault."

Ethan gave Landon a mock salute in parting and took off through the maze of cubicles toward the far end of the main office. As he contemplated their conversation, Landon couldn't help but wonder if Emma's frequent visits to the federal prison weren't part of a motive completely separate from a daughter's concern for her ailing father. *Come to think of it* . . . Landon made a mental note to have Ruiz's medical records subpoenaed. Maybe the bastard wasn't quite as sick as he let on.

He pulled up his contact list on his phone and dialed Galen's cell. After four rings, he finally answered, "Kelly."

"You know, when you sound all professional and tough like that it makes my heart skip a beat."

"Funny," Galen replied, "Harper tells me the same thing."

Gag. The last thing Landon wanted to hear about was Galen's oh-so-perfect relationship with *The Oregonian*'s star political reporter. *Moving on . . .* "Has the prison transport team been questioned yet?"

Something didn't add up. No way could Ruiz have escaped without help. Granted, he was a minimum-security prisoner, but still, he would have been outnumbered three to one. Even healthy, he would have had a tough time getting free without outside help.

"The warden sent over their official statements right after the escape, but Monroe and I are headed to Sheridan later today to conduct formal interviews. Want me to look out for anything specific?"

Specifics were tough when Landon wasn't sure what he was looking for. He knew their chief deputy would be thorough, but he couldn't shake the feeling that this was somehow an inside job. "All I know is that something about Ruiz's escape doesn't add up. I'm pretty sure he had help. If it wasn't inside assistance, it was someone who was pretty damned connected. The prison staff could know something. It might not be a bad idea to shake them up a bit. Give them a reason to fold. Damn it, I really should be conducting these interviews myself."

"Kind of tough to be in two places at once," Galen said with a laugh.

"No doubt. Morgan is bringing Emma in for questioning soon. We'll rattle her cage a little, too, because I'm sure she knows more than she's letting on."

"So you didn't charm the information out of her this morning?" Galen joked.

Landon scoffed, "Not even close."

"She still hot?"

Despite the fact that she'd been only eighteen when they'd first arrested Ruiz, his daughter's good looks had often been a topic of conversation amongst some of the deputies, Landon and Galen included. Landon considered her long, dark, curling hair, large brown eyes, and full, pouty lips. And he'd been trying *not* to think about the way the lush, more filled-out curves of her body had looked in that little top and spandex pants all goddamned morning. "She's still hot," he said. Hotter. Like, surface-of-the-freaking-sun hot. "But she's still a raging pain in the ass, too."

"If anything, she'll keep you on your toes. I'll check in after we've interviewed the prison staff."

"Sounds good," Landon said. "Later."

He ended the call, the gears in his mind spinning faster than his thoughts could keep pace with. The Ruiz case had always rubbed him the wrong way. The man had money to spare and so his motives in extorting money from Mendelson in exchange for a favorable ruling in their case had never quite added up to him. And when they'd arrested the judge, Ruiz hadn't proclaimed his innocence or acted overly offended by the charges the way some suspects did.

Nope, the dude had just whispered something in his daughter's ear, kissed her on the cheek, and gone with them willingly.

After all this time, the case still bothered him. Six years, and Emma could still get under his skin. But he was on the job and no matter how beautiful or tempting she was, Emma Ruiz was *off-limits*. Landon hoped that he could follow his own advice and keep her at arm's length. Otherwise, he was as good as fired. With nothing more than a look, she could make him feel a rush that equaled diving headfirst out of a plane. It was a feeling he craved. Couldn't get enough of.

And that was a huge fucking problem.

Emma fought the disappointment that settled on her like a black cloud when she answered her door to find two deputy U.S. marshals—neither of which were Landon McCabe—waiting to escort her to their office for an interview. And how pathetic was she that even though she should hate him right down to his trendy leather loafers, she still wanted to see him? Pretty damned sad.

"Miss Ruiz, I'm Deputy U.S. Marshal Ethan Morgan, this is Deputy Kevin Courtney. I believe Deputy McCabe mentioned we'd be by?"

Emma eyed the two marshals, cocking her head to the side as though trying to recall if she had, in fact, been visited by McCabe, and took a moment to size them up. Morgan was cute enough, with bright green eyes and short-clipped, russet hair. His partner wasn't too bad, either, though maybe a little rougher around the edges. What was it with law

enforcement guys, anyway? Did they all get their hair
cut at the same salon? *U.S. marshal special, please.* But
neither of them appealed to her the way that blond,
snarky pain in the ass McCabe did.

"Am I under arrest?" she asked.

Morgan smiled. He was definitely cuter when he
smiled. "No, ma'am. We just want to ask you a few
questions."

Ma'am? For the love of all that was holy, she was
barely twenty-four. Didn't these guys know that the
fastest way to insult a woman was to call her *ma'am?*
Emma leaned against the door frame and positioned her hand at her hip. "Can't we talk here,
then? I don't have any more to say to you two gentle-
men than I did to Deputy McCabe this morning."

Morgan's eyes hardened. Emma wondered if he
liked playing good cop or bad cop. "Regardless, I'm
going to have to insist that you come with us."

"Or . . . ?" She let the word dangle, daring him to
throw down.

"Or I'll consider you hostile. *Then* you'll be under
arrest, Miss Ruiz."

Oh, he totally liked to be the bad cop. "All right.
But give me a minute. I'm not really dressed to go
out."

Morgan gave her a tight smile. "You don't mind if
we wait inside?"

Deputy Bad Cop was looking for an excuse to
snoop around. Or was totally paranoid. What did he
think she was going to do? It wasn't as if her apartment had a back door. The only other escape route
was to jump off the balcony, and Emma wasn't planning any daredevil stunts quite yet. "Of course," she
said, every word dripping with honey. "Make your-
selves at home. Watch TV. Raid the fridge. I won't

be too long." She turned, leaving the door wide open, and stalked through her living room without a glance back. Once inside her bedroom, she closed the door behind her and collapsed on the bed. She hoped they liked mindless morning TV, because she wasn't even close to being ready to leave with them.

Emma stared up at the ceiling and took a deep, cleansing breath. And then another. Nervous energy skittered through her limbs as her heart pounded in her chest. "I can do this, I can do this, I can do this. . . ." She repeated the mantra over and over again, psyching herself up for what she had to do. Cesar had made it perfectly clear what was expected of her, not to mention what was at stake if she failed to deliver.

If the only thing she had to contend with in the interview room was Deputy Bad Cop and his less interesting partner, Emma was pretty sure she'd be fine. But if they brought McCabe in on her interrogation, she doubted she'd be able to keep it together and her dad's life depended on her maintaining a level head.

"Miss Ruiz?" Deputy Morgan's voice came on the heels of a knock at her door. "You need to get moving."

A not-so-subtle reminder that he'd arrest her ass if she didn't get it in gear. The media was already going to have a field day with her, and they'd crucify her if they saw her looking anything less than perfect. So, she pushed herself off the bed and headed for the bathroom. "Almost ready," she called. "Give me ten minutes."

"I'll give you five," Morgan replied. "And not a minute more."

* * *

The media circus camped outside of her building was no less than Emma expected. And though they'd avoided the bulk of reporters by leaving via the underground parking garage, another crowd of gawkers was waiting for her at the federal building. Which piqued her interest, since no one should have known where she was headed. A leak in the Marshals office, maybe? It was something to consider. When she was younger, she'd reveled in the attention, posing for the cameras as she hopped from one nightclub to another. With her father in prison, she'd used the party scene and crowds of people to banish the bone-deep loneliness and depression that had threatened to lay her low.

"Emma, Emma!" Several reporters shouted her name, and questions that ranged from, "Do you know where your father is?" and "Are you under arrest?" to "Who are you wearing?" assaulted her ears. In the confusion, she could do nothing but allow Deputy Morgan to help her out of the car and escort her into the building. For once, Emma wished for quiet anonymity. Couldn't these guys find someone more exciting to follow around? Wasn't Lady Gaga in town this weekend for a concert or something? Emma wasn't even that interesting, for shit's sake. And seriously, *Who are you wearing?* What was wrong with people?

Conversation was nonexistent as Emma checked in as a visitor at the front desk and was issued a temporary ID badge while her purse went through a scanner. She walked through the metal detector, glad she wasn't wearing anything that would set off an alarm. The last thing she needed was a full-body search. Especially with the paparazzi outside doing their best to get a glimpse of her.

"This way, Miss Ruiz."

The sound of Deputy Morgan's voice woke her from her stupor, and she followed him to a set of elevators. For the most part, the ride to the seventh floor was just a notch below excruciatingly uncomfortable. Right now they were treating her with a modicum of respect and professionalism. But once they stepped into that interview room, she knew without a doubt that the gloves would come off.

When the elevator doors finally slid open, Emma released the breath she'd been holding—and then choked on the intake as she came face-to-face with McCabe. "No cuffs?" he teased as she stepped out into the hallway.

"I'm cooperative, Deputy McCabe," she replied as though offended. She followed Deputies Morgan and Courtney out of the elevator and McCabe fell in step beside her as they made their way down the hall. "I even got all dressed up for you."

Since she was sixteen, Emma had used flirting as a shield. Worn sweet smiles like a suit of armor, and perfected the art of steamy stares to black-belt level. She never felt as if she could truly be herself, and so she'd developed her femme fatale persona, an alter ego to hide behind when it was too hard to be the real Emma, the girl who liked to lounge around in sweats and watch football on Sundays. The woman who preferred peace and quiet, and would rather spend the evening writing code or working on developing a high-functioning website than tossing back drinks and shaking her ass on the dance floor. The duality of it all wore her down. But she guarded that secret part of her with the fierceness of a pit bull. She trusted very few people—less than a handful— and not even Landon McCabe was worthy of anything more than the façade.

His gaze swept the length of her body, from her knee-high stiletto boots, up her thighs clad in clingy denim, and the short leather jacket covering her black silk tank top. A momentary flare of heat sparked in the depths of his blue eyes, but he quickly recovered, replacing the expression with disinterest. "I'm interested in one thing and one thing only, Emma: finding your father before he gets himself into any more trouble." He turned his attention to Deputy Morgan and said, "Ethan, where would you like to do this?"

Morgan and Courtney continued on ahead of them, and Morgan answered, "There's an interview room two doors down to our right. We'll use that one."

Without a word—or a second glance—McCabe caught up with the other two deputies and led the way down the hall. Crap. Okay, so maybe she hadn't been able to dazzle him on her first attempt, but she was still in field goal range and, as far as Emma was concerned, had another down to go. Her flirty behavior was nothing more than an artfully planned defense. A sleight of hand meant to distract. To deflect scrutiny. Flirting was all about showing interest. As a general rule, people enjoyed attention—it was human nature. By giving attention, she was taking it away from herself. And most people didn't even realize they were being maneuvered. The question was, would she be able to pull one over on McCabe and his cronies?

Or would they see right through her act?

Chapter Three

How in the hell could Landon possibly be expected to concentrate while cooped up with Emma in a room the size of a closet? Her scent enveloped him, a cloud of vanilla and honeysuckle that dulled his mind and heated his blood. *I even got all dressed up for you.* Jesus. His mouth had gone dry at her seductive tone even though he knew she was playing him, trying to draw his focus and scramble his thoughts. Well, it fucking worked. Putting one foot in front of the other was damned near impossible when all he wanted to do was turn around and drink in the sight of her in those ridiculously tight jeans and that black leather jacket that just barely skimmed her waistband, hugging every curve.

That outfit, coupled with the wild curls of her dark hair and smoky eyes, made Emma look like sin that was worth going to hell for. And right about now, Landon could feel the flames licking at his skin. *Do not let her get the upper hand here. So what if she's gorgeous? You're in charge here, not her.* Yeah, right. As though that little bit of self-coaching were going to do anything about the blood that was slowly draining from his brain and venturing south.

As a professional courtesy, Morgan and his partner hung back, allowing Landon to run point. They flanked him on either side of a rectangular table, all three of them facing Emma. If that wasn't intimidating, he didn't know what was. If they played this right, they'd have her singing whatever song they wanted by the time this interview was over and he'd have Javier Ruiz in custody before dinner. *Great. Awesome. Fan-freaking-tastic.* The sooner he could get away from Emma and her intoxicating, adrenaline-spiking presence, the better.

"All right, let's get to it." There was no point in wasting time on pleasantries. "When was the last time you spoke with your father, Emma?"

"Hmm . . ." Emma tilted her head to one side, exposing the long column of her neck. Landon swallowed and reached for the carafe of water and one of the glasses that had been left on the table. She shrugged out of her jacket, revealing a flimsy top, the fabric soft and clingy, exposing the curves of her breasts. Had someone turned the heat up? He could barely take a breath it was so damned stifling. "I try to visit him at least twice a month. More if I'm able. You can check the records at the prison to corroborate, but I have nothing to hide. The last time I spoke to him was two weeks ago. On June seventh. I drove up to Sheridan to see him."

She'd spoken to her father eight days before his escape. The timing could certainly put her in a position to be considered an accessory. "And where were you last week on the morning of June fifteenth? The day that your father escaped federal custody?" Landon swallowed down half a glass of water, allowing the liquid to quench the heat of Emma's dark gaze. A surge of adrenaline coursed through his veins, the high miraculously steering his focus. He wasn't some twenty-four-year-old rookie anymore. He refused to let Emma get one over on him.

"I was with Tyson Kennedy that night," she replied. "From about . . ." She pulled her bottom lip in between her straight, white teeth, as her eyes gazed high and to the left—an indication that her story might be fabricated. "Eight in the evening until two or three the next morning. We visited several clubs downtown. I'm sure if you asked around you could find two or three people who saw us out that night."

"We'll check it out," Morgan replied from his right side. "We'll need the names of those clubs, Emma."

"Oh, sure," she all but purred. "The War Room, Sixty-Nine . . ." Emma paused, and this time her gaze was focused squarely on Morgan. Her time frame might be fabricated, but the clubs she'd been to weren't. "Oh, and a hot little dive bar in Belltown called The Pit. I remember because the bartender there, Levi, is *hot.*"

Morgan scribbled the names on a notepad and reclined back in his chair as Landon asked, "And what about the week since your father's escape? Has he called, dropped by, sent you any e-mails? Had any contact whatsoever with you?"

Emma rolled her eyes and let out a derisive snort. "You know what your problem is, McCabe?" No, but he was pretty sure she was about to tell him. "You always jump to conclusions. You've got that self-righteous cop attitude down pat, and because you have the so-called *law* on your side, you fail to look past the obvious answer to any question."

"Spoken like someone who's *breaking* the law," Landon remarked. Truth be told, he had no idea what she was talking about. There were no obvious answers where Javier's escape was concerned. If there had been, he'd be in custody right now. "But since you're so keen to enlighten me on my short-comings, tell me, Emma, what is the obvious answer I'm missing?"

Emma let out a slow sigh as her gaze shifted low and to the right. Now she was hiding something. "No, he hasn't called, e-mailed, or stopped by for a visit. I haven't seen or heard from him since the day I drove to Sheridan to visit him."

Not a lie, but not the truth, either. "Would you tell me if he had contacted you?"

Emma leveled her gaze on Landon, and those big brown eyes of hers all but swallowed him whole. "No," she said. "I wouldn't."

Landon leaned back in his chair and studied Emma for a quiet moment. He was getting nowhere with her, which was exactly what he'd expected. His only choice at this point was to treat her as hostile, which, knowing Emma, would only make her more antagonistic. This was a lose/lose situation no matter how Landon approached it so he'd give her one last chance to play nice.

"Emma." Her name rolled off his tongue, and though it was a technique used to make her feel a sense of familiarity, Landon couldn't ignore how the sound of it punched into his gut with a pleasant ripple. Sort of like diving off of a high cliff into the ocean below. His breath caught as though he were under water, and it took a conscious effort to breach the surface and convince his lungs to work again. "We're on the same side here. We both want to find your dad. I know he's not well and he's not going to get the medical attention he needs on the run. Help us help him."

"Don't talk to me about my dad's health," she snapped. Well, that tactic crashed and burned. "He wouldn't even be in this situation if you'd done your job right the first time. We are not on the same side, McCabe. We never will be. You don't care about my father's health, so do me a favor and *don't* use it in your attempt to psychologically manage me, okay?"

Damn. For a minute, Landon wished he had the flirty, vapid representation of *Emma Ruiz, Spoiled Socialite* that she'd thrown at him upon exiting the elevator. He could deal with that aspect of her personality because he knew it was a front, a wall she put up to keep others out. This fiery, intelligent, assertive, no-holds-barred woman sitting in front of him was the real Emma. And, damn, did she ever turn him on.

"Oh, you'll know when I'm managing you." Morgan gave him a look, but Landon couldn't be bothered to feel repentant over his own flirtatious tone. Where Emma was concerned, caution and good sense didn't exist. "Do you know what conspiracy is, Emma?"

"Do I look like a child to you, McCabe? Or an idiot?"

No, she certainly didn't look like either. He dragged his gaze from the tantalizing swell of her breasts as a tight smile tugged at his lips. "You've got a good life, a career, friends . . ." Was there a boyfriend in that mix? "I don't want to see you throw it all away. I know your dad wouldn't want you to, either."

"You know nothing about my dad," Emma bit out. "You know, for the record, McCabe, putting cuffs on a man doesn't make you BFFs."

Landon shrugged a shoulder. "You're probably right, but I do know that he loves you and that he wouldn't want to see you throw your life away to protect him. If you tell us what you know, his punishment might be less severe. If not, there's a pretty good possibility he'll spend the rest of his life in prison."

Emma regarded Landon, again tilting her head to the side and giving him an unhindered view of her lovely throat. "Well, in that case, I guess I'd better spill my guts."

Seriously, did McCabe's *I'm on your side, help me to help you* routine ever gain him any ground with suspects?

Either the criminal set he was used to dealing with was way dumber than Emma expected or McCabe was *so* full of himself that he couldn't smell his own ripe bullshit. Well, he was about to have a rude awakening. He could threaten her all he wanted, spew concern and tell her he was on her side until the cows came home, she still wasn't going to play ball. Not now or ever. And as far as arresting her? Let him try. He had nothing on her. She'd be out by dinner.

All three deputies sat up straighter in their seats at her words, their eyes round as they waited for her big reveal. It didn't take much bait to hook these eager fish. It was almost too easy. Emma leaned forward in her chair as though about to share a coveted secret. "Here's what I *know*. The male seahorse carries the babies, not the female. The top speed of a cheetah clocks in at about sixty miles per hour. More men than women are color-blind. The first computer programmer was a woman—which, in my opinion is pretty damned awesome. And, the first programming language was called Fortran—sounds super sci-fi, right? There are more than three hundred and fifty of those little dimples in a golf ball, and tug-of-war was an actual Olympic event in the early nineteen hundreds." Emma took a deep breath and watched as Landon's cheeks turned a lovely shade of scarlet. A couple more random facts might cause steam to billow out of his ears. "Babe Ruth used to wear a cabbage leaf under his hat, and—"

"I can arrest you right now, Emma. Is that what you want?"

McCabe's tone was no longer playful or even friendly. Instead, it carried a dark edge that caused a pleasant shudder to fan from the center of Emma's stomach as it rippled outward through her limbs. She couldn't resist pushing him a bit further and held out her hands, wrists upturned. "I've always wondered what it would be like to have you cuff me, McCabe."

Without a word, he shoved his chair back, the feet scraping on the floor tiles as he stood. His jaw was clenched tight, the muscle at his cheek twitching as he headed for the door and yanked it open. He slammed it behind him and Emma jumped in her seat, startled despite feeling just a tad smug over the way she'd managed to rattle his chain. She turned her attention to the remaining two deputies and said, "Want me to keep going? I know so much more than what I've already told you."

Truth be told, now that McCabe was out of the room, Emma finally felt like she could take a decent breath. If he had any clue that his very presence was more disarming than any hard-lined questioning, Emma would have sung like a canary the moment she sat in her chair. He wanted to talk to her about crimes? It was downright criminal for him to look so damned good in his designer jeans, crisp dress shirt that hugged every tight muscle of his body, and gray suit vest with matching white and gray striped tie. His outfit must have cost more than a couple days' pay, but one little factoid Emma hadn't spilled in her long confession: she happened to know that Landon McCabe was *loaded*. Like, my-other-car-is-a-Bentley loaded. It had always piqued her interest, why a guy who could live comfortably off of a generous trust fund would choose to work in law enforcement. She wondered how many of his colleagues knew that little tidbit about him. A simple Google search would tell them all they needed to know.

"While I'm sure you find yourself very entertaining, Miss Ruiz," Deputy Morgan began, interrupting her train of thought, "this is serious business and I think we'd better get back on track. Don't you?"

Sure. Why not. Now that McCabe was out of the room, there was nothing here to interest her. She'd answer their questions, though she doubted she'd say anything they wanted to hear. "All right, Deputy. Step up to the plate. Let's see what you've got."

* * *

Landon raked his fingers through his hair as he let out a frustrated gust of breath. Emma needed someone to take her across his knee and give her a good spanking. Unfortunately, the thought of having Emma's tight, round ass within touching distance didn't evoke images of punishment. Rather, Landon took it to an erotic extreme and it only caused the blood to pump harder in his veins. *Damn.*

She wound him so tight he felt as if he might spring a hundred feet in the air at any moment. Her smart-ass responses revved him up for a challenge he was more than ready to accept. Landon prided himself on being one step ahead of the criminals he hunted, and this interrogation had only managed to prove that, when it came to Emma, he was going to have to step up his game. She taunted him with her very presence, that tight outfit leaving nothing to the imagination. And those boots! He couldn't help but picture her naked wearing nothing but the knee-high leather with the four-inch heels. And what's worse, he knew that she'd deliberately dressed that way to throw his focus. Hell, she'd all but confessed it to him the second she'd stepped out of the elevator.

And what the fuck was wrong with him that he fell for it?

The unflappable Landon McCabe, tilted off his axis by five feet four inches of fiery female. *Stellar.*

Landon continued to pace, allowing the *tap, tap, tap* of his shoes on the industrial carpeting to calm his roiling temper. He counted each step, one to ten and then ten to one, until his mind was no longer clouded with visions of Emma's face and he no longer smelled her lingering floral-vanilla scent. His head snapped up on his tenth pass down the hallway as the door to the interview room swung open and Emma emerged with Morgan and his partner a mere step behind her. Emma paused and glanced down one end of the hallway and then the other, her full mouth curving into a sweet smile when her eyes landed on him.

Morgan's gaze followed and his brow furrowed. "This way, Miss Ruiz. Deputy Courtney will take you back to your apartment." He held up a palm indicating the way they'd come and she fell into step beside Morgan's colleague. Landon stopped dead in his tracks, nothing more than a hunk of metal drawn to the magnetic sway of her hips. She walked down the hallway to the elevator and stepped inside. Turning to face him, her dark eyes smoldered as she stared a hole straight through his chest. As the doors slid shut, she lifted her hand and wiggled her fingers in a silent good-bye.

He was so, *so* fucked.

Morgan made a beeline for him, his own steps precisely placed and his face an impassive mask. *Way to make an impression on the Seattle boys, you dumb ass.* No doubt his behavior instilled them with all sorts of confidence in his ability to locate Javier Ruiz and wrap this case up in a pretty bow. "You okay, McCabe? You look pretty wound."

Tight as a motherfucking spring.

"Yeah, well, you'd think after six years, she wouldn't be able to push my buttons. Guess I was wrong."

Morgan laughed. "She's something, no doubt about that."

"Did you get anything out of her after I left?" He figured that *in a huff* went without saying.

"Nothing. She knows how to evade questioning. In fact, she deflects better than anyone I've ever seen. But I do think she knows something. If she doesn't know exactly where he father is hiding, she's at least been in contact with him."

"Agreed." She wouldn't have been such a smart-ass if she weren't trying to lead them off the scent. "I'll keep an eye on her tonight. Maybe we'll get lucky and she'll do something other than club hop for a change."

"Could be," Morgan said, thoughtful. "Has it occurred to you that she might be using the clubs as cover? Maybe she's meeting someone inside who's using the crowds to hide out."

"I was thinking the same thing," Landon admitted. "If she goes out tonight, I'll follow her inside, keep a close eye on her. Are you up for a stake-out?"

Morgan smiled. "Sure. I've got nothing going on tonight. Might as well."

"Great. Get set up and I'll meet you outside of her apartment at around seven."

"Sounds good," Morgan replied. "See you then."

Another night spent watching Emma Ruiz. As Landon followed Morgan back toward his office, he had to wonder, how long could he look and not touch?

Chapter Four

Landon took the ticket from the valet and slid it into his pocket. He'd dressed to blend in, so nothing about his outfit screamed, *I could totally arrest your ass.* Rather, he'd opted for a pair of True Religion jeans, a Bogosse button-up, and a pair of Corvari high-top biker boots. The only accessories on his body were the Bulgari watch his parents had given him on his twenty-first birthday and a nearly invisible earpiece and remote mic. He'd left his sidearm and cuffs locked in the glove box of his SUV along with his badge. For all intents and purposes, he was nothing more than some random guy, hanging out and seeing the sights. Morgan and his partner were staking out the downtown club they'd followed Emma to tonight, and Landon's job was to be their eyes on the inside.

Landon had to agree with Morgan that her recent outings were suspicious to say the least. Despite her party-girl rep, there was no way Emma would be clubbing while her terminally ill father was on the run. She liked to pretend that she didn't have a care in the world, but in his previous dealings with her, Landon had seen another side to the wild child. Emma truly cared about her dad. The only explanation for her going out tonight was that she was planning to meet with someone and needed the club as cover—or she was drawing the marshals' focus in order to sneak something past them. Both were viable possibilities, which was why Morgan had filed a request for a wiretap in Emma's condo. All they were waiting for was a federal judge to sign off and a team would be in place, ready to roll and perform the installation.

So really, Emma's leaving her apartment was a win for them either way.

The trick to gaining admittance to these "hot spots" was knowing someone at the door, having the cash to buy your way in, or looking like you belonged. Luckily, Landon had the cash and the look. If Galen could see him now, his friend would be laughing his ass off, right after he ridiculed him mercilessly for his taste in clothes. Galen hadn't grown up with money. Fuck, the guy hadn't even had parents who could get it together enough to take care of him and his sister. But they'd done well enough on their own. Though Galen didn't have a lot of money or status, he was one of the most level people Landon knew, and there was no one he'd rather have at his back.

While Galen had spent most of his adolescence scraping by, Landon's experience swung toward the opposite end of the spectrum. His family had wealth, privilege, and high-society clout. Landon's own trust fund was large enough to set him up for the rest of his life. All he had to do to get his hands on the bulk of it as opposed to receiving a monthly stipend was to ditch the U.S. Marshals Service.

Well, fuck that shit.

His old man could go to hell. No way was Landon turning his back on the only thing he gave a shit about for a few bucks. Okay, so maybe it was closer to several million, not that it mattered. Though he'd grown up surrounded by old money, tight-assed corporate CEOs, and big shots without compassion or morals, apparently the worst thing his father's only son could do was choose law enforcement as a career. There were days when Landon thought his dad would've been more proud had he become a drug czar or inside trader. For his dad, it was all about having weight to throw around, people to intimidate, and wealth to lord over those who would never be your better. Apparently the badge, honor, dedication to justice, and the clout that carrying a .40-caliber sidearm brought weren't good enough.

Hugh McCabe was exactly like the assholes at Mendelson Corp. He was the sort of rich, entitled asshole who didn't think twice about paying someone off to keep his company out of the news—or out of court. Maybe that's why the Ruiz case had stuck with Landon after so many years. Because Javier and that dick Mike Shanahan at Mendelson reminded him of the family he tried like hell to distance himself from. Yeah, that was it. It had absolutely nothing to do with a certain fiery, dark-eyed beauty.

At any rate, Landon didn't need his uptight family or anyone else to feel validated. Galen and the Marshals Service were his family now. At least they didn't turn their noses up at him when he was jonesing for fast food—

"McCabe? You copy?"

Morgan's voice came through his earpiece and Landon snapped to attention. He was on the job and needed to get his shit straight and focus. "Yeah, I copy."

"Do you have eyes on Ruiz?"

Landon scanned the club as he walked, weeding through the throngs of people in search of Emma. Near the VIP area, he spotted a large group of people surrounding some point of interest. It didn't take an investigative genius to discern who was at the center of all the attention. He edged his way closer, careful to keep his profile turned to the group. Through the press of bodies, he caught sight of her dark, curling hair and his chest constricted. Okay, so maybe his obsession with the case had to do with more than just her dad. . . .

"I've got eyes," he said after a moment. "She's in the VIP lounge."

After the initial excitement of her appearance subsided, Landon finally had an unobstructed view of the subject. It was easier to think of her as simply another suspect, rather than focus on her shapely legs, showcased by the short black skirt she wore, or the plunging neckline of her top that bared one shoulder and left little to the imagination. The way her skin glowed like oiled bronze in the low light of the club, flawless and smooth made his fingers itch to touch her. *Jesus.* Landon gave himself a mental slap to the face. *Snap out of it, you dumb son of a bitch. The last thing you need right now is to be obsessing over someone who's a person of freaking interest!* He might be a smart-ass, but Landon prided himself on his professionalism. And fantasizing about touching Emma Ruiz was less than upstanding job performance.

"We got word our wiretap was approved. I have a team heading over to the Aspira to do the install. What's up on your end?"

Damn. The boys in Seattle moved fast. Which was good for Landon, because he needed to get this shit wrapped up so he could get his ass home and as far from Emma as possible. "Not much. I'll let you know when she's on the move. So far, looks like she's just out to be out."

"Ah, well," Morgan responded. "Even if tonight doesn't produce anything, at least we got the wiretap."

Landon shifted so that a trio of girls blocked him from Emma's line of sight. "Yup. It's a win."

The hip-hop and top-forty crap the DJ was spinning did little for Landon's deteriorating mood. As he watched a guy who was pushing seven feet tall bend over Emma and kiss her on the cheek, he could damned near hear the enamel of his molars grinding together. And when she squealed with surprise and threw her arms around him, Landon was pretty sure his jaw permanently locked. Who the hell was he? And why did it cause his chest to burn and his muscles to contract at the thought that this guy meant something to Emma?

He sipped from a glass of ginger ale, not even bothering to hide the scowl that had settled on his face. Emma and the tall bastard hanging on her every word seemed to be enjoying themselves. He could tell from her easy expression that she was comfortable with this guy. Enjoyed his company. Her smile was bright and genuine, and it caused something in Landon's chest to crack. He imagined what it would feel like to have her look at him with that same expression, so honest and happy. Totally and completely at ease. She sipped from a wineglass as they talked and laughed, virtually ignoring everyone around them. Tall, dark, and annoying put one large hand on Emma's bare shoulder, and Landon shot to his feet, anger burning in his gut at the intimate contact.

As if you have any right to be jealous, you dumb asshole.

From the corner of his eye, Landon caught a man making his way toward the VIP room. This one made his hackles rise as years of training triggered his intuition. No way was this guy here to party, and the way he sauntered through the crowd, his left arm tucked tight against his body, made Landon think that he might have a piece holstered under his shoulder. Crafty bastard too, to get a weapon past the bouncers frisking people at the door. It might have been a good idea to alert Morgan of a potential problem, but Landon held back. He watched as the man pushed through the crowd, clubbers moving away from him as though spurred by some warning instinct. This guy was no stranger to intimidation. He wielded it as sure as the weapon he had stashed under his jacket.

Landon brought his phone up as though he were reading something on the screen and snapped off a few shots with the camera. Odds were they wouldn't turn out. It was too dark and the zoom feature sucked balls. But maybe they could enhance the image back at the office and get it clear enough for the facial recognition software to pick something up. Their techs were wizards with that shit.

Landon worked his way closer to the VIP lounge, all the while committing every detail of the guy headed for Emma to memory. Hispanic male, mid-thirties, dressed like he had the cash to back up his swagger, buzzed hair tight to his skull, five-eight or so, a buck eighty at the most, with a scar below his left eye and a nondescript tattoo on his left forearm. Maybe gang-related? His lip seemed to be upturned in a permanent sneer, and his dark eyes were narrowed with suspicion. He shouldered his way past the tall, possible pro athlete Emma had been hugging and grabbed her by the arm.

A burst of adrenaline shot through Landon's system as a protective urge spurred him forward. She did a good job of masking her panic, and there was recognition in her eyes. Emma knew the guy, but it was obvious they weren't friends. The maybe-athlete was elevated in Landon's opinion when he stepped in to help. Actually, he could have been more interested in asserting himself as the alpha after being shoved over, as the guy disregarded Emma's well-being entirely for a *real* manly chest-bumping session. What was it with guys like that? They thought invading each other's space was a show of dominance. Landon didn't bother with trivialities. He threw punches first and asked questions later.

The look of alarm on Emma's face commanded Landon's attention as she stepped into the fray. As though she needed to diffuse what was about to become a very dangerous situation, she placed her hand on the chest of the athlete, careful to avoid touching the would-be gangster.

Interesting.

What in the hell have you gotten yourself mixed up in, Emma?

Emma had agreed to meet Cesar here because it creeped her out to be alone in her condo with him. She didn't expect to be accosted by a crowd since it was a weeknight, nor did she think Jeremy would show up since he was supposed to be out of town doing a press junket for the line of athletic wear he was getting ready to launch before the Seahawks' preseason began. Could the night get any worse?

Don't tempt fate by asking, Em.

"It's okay, Jeremy. I know him." Cesar wasn't doing a very good job of *not* drawing attention. And why the hostility? It wasn't like she was avoiding him. It had been her idea to meet him here. There was no need for him to manhandle her. Though she doubted he knew of any other way. What a jerk.

"Yeah, well, someone needs to teach him how to treat a woman." Jeremy's deep voice rumbled in her ear. The tension in his muscles told her that he wasn't ready to back down, and she reached up, guiding his gaze to hers.

"It's okay. I'm okay. Just give me a minute?"

"Alone? Not a good idea, Em. Especially with everything that's going on with your dad right now. Who is he?"

The problem with good friends was that they could occasionally be overprotective as well as nosy. And there was no way she was going to open up and

share. "I'm a big girl, Jer. I can take care of myself."
He flashed her a swoon-worthy smile that would
have crumbled the resolve of any number of girls.
"Don't you dare try to charm me with that trademark grin. I'm not one of your groupies. Order us
a couple of drinks and snag a table. I'll be back in
a few."

"All right, but hurry." He pointed an accusing
finger, and Emma marveled at how Cesar wasn't
intimidated by Jeremy's sheer size. The guy could
have broken Cesar over his knee as though he were
a twig. "I'ma come after you if don't get your ass
back here."

Thank God the music was too loud for him to
hear the nerves in her laughter. If she didn't tell
Cesar what he wanted to hear, the odds were good
she wouldn't be coming back any time soon. "Let's
go," she said as she guided Cesar out of the VIP
lounge and toward the rear exit.

"You're quite the actress, *chica*," Cesar said in that
low, sinister voice that caused chills to freeze her
very bone marrow. "Did the marshals get a dose of
that skill today?"

The fact that he even had to ask was enough for
Emma to doubt his intelligence. "I did what you told
me to do."

"Don't get lippy with me, *niña*," Cesar said from
between clenched teeth. "The trouble you're in is
your own doing. I wouldn't be here at all if you
hadn't tried to shake down *mi patrón*." He dragged
her along, his fingers biting into her flesh.

Such a gentleman. Cesar's mama must have been
so proud of her son, handling a woman like that.
What an ass. "I know why I'm in this situation. As

well as what's at stake if I don't play ball. I didn't say anything at my interview today. And as far as I can tell, the marshals don't have any leads either."

"That's good," Cesar replied. His jacket gaped away, and Emma caught sight of a gun resting in a holster under his arm. The sound of her pulse in her ears echoed the frantic beating of her heart, and she swallowed down the anxiety that threatened to overtake her. "Keep doing what you're told and we won't have any problems. Stay away from those *puto* marshals. I'll be watching you, *chica*. And I'll be contacting you again soon."

Cesar turned to leave and Emma shouted, "What about my father?" How much longer was this to go on? Because at this rate, she wouldn't last the week. He promised her they'd make the exchange after tonight. "You told me—"

"I told you I'll be contacting you soon." Cesar rounded on her with a snarl, his nose inches from hers. He smelled like bourbon and cigars, and Emma's stomach convulsed. "You don't ask me anything, *entender*? I make the rules, not you. You do nothing but sit and wait for my call."

He turned and strode away, shoving anyone in his path to the side. Yes, she understood Cesar perfectly. She'd screwed up and he was going to make her suffer for it. Emma slumped against the wall, her limbs shaking as her breath sped in her chest. There was no use fighting the undercurrent that was slowly pulling her away from the shore of her composure. It would only be a matter of time before the tide of her actions swallowed her completely. Already she felt as though she were drowning.

She couldn't go back to Jeremy and act as though

nothing were wrong. Not while she was still so worked up. He'd see right through the act. Emma pushed herself away from the wall, and rather than head for the exit, she made her way down the employees-only hallway. Most patrons didn't know about the back stairs that led to the roof, but Emma had been coming here for years and the manager let her use the roof access when she needed a little air. Or perspective. And right now, she was desperate for both.

As she walked out onto the roof, the early summer air cooled by the recent rain was a balm on Emma's heated skin. She drew a breath into her lungs and held it, enjoying the cold bite. God, how she'd wanted to come clean to McCabe today in the interview room. She experienced a pleasant rush of excitement at the memory of his intense gaze. His blue eyes seemed to see into the most secret part of her, but obviously that wasn't true, was it? Otherwise he would have forced the truth out of her. Instead, she'd snowed him exactly like she had his clueless partners. They didn't deserve her honesty. If the U.S. Marshals had done their job right the first time around, none of them would be in the positions they were in now.

Emma took in the city sounds as she strolled across the roof to the edge of the building. The white noise helped to quiet her tumultuous thoughts, along with the breeze that whooshed over her ears. Her upper arm still ached where Cesar had grabbed her, and she rubbed at her skin, wishing that the gentle wind could banish the memory of his hands on her. He was corrupt, heartless, and soulless, and it made her feel dirty having shared the same air as that son of a bitch. Without thinking, Emma stepped up onto the ledge of the building to look down at the street below. Only a couple of stories up, it still felt like miles from the ground and she swayed on her feet as the heel of her stiletto caught in a crack on the ledge.

"Jesus Christ, Emma!"

Before she could make sense of what was happening, strong arms wrapped around her waist and the ledge fell out from beneath her feet as she was ripped from her perch. The world spun in a blur, hauled against a wall of muscle before being deposited back on her feet.

"What in the hell were you doing?" McCabe's incredulous voice was warm in her ear. He held her tight against him, and Emma's head swam with his scent, clean and masculine with a hint of expensive cologne. She trembled in his arms, but whether from fear or excitement, she had no idea. Wait a sec. . . . What in the hell was *she* doing . . . ?

"What in the hell are *you* doing, McCabe?" Emma pushed at Landon's chest, stumbling backward. "Why are you here? Are you following me?" Panic flooded her at the realization. What if Cesar had noticed? *Oh, God. Dad . . .*

"I'm saving your ass, that's what I'm doing!" McCabe said as though Emma had lost her mind. *As if.* She wasn't the one grabbing people and tossing them around. "Do you want to explain what in God's name you were doing on that ledge?"

Had he actually thought she was about to jump? His eyes were alight with blue fire and his forehead creased right above the bridge of his nose where his brows were drawn tight. Despite the fact that she'd pushed him away, he closed the space between them, giving Emma nowhere to go but backward. Her back pressed against the cold brick of a tall air vent, and she shivered from the cold. Damn it. It was pretty tough to be enraged with McCabe when his anger made him look so freaking *good*.

"It's none of your damned business what I do, McCabe." Emma infused her voice with as much indignation as she could muster. No way would she give him any clue how his proximity affected her. Already, she found it hard to take a deep breath. "I haven't done anything wrong. You have no right to follow me. Stay out of my life!" The last words left her mouth in a strangled shout. If he didn't back off, he'd ruin everything she was working to fix.

"Who is he, Emma?" Landon demanded, wrapping his hands around her upper arms.

She bucked her chin in the air. "Who?"

His grip tightened, but not with the same painful bite of Cesar's grip. Rather, he was careful to keep his strength in check, restraining her while not hurting her. His touch set Emma's skin on fire, every nerve ending awakened to the sensation. Little pants of breath sped in her chest and she averted her eyes from the intensity of his stare. "Don't play games with me," he said, low. "Tell me who he is."

With the building at her back and Landon's chest a wall of unyielding muscle in front of her, Emma was effectively trapped. She couldn't deny that she found her helpless state—being at McCabe's mercy—a little exciting, but this wasn't a game she could afford to play with him. Too much was at stake. "Go to hell, McCabe."

One strong arm came up to rest on the wall behind her. Emma was caged in, pinned by his accusing stare and the sheer size of him. A muscle twitched at his jaw and his nostrils flared. "Are you in trouble, Emma? I can help you, but you've got to stop being so goddamned stubborn and *trust me.*"

Trust him? He was the enemy. The man who'd put her father in prison without even blinking an eye. How could she possibly trust him? Still, her resolve crumbled under the sincerity of his tone. The words cut through her like a blade, and the guilt of her actions was a bitter gall Emma forced herself to swallow down. If she let him continue to press her, she'd confess everything, including the time she'd shoplifted a tube of lipstick when she was fifteen. Damn him.

Without thinking, Emma pressed her body tight against his chest and put her lips to his. It seemed the best way to silence his persistent questions, and she knew of no better way to throw a man off track.

Dios mio! Her brain went fuzzy as his mouth moved over hers, his lips firm and demanding. She hadn't expected him to answer to her kiss, but holy crap, he wasn't holding anything back. He shifted his weight against her, pushing her flush against the wall. His free hand wound around the back of her neck, his mouth parted, and his tongue flicked out at her bottom lip. Talk about the mother of all backfires.

Emma was officially thrown.

Chapter Five

"McCabe? We've lost audio. McCabe? Do you copy?"

Morgan's voice in his ear was doing nothing for Landon's state of mind. He pushed his free arm from the wall and reached for the battery pack secured to his belt, double-checking to make sure the receiver for his mic was still off.

What in hell are you doing? As he'd emerged from the stairwell to find Emma standing on that ledge, he'd flipped off the mic for no good reason. When she'd slipped, it had stolen the air from his lungs, and all Landon had known was that he had to act. Career suicide hadn't been on his agenda today, but here he was, delivering the deathblow with his own two . . . uh . . . lips. But holy hell, how could he even think about pulling away when she felt so damned good in his arms? Her lips were silky soft against his, her mouth sweet with just a hint of red wine. Emma arched into him, and through the thin fabric of her dress, the tight points of her nipples rubbed against his chest. Landon couldn't help the groan that worked its way up his throat, and when she reached up and guided his hand to the swell of her breast, his composure took a nosedive.

Kissing Emma was a free fall from six hundred feet. An unparalleled rush. Adrenaline coursed through his body, the high so intense all he could think was, *More.* He wanted as much of her as he could get. His mouth slanted across hers as he deepened the kiss and she responded, her tongue sliding against his as she threaded her fingers through his hair and dragged her nails across his scalp.

The way she held him tight against her was maddening; the thin fabric of her dress with no bra underneath allowed him to feel her as though she had nothing on at all. His hand wandered to cup her breast through the silk and she moaned into his mouth. When his thumb flicked over one pearled peak, she shuddered against him. "Oh, God, McCabe, do that again," she gasped as she broke their kiss, her head rolling back on her shoulders.

Something inside Landon's chest tightened when she called him McCabe and not by his first name. As if the moment was totally impersonal to her and he was nothing more than a body filling up the empty space in her arms. His teeth gnashed together as he tested the tight peak again and a low, sensual moan escaped her lips. The thrill of a challenge spurred him as he tasted the flesh beneath her ear and downward to where her shoulder met her neck. The same deliciously delicate column of skin she'd taunted him with earlier today. By the time he was through with her she'd never call him "McCabe" again.

He reached down and cradled her ass in his

palms, lifting her until one leg straddled his waist. Emma's skirt hiked up around her hips and his fingers found the bare skin of her ass. Worst. Angle. Ever. He regretted their current position because he was now obsessed with her soft skin and desperate to see the sexy underwear that bared her to him in the most torturous way possible. Landon firmly believed there should be a shrine somewhere dedicated to thongs. Emma gripped his shoulders and pressed her back into the wall, which, coincidentally, jutted her high, pert breasts closer to his face. Landon took the opportunity that presented itself and kissed the swell revealed by her deep plunging neckline.

This is wrong. This is so, so wrong.

But seriously, Landon couldn't be bothered to give a shit about right or wrong when she thrust her hips against him, rubbing her nearly naked core against the erection straining against his fly in a way that made him ache to move the thin strip of fabric aside and bury himself inside of her and—

"McCabe, we're moving in."

The voice in his earpiece was as effective at cooling his lust as a dunk in a pool of ice cubes. It probably wouldn't do much to advance his career if Morgan found him up here with Emma wrapped around him like a boa constrictor. How in the hell would he explain himself? *I was just grilling her for information and she tripped and fell on my cock.* Right. That'd work.

"Emma." His voice was thick and lazy. He cleared his throat as he guided her leg from his hip. "Listen to me, I need you to go back down to the club. Don't stop to talk to anyone. Blend in with the crowd, head for the exit, and go home. Do you understand?"

Emma's brow knitted. She straightened her clothes as though ashamed, and Landon's stomach bottomed out. He'd fucked up and she was suffering the emotional fallout because of it. *Goddamn it.* "What's going on?" Her voice quavered and she refused to make eye contact.

How much should he tell her? She was a suspect in a crime, for shit's sake, and it wasn't as if she'd spilled the beans about the identity of the guy who'd grabbed her arm earlier in the night. Despite his rough treatment of her, Emma had protected his identity. Which not only stoked a raging fire of indignation in his gut, but further convinced Landon that she wasn't an innocent party in her father's escape. The last thing he needed right now was for Morgan to catch them together, though. He could deal with whatever she was hiding tomorrow. "Just do what I say, and don't ask any questions. Go. Now."

She finally met his gaze and her dark eyes glistened with emotion. It tore at Landon's composure to know that he'd hurt her, which made him even angrier. He prided himself on his tough demeanor. Suspects *did not* get under his skin. *Ever.* And what had just happened between them went way beyond simple emotional manipulation. Without a word, she turned and ran for the door, her heels clicking with every step. She threw the door open and it bounced off the wall, rebounding with a slam to signal her exit. Landon exhaled a long, slow breath and slumped against the wall he'd moments ago pressed Emma up against, her body soft and warm against his.

Holy shit.

His limbs still shook from the adrenaline rush

and Landon's heart pumped in his chest as though he'd just rappelled from the top of Everest. Morgan's chatter in his earpiece reminded him that he didn't have time to sit and relive what had happened—or think about the consequences of his actions—and he reached back to flip the switch on his mic. This was still Morgan's show, and Landon needed to keep his shit together before his invite was revoked. "Morgan, you copy?"

"What's your twenty?" Morgan responded, sounding not a little annoyed. "What happened? I lost communications for a few minutes."

"Malfunction, I think. I lost eyes on the target. I'm on the roof."

When Morgan opened his mic, Landon heard the thump of the base and roar of the crowd inside the club. "We're sweeping the interior now, no sign of her. Stay put."

Gladly.

Landon braced his arms on his knees and dropped his head between his shoulders as he took several cleansing breaths to slow his racing heart. When his eyes drifted shut, his mind was assaulted with visions of Emma, her head thrown back on her shoulders, dark eyes heavily lidded and her mouth parted on a silent moan. His shoulders tingled, every contact point of her fingers seeming to sear his flesh with a permanent mark. Landon straightened his spine and knocked his head against the concrete wall behind him as though a concussion might banish the memory of her soft skin from his mind. Just thinking of the moment they'd shared caused his cock to grow hard and throb in his jeans. The evidence of his renewed arousal wasn't exactly something he wanted his colleagues to see. *Cool your jets, dude. Jesus, you're not sixteen anymore.*

Behind him, the door to the roof swung open and Morgan and his partner stepped out onto the roof. Great. Fucking *awesome.* "What in the hell's going on, McCabe? Are you hurt?"

Landon imagined he might look a little dazed, what with banging his head against the wall and all. And he was sort of doubled over now, dragging in a few deep breaths of the cool night air in an effort to tame the raging erection that threatened not only to embarrass him, but to rat him out to Morgan. This was so much worse than your mom catching you jerking off to *Playboy.* And a hell of a lot harder to explain, too. Thank God he'd kept his damned pants on.

"Just winded," Landon offered by way of an explanation. Wow, as if that weren't the lamest excuse ever. "I thought I spotted Emma heading for the stairs and I followed."

"But she isn't up here?" Morgan responded, raising a dubious brow.

Yeah, it wasn't even a passable excuse to Landon. "No. She might have used a back office exit or something."

"Was she alone?" Morgan's partner, Kevin, piped in. Up until now, Landon had wondered if the dude was mute.

"She was when I trailed her; I thought maybe she was meeting the male suspect up here." At least that wasn't a lie. If anything, Landon was determined to uncover the identity of the asshole with the grabby hands.

"Wait a sec," Morgan said, pinning Landon with

an accusing stare. "Male suspect? Why is now the first I'm hearing of this?"

Uh-oh. Landon had a lot of 'splaining to do. It was going to be a long goddamned night.

Emma slid into the passenger seat of Jeremy's Mercedes amidst the flash of cameras and curious shouts that were incoherent to her racing mind. She knew that the pics would be all over the Internet the next morning. It wouldn't be long after that before the local news picked up on her little outing, which would more than likely set Cesar's temper off like a powder keg. *So* not good. She'd really screwed up tonight, and it was a testament to her poor decision-making skills that the problems with Cesar were becoming the least of her worries.

Had she really made out with Landon McCabe tonight while trying to climb him like a tree?

"You okay, Em?"

She turned to Jeremy and smiled. "Yeah, just tired." Her fingertips brushed her lips, still warm and a little swollen from McCabe's kisses. Damn, did that man ever know how to use his mouth. The memory heated her skin and caused her heart to race in her chest. She couldn't help but wonder what it would have felt like to have that wet warmth on other, more sensitive parts of her body.

"Not to pry or anything, but what was up with that dude earlier?"

"What dude?" she asked, hoping he hadn't noticed McCabe follow her up the stairs.

"You know who I'm talking about. The one who looked like an extra from *Scarface*."

Of course he was talking about Cesar. It was unlikely anyone had seen McCabe follow her. Anyone but Cesar, that is. He watched her like a hawk and probably had a tally of every time she'd visited the bathroom. Which totally squicked her out. "Just a guy. Don't worry about it, Jeremy."

"Em, I don't wanna sound like I'm telling you what to do, but if it has anything to do with your dad—"

"You don't want to sound like it, but you're totally about to tell me what to do," Emma said, cutting him off. "I know you're concerned and I'm glad you've got my back, but really, I'm okay." The last thing Emma needed was to get Jeremy involved in this business with Cesar. She'd messed up enough people's lives already. No need to add to the tally. "He's a little . . ."

"Pushy? Rude? Rough?" Jeremy ventured.

"Intense," Emma said. "But I know how to manage him."

"You're not seeing him, are you?"

Emma almost laughed at Jeremy's appalled tone. "No," she said with a sad chuckle. "I'm *not* seeing him."

"Good. Because if you were, I'd have to have a talk with him about how you deserve to be treated. And then with you about your questionable taste in men."

Though Emma and Jeremy had dated once or twice a few years ago, they'd both decided that they could never be anything more than friends. And that was totally okay. Emma didn't have many close friends—people she truly trusted—in her life and that made Jeremy worth more to her than a simple hookup. Which was exactly why she couldn't drag him into this business with Cesar.

"So, I've got some time off. Preseason doesn't start for another three weeks and my press tour was pushed back until next Friday. You wanna bounce and hang out at my place in Malibu for a while?"

Emma loved the beach and Jeremy's suggestion was exactly what she needed right now. Too bad she couldn't take him up on his offer. "I can't. With the investigation going on, it would look suspicious if I left. I need to play it cool for a while so the Marshals office will back off."

"I guess it would look sorta bad. But damn, Em, I wish they'd lay off. It's not like you know anything."

"Yeah." Emma let the conversation die, unwilling to lie to Jeremy outright. And if anyone wished the marshals would lay off, it was her, except . . . if they did, it would mean that McCabe would go back to wherever he came from. After what had happened between them tonight, Emma wasn't sure that was what she wanted. Sure, she'd kissed him to shut him up and to keep him from asking too many questions she couldn't answer. But she'd never expected him to respond so enthusiastically. In fact, she'd expected nothing more than a cool rebuff from the hotshot deputy. Instead, what he'd given her had left Emma breathless and craving more. *Damn you, McCabe.*

She was so wrapped up in reliving tonight's escapades, she didn't even notice when Jeremy pulled into the underground parking garage of her building. As if she were waking up from the best dream ever, her mind and body conspired together to keep her in a relaxed state. Sweet Lord, the way McCabe's fingers had felt against the bare skin of her ass had been nothing short of bliss. And she shuddered as she recalled the hard length of his erection pressing up against her as she straddled his hip.

"Do you want me to walk you up?"

But then, McCabe had simply pulled away without any explanation. His once-fiery demeanor replaced with something cold and indecipherable. A heavy lump of disappointment settled in Emma's stomach as she remembered his commanding words. How his handsome face had hardened and made her feel so ashamed for throwing herself at him the way she had.

"Oh, God."

Her embarrassed groan was answered by Jeremy's large hand covering her own. He squeezed gently and his deep brown eyes were wide with concern. "What is it, Em?"

Oh, nothing much at all. I acted like a sex-deprived slut and jumped a federal cop on the roof tonight. My mother would be so proud if she were alive to see it. "Nothing, I'm just tired. I don't need you to walk me up, I'll be fine."

He smiled. "You sure?"

Emma nodded. No need to admit that she didn't think she'd ever be fine again.

"How 'bout we grab lunch next week? McCormick & Schmick's?"

That ought to be fun with Cesar *and* the Marshals tracking her every move. "Sure. Sounds like a plan."

"I'm holding you to it," Jeremy said with a wink. "Night, Em."

He held out his fist and she bumped his knuckles with her own. "Night."

Emma focused on the soft purr of the engine as Jeremy pulled out of the garage. She headed for the elevators, each step carefully placed. She counted them off in her mind—*one, two, three, four, one, two, three, four*—in an effort to center her thoughts and draw her focus from her current worries. And they were many. Too damned many for a woman her age, yet she was in too deep to do anything about it now.

Emma was the classic overthinker. For as long as she could remember, she obsessed, overanalyzed, turned things over again and again in her mind. And that obsessive brain of hers had caused her countless sleepless nights and not a few anxiety attacks when she was young. It took concentrated focus to redirect her thoughts. That's why she counted her steps. If she didn't preoccupy her brain with something new to obsess over, she'd drive herself crazy. When she was eighteen, and stressed to the point of an ulcer over her dad's investigation, she'd used Deputy U.S. Marshal Landon McCabe as a distraction.

She'd only seen him a few times in the initial phase of her dad's investigation, but that was all it had taken for her obsession with him to root firmly in her mind. Tall, with a lean swimmer's build, and as blond and fair as she was dark. His smile had been snarky but infectious and when he was upset or concentrating really hard, the most adorable crease had cut into his brow. Then she'd realized that he was gunning for her dad. He'd quickly become the man she loved to hate, the gorgeous villain of her nightmares. And even though her dad insisted that she harbor no ill will toward the good men doing their jobs to uphold the law, she couldn't help but feel a certain amount of animosity. Still, his good looks haunted her waking thoughts. More than once she'd used McCabe as a distraction from the crippling anxiety that weighed on her every time she thought of how alone she'd be if her father was convicted and sent to prison. She'd even tried to count each of his eyelashes once during a particularly hostile interview with her dad. His lashes were long and so dark. In the long run, it was impossible to count them and she found herself feeling jealous that God had given him such pretty lashes. What did men need great lashes for, anyway?

And now she was counting her own footsteps to the elevator to distract her from him. Funny how life worked out sometimes. If by funny, she meant crushing and humiliating. Emma's phone vibrated in her back pocket and her heart leapt up into her throat. A quick glance at the caller ID confirmed her fears and she said a silent prayer before answering. "Hello?"

"*Mija*?"

Tears sprang to Emma's eyes at the sound of her father's voice. "Dad!" *Oh, thank God.* "Dad, are you okay?"

"I'm fine. Try not to worry. I need you to listen very closely to what I'm about to say, Emmalina. If you do what I tell you, everything will be fine. I promise."

He'd promised her the same thing six years ago. And nothing had been fine since that day. But at this point, what choice did she have?

"Okay, Dad. I'm listening."

Chapter Six

Landon didn't feel any better this morning than he had when he went to bed last night. Which might've had something to do with the fact that he'd slept a grand total of fifty-two minutes the entire night. His head was still swimming with Emma's intoxicating scent, floral with a sweet edge that made him hungry and horny at the same time. How fucked up was that?

"Here's your harness. Sorry, but those are the rules, man."

He looked at the guy behind the counter as if he'd only now noticed he was standing inside the indoor climbing facility. Landon needed to clear his head and he knew of no better way to focus his energy than a climb. And since he didn't have time to drive out to the mountains, the indoor walls would have to do. Despite the fact that he wanted a free climb without the restraint of the harness, it looked as if he'd be forced to follow the rules if he wanted to use the facility. Rules shouldn't have been a big deal for him. He was a deputy fucking U.S.

marshal for shit's sake. Rules were his *business*. So why, this morning, did he want to punch this guy in the face because of a rule?

Landon gave a derisive snort. *Why?* He could answer that question in two words: Emma Ruiz.

"Uh, sorry," he said when the guy behind the counter gave him a dirty look. "Yeah, the harness is fine. No worries."

"You're going to need a belayer, too," counter guy remarked. "Josh is out on the floor this morning. If he's not helping someone else, you can snag him. Tall guy with shaggy brown hair. Over there."

Landon looked to where the guy pointed and gave a nod. "I see him. Thanks."

Really, the harness probably wasn't a bad idea. As distracted as he was, he was as likely to fall as he was to make it to the top of the wall. A broken back would pretty much wrap up his month in a nice little bow. He took his credit card from the now disgruntled counter manager and headed into the main gym with the harness in one hand, his gym bag in the other. He found an empty public locker and grabbed his chalk bag before he stuffed his duffel inside and headed for the wall.

Landon slipped on the harness and secured the carabiner from his harness to the belay attached to a rope dangling from the ceiling. Josh, who definitely looked like he could use a haircut, caught sight of Landon and headed over. "'Sup, man," he greeted Landon as he grabbed hold of the length of rope. "Ready to get your climb on?"

"Uh, yeah. Sure." Get his climb on? Josh must be new to the job. He had the eager-camp-counselor act down pat. Which made Landon wonder if Josh had experience with belaying anyone over the age of twelve. Shit, a free climb might have been safer than trusting a newb to manage the tension in his rope while he climbed. It was too late to worry about it now, he supposed. At any rate, maybe he'd be too worried about Josh's belaying skills to think about last night. He'd take whatever distractions he could get at this point.

Landon massaged the chalk bag in one hand and then the other, stuffing it under the harness strap before grabbing a handhold and hoisting himself up on the wall. The first twenty feet were an easy climb, like going up a ladder. But from there, the wall became steeper and angular, presenting Landon with a more challenging ascent. By the time he hit forty feet, the endorphins should have kicked in.

Usually, a good climb gave him a nice, mellow buzz. His breath quickened and his heart rate increased, but the excitement factor was absent. Landon continued to climb as the angle of the ceiling bent to almost forty-five degrees. His teeth clenched to the point that he could hear the enamel grind as he reached up, his fingers barely making purchase on the handhold and still, he felt nothing. Until his mind wandered to the memory of silky soft lips, supple breasts, and the sound of Emma's low moan when he passed his thumb over the stiff peak of her—

Whoof! Landon's chest made contact with the wall, knocking the air from his lungs. His palms warmed from the friction of the rope as it slipped through his hands during his rapid descent, and his face pulsed where it met the sharp edge of the polyresin hold he'd lost his footing on. Below him,

Josh's amused snicker echoed through the gym, joining in with that of the snarky counter guy. Landon cursed under his breath. Nothing like having an audience when you biffed your face against the wall. Especially when one of those witnesses already thought you were a jackass and the other treated you like a kid at day camp. Awesome.

He never should have let things go as far as they had last night. Hell, he'd known what Emma was up to the minute she'd leaned toward him. He could have pushed her away, taken a step back. Told her to stop. But he hadn't. No, like the fool he was, he'd taken her in his arms and played right into her plans, effectively distracting him from questioning her about the man at the club. And like the dumb son of a bitch he was, he would do it all over again given the chance.

Landon had been a rookie straight out of the academy when he'd been assigned to the Ruiz case. Despite the guy's wealth and clout, the case had been cut and dry, with more than enough evidence to support an arrest. A cake assignment to ease him into the job with a senior deputy supervising him. When it came to work, to procedure and protocol, Landon did everything by the book. But the second he'd taken in the sight of Javier Ruiz's daughter, his brain had gone on a vacation south and suddenly procedure became the last thing on his mind.

Now, he was right back where he'd started. What did he expect? That in six years' time she'd become less attractive? If anything, she'd grown more beautiful and lived enough to know how to work her feminine wiles. Landon groaned as he reached for a difficult handhold and pulled himself higher on the wall. She'd been making the rounds with celebrities and dating fucking sports superstars for the past six years. And it wasn't like she'd ever been the innocent, wide-eyed girl, even at eighteen. He thought about the pictures pasted on the Internet and the soccer star's arms around her as he shielded her from photographers. His stomach burned and his jaw clenched as Landon propelled himself to another hold farther up the wall. The thought of another man touching Emma made him want to break something. Namely, the bastard's face.

His foot slipped on the hold and Landon cursed. He'd come to the gym this morning for a workout and to clear his mind. But an hour and fifty vertical feet later, he still felt like shit and his brain was nothing more than a tangle of knotted thoughts. The only thing that was going to clear his head at this point was distance. From this case. From her. If he didn't wrap it up and get a lead on Ruiz soon, it wouldn't be only his success rate on the line.

It would be his badge.

Landon pushed away from the wall as he fed the nylon rope through the belay. He dropped from the top of the wall to the floor in a matter of seconds, and his stomach gave a pleasant flip with the quick descent. He landed on his feet, unclipped the carabiner, and shed the harness, handing it over to Josh. "Thanks, man," he offered without eye contact as he headed for the lockers. The only thing he'd gotten out of this morning's climb was a bruised ego and a shit ton of frustration. He dug his phone out of his gym bag and passed the counter without a second glance at the smart-ass giving him a superior smirk. Sometimes caution was the better part of valor and he didn't think Morgan would appreciate it if he decked anyone for no good reason while visiting the deputy's city.

As he hoofed it for his car, Landon called Galen. He needed tunnel vision for the rest of his time in Seattle if he was going to keep Emma out of his head and get down to business. "What did you find out from the prison staff?" he all but growled when Galen answered his phone.

"Wow. Good morning to you, too, sunshine. Rough night?"

You have no idea. "I just want to wrap this shit up and get home, that's all."

Galen's answering silence only served to annoy Landon more. "Oh reeeaaallly?" Galen replied, obviously smug. The bastard. "Who could possibly make you want to ditch the Emerald City?"

"Why does it have to be a who?" Landon asked as he unlocked the car and threw his gym bag in the backseat. "In case you've forgotten in your quest for celebrity status, the Portland field office is where I work. I'm not exactly fond of living out of a hotel room."

"Oh, it's a who," Galen responded. "Because I know for a fact that you don't mind Seattle or hanging out in hotels."

Okay, so *one time* he took an unscheduled two-week vacation and shacked up with a park ranger at a Best Western. But it wasn't like he whored around Seattle regularly. The hiking in Olympic National Park was great. "How about you fill me in on the prison guards before I call Harper and give her the scoop on some of your more questionable past relationship choices."

"Are you suggesting that there's someone in Seattle you'd rather not know about yours, too? Because I've got some hard-core ammo for retaliation."

As if Landon would give Galen the satisfaction of confirming his suspicions. And, seriously, why was he even considering the possibility? Of course there wasn't anyone in the city he cared about. No one. At all. Period. "The prison staff? I haven't got all day, Galen."

Galen chuckled and it was all Landon could do not to throw his phone. "All right. Fine. It's no fun razzing you when you're in a shitty mood, so let's get to it. You were right that Ruiz didn't do this alone. At least, that's what I gathered after filling in the blanks."

Finally they were getting somewhere. "Do you think it was an inside job?"

"I think whoever helped Ruiz escape was coercing information from someone who worked at the prison, but I don't think any employees were actively involved in his escape." Galen paused, and Landon grabbed a notebook and pen from the glove box and started to scribble down a few notes. "The initial report suggested that Ruiz escaped prison custody without any help. He was being transported to Willamette Valley Medical Center for a chemo treatment, and it's only seventeen minutes from Sheridan. Doesn't leave a lot of time for an escape. Plus, dude was *not* in any shape to overpower two guards and a driver. They were most likely drugged. We're running tests on blood samples to see if we can find anything, though it might be out of their systems by now. All three guards are reporting gaps in their memory. Anyway—"

"Wait a sec," Landon interrupted as a thought struck. "Do you think Ruiz could have been kidnapped?"

"Kidnapped?" Galen asked as though he'd never heard the word before. "Who would want to kidnap him? And why?"

Exactly. "Can you e-mail me the complete report from the interview?"

"Sure, but there's not much more, just a few jumbled details."

Landon tossed the notebook into the passenger seat and turned his key in the ignition. "And send me the tox reports on the guards' blood."

"Can do. You wanna fill me in on what you're thinking?"

Right now, it was only a hunch, but until Landon discovered the identity of Emma's grabby admirer last night, a hunch was all it was going to be. "Not yet. I need to dig a little deeper."

"Secrets don't make friends, you know," Galen quipped, though his tone was light.

"Neither does being a dick," Landon shot right back. "I'll call you when I have something concrete."

"Later," Galen responded with a laugh and ended the call.

Landon pulled out into traffic, antsy to get to work. Jesus. Until now, he'd never considered the possibility that Ruiz might be a victim rather than an escapee. And if the former judge had, in fact, been kidnapped, Emma might be in more danger than she realized.

An image of the rough-looking gangster grabbing onto Emma's arm flared in Landon's mind, and he gripped the steering wheel until his knuckles turned white. Maybe Emma knew exactly what sort of danger she was in. And maybe he was already too late to do anything about it.

"She's famous for being famous. Sort of like Paris Hilton or one of the Kardashians, but on a smaller scale."

Emma cringed as she overheard the whispered words of the girls behind her in line at Starbucks and pushed her sunglasses down from her forehead and back over her eyes. For the record, she had zero sex tapes floating around the interwebs, and no matter what anyone thought to the contrary, she was hardly famous for being famous. More like, she was accidentally famous. And on the celebrity radar, she was barely a blip.

Growing up, Emma's friends had always been guys. And being a sports junkie, she had a tendency to hang out with guys who played sports. Tyson Kennedy had been her best friend since childhood. And because he'd gone on to become a famous pro athlete and Emma was always hanging around, she'd sort of gained notoriety by default.

"I heard she was dating Jeremy Blakely from the Seahawks. And that her dad's some sort of Mexican cartel drug lord."

Emma snorted. Jeremy would get a kick out of that little bit of news. And her dad was about as dangerous as a springer spaniel. God, how she hated the rumor mill.

"Venti caramel macchiato for Ella?" the barista called out from the counter.

She'd drop dead the day one of them got her

name right. Still, Ella was better than Nanna, which someone had scribbled on her cup last week. Seriously? *Nanna?* Emma grabbed her coffee and headed for the most isolated table she could find. Most days, this was her go-to place to sit and relax and catch up on work. Aside from her more public notoriety, Emma had built a professional reputation as a general computer-geek-gun-for-hire. One of the top programmers in her field, she was known for constructing practically unhackable security systems. She contracted for multinational corporations as well as mom-and-pop outfits. She'd even consulted for Rosenbaum's, a large supermarket chain that had made headlines last year after a security breach had occurred, giving hackers thousands of their customers' credit card numbers. She'd jumped in and restructured their security protocols and it had only helped to elevate her growing business.

Being an independent contractor gave her the freedom of a mobile office as well as setting her own hours. Sure, the gossip sites claimed she was a trust fund brat who lived off Daddy's money, but that wasn't entirely true. Her dad had set aside a trust to help her out, but it wasn't enough to set her up for life or anything. She didn't have Buffett or Hilton money. Hell, in the course of her obsessive research into McCabe six years ago, she'd discovered that her family didn't have *McCabe* money. No, Emma had never been über rich. Her family had simply been better off than most. The trust had put her through college and afforded her the benefit of graduating without the burden of thousands of dollars of student loan debt. And now, that trust helped to pay for her condo in a building that made her feel safe. Until recently, that is. That's all her dad had ever wanted: that she be taken care of. Protected. And now, it was Emma's turn to take care of him.

She set up her laptop and angled the screen away from anyone who might've been able to glance at the content. It took only a moment to connect to the coffee shop's Wi-Fi, and she placed her cell on the table beside her, waiting for a call she didn't really want to answer.

Minutes ticked by. Emma sipped her macchiato, reviewed a couple of client projects, and answered an e-mail. She checked Twitter and her Facebook page—great, someone had tagged her in a couple of candids with Jeremy last night—and, disgusted, she closed the windows, vowing to stay off social media for the rest of her life. She checked the time on her phone, and her stomach did a nervous flip. She'd followed her dad's instructions to a tee and set up her laptop in a public place, hopefully far from prying eyes. If everything went according to plan, this would all be over soon. But Cesar's call was now officially ten minutes late. What in the hell did that mean?

"Meeting someone this morning?"

Emma jumped about a foot in her seat at the sound of McCabe's voice. Damn him and the pushy bastards tailing her! He was going to ruin everything. She pushed her glasses up on her forehead and leveled an icy stare at him. "Not that it's any of your business, but I'm working. I usually come here to avoid nosy jerks who have nothing better to do than follow me around. Looks like I'm going to have to find a new hangout."

His sardonic smile jacked her pulse rate up and turned her insides to mush. How he could be equal parts sexy and annoying was a mystery. "We need to talk."

About what? she wondered. The fact that she was still under investigation in connection with her father's escape or the fact that he'd kissed her dizzy last night. Would it be in poor taste to bring up the latter first? Probably. "I have nothing to say to you, McCabe."

His eyes hardened almost imperceptibly and Emma could only guess as to what had triggered his animosity. He apparently expected her to play nice after their escapade last night. Maybe that's why he'd kissed her back, thinking to buy her cooperation with a few sweet—okay, hot—kisses. Well, toe-curlingly good or not, those lips of his weren't going to buy her cooperation now or ever.

"You are going to talk to me, Emma. Right now. You're running out of time and this attitude of yours isn't getting you anywhere." He raked his fingers through the short thatch of his blond hair giving it a way too sexy, bed-head look and sighed. "Damn it, if you're in trouble, I can help you. Why are you being so stubborn?"

"I don't know what you mean, McCabe. I've cooperated with your office."

Again, when she said his name, his eyes seemed to grow cold, and it only served to further pique her curiosity. "Do you want me to jerk your spoiled ass out of that chair and arrest you like some sort of criminal? Lay you out on the table and read you your rights in front of everyone here? Because I'll do it and I won't even think twice about the phones poised and ready to record the video."

Emma felt the sting of tears at her eyes, but she bit them back. McCabe's detached cruelty was a far cry from the heat she'd felt from him last night. Then again, after his rebuff, maybe this was his way of setting the record straight and letting her know that what happened was a mistake. He might as well cuff her right here and now. Kick her while she was already down. He seemed to enjoy it well enough. "Just leave me alone, okay?" Emma simply couldn't muster the energy to snap at him. She checked the time on the bottom of her laptop screen. McCabe needed to get the hell out of there before Cesar called. "I haven't done anything wrong, and technically this is harassment." And how deranged was it that what she was the most upset about was the fact that he wasn't harassing her with his mouth right now. Totally sick. "I'll call my lawyer if you want."

"No, you won't." McCabe leaned back in his chair. "You would have lawyered up the second you heard Javier escaped custody, and since you didn't bring counsel with you to your interview, I'm going to go ahead and assume that you're hiding something that you wouldn't even trust a lawyer with."

"I know how you guys operate, McCabe." Now that she sensed it riled him up, she couldn't wait to use his last name often and with inflection. Like it was a curse word. Ha! "Intimidation gets the job done, right? You pretend like you know all of my dirty secrets in the hopes that I'll fold like a house of cards and fess up. But see, there's a problem with that, *McCabe*. I don't have any secrets to spill. Sorry, dude, but you're barking up the wrong tree."

His gaze burned with a heat that simmered in

every pore of Emma's body. A corner of his mouth lifted, hinting at a smile, and he said, "Am I?"

She flushed with warmth, aware of the turn the conversation had taken and the innuendo in his tone. But Emma wasn't about to play into it. Not after he'd pushed her away and treated their kiss as something as casual as a handshake. A snappy comeback sat at the tip of her tongue, but when she opened her mouth to speak, the display of her phone lit up, vibrating loudly on the table's surface.

Shit.

Shit, shit, shit! Of all the crappy timing. Her stomach rocketed up into her throat and her heart beat so fast she was afraid it was going to break a rib. The unlisted number on the caller ID could only mean her late caller had finally gotten his act together. How could she do what Cesar wanted her to do while McCabe was sitting right next to her, remotely connected to God knew who else with the Marshals Service? Should she let it go to voice-mail? Answer and pretend nothing was wrong? Warn Cesar somehow? Black spots swam in her vision and her head pounded as her anxiety increased tenfold. Emma's vision darkened at the periphery as a hundred scenarios played out in her mind. Shit, she was going to pass out. She wasn't up for this. Couldn't do it. And she had no one to turn to for help.

Landon's gaze lingered on her phone before he brought his eyes up to meet hers, pinning her with his stare. "Well, are you going to answer it?"

Chapter Seven

"Answer the phone, Emma."

Landon refused to break eye contact with Emma and she looked like she might throw up. Her eyes grew wide and her chest inflated with her rapid breath. The expression on her face was a study of indecision. And fear. A protective urge spiked in Landon and he reached for the phone, bound and determined to shut down the cause of her distress.

"No!"

She tried to stop him, but his reflexes were quicker and he snatched the phone into his grasp. Landon noted the "unknown" ID of the caller before swiping his finger across the screen and hitting the speakerphone function. "Hello?"

"Hi! This is Tammy from bank card services. I'm calling in regards to a promotion we're running and—"

Landon hit the button to switch the call back to the handset and placed it in Emma's hand. The look of shock on her face didn't go unnoticed, nor did the quaver in her voice as she brushed off the credit

card solicitor's offer. If anything, this was the proof
he needed that Emma was not only hiding something, but also in a shit load of trouble.

Emma ended the call and stuffed her laptop and
her phone in a briefcase. Her hands shook as she
pulled the zipper closed and she tipped what was left
of her coffee over in her haste to put everything
away. Landon grabbed a napkin and began to mop
up the mess while Emma pushed her chair away
from the table in a growl of wood against tile.

"Don't leave, Emma," Landon warned as he reached
out to grab her hand. The contact was electric. God,
he wanted to pull her into his lap and hold her tight
in his arms while he kissed her senseless.

A quick look around the coffee shop must have
confirmed that people were beginning to stare because Emma sat back down slowly and leaned over
the table, though she did nothing to disengage her
hand from his. Landon wanted to close his eyes and
soak in the physical contact. Revel in the warmth of
her touch, softness of her skin, the weight of her
hand resting in his. Which was so goddamned wrong
and he knew it. But his career be damned, he did
nothing to stop it.

"Let me ask you something. If you were in my position, and it was your dad, would you cooperate?"

Landon thought about that for about a half a
second. "I would."

"Because you're just *so* right? Is that it? Black and
white. Good or evil. There's no gray area for you,
and if your dad was in prison, it's because he belongs
to be there. Is that it?"

She had no idea how close to home she was
hitting. Landon wouldn't put it past his father to

engage in some of those "black area" dealings that—if he didn't have the best attorney money could buy—would land him in a federal prison somewhere.

"You can't ask me to pass judgment on your father and what he might or might not have done. He was convicted and sentenced. And he escaped from federal custody. It's not my place to determine if he's guilty or not. My job is to find him and bring him in." It was a hard truth that pained him to speak, but he wasn't about to sugarcoat anything for her. "I'd cooperate because if my dad did something to land him in prison, he'd be there because he damn well deserved it."

"Yeah, well, my dad is *innocent*," she said, her voice thick with emotion. "He didn't deserve to have his career ruined by a federal investigation, and he sure as hell didn't deserve to be thrown in prison."

"Emma, he made a full confession."

She gave him a sad shake of her head as though he were pathetic, not to mention dense. "Oh, and I'm sure no one in the history of history has ever been coerced into a false confession."

Landon sighed. This was too damned hard. "That's what you think, Emma? That he was coerced?"

"I don't think. I *know*."

"Emma—"

"You have no idea what it's like to be alone. Do you, McCabe?"

It aggravated him to no end that she refused to call him Landon. He craved that small intimacy between them even though he had no right to it. Emma's voice was soft and sad, slicing through him like a knife, and he stroked the webbing between her thumb and forefinger with his own as if the small gesture could comfort her. "I have a better idea than you think."

A curious expression accented her features as she canted her head to one side. Her dark eyes bored through him as though trying to break down the door into his memories. "You think you know me, but you don't. You only know what the gossip rags tell you or what you saw during your investigation six years ago. We're not friends, McCabe."

"Really? You seemed pretty friendly last night." The words slipped from his lips before he could think better of it. Now might've been a good time to bash his head against the table. *How does the sole of your shoe taste, you fucking idiot?*

She jerked her hand from his grasp, her expression that of utter disbelief. Or was it disgust? It was hard to tell which way her emotional compass was swinging at this point. All Landon knew was that his foolish words had spooked her, and in his experience, that led to all sorts of bad decisions. He couldn't let her take off before he found out what was going on.

"You can't run away and expect it to fix anything."

"I'm not running anywhere," she said, bucking her chin a notch. "I just want to get the hell away from you."

Landon got up from his chair and blocked her path to the exit, not giving a single shit who might be witnessing their little drama. "You have to trust me, Emma."

"Trust you?" The words tumbled from her lips in

an incredulous burst. "You put my father in prison! Why in God's name would I ever trust you?"

She had a point. To Emma, he was nothing more than the sanctimonious son of a bitch who took her dad away from her. How could he possibly earn her trust?

"Emma, I was doing my job."

He was answered with a derisive snort as she rolled her eyes to the sky. "Right. Sorry to break it to you, McCabe, but you weren't doing your job when you arrested my father. And now, because you didn't do your job right the first time, I'm paying the price. Get out of my way before I sic my *very* expensive lawyer on you."

No matter how badly he wanted to cuff her to him and force every last secret from her, he knew that his only option at this point was to give her a little space. The last thing he needed was for her lawyer to get involved and have the Seattle office coming down on him. And while Landon still believed Emma wasn't about to bring a lawyer into whatever mess she was in, it was a chance he wasn't willing to take. Lawyers had a tendency to fuck everything up and bring the pace of an investigation to a standstill. He did *not* need that kind of headache right now.

He took a single step to the side, his face devoid of emotion, and Emma brushed past him without another word. The sound effects mimicking camera shutters sounded off around him, and Landon closed his eyes while he expelled a low, slow breath. *Fucking smartphones.* Christ, smacking his face against the climbing wall had been a cakewalk in comparison to the humiliation he felt right now. Emma would suffer for their argument when photos went live all over the Internet. He probably wouldn't undergo an ounce of scrutiny—nothing more than a deputy marshal doing his job. She'd look guilty while he played the hero, and that made him a king-sized asshole, didn't it?

So before the eager tweeters and Instagramers could work their social networking magic, Landon banked on the fact that most of the patrons in Starbucks this morning would be oblivious to proper procedure. "Deputy U.S. marshal," he announced as he flashed his badge to the coffee shop at large. "I'm going to have to ask everyone who documented that little scene to step forward with your phones."

"You can't stifle free speech, man!" some idiot called from the back of the room.

"I can arrest you for interfering with a federal investigation," he said. Which, of course, he couldn't. Nothing about what had happened between him and Emma a moment ago would hinder his case. That he knew of. "So, step up and delete any pics you might've snapped, or spend the day in jail. It's your choice."

A collective grumble spread through Starbucks as reluctant gossipmongers gathered near his table. He hated that people who didn't even know her dehumanized Emma, turning her into some kind of media spectacle. And worse, he'd helped to fuel the fire by calling her out in a very public place. The least he could do was try to minimize the backlash by making sure as many photos of their encounter were erased from existence as possible. He had a feeling that, right now, she could use all the help she could get.

Emma rushed down the street, swiping at a traitorous tear that escaped her eye and rolled down her cheek. She'd always fought against the insecurity that plagued her when she was out in public—especially when people recognized her like the two girls at the counter had this morning—but McCabe had managed to decimate any bravado she had left.

As she hailed a cab, her phone vibrated in her pocket. Nervous energy sent her hands to shaking as she dug the phone out of her pocket, nearly dropping it into a gutter in the process. A taxi pulled up to the curb, but she waved it on. Instead, Emma ducked into an alley off Pike Street and answered.

"I thought you said you had the Marshals managed, *chica.*"

How could Cesar possibly know that she'd been with McCabe, unless he'd been watching her as well? Great. Was there anyone in the city not following her every move? "I told you, the Marshals aren't a problem. But honestly, what do you expect, Cesar? My father's missing and I'm his only living relative. Who else are they going to pester?"

"Nah, your papa ain't missing. He *escaped.* Don't you watch the news?"

What a raging douchecanoe. Emma had never hated anyone in her entire life, but she hated Cesar deep down in the pores of her skin. She knew he was trying to get a reaction out of her. Most likely so he could retaliate. And no way would she give him the satisfaction. "Are we going to do this, or what?"

"Not now," he replied as though the suggestion

was asinine. "Too much heat on you. *Mi patrón* wants to lay low for now. Until you can figure out a way to get the Marshals off your back."

"How in the hell am I supposed to do that?" Panic choked the air from Emma's lungs as the weight of the world seemed to press down on her.

"You'll think of something, *si*?" Cesar remarked in his smooth, oily voice. "*Tu padre* is depending on you."

"Yes," Emma said. "I'll think of something."

"Good. We'll talk soon."

Emma looked around at the dingy wall lining the alley as though the answer to her problems might be scrawled on the bricks. She wanted to scream. To throw something, break everything in her path, and leave a swath of destruction that would make Cesar and his asshole boss cower in her wake. The helplessness she felt was nothing new and it was a cinder burning in the pit of her stomach. She'd experienced the same helplessness when her dad had been convicted of a crime he hadn't committed. And she'd spent the entire six years of his incarceration working, and digging, and nosing around where she had no business doing so to prove that fact.

McCabe's presence in her life had only made matters worse. Their hot make-out session aside, she believed that he wanted to help her. If only in the course of doing his duty. But she couldn't trust him with the information she had. She couldn't trust anyone. If she did, her dad would pay the price with his life, and she knew that neither Cesar, nor the man who employed him, bluffed when it came to their threats.

The thought of impending violence caused Emma's knees to buckle, and she leaned against the wall for support. She wished she were stronger. Not just stronger, *tougher*. Like Cesar and those bastards who'd framed her father. Ruthless and devoid of emotion, ready and willing to do whatever it took to keep herself and her loved ones safe. Instead, she'd become a pawn in their game, and in trying to fight back, she'd enabled them to use her. Pathetic.

The text alert went off on her phone and she opened the message to find a thumbnail image that caused the air to stall in her lungs. She enlarged the image and stared for a long second before her mind grasped exactly what she was looking at. A strangled sob worked its way up her throat, and the image blurred as tears welled in her eyes.

Her dad was tied to a chair, gagged and blind-folded in a nondescript room that could have been anywhere. The walls appeared to be constructed of steel and there was a crude metal staircase directly behind him and huge crates in the background, in-dicating he was being held in some kind of storage facility, though Emma had no idea where. Still in his orange prison jumpsuit, the garment hung from his gaunt frame and he looked worse than he had a couple of weeks ago, the last time she'd seen him at visitation. Emma bit back the tears as she noted his bald head, which had once sported a mop of salt-and-pepper hair. He was too sick to endure what these bastards were putting him through. Appar-ently, Cesar didn't trust that she'd get the marshals off her back and this picture was insurance to help guarantee that she would.

All she had to do was make Landon McCabe go away for good.

Chapter Eight

I don't think. I know.

The conviction in Emma's voice when she'd spoken the words still had Landon a little rattled hours after their encounter. He tried not to weigh the possibility that he could have been wrong—or misled—in the course of conducting the Ruiz investigation six years ago. Evidence never lied. It didn't mislead or play him false. He depended on the evidence gathered in the course of an investigation to justify his actions. Once gathered, evidence became fact and fact could never be disputed.

Right?

Javier Ruiz had confessed to the extortion charge. Looked Landon right in the eye when he said the words. Signed his name to the statement without a second thought or falter in his actions. What could have possibly prompted a man with a flawless reputation and flourishing career to admit so willingly to a crime he hadn't committed?

"McCabe, you got a second?"

Morgan's voice startled him from his musings,

and Landon swiveled in his chair to face the deputy. "Sure. 'Sup?"

Morgan leaned against the desk in the cubicle Landon had taken over and folded his arms across his chest. "I thought you should know that we found something in regards to Emma's involvement in Javier's escape. My chief deputy has been on the phone with the Oregon district office all morning, and he wants us to make an arrest by the end of the day tomorrow."

Landon's pulse jacked up as his mind raced with too many thoughts to find a single coherent thread. "What did you find?" was all he could muster. He knew Emma was hiding something, but he'd hoped her involvement was minimal.

"A couple of weeks before Ruiz's escape, an account in the Cayman Islands was opened in Emma's name. She's the primary signer on it, probably a dummy corporation. Azul LLC. We had a hard time getting a peek at the transaction records, our techs couldn't break past her security protocols. But I made a couple of calls and found a reformed hacker on the FBI's payroll who managed to find a backdoor into the account. Five separate deposits were made that total ten million dollars. And we're assuming that she's planning to make another deposit in the next few days. She also notified a few of her clients that she was going to be taking some time off. Your chief agrees that she might be planning to flee the country with her father, and my chief thinks we should bring her in now rather than wait and risk the chance of losing both of them later."

This new development was putting a serious fucking monkey wrench in Landon's plans. If they took

Emma into custody, she'd shut down completely, and there'd be nothing he could do to get her to confide in him. Already, she refused to put any faith in his ability to help her. How was he going to gain her trust if he was forced to arrest her?

"Why do you assume there will be more deposits?" *And where in the hell did she get ten million dollars?*

"Ruiz's extortion money was never recovered. Isn't that about three-quarters of what he demanded from Mendelson?"

According to Mike Shanahan, Mendelson's CEO, Ruiz had demanded fifteen million dollars for his cooperation. And the deposits didn't do much to proclaim Emma as an innocent party in all of this. Had they been hiding the money all this time? If so, where? And why, when there was so much attention being focused on them, would Emma choose now to shuffle the funds around? None of it made sense. "When are you planning to bring her in?"

"Tomorrow sometime. You have to admit, McCabe, the time line fits. Emma admitted that her last visit with her dad was a couple weeks ago, right after the deposits were made. We want to keep an eye on her for the next eighteen hours or so. Monitor her phone calls and see if she gives anything up. I put in a request this morning for a tap on her cell phone since it's more likely she'd use it than her landline at this point. They're tough to get so I'm hoping we have approval within the week. We've also put an extra set of eyes on her condo and we're watching her known associates. She could have enlisted help from her more powerful friends."

Known associates? Jesus, Morgan was already

treating her like a criminal. "What about the guy I saw her with at the club last night?"

"The banger?" Morgan asked. "Your pics weren't great and our facial recognition software isn't able to match him up with anything. Without a name, it's pretty tough to identify him. At this point, we have to hope he comes around her place or calls her."

Fucktastic.

"All right. I'll do some more digging as well, see what I can find out. Maybe if I question her again, I can get her to cooperate."

"The word from Portland is they don't want us making contact."

Okay, since when was Morgan getting info out of Landon's home office before he was? What the fuck? "This came down from Monroe?" The chief deputy would have surely called him if that was the case.

"I'm just telling you what my superior told me, Landon. I don't know who else is involved in this or how high it goes. All I was told was to bring Ruiz's daughter in tomorrow."

With zero leads on Ruiz's whereabouts and the mysterious offshore account, Emma was the only suspect to pin the escape on at this point. But arresting Emma right now was only going to make things worse, and he knew it wouldn't get them any closer to finding Javier. She'd clam up as tight as . . . well . . . a clam if they pressed her for information and Landon knew for a fact that Emma would gladly go to jail if it meant ensuring her father's safety.

The only problem with that scenario was that Landon wasn't entirely convinced that Javier would be safe whether Emma went to jail or not. "Thanks for the heads-up." What else could he say at this point? Thanks for fucking up my investigation?

Morgan was simply doing his job. "Let me know if you get anything from the wiretaps."

"Will do."

Landon turned back to his computer, staring blindly at the swirling animation of the screen saver. Emma had a solid alibi that covered her on the day of Javier's escape. The man was on chemo. Weak and sick. Yet he'd single-handedly managed to enlist outside help and plan an escape that had allowed him to disappear into thin air?

Yeah, right.

No fucking way.

The gears in Landon's mind cranked as he tried to make sense of the situation. He was more convinced that it wasn't an escape they were dealing with. He racked his brain as he replayed every conversation he'd had with Emma since arriving in Seattle. She'd kept her cool, remained detached, and let very little slip. But Landon had always known that Emma was too smart for her own good. Despite her levelheadedness, she'd been spooked this morning. The phone call she hadn't wanted to answer in Landon's presence was perhaps the most damning piece of evidence that she'd gotten herself into trouble. Who had she been expecting a call from? The banger from last night? And why had there been so much fear in her deep brown eyes?

The possibility seemed so out of left field that Landon wanted to laugh, but he couldn't shake the notion that Javier Ruiz hadn't planned any escape at all. With or without Emma's help. What if someone had abducted him instead? And what the fuck information did he have that would warrant a kidnapping? Landon's stomach twisted into a nervous knot as he pushed the chair out from his desk and grabbed his jacket. He checked the magazine of his Glock, slammed it back into place, and settled the firearm into his shoulder holster before heading out of the office. Emma had declared that she knew her father was innocent. And if she had proof of his innocence, maybe someone wanted to make sure she and her father kept that information to themselves.

Now, if Landon could convince the entirety of the northwest divisions of the U.S. Marshals Service to get on board with that theory, he'd be golden. He just needed Emma to cooperate.

Piece of cake, right?

Climbing Everest might be a less daunting feat.

Emma stared at the Web page displayed on her iPad proclaiming her bank account balance to be ten million, two hundred thousand dollars and some change. At first, this had been about getting one up on the men who'd ruined her—and her father's—life. Showing them that they weren't the omnipotent figures they thought they were. It was a game. Something that had spurred Emma's competitive edge as she set about proving she was the more skilled opponent. Win at all costs. Decimate the other team. It had driven her past reason until she crossed the finish line, victorious. If only she'd thought it through before she'd acted, weighed the consequences of her actions. Now it was too late and she was in too deep to do anything but play their game. Emma hadn't crossed any finish line. She'd *lost.* With a flick of her wrist, she tossed the tablet aside, disgusted, and walked to the large picture window in her living room that overlooked the city.

The sun had set hours ago and through the dark panes of glass, she stared out at the twinkling artificial light dotting the skyline like its own solar system. Seattle might as well be a universe, vast and dark, making Emma feel small and insignificant. A flash of lightning streaked across the sky, followed moments later by the distant rumble of thunder. The first raindrops tapped at the large picture window in slow succession, building to a roar that almost drowned out the sound of her television. Maybe the rain would send the marshals back to their holes for the night. Without a doubt, they were down there on the street, watching her. Waiting for her to leave, to meet someone. To slip up. To hand her father over to them on a silver platter.

At this point, she almost hoped they'd get it over with and arrest her.

Emma's ears perked up as a low *tap, tap, tap* registered under the sounds of the rain and her TV. Almost too quiet to hear at all. She paused. Tilted her head toward the sound. *Tap, tap, tap.*

With slow, quiet steps, she crossed the room. Her heart rate jacked up to about five hundred beats per minute as she made her way to the door. How could she live alone in the city and not even have a can of pepper spray handy? Good Lord. Up until now, she'd existed under the false sense of comfort that came from living in a building with great security. But in the course of a few weeks, not only had the U.S. Marshals barged in without anything more than a heads-up from security, but Cesar had wandered up to the twenty-first floor like he owned the place. Emma grabbed the first heavy object she could find and finished her trek to the door, decorative vase in hand. It might not do a lot of damage, but if push came to shove, she might be able to immobilize an attacker.

The fear that crept up her spine made her want to cringe away from herself in revulsion. She couldn't afford to be afraid.

She took one last calming breath before rising up on her tiptoes to look through the peephole in the door. Landon McCabe stood on the other side, one arm braced against the door, his head hung between his shoulders. Jeez, he looked as tense as she felt. She placed the vase back on the end table and went back to open the door. So, Cesar wasn't here to finish her off, but it looked as if she was about to be taken into custody. She should have felt relief. The way her hands shook when she turned the doorknob, though, told a different story.

McCabe pushed his way in and placed his palm over Emma's mouth, gently shutting the door behind him. Emma tried to back away and struggled against his iron grip, but he wrapped his free arm around her waist and pulled her tight against him. Her hands came up between them to push against his chest and his warmth soaked into her skin, jacking Emma's pulse in a way that wasn't entirely unpleasant. Damn him. She was *trying* to be outraged.

"Is there anyone else here?" Chills danced over Emma's skin as the warmth of his breath brushed her ear. She shook her head in response, and he said, "I'm going to let you go now. Don't say a word, do you understand?"

What in the hell was going on? She pulled back so she could look into his face and the hand that was wrapped around her waist moved to cup the back of her neck. He leaned in and his lips brushed her cheek when he said, "Not. A. Word. Nod your head, Emma."

Bossy.

But she obliged him anyway, giving a sharp nod of acknowledgment. McCabe let her go, and Emma almost melted into the floor without his firm grip to keep her upright. She followed him into the living room, bemused at his strange behavior. As if she thought her situation couldn't get any weirder. By all rights he should have barged in flashing his badge and gun, being seven different kinds of cocky while he tried to intimidate her into cooperating.

Was she in the Twilight Zone?

No, seriously.

McCabe grabbed the TV remote from the coffee table and turned up the volume until it was a notch below annoyingly loud. He crossed back to Emma and again, leaned in so close that their bodies touched. "Your apartment, phone, and cell are tapped and you're going to be arrested tomorrow for conspiracy, aiding and abetting, and a handful of additional charges. Since we can't find Javier, you're going to be the scapegoat, Emma. I know you didn't do this alone. Tell me what's going on so I can stop this arrest. Let me help you."

The conviction in his words didn't go unnoticed. Nor did the way his body tensed when his hand brushed her hip. Electric energy charged the narrow space between them, and Emma's breath sped in her chest. "I can't." She felt as though she were being torn in two. The pressure Cesar put on her was too much. Landon's urging was too much. She was breaking under the strain. "Please, McCabe, go.

Or arrest me right now." Would he? Could he simply slap the cuffs on her right here and now and haul her out into the rain? At least then the situation would be out of her hands.

He took a step back. His eyes drifted shut as he held a breath in his lungs. On the exhale, he raked his fingers through his hair and when his eyes finally opened, there was an unmistakable fire burning in his gaze. "For *once*, can you please not behave like a spoiled child? You're going to go to federal prison, Emma. You think the gossips are up your ass now? They'll have a field day once you're taken into custody!"

Wow. Flag on the play! Personal foul. For someone keeping his voice to a seething whisper, McCabe sure projected his insult well. Did he think this was easy for her? Some kind of game? Let's see how far the spoiled Emma Ruiz can push the U.S. Marshals before they crack?

"Do you think *any* of that matters to me?" McCabe wasn't the only one who could pack a punch while talking like a girl at a slumber party after lights out. She poked a finger into his chest to accentuate her words. "You don't have any idea what I'm dealing with! And don't you dare call me spoiled. You know *nothing* about me."

With the last poke at his broad chest, McCabe caught her wrist in his grip, firm but not tight enough to hurt her. He hauled her against him, and she bucked her chin in the air, meeting him glare for angry glare. "I'm putting my job on the line for you, Emma. If anyone finds out I'm here, alerting you to the fact that you're about to be arrested, I could be fired."

"I didn't ask you to do that. Go. Away."

McCabe had no idea the sort of people Emma was dealing with. Cesar would kill them both and not even bat a lash. The only thing keeping her alive at this point was the information she'd gathered over the past six years and the money she'd stolen a few weeks ago. Once Cesar and his boss got their hands on it, she was as good as dead. Didn't it count for something that she was trying to keep McCabe out of this mess? But if he refused to butt out, there wasn't much she could do to protect him.

"I'm not leaving until you tell me what's going on."

There was no escaping McCabe's tenacity. She had no doubt that he'd park his ass on her couch until the sun rose and his buddies showed up to take her away. And likewise, Emma was no shrinking violet. No way was he going to coerce information out of her. So if she couldn't get rid of him without coming clean, maybe she could misdirect him. Just long enough for her to put his information to good use and get the hell out of there before the marshals screwed everything up.

But what could she tell him that he'd believe? This was why she was way over her head. Emma wasn't a good liar, and aside from the few pranks she'd played on the marshals when she was younger, she didn't exactly do underhanded like a boss. "If I tell you what you want to hear, will you get the hell out of here and leave me alone?" Truth be told, his presence was a safety net she didn't want to let go of, but Emma refused to put anyone else in danger. Even bossypants McCabe.

"If you tell me what I want to hear, I'm going to assume it's a lie," he remarked. The way his blue eyes bored into her, she swore he could see right into her soul. "So whatever you tell me, you'd better make it good."

"Then what in the hell do you expect from me, McCabe?" The man was exasperating. She couldn't decide if she wanted to sock him in the face or kiss him. "Because at this point, I really don't know."

"What I want is for you to quit playing games. What I want is for you to grow up and take this situation seriously." With every second, he grew more agitated, every word forced from between clenched teeth. "What I *want* is for you to stop looking at me like that because if you don't, I'm going to flush my career down the toilet and kiss you again. And I won't stop there, Emma. You can believe that."

Talk about a yo-yo. Emma couldn't keep up with the constant ups and downs of McCabe's moods. Just this morning, he'd thrown their intimate moment in her face, all but mocking her for it. Now . . . well, he'd pretty much said point-blank that he was thinking long and hard about getting them both good and naked.

"How am I looking at you?" She knew she was pressing her luck, but she didn't care. She might be dead by tomorrow afternoon, or worse. Why not live a little?

McCabe took a step closer. So close that Emma had to tilt her head up to look at him. "Like you're dying for me to kiss you. Touch you. Maybe even fuck you." Fire burned in his gaze and his brows drew sharply over his eyes. He reached up and his fingers dove into the hair at her temple. Emma's eyes drifted shut.

Pop! Pop!

The loud burst of sound confused her, and Emma opened her eyes in time for McCabe to tackle her to the floor. She landed with a *whoof!* as all of the air left her lungs in a mad rush. McCabe threw himself on top of her, his arms shielding her head as he tucked his body into hers. The picture window shattered into a million pieces, raining down pebbles of glass that bounced over the surface of the hardwood floor.

"Stay low, and head for the door," McCabe barked. "I'm right behind you, Emma. Don't look back."

"But—"

"No buts," he shouted. "Just move!"

Chapter Nine

What. The. Fuck.

Emma didn't exactly live on the ground floor, which meant someone with a high-powered sniper rifle had them in its crosshairs. It was a miracle they both were still alive, but if they didn't get the hell out of her building in the next five minutes, that status might change.

Landon did a quick assessment of their situation as Emma scrambled to her feet. She wasn't exactly in good shape, running out the door in her bare feet, but at this point, they couldn't afford to stop for her to grab a pair of shoes.

"Where is it coming from?" Emma's voice shook with panic, but she didn't turn around as she raced down the hallway toward the elevators.

A moment of indecision caused Landon's step to falter. The elevator wasn't the safest escape route, but at this point neither was the stairs. As far as he knew, the sniper fire was a tactic to flush them out of the building to make them easier prey. The stairs left them more exposed. But a well-trained assassin could easily ambush them in the elevator. *Fuck it.*

He followed her into the elevator and chambered a round in his Glock. "Hit the fourth floor," he said. "We'll take the stairs from there."

The parking garage could be staked out. And likewise, whoever was after Emma might assume they'd come out through the lobby. Odds were good that Morgan or one of his guys was parked out on the street and even better that, with the wiretap in her apartment, they'd be on their way up to investigate. He should call Morgan and form a plan to get Emma safely out of the building. Damn it, he should. But all the guy would do was take Emma into custody, and that really wasn't going to work for Landon.

"What am I going to do? Oh my God, what am I going to do?" Emma spoke the words under her breath like a mantra, obviously not intending for Landon to offer up a suggestion. "I mean, I'm barefoot. Barefoot! Can you say Britney Spears?"

"Hey." Landon felt an epic meltdown coming on and he needed Emma to keep a level head. "Listen to me. You're going to be okay. I won't let anything happen to you."

She laughed. A loud, manic, disbelieving chuckle that solidified to a cold lump in Landon's gut. Yup, definitely on the verge of freaking out. "You can't protect me, McCabe. You have no idea who you're dealing with." A strangled sob worked its way up her throat. "And if they're trying to kill me, it means my dad is probably already dead, too."

If he'd known a few stray bullets would loosen up her lips, he would have shot at her a couple of days

ago. This was progress. He didn't like the direction
they were headed, but he couldn't do anything
about that. He'd take what he could get. The elevator came to a stop at the fourth floor, and Landon
threw an arm out, guiding Emma away from the
door and out of sight. He held up a finger to his lips
and brought his gun up, ready to fire at the first son
of a bitch who crossed his path as he checked the
hallway.

"Okay, we're clear," he said. "Don't run, don't act
as though anything out of the ordinary is going on.
Just head for the stairs."

"Sure, it's easy for you to act ordinary," Emma
remarked. "You're wearing shoes."

Well, at least she wasn't freaking out and mutter-
ing about Britney Spears anymore. But the comment
did raise a question Landon hadn't thought to address. It was one thing to slip out of the building by
himself, but Emma had a posse of camera-wielding
fanatics camped outside of her building waiting to
memorialize her every move. Really, the Marshals
Service should take a cue from the paparazzi. They
knew how to track someone down. Landon grabbed
Emma's hand and kept her close by his side as they
made their way to the door marked EXIT, which led
to the stairwell. "Okay, Emma, it's time to level with
me. I need to know what we're dealing with before
we hit the street. I can't protect you if you're not
honest with me."

Silence answered him. Great, they were back to
this. . . . "Emma, someone tried to kill you. You can't
keep secrets any longer." He pulled open the door
to the stairwell and paused. "Are you hearing me?"

Behind her veiled expression, storm clouds of

doubt gathered in the dark depths of her eyes. She still didn't trust him. Considered him the enemy. For a minute, he thought about grabbing her by the shoulders and shaking some sense into her, but he knew it wouldn't do much good. He'd never met anyone as stubborn as Emma Ruiz in his entire life.

"Can you get me out of here, McCabe?" Her tone hinted at defeat, but Landon wasn't about to get his hopes up. "And then, we'll talk."

Either Emma wasn't sure what they were up against, or she didn't want Landon to know. Both options left him screwed and he was seriously beginning to doubt his own sanity at trying to get her out of the building without any backup. "Okay, first things first. We've got to ditch our phones." Emma's was being monitored; his relayed his GPS coordinates to anyone with the Marshals Service who wanted a look. They might as well be running around with a big red light flashing above their heads.

"I—I can't," Emma stammered. "There's a number that I need. . . ."

"Your phone is being monitored. If we know where you are, there's a chance the people shooting at you know, too. Lose the phone. It's not up for debate."

She pulled her phone out of her pocket and a sigh escaped her lips as she handed it over to Landon. He stashed it, along with his own, at the top of the stairs. "Okay, now what?"

Shit, he wished he knew. Landon was usually the guy chasing the suspects, not the one helping them to escape. In any other sticky situation, he'd call Galen to get him out of a jam, but since he was three hours and about a hundred and seventy-five miles away, the chances that he'd get here in time to be of any help were pretty slim.

"Is there anyone in the city that you trust? And I don't mean like one of your party pals. Someone who'll do anything for you, no questions asked?"

Emma stared at him for a long moment. "I don't want to bring anyone else into this," she said. "It's bad enough that you're involved."

"Does that mean you're concerned for my safety?" Okay, so maybe this wasn't the time to feel smug satisfaction, but Landon couldn't help himself.

"It means that if you would have stayed out of my business, you wouldn't be dodging bullets and worrying about job security right now. God, McCabe, why couldn't you be a slacker like everyone else in law enforcement?"

She was trying to pick a fight with him, but he refused to acknowledge her slight against his profession. "You can put as many walls up as you want, Emma, but it doesn't change the fact that we're in this together now. You'd be better off accepting it."

"I don't have to accept anything."

Landon opened his mouth to lay into her when the sound of a door slamming open echoed down the stairwell. In an instant, he had Emma's back to the wall, his body pressed up against her and weapon held at the ready. Her body molded to his and each rise and fall of her chest was a distraction Landon couldn't afford as her breasts brushed against his back. Warm breath tickled the back of his neck and his gut clenched tight. Damn it, of all the moments to be living one of many fantasies he'd concocted as a teen . . . Badass cop. Sexy witness.

Danger at every turn. The adrenaline rush was fucking amazing.

Morgan and his partner wouldn't have had time to get into the building yet, so either someone else was a fan of taking the stairs, or they needed to get their asses in gear, like, now. Landon turned to face her and was taken aback by the fear in her dark eyes. He'd always thought of Emma as courageous and stubborn, unwilling to show any sign of weakness. But the vulnerability that marred her soft features was a vise that squeezed every last particle of air from his lungs.

With slow deliberation, he took Emma's hand in his and a wave of tremors passed down her fingers and into his arm as though he was a conduit for her fear. A haze of anger slammed him, damned near blinding Landon as he guided her down the stairs, careful to make as little sound as possible. Her bare feet were nothing more than a whisper on the industrial rubber matting and he tried to keep his own steps as light and soundless as hers. Running would only draw attention to them, and likewise, he wanted to be able to hear any approaching danger. So far, the telltale sounds of anyone charging after them or toward them were eerily absent from the stairwell. Either this was a false alarm, or whoever tracked them was a stealthy motherfucker.

When they hit the lobby floor, Landon peeked out of the doorway first, in case someone was waiting to ambush them. Clear. He grabbed Emma's hand so he could guide her out in front of him and protect her back once in the lobby. He tucked his sidearm into the holster so as not to cause a panic if someone should notice. Law enforcement had a tendency to put even innocent people on edge, especially with a drawn weapon. He wasn't interested in creating a scene—what they needed right now was a quiet, low-key exit. Unless . . . Shit, how could he have overlooked the possibility that a flashy escape was *exactly* what they needed to get out of this alive?

He turned to her and smiled. "Okay, Emma. Let's get the hell out of here."

There wasn't enough oxygen in the world to properly fill Emma's lungs. Landon paused, hand on the levered doorknob of the stairwell exit, listening. The sound of sirens grew louder, and from the tiny square window in the door, Emma watched as the lobby staff jumped into action, answering the phones that had begun to ring in succession. She supposed it wouldn't take long for the building to go on high alert, what with the marshals tracking her every move and the windows of her condo being shot out of existence. Her brain had gone numb around the time McCabe had dragged her out of her condo, and she had a feeling that when the numbness finally wore off, she'd have a hard time keeping it together.

She couldn't think about her father, or what might or might not have happened to him, or what her own attempted murder meant in the grand scheme of things. Right now, her focus was on staying alive, and the only way that was going to happen was to rely on the one man she'd sworn she'd never trust.

"Where are we going?" Emma asked, low, as McCabe guided her toward the door that would take them right into the middle of chaos. He couldn't possibly think it would be better for them to simply walk out onto the street.

"We're going to mingle," McCabe said. Okay, so he'd officially lost his mind. Maybe something jogged loose when he'd taken her down to the floor up in the condo.

"Out there?" Emma's voice climbed an octave as she dug her heels into the tile. "Are you insane?"

"I need to hide you, Emma." He pulled her along and she nearly tripped on her own feet. "And right now, hiding in plain sight is what's going to get us out of here in one piece. Just follow my lead and everything will be okay. Trust me."

Trust him? She wanted to slap some sense into him. "I've got nothing but the clothes on my back, I look like I just rolled out of bed, and don't even get me started on the fact that I'm *not wearing shoes*." She took a deep breath to keep from freaking out. "And you want me to walk out there and face the marshals casing my place, the rabid media, and maybe the person who's trying to kill me?"

"Yup."

Dios mio. His calm self-confidence was going to give her a heart attack. "I can't do it."

"You can." McCabe looked at her from the corner of his eye and a half smile curved his lips. "If you don't, I'll throw you over my shoulder and haul you out the door against your will if I have to."

Why was he doing this? By all rights, she should be handcuffed and in custody right now. She'd never met a straighter shooter than McCabe— seriously, the guy had admitted that he'd arrest his own father if the situation called for it. "I think you should arrest me." The words left her mouth before she could think better of it. Too late to take it back now.

Landon pinched the bridge of his nose between his thumb and forefinger and let out a long-suffering sigh that Emma suspected he saved for moments like this. He was such a drama queen. He leveled his gaze on her, the intensity almost hypnotic, and his mouth formed a hard line. "If you don't get your ass out that door in the next sixty seconds, I'm going to—"

"What, Deputy McCabe?" A man in a pristine black suit strode through the stairwell doorway, an amused smile playing on his lips. "Is this how a decorated U.S. Marshal conducts business? By sneaking around with suspects?"

Landon reached for his sidearm, and the man in the suit gave him a calm but stern appraisal. "Think very carefully before you pull that piece, McCabe."

Emma's heart jumped up into her throat, and she turned to run the opposite direction, only to find her way blocked by similar serious-looking men in suits. Who were they? Because they sure didn't look like anyone Cesar would hang out with.

"Bill Crawford, SOG supervisory director," the man said from behind her. She didn't know what SOG stood for, but she had a feeling this guy's involvement was going to further complicate an already messed-up situation.

Emma turned to face Bill Crawford, supervisory whatever. Why bother to run, or put up a fight? The moment her living room window had shattered into a million pieces, she'd known that she was screwed. Landon's expression was an impassive mask, his eyes glued to Bill Crawford's face as though he doubted every word out of his mouth.

"How do we know you're who you say you are?" She might as well put what she suspected were Landon's thoughts into words. He could be one of Cesar's lackeys come to collect for all she knew.

Bill smiled, and Emma noted that there wasn't a bit of malice in the expression. He fished a badge out of his pocket and held it up for inspection. "You're going to have to trust me, Miss Ruiz."

Yeah, right. Like that was going to happen. "And SOG is . . . ?"

"Special Operations Group," McCabe replied, his voice clipped. He hadn't taken his eyes off of Bill, and Emma couldn't help but notice how he'd positioned his body so that she stood behind his left shoulder. Was he trying to protect her? And if so, why did that make a riot of butterflies swirl in her stomach? Because, really, she should find that totally annoying.

While Bill from SOG and McCabe sized one another up—why did men do that?—yet another guy in a suit opened the door to the stairwell and stepped up beside Bill to murmur something in his ear. Through the little window at the top of the door, Emma noticed a swarm of Seattle police personnel enter the building. To their credit, they kept a low profile and did their jobs without sending the innocent residents milling around the lobby into a full-out panic. Emma didn't know what she expected. Maybe for them to run in screaming, "Shots fired! Shots fired! Everyone on the ground, now!" Sort of anticlimactic, really. Or it was merely a sign that she needed to lay off the cop dramas. Either way, the business-as-usual attitude on display did wonders for her heart rate, and even though she realized she'd probably be spending the night in a jail cell, at least no one would be shooting at her.

"Hell. No." McCabe's outraged voice sliced through the calm of Emma's thoughts as the door slammed, once again shutting them out from the rest of the world.

She shook herself from her thoughts and looked up to find McCabe standing nose-to-nose with the SOG guy. Apparently she'd missed their entire conversation. And while McCabe looked strung tight enough to snap at the slightest pluck, Mr. SOG was still as calm as a newborn. Maybe when your group operated under the label of "special," a Zen attitude got the job done.

"I didn't ask your permission, Deputy."

"It wouldn't matter if you had," McCabe snapped. "You're not taking her into custody. The Ruiz case is mine, and as far as I've been told, the SOG has *zero* reason to be involved."

"Crawford?" One of his fellow suit-wearing associates approached as though McCabe were a bear trap about to snap down on Crawford's leg. She'd never thought of him as particularly threatening until now. Dude was pissed enough to blow a gasket at any second. "The lobby has been secured and our guys have Seattle PD under control. How do you want to move forward?"

Bill all but ignored McCabe, who was still all up in his grill, and replied, "Call forensics in to process the condo. And tell them to be thorough." He cast a side-long glance at Emma. "Treat it as a murder scene."

"Murder scene?" McCabe spat, his composure evaporating before Emma's eyes.

"Unfortunately," Bill said, turning his gaze back to McCabe, "Miss Ruiz died en route to the hospital."

Chapter Ten

As though on cue, the sound of a siren howled in the distance. Her stomach coiled tight and a lump formed in her throat. Her brain couldn't process what was happening and threatened to shut down at any second. Murder scene? Died on the way to the hospital? *"What?"*

Crawford cracked the door leading into the lobby, and Emma watched as a trio of emergency service personnel wheeled a gurney past the front desk and toward the stairwell. "For now, that's the story. It's the best we can do on such short notice. You have no choice but to play along."

Emma's breath stalled in her chest. Her vision darkened at the periphery and the floor tilted at a strange angle. *Oh shit.* She was going to pass out. No way could she let McCabe see her crumple like a discarded piece of paper. Time out. Time out on the field! Emma was tough, damn it. She could hold her own, and despite everything that had happened, life hadn't managed to beat her down yet.

"Emma?" McCabe's voice went from growly to concerned in a beat. Go figure. "Are you okay?"

She supposed the gurney wasn't a bad idea considering her legs were about to give out on her. The adrenaline high that kept her going thus far began to wane, and wouldn't you know it, at the worst possible time. McCabe took a step toward her, and Emma's spine went ramrod straight. "I'm fine, McCabe. Don't get your panties in a bunch."

Vulnerability wasn't something Emma could afford right now. And likewise, she refused to give anything up to these SOG guys that would confirm the fact that McCabe had been trying to sneak her out of the building under everyone's nose. He'd saved her life tonight, it was the least she could do for him.

"What are you guys doing here and what makes you think I'll play along with your little murder scenario? I don't exactly look like I'm about to keel over."

Bill smiled, and what she'd first thought of as calm and friendly came off as a little devious and creepy. He took two quick steps toward her and smashed his palm into her chest right above her left breast. With a quick tug to open the stairwell door, he shouted, "She's bleeding! I need an EMT over here!"

Emma looked down at her pink T-shirt as a sticky pool of red spread out on the cotton fabric. Eyes wide, she watched as Bill removed a handkerchief from his pocket and casually wiped the crimson liquid from his palm. "I suggest you play along and hit the deck, Miss Ruiz. Otherwise, I don't know if I'll be able to save your father."

She shifted her gaze to McCabe, jaw slack. His expression echoed her own, and once again she felt her legs turn to spaghetti beneath her. Emma kept her eyes glued to Landon, watching as it took a split second for him to regain his bearings and rush to her, arms out moments before she felt her legs give out.

Well, shit. So much for being a tough girl . . .

Emma lay on the gurney, eyes closed and body still, as a media storm swirled around her. She didn't look so hot, and that made Landon's chest tighten. He wouldn't have thought it possible for her to look so pale, a sheen of sweat glistening on her brow. Even her breathing appeared shallow. He shot a glare at Bill Crawford as the paramedics loaded the gurney up into the waiting ambulance. It took all the self-control he had left not to pop him in the face for hitting her with the red dye pack. Who knew the SOG guys were so goddamned devious? He was definitely going to have a talk with Galen about that. They even made sure to keep that telltale stain visible as the paramedics wheeled Emma out of the building. By tomorrow morning, the Internet would be smeared with the dramatic photographic evidence and Landon would be surprised if the local news stations weren't already running the story: Socialite daughter of escaped federal prisoner shot in her downtown condo. . . . *Wonderful.*

"Better get in, Deputy," Crawford said, inclining his head toward the ambulance. "She's technically a suspect in custody."

Landon would be sorely tempted to put his badge on the line for one shot at Crawford. But since giving up his badge would give him no choice but to crawl home to his family, he gritted his teeth and swallowed down the anger that caused his hands to curl into tight fists at his side. "I'll see you at the hospital?" he asked.

Crawford answered with a single nod.

Landon poked his head inside before stepping up into the ambulance. The paramedics had been ushered to the front of the vehicle, and a couple of Crawford's suits were sitting to one side of Emma on a bench. He took the opposite bench—no way was he sitting with any of those MIB-looking dudes—and cradled his head in his hands. He'd reached new heights of fucking up with this investigation. Monroe was going to have his ass in a sling when he got back to Portland.

"Do I look like I'm dying?" Emma's eyes were still shut and her voice nothing more than a whisper.

Landon leaned in until his mouth hovered near her ear and said, "I'm going to get you out of this mess, Emma."

If Landon knew what was good for him, he would've kept his fool mouth shut. What was it about her that spurred every protective instinct he had? And why, for the love of God, couldn't he do his damned job without making promises he didn't know if he could keep? *Maybe it has something to do with the fact that you're craving one kiss more from her?* Or how every time she touched him, his heart rate elevated, adrenaline coursed through his veins, and he experienced the most intense rush he'd ever felt? Yeah, that *might* have something to do with his bad decision making over the past couple of days.

"What makes you think I deserve to be gotten out of anything?" Her breath was warm on his cheek.

Landon leaned back to study her, but Emma kept her eyes closed good and tight. Was she admitting to something? The SOG guys were eyeballing him from across the gurney. Can you say awkward? Emma tried to sit up, fiddling with the buckles holding her secure on the gurney, but one of the suits held out his hand.

"I need you to stay down, Miss Ruiz."

Landon rolled his eyes. It wasn't like anyone was going to get a peek inside of a moving vehicle with two little tiny windows. "Look, McCabe, I get that you feel bad about how all of this has gone down, but . . ." She turned away from the SOG guys and lowered her voice to a whisper. "You shouldn't feel obligated to do anything for me because of what happened the other night."

Obligated. She thought he felt *obligated*? Did she have any clue how that came off? *Obligated* translated to *responsible* as far as he was concerned. As though he'd taken advantage of her somehow. He caught Crawford's men from the corner of his eye watching their exchange with a little too much interest. Great. Now his life had been reduced to cheap, dramatic entertainment. "I don't feel obligated." His eyes narrowed with annoyance, and he sat up, crossing his arms across his chest. "I still have a job to do, Emma. And I'm going to do it."

"Well, looks like you'll be on your own from here on out, McCabe, because if you hadn't noticed . . . I'm dead."

Landon had no fucking clue what was going on or how the Special Operations Group had gotten involved in the Ruiz case, but he'd be damned if he let Crawford and his colleagues give him the runaround. He was starting to wish he hadn't ditched his phone in the stairwell because this entire setup reeked of something dirty. He would have liked to at least touch base with Galen—you know, in case these SOG guys buried him in a shallow grave or some shit.

Because if SOG was involved, it wasn't a stretch to think the FBI or CIA might be as well. And those central intelligence dudes were some scary mother-fuckers.

He decided that trying to reason with Emma right now would get him nowhere. If they'd made it out of her building, Landon knew he could have con-vinced her to open up to him. But now she was locked down tight and no amount of arguing was going to convince her to come clean. Just one more thing for him to lay at Bill Crawford's feet. Landon leaned back on the bench seat and rested his head on the rack behind him. A slow, measured breath re-leased from his lungs as he closed his eyes and tried to center himself.

Emma had him tied into goddamned knots.

He needed a plan of attack. A course of action that he could implement once he had some idea of what kind of mess they'd wound up in. Chances were good that once they took them to wherever they were going, Landon would be debriefed—meaning they'd question the shit out of him and then reciprocate by giving him as much information as his pay grade allowed—and send him on his way. And if they thought for a second that he'd simply tuck tail and head home, deserting Emma, well, they had another fucking think coming.

The ambulance pulled into an underground

parking garage at the University of Washington Medical Center. Smart. The city's top hospital would undoubtedly have the best security. When the ambulance pulled to a stop, Bill Crawford was waiting outside the doors. Landon wondered if the dude realized he was giving off a sort of creepy vibe. Like Lurch from *The Addams Family*. He exchanged a few inaudible words with his colleagues and directed the paramedics as to where to take Emma. "Sorry, Miss Ruiz, but you're dead," he said as he covered her head with a white sheet. She stared upward as she was covered, displaying no outward show of emotion. Her seeming resignation burned in the pit of Landon's gut. Surely she wasn't beaten down so easily? Not the tough, snarky Emma Ruiz he knew.

"Follow me, Deputy McCabe," Crawford said as the gurney was wheeled into the hospital.

"*No fucking way* am I leaving her unattended," Landon snarled. "You've got a pair on you if you think—"

"You don't get a choice," Crawford interrupted as his team veered off to follow the paramedics and Emma. "As of now, you're off this case, Deputy. And unless you want an armed escort to take you back to Portland, I suggest you play ball. Understand?"

Landon gnashed his teeth so hard he damned near ground his molars to dust. He was itching for a fight, and Crawford might be the bastard to give him one. "I think my office might have a thing or two to say about that. Fugitive recovery falls under our jurisdiction."

Crawford let out a long-suffering sigh, as though dealing with Landon was one too many things for him to handle. Well, too damned bad. "Ruiz isn't a fugitive, McCabe. He's a hostage."

I fucking knew *it.* "I think I know who has him." That son of a bitch from the club. It had to be. Maybe Landon could use his knowledge to keep him on the case and by Emma's side.

"We already know who it is," Crawford replied.

Well, shit. That took the wind out of his sails. He might have been down, but he was far from out, though. Crawford headed inside the hospital and Landon followed, keeping pace as they walked to wherever Crawford was taking him. "How does Emma fit into this? At this point, I find it hard to believe that she orchestrated her own father's kidnapping and is holding him hostage. Why not turn her over into our custody and let us put her into WITSEC until this is wrapped up?"

"Witness Security is off the table at this point. It's not that simple."

Crawford ushered him into an empty meeting room and shut the door. He motioned for Landon to take a seat and he leaned a hip against the table instead. "Thanks, but I think I'll stand."

"Suit yourself," Crawford replied with a shrug. "I'm sure I don't have to tell you this, but the Ruiz case goes way above your pay grade, McCabe. I don't have to supply you with shit. *But,*" he stressed as Landon opened his mouth to protest, "out of professional courtesy, I'll tell you what I can."

Well, wasn't that *courteous* of him. What a crock. "All right, then. Tell me."

Crawford leveled a laser-intense gaze on Landon before he said, "About eighteen months ago, one of our undercover agents was working a tip we'd received about an arms dealer who was funding the weapons end of his organization via human trafficking. We've been partnered up with Department of Homeland Security and the FBI on this case for almost a year and were getting close to making an arrest."

"Does the dealer have a name?" Landon took a chance and asked even though he doubted Crawford would play ball.

He simply smiled. "From what we've been able to determine, he's trying to get his hands on something big."

"A dirty bomb?" Landon ventured.

Crawford nodded. "Nuclear and ready to be shipped to the highest bidder."

A dull ache throbbed behind Landon's eyes and he massaged his temples. The pain in his head was nothing compared to the spike of adrenaline dumping into his system as the weight of the situation came crashing down on him.

"And Emma? How does she fit into this?"

"Now *that's* above your pay grade."

Of course it was. Landon raked his fingers through his hair, the gears cranking in his mind as he tried to think of a way to get Emma out of this mess. "Why the cloak-and-dagger act, then? If she's involved, and obviously valuable to you guys, why stage her death?"

"To be honest, we didn't think you'd be quite so good at your job, McCabe." The backhanded compliment was laughable, but Landon let it slide. "We figured you'd question Emma, but her alibi was airtight, so I didn't think you'd stay on her for long. I guess I was wrong."

Not merely wrong. Crawford was straight-up stupid.

"Emma's been working with your office all this time?" Landon waited for an answer, gauging Crawford's reaction. Emma was just as surprised as he'd been when SOG showed up on the scene. No way was she that good of an actress.

"Unintentionally," Crawford replied.

Anger surged in Landon's chest and he pushed himself away from the table, going nose-to-nose with Crawford. "You mean you used her as *bait*?"

Crawford shrugged, and it was all Landon could do not to deck the son of a bitch. "This is a national security issue, McCabe. I don't have to explain myself to you or anyone else. I'm getting the job done, and that's all there is to it."

"By risking the life of an innocent woman?" Landon all but shouted. "What the hell sort of crackerjack operation are you guys running, Crawford?"

Landon released a deep breath as he tried to calm the fuck down. Crawford wasn't the enemy. They played for the same team, for Christ's sake. Worked for the same damned agency. In any other situation, Landon would be nodding his head, agreeing with every single tactic Crawford or any other agency sought to employ in order to take down their target and get the win. The animosity he felt toward the other man had nothing to do with proper procedure or even the way he conducted his operation. Rather, this had *everything* to do with Landon's irrational need to protect Emma at all costs.

"What about Javier?" he asked. "How does Emma's dad fit into all of this?"

"Again, McCabe. This is a national security matter and the details of this operation are classified. I'm telling you this much because I think you're good at your job and you deserve to go back to Portland with some sort of explanation. I wish I could tell you more. But I can't."

Frustration pooled in his gut like acid. The feeling of helplessness threatened to drive his anger to a point he doubted he'd come back from. Professionally, anyway. One misstep and you could bet Crawford would have his badge. But Landon refused to simply abandon Emma and let the U.S. government continue to use her like some sort of expendable pawn.

"I'll be on the phone with your chief deputy when I walk out of this room," Crawford warned. "I suggest you don't waste any time getting back to Portland. We appreciate your work on this case, but this is where your involvement ends."

"So that's it?" Landon asked as Crawford headed for the conference room door. A swath of light cut through the darkness as he pulled it open, casting a long, ominous shadow behind him. He understood working a case close to the hip, clearance levels, national security, and the need to keep secrets safe. But what Landon couldn't get behind was the way they'd decided to use Emma to get what they wanted without her consent. "What if she cracks? She was barely keeping it together before any of this went down. What makes you think she'll play ball?"

Crawford turned, his face partially hidden in shadows. "They have her father, McCabe. She's been playing for quite a while now."

The door closed with an echoing finality that made Landon's gut clench. He'd spent years building his career into something he could be proud of, even at the expense of his family's disapproval.

Exhaustion won out as Landon slumped down on the table's surface, his own indecision warring with common sense.

He should walk out that door. Right now. Take a cab to Emma's apartment, get his car and his shit, and go home. Work a new case and move on.

Forget all of this.

Instead, Landon crossed the room to the far wall and picked up the landline. He accessed an open line and dialed.

"Hello?" Galen answered after a few rings.

"It's me," Landon said.

"Oh, hey," Galen replied. "Where are you calling from? Making any headway up there?"

"I need a favor," Landon said. "And no one, not even Monroe, can know about it."

There was a long pause, and then Galen replied, his tone somber, "What do you need?"

Chapter Eleven

Emma waited in a room that she assumed was reserved for trauma patients. People in serious need of medical attention who might be teetering on the precipice of death. It didn't sit well with her that she was occupying a space that someone might need. That the tools and machinery surrounding her could save someone's life, and instead they sat there, useless, nothing more than a bunch of props to help perpetuate the story that she'd died from a gunshot wound earlier in the night.

Outside the door, Bill Crawford's men stood guard like a couple of gargoyles, showing no outward sign of movement. Emma couldn't help but wonder if her appointed sentries were there to keep curious onlookers out, or to keep her in. Either way, a spasm of nervous energy skittered through her veins as she tried to control the frantic beat of her heart.

Because she had a feeling that these SOG guys were totally off sides.

Running their offense ahead of the allowable

defense, they'd managed to tip the scales in their favor by orchestrating her fake death. And the fact that they'd stepped in and walked all over McCabe as though he were no more important than a second-stringer on the sidelines told her that not only did these guys mean business, but they knew what she was up to as well.

Crap.

As she waited for Crawford to show up and work his intimidating secret-government-guy mojo on her, Emma craned her neck toward the door hoping to spot some sign of McCabe. She had to admit that she felt a lot better when he was around. Safer. Even when she had been a rash, impulsive teenager and she'd known he was the enemy, she'd felt safer when he was in the room. As though he'd never let any-thing bad happen to her. It was totally lame and childish, she knew. But right now, she felt as helpless and afraid as she had when she was that eighteen-year-old girl watching as her father was handcuffed and taken to prison.

Once again, she was alone.

"Sorry to keep you waiting, Miss Ruiz."

Bill Crawford strolled into the room with all of the confidence of a man in his position. If she'd learned anything over the years, it was that when you gave some people an inch, they took a mile, and that went for power plays, too. If she let Crawford think he was running the show, he'd steamroll her. The only option at this point was to beat him at his own game.

It was still too soon to know what the SOG's inten-tions were. And even though, deep down, Emma knew they were the good guys, there was still that part of her that harbored a deep mistrust of anyone in law enforcement. The marshals had helped put her father away without batting a single lash, so sure he'd been guilty. Hadn't any of them seen past those ridiculous accusations and realized that they were prosecuting an honorable, decent man?

How could she possibly trust any of them?

"I know my rights and I want to contact my lawyer. I'm not going to say a word to you or any of your people until I have legal counsel present."

Crawford chuckled, making it clear how entertaining he found her request. "As it pertains to issues of national security, I'm afraid you have no rights, Emma."

National security? What in the hell was he talking about? "Look, buddy, I've been through this before and you feds are all alike. You think you can push me around, threaten me, scare me into cooperating. It's not gonna happen. Not without my lawyer present."

Crawford gave her a cold, emotionless smile that seemed to bring the air temperature down twenty or so degrees. "As of this moment, I have more than enough evidence to slap you in a prison so far away and so secret, I'll have no problem convincing people that you're dead. The fact of the matter is, you're in way over your head here, and unless you cooperate, Teyo Sousa won't hesitate to instruct Cesar Molina to kill your father."

If there was one thing her dad had drilled into her head, it was that rash decisions and hasty words didn't do anyone a bit of good. By dropping two tiny names, Crawford had shown her that he knew way more about her situation than she'd thought. She needed to move forward cautiously. After all, he'd said he could help save her dad. That wasn't an offer she could discount quite yet.

"You wouldn't be trying to leverage me if you didn't need something from me. And it's totally shitty of you to hold prison and my dad's life over my head in exchange for what you want."

"In the course of trying to exonerate your father, you managed to stir up a hornet's nest, Emma. So you can think this is as shitty as you want, but you're in this situation by your own doing. Believe me when I tell you that Teyo Sousa isn't someone you're equipped to tangle with. If you go this alone, you and your father will be dead. No pretending. I'm offering you an end to this once and for all: your father's life for your cooperation. I'd think the decision would be an easy one for you to make."

Emma's mouth went dry. Her pulse jacked up as her heart threatened to break out of her chest. All she wanted was to clear her dad's name and take care of him while he was sick. Nothing was happening the way she'd planned it to. She wanted to trust Crawford. But . . . "I want to see Landon McCabe."

Crawford's expression soured. "I'm afraid that's not possible, Emma. Deputy McCabe is no longer working this case. I doubt he's even still in the building."

By getting rid of McCabe, Crawford had managed to cut Emma off from any possible support system. She struggled for a deep breath, but found that there wasn't enough oxygen to fill her lungs. "Well, that's too bad for you, then." She infused her voice with every ounce of strength in her reserves. She didn't know if she could trust the SOG bigwig, but she was starting to believe that she *could* put her trust in McCabe. She'd been going it alone for so long that the prospect of having a little help gave Emma hope that she might get her dad out of this situation after all. She didn't want to be alone, not anymore, and Crawford needed to know she wasn't going to let him make an island out of her again. "Because I'm not saying another word until you find him."

Emma leveled her gaze on Crawford and stared him down. She clamped her jaw down tight for good measure to drive home her point. A few moments passed, a battle of wills that was laughable when Emma considered her situation. The sound of Crawford's phone sliced through the quiet, effectively ending their standoff. With a curse under his breath, he pulled his cell from his jacket pocket and answered with a curt, "Crawford."

As he listened to whoever was on the other end of the call, his gaze landed on Emma and he shot her a glare that should have killed her right where she sat. "You've got to be fucking kidding me," he growled into the receiver. Without a parting word, he spun on his heel, phone still glued to his ear, and stomped out of the room.

Despite the interruption, Emma considered herself the winner of round one.

Landon waited in the dark conference room, laid back in his chair with his feet propped up on the table. When he heard the door open behind him, he let his eyes drift shut, a pleasant, albeit triumphant smile playing on his lips. Sometimes, having influential friends paid off, and though he'd owe Galen for the rest of his damned life, it was totally worth calling in the favor.

"I suppose you think you're hot shit, Deputy. But all you've proved to me is that you're willing to risk national security by running off at the mouth."

Landon didn't need to look at Crawford to know the man was absolutely livid. Each word he spoke was clipped with barely restrained rage. And he knew Crawford hadn't counted on Landon being quite as connected as he was. Well, to tell the truth, it was Galen who had all the fancy-dancey political connections, but Crawford didn't need to know that. Besides, it wasn't as though he was going out of his way to ruin Crawford's operation. He wasn't that big of an asshole. First and foremost, Landon was a professional. What he'd wanted to get from the strings he'd pulled was the chance to be close to Emma. To watch out for her. She needed someone who had her best interests at heart. Instead of being a hindrance, he wanted to be an asset to the investigation.

"Pull your Hanes out of your crack and try to settle down, Crawford. I didn't compromise your mission. I just want in."

"You want in all right, but I doubt it has anything to do with this operation."

The innuendo in Crawford's words ignited Landon's temper, and he swung his legs down from the table, turning in his chair to face the other man. He leveled his gaze on Crawford and stood slowly, his fists clenched at his sides. "You make an insinuation like that again and you'll be picking your ass up off the floor. I don't give a shit who you work for or what kind of weight you can swing around. Get me?"

"Get this, McCabe," Crawford said as he opened the door and held it open in invitation. "You step a toe out of line and I'll show you exactly what kind of weight I have. You won't be able to land a job as a security guard at the local mall when I'm done with you."

Landon smiled as he walked out into the hallway ahead of Crawford. He'd like to see him try.

They headed down a long corridor into a section of the emergency room reserved for trauma patients. All around them, nurses and doctors hustled from one room to the next, machines beeped and buzzed, and no one paid them a bit of attention. For all intents and purposes they were ghosts. And Landon was willing to bet the SOG had little trouble maintaining their obscurity.

At the end of the corridor, Landon noticed a couple of Crawford's men standing guard outside of a room. He moved out ahead of the other man, shouldering his way through the door, daring either one of them to make a move to stop him. Once inside, he stopped just shy of the doorway, his gaze drinking in every last detail of the woman seated on the hospital bed before him. Her T-shirt and chest were stained with red dye. Her curls were wild and disheveled. She was obviously worked over and exhausted.

And she looked damned beautiful.

"Are you okay?"

She nodded in response and gave him a wan smile. "I have no idea what's going on, though."

"Well, that's not going to be a problem because we're about to get down to brass tacks, right, Crawford?"

The door closed quietly behind them, and Landon gave Emma a reassuring smile.

"Thanks to your stubbornness and McCabe's . . . *resourcefulness*, you've both created a problem we'll be forced to deal with before we can even let you out of here."

"Which is . . . ?" Landon asked without turning to face Crawford.

Crawford walked deeper into the room and settled down on a stool next to Emma. He propped his feet up on the rungs and leveled his gaze on Landon. "The whole point of orchestrating Emma's death was to give the appearance that you—and the Marshals Service—were off her back. How am I supposed to explain your presence to our target and his associates? I can't exactly have you hanging around."

Emma's expression went from zero to abject panic in less than a second, which told Landon that Emma knew even less about what was going on than he did. "Okay, let's back up a bit." Landon didn't dare take another step closer to Emma because he didn't know if he could keep himself from reaching out to take her hand. Her apprehension was palpable, and no matter how mad he was at her for keeping her damned secrets, he doubted she deserved what Crawford was putting her through. "We need to start from the beginning before we can even think about making a decision about how to proceed."

"We don't have all night, and now I've got to deal with debriefing not only the Portland chief, but Seattle's as well. So let's get to it before this whole plan goes to shit." Crawford propped his elbows on his knees and leaned in toward Emma. "In digging for information to exonerate your dad, you inadvertently landed in the middle of an arms deal, Emma. And if Cesar Molina's employer gets his hands on the weapon he's trying to buy, a lot of people could lose their lives."

"Wait." Emma's brow furrowed as her gaze darted to Landon for a split second. "Arms deal? What are you talking about? Cesar and his boss are human traffickers, not terrorists. They've been smuggling women out of Mexico for the past ten years and selling them into the sex trade. They used Mike Shanahan to launder their money through Mendelson. And when the FTC brought insider-trading charges against Mendelson, they framed my dad with some bogus story about extortion to divert the feds' attention from finding out what they were really up to. I've got all of the records to prove it."

Oh, shit, Emma. A renewed sense of anger boiled in Landon's gut at the thought of how deep this went. And by nosing around where she clearly didn't belong, Emma had landed herself right in the middle of an international terrorism investigation.

"I was getting ready to contact the FBI when they kidnapped my dad."

Landon rolled his head on his shoulders in an effort to banish the tension holding his neck in a vise. "They couldn't have known you were going to the feds, Emma. What did you do that would prompt them to kidnap Javier?"

She worried her bottom lip between her teeth as she looked askance at Crawford. Landon tried not to let her mouth distract him, but he couldn't seem to tear his gaze away. "About six months ago, right after my dad got sick, he told me everything. He said that when the FTC and DOJ was investigating Mendelson, a man by the name of Teyo Sousa reached out to him. Apparently they'd grown up together and Teyo figured that my dad would do him a solid for old time's sake. A grand jury was being convened to indict Mike Shanahan and more arrests wouldn't be far behind. Sousa couldn't afford for Mendelson to be investigated because it would lead back to his organization and money laundering. When he refused to help him, Sousa sent Cesar to visit my dad and he told him that if he didn't throw out the case and the indictments, they'd make his daughter suffer. So Dad did everything they asked him to do. Then, to make sure he wouldn't talk later down the line, they framed him, had him thrown in jail, and told him that I'd never be safe unless he kept quiet.

"But I couldn't let Dad go to the feds without information to back up his confession. So I hacked Shanahan's private files, looked into Mendelson's finances and followed the trail back to Sousa. I can't prove the human trafficking, though I know without a doubt it's going on. But I have enough to put him and Shanahan away on money laundering and conspiracy. And I thought that with what I had, and the information my dad was going to give them, that the feds would negotiate his release from prison."

"That's not all, though, is it, Emma?"

A dark cloud passed over her expression as she said to Crawford, "I also hijacked all of Sousa's financial records, siphoned the money from his accounts, and buried it so deep he'd never find it. I wanted him to pay for what he did to my dad and so I took something away from him that he cared about. His money. And"—she cringed—"I might have dangled the fact in front of his face to show him what it felt like to have something important taken away from him. I got cocky. Thought I had him right where I wanted him. I gathered up everything I had on Sousa, and he took my dad before I could go to the FBI with it."

Landon thought his eyes might bug right out of his head. *Holy fucking shit.* Crawford gave him a look. The only reason Emma was still alive was because she had a badass arms dealer's money. And what she'd taken as the spoils of her personal war were now being used as ransom to secure her father's safety.

"Emma . . ." Landon didn't know what to say. Where to begin. "You're lucky you're not dead right now!" He hadn't meant to raise his voice, but the gravity of the situation hit him with the force of a jackhammer to the chest. No wonder Crawford was wound up. This was a disaster! "Do you realize what you've done? Who you've pissed off? Jesus Christ." The danger she was in was not only real, it was god-damned severe. Because they were dealing with a WMD, Crawford and his people would put Emma's safety second to making an arrest. Their only concern was intercepting a bomb. In their eyes, she was an acceptable sacrifice. A casualty of war. And Landon had no clue how he'd manage to get them out of this mess in one piece.

Not when Emma was already in too deep.

"So with the Marshals Service bringing heat down on Emma, your guy on the inside suggested to

Sousa's number two that he could find a way to fake her death, am I right?"

Crawford nodded. "More or less. My undercover man was on the other end of that sniper rifle tonight. We were hoping to get to Emma before you did, but it didn't work out that way. We certainly hadn't intended to let you think someone was trying to kill you, Emma. You weren't ever in any real danger tonight."

Landon was thankful that Crawford was being more upfront, but he knew that he was intentionally leaving out more than a few details. He'd let Landon fill in most of the blanks and confirmed the truth when it was absolutely necessary. That way, he wasn't offering up more information than he needed to, keeping the hows and whys to himself and holding just enough back that Crawford still maintained control over the situation and the safety of his undercover man.

"The buy is supposed to happen in less than a week. If Sousa doesn't get his money back, he'll miss his one and only opportunity to get his hands on the merchandise. They need Emma. Right now, she's holding all of the cards."

Landon expelled his breath in a single gust. "Yeah, she is."

Their gazes locked and for a moment, Emma merely sat there. She was too damned smart for her own good and he was waiting for the moment when everything clicked into place for her and she lost it completely.

"What now?" Her voice was quiet, but not even a little unsure. Landon respected that. He'd always known she was stubborn, but she was also tougher than he'd given her credit for.

"Now, we put you up somewhere for the night. The PIO for the Marshals Service will be making a statement to the press soon, confirming that you were shot at your apartment this evening and died en route to the hospital. Once we make contact with our man on the inside, we'll proceed. If we're lucky, we can trade Sousa's money and the information you have on him in exchange for your father. We'll take it from there."

Sounded simple enough, but Landon knew from experience that even the best plans were never as simple as they sounded. "Luckily, witness protection is sort of my business. My hotel is outside the city limits. It's low-key, easy to patrol, and if it comes down to it, I could set up a security protocol with little to no effort. Emma can stay there tonight."

"In your room?" Crawford cocked a curious—and not a little mocking—brow.

"Why not?" Landon kept his tone level, though what he wanted to do was pop Crawford in the face for his snarky bullshit attitude. "I'm already set up and no one will notice if I bring a woman in with me."

Crawford let out a derisive snort.

"And what makes you think we'll remand custody of Miss Ruiz over to you, McCabe? As far as I'm concerned you were trying to sneak her out of her building under your own people's noses when we intercepted you. What's to say you don't take off with her the second we let you two out of here?"

Though he was sorely tempted to do just that, Landon knew that Emma would never abandon her dad. And likewise, he would never abandon his duty. "You're just going to have to trust me, Crawford."

"I guess I am." Crawford stood and came at Landon head-on, poking a finger at his chest. "But if you step even a toe out of line, I'll have your badge, McCabe."

He might have been ready to throw down with Crawford earlier, but this was a completely different game now. Too much was at stake for him to be anything less than one hundred percent from here on out. "Not a toe, sir. You won't have to worry about it."

Chapter Twelve

Emma spent the drive to Landon's hotel, the walk across the parking lot to the back entrance of the hotel, the short ride up the elevator, and the long— *oh so long*—walk down the hallway to his room contemplating the many downfalls of her current situation. One of which being how she was going to handle being locked up in close quarters with a certain deputy U.S. marshal for God knew how long.

Landon closed the door behind them, and Emma reached to pull the obnoxious blond wig that Crawford had made her wear from her head. It itched like crazy and made her entire skull feel as though it were encased in flames. Humid flames. Humid, itchy, hot, annoying flames. *God, how do women wear these things?*

"Hold up," Landon said as he crossed the room and pulled the drapes closed. "We can't run the risk that anyone will see you. You're dead, remember?"

His harsh tone was salt in an open wound, and Emma didn't appreciate it a bit. After Crawford's come-to-Jesus, it had been another two hours' wait for his people to get Emma a change of clothes, shoes, and a wig—which made her stand out even more in her opinion—before they let Landon take her to the hotel. She checked the clock on the bedside table, a little past one in the morning. It would be a miracle if she slept at all tonight, and though her mind raced with innumerable thoughts, her body was ready to go down for the count.

"I don't know why you're so bent out of shape, McCabe." His attitude was getting on her nerves, all growly with his brows drawn sharply over his bright blue eyes. She didn't like the Crankypants version of McCabe in the least. "You wanted to know the dirty details of my dad's escape. Well, you got them. It's not my fault the story wasn't the one you wanted to hear."

"Yeah," he scoffed. "There was no escape. Javier was kidnapped because you stole millions of dollars from arms dealers." Landon flopped down on the armchair in the corner of the room. "No wait, not *just* arms dealers. *Terrorists*. Do you have any idea what you've done, Emma?"

"I wasn't going to keep the money." Did he think she was stupid?

His eyes widened with disbelief. "This has *nothing* to do with the money!"

"I didn't know they were arms dealers."

Landon gave her a pointed look.

"Okay, so maybe I didn't dig deep enough. But in my defense, I didn't know what I was looking for."

"Emma." Landon's frustration stifled the air, stole the breath from Emma's lungs. "You shouldn't have been looking at all!"

Jeez, why the sudden hostility? If he didn't stop

shouting at her, someone was going to call in a noise complaint. That'd help her keep a low profile. "You know, I'm starting to think that you're just pissed off that I took your precious case away from you," Emma spat. "Does it rankle the great Landon McCabe to know that you were *wrong* when you arrested my dad six years ago? That you were *wrong* when you rolled into town thinking you could scare me into giving him up? And that you were *wrong* in thinking that you were the biggest, baddest, most intimidating federal cop around?"

McCabe shot up out of his chair and crossed the space between them in a few long strides. Emma's heart thundered and her stomach wrung itself into an anxious knot as she backed away from him, stopping only when the wall gave her nowhere else to go. She shouldn't have tried to get under his skin, but he was so far off base in chastising her that he didn't even have a foot on the damned bag. Did he not realize how scared she was? How utterly ashamed that she'd endangered not only her own life, but her dad's? She already felt like crap. She didn't need McCabe to bring her even lower.

His large frame seemed to take up all of the available space, crowding her until Emma found it difficult to focus. Her head swam with his masculine, outdoorsy scent, and his breath feathered across her cheek, prompting her to look him square in the face. "You think that's what this is about?" McCabe caged her in with one arm, bracing it on the wall behind her. His voice was low with a dark edge that heated Emma's skin. "My *ego*?"

It had been a long night and Emma had reached her threshold. Any more stress and her brain might explode. McCabe's face loomed above hers, his blue eyes sparking with anger. A muscle ticked at his cheek as his jaw clenched tight. Holy mother of God, he was the most beautiful man Emma had ever laid eyes on. Even in his anger, he was magnificent. Emma balled her fists at her side, resisting the urge to reach up and stroke her fingers along the strong line of his jaw and the rough stubble that shadowed his cheek. "Look, we're both tired and wound up." A shiver traveled the length of Emma's body as his gaze all but devoured her, and she was shaken by the memory of how good it had felt to have his hands on her bare skin, his mouth, soft yet unyielding, on hers. "Let's just drop it, okay?"

He reached up with his left hand and braced it on the wall right above her waist. She couldn't move if she wanted to and they were standing so close, Emma could feel the heat from Landon's body brushing against her, igniting all of her nerve endings to a state of hyperawareness. Her breath caught in her chest. Silence stretched out between them; the only sound in the quiet room was Emma's own pulse racing in her ears. "McCabe . . . I . . ." Stringing two words together to form a sentence became a struggle as Emma's mind clouded with erotic images. His hands groping at her flesh. His mouth, hot and urgent, as he kissed her. A rush of warmth spread between her thighs, and Emma's stomach clenched tight with lust as she imagined what it would feel like to have his hard length buried deep inside of her. She shuddered. "I know this situation didn't turn out the way you wanted, but—"

"Landon."

Emma's brow furrowed. "What?"

He leaned in closer and Emma inhaled deeply

taking his scent into her lungs. "My name. Is Landon. Not McCabe. Not Deputy. *Landon*. Say it."

Emma tried to swallow and found that her mouth had gone completely dry. The sensual undercurrent of his voice dizzied and addled her, made her excited and deliciously drunk all at the same time. "I . . ." She was at a loss for words. Well, for the one word he wanted her to say anyway. She'd never been tongue-tied. Not once in her entire life. But Landon McCabe could bind her in knots with nothing more than a look and the low, sensual thrum of his voice.

He leaned in even closer, if it was possible, his mouth hovering over hers. Emma's breath came in shallow bursts of air as she tilted her chin up toward his face, and her heart pounded in a staccato against her rib cage.

"Say it."

"Landon." The word rushed out in a breathy whisper that ignited something low in her belly, and Emma found that she couldn't tear her gaze away from his no matter how she tried. She felt like that eighteen-year-old girl again, dazzled by the stunning, confident U.S. marshal. The man her father made her promise not to harbor any ill will toward despite the fact that he was taking her sole support system away from her.

He put his mouth next to her ear, and Emma held her arms tight at her sides to keep from reaching out to touch him. "Again."

"Landon."

This was thin ice to tread and he knew it. Landon's entire body vibrated from the effort it took to keep his arms braced against the wall and his mouth at Emma's ear and not on her lips. She smelled like heaven, delicate and sweet, warm vanilla and honey. He wanted to lick every inch of her, for no other reason than to see if she tasted as good as she smelled. The way she said his name, all breathy and soft, was enough to make his cock hard as stone, and he yearned to hear his name on her lips when she came. Would it sound the same, or would passion infuse the word with heat and intensity?

Fucking hell.

Landon bent at the elbows, fully prepared to push himself away from the wall. His chest brushed against her soft breasts and he stifled a groan. It would take an act of God to move him at this point. Hurricane-force winds or a bolt of lightning. Once again, he considered that Emma was a powerful magnet and he was nothing but useless metal. He couldn't pull away from her if he tried.

"Goddamn it, Emma." His own voice was ragged in his ears. Each word strained. Tortured. "Do you have any idea how hard it is to be this close to you? The things I want to do to you right now?"

Emma reached up and grabbed the fabric of his shirt in her fists. She tilted her head up until her silky lips brushed his cheek and murmured in his ear, "What's stopping you?"

Those three simple words were all it took to crumble his resolve.

Landon pressed his body against hers, forcing Emma tight against the wall as he slanted his mouth across hers in a ravenous kiss. He didn't trust himself to touch her, not yet. Not when the very thought of having her carried him over the edge of reason. Her arms snaked around his neck, holding him to her as Emma's tongue flicked out at the seam of his lips, a slow, sensual caress that Landon felt from one end of his body to the other.

Her fingers combed through his hair from the base of his neck upward, and Landon groaned into her mouth as his teeth grazed her bottom lip. As though she couldn't get close enough, Emma molded her body to his, her fingers curling into fists in his short hair, pulling the strands just hard enough to drive Landon crazy. He kissed her as though he were starved for her, his tongue thrusting into her mouth, his hips rocking against her in tandem. Emma's taste, her scent, her very presence enveloped Landon in a cocoon of sensation until he felt her in every pore of his skin, every inch of his body. His want of her overwhelmed anything else he'd ever longed for in his life, and tonight, he was going to have her.

"Landon?" Emma's voice was tentative as she pulled away, her brow furrowed.

He studied her for a bare second before lunging at her, greedy to taste her mouth again. She put her palm between them, her brow arched curiously and a bemused smile curving her lips.

"The phone?" He looked at her, confused. Logical thought was impossible at this moment. All the blood had rushed from his brain a while ago, and like a caveman, he was pretty sure he was only capable of unintelligible grunts. "Landon," Emma said again. "The phone's ringing. Don't you think we should answer it? It could be important."

Phone? Ringing? "What?"

"Landon." Emma's voice transformed from soft

and sweet to agitated in an instant. "Answer the phone. Please."

The worried expression marring Emma's features was like a bucket of ice water cooling Landon's lust. *Get your shit together, man.* The whole point of forcing his way into Crawford's operation was to keep an eye on Emma. An *eye.* Not his hands and certainly not his dick. If he let his focus wander . . . his gaze drifted to the swell of her breasts just visible above the V-neck of her shirt. He needed to get his head on straight. Now.

With more effort than he thought possible, Landon shoved himself away from the wall and turned his back on Emma. The phone continued to ring, the sound drilling into his skull like a thousand sharp screws. He rolled his head back from one shoulder to the other. *What a night.*

He strode over to the bedside table, jerked the phone off the cradle, and brought it to his ear. "This is Landon McCabe."

"I think you and Galen are trying to force me into early retirement," Chief Deputy Curt Monroe remarked with less than good humor. "Why in the hell aren't you answering your phone?"

Landon pinched the bridge of his nose between his thumb and forefinger and let out a measured breath. Wasn't there a rule somewhere that said you didn't have to talk to your boss while sporting a raging hard-on? "I left it at the scene of a shooting earlier tonight. I haven't had a chance to get it back."

"Was that before or after you tried to flee the scene of a crime with a person of interest in an active investigation?" The accusation didn't go unnoticed and Landon cringed.

"That would be before, sir." No use trying to bullshit his way out of anything. Crawford had obviously ratted him out.

"Ah, I see." A moment of silence passed, and Landon wondered if Monroe was too busy filing his release papers to speak. "And when was it that you brought Kelly into this? From what I understand, he's had a busy night calling in favors to a few politicians, not to mention the U.S. ambassador to France and Jim Daniel with SOG ops down at Camp Beauregard. Have you lost your goddamned mind, McCabe?"

He chanced a glance to his side, where Emma was still leaning against the wall. He was waist fucking deep in it, that was for sure. "Crawford and the SOG hijacked *our* case. Our person of interest. And refused to share information. As the original lead deputy on the Ruiz case—"

"The SOG has every right to hijack whatever the hell they want," Monroe snapped. "Including our person of interest. Unless you've forgotten, McCabe, there is no them or us. We're all on the same team. You bullied your way into Crawford's operation and I'm the one taking heat for it. Do you know what time it is, McCabe?"

Landon leaned to his right to get a good look at the digital alarm clock and swallowed down a groan. "It's almost two A.M., sir."

"Yeah. And I'll tell you what, I'd be a hell of a lot happier if I was asleep right now and not tracking one of my deputies across Seattle. Get your damned phone back. As soon as possible. And McCabe, if I get one more report—just one—that you're fucking up over there, you're on suspension. Understand?"

"I understand, sir."

"All right then. Get some sleep."

"I will. You too, sir."

Monroe snorted in response and hung up.

Landon let out a huff of breath and let his head hang between his shoulders. A knot of tension the size of a freaking boulder formed between his shoulder blades and he doubted he'd find any relief until this operation was wrapped up.

"Is everything okay?"

No. Everything was *not* okay. "Yeah, everything is fine. That was my chief deputy back in Portland. Apparently he got a dose of Bill Crawford charm tonight. But it's no big deal."

"Are you sure?" Emma's footsteps whispered across the carpeting and the hairs on the back of Landon's neck stood on end as she came up behind him. So close the warmth of her breath caressed his skin. *Damn.*

Landon took a step to the side, putting some much needed distance between them. He couldn't think straight when she was so near. Couldn't make a rational decision to save his life. And he needed to be at the top of his game if he was going to keep Emma out of danger and the SOG off his back. Which meant he couldn't give in to his desires. No more temptation. No more close contact with her. He needed to end this dangerous flirtation before it turned into something he could no longer control.

Flirtation? Yeah, right. They'd passed *flirtation* a few miles back. Before Monroe's interruption, Landon had been racing down the road toward hot, dirty sex. His body reacted as he thought about kissing Emma. Touching her. Tasting . . . *O-kay. Time to call it a night. Fuck.* How was he supposed to stop thinking about Emma like that when all he wanted was to think about her like that?

"It's late, Emma." Landon infused his voice with a calm he wasn't even close to feeling. "I think we'd better go to bed."

A slow, sensual smile spread across Emma's lips, still swollen and pink from their kisses. Her dark eyes smoldered with a heat that promised all sorts of wonderful things as she took a step closer. Jesus, she was *killing* him. Landon averted his gaze and grabbed a pillow from the king-sized bed. "I'll take the chair. You can have the bed. You need to get some sleep. I guarantee tomorrow is going to be a busy day."

Her expression fell, the disappointment slicing through Landon like a razor blade. "Oh, okay, then. But you don't have to sleep on the chair, Landon. There's plenty of room in the bed."

Distance would be a hell of a lot easier if he hadn't demanded that she call him Landon. The way his name rolled off her tongue was bliss. Each syllable sweetened by her voice. "I'll be all right. Believe me, I've slept in worse places. Tomorrow, I'll try to get us two adjoining rooms, or one with two beds at the very least."

A deep crease cut into her brow, her beautiful mouth turned down in an almost pout. Adjoining rooms? Separate hotels would be better. Separate states. Landon doubted a cross-country divide would be wide enough to keep him from wanting Emma with anything less than raging desire. But he had to keep himself in check. She deserved him at one hundred percent. And he wasn't going to give Crawford or Monroe any excuse to shit-can his ass.

Emma turned her back on him and a deep ache took root in Landon's chest. From the edge of the bed, the sound of several hitched breaths made its way to him before she reached over to turn off the light. In the blinding darkness, Landon waited for the telltale sounds of the bed linens rustling as Emma crawled under the covers. Once she settled in, he took his place on the chair, propping his feet up on the ottoman as he tucked the pillow beneath his head. He stared at the ceiling, unseeing, every nerve on his body aware of the woman lying not five feet from him. Minutes passed. And then an hour. The silence gutted him, but he kept his ass parked right where it was despite the urge to go to her.

Emma let out a gentle sigh, and after a few minutes her breathing finally became deep and even. Landon shifted on the chair—his holster was digging into his ribs—and he moved the damned Glock out of the way lest he wake up with a bruise the size of a baseball. She'd never given up on her dad, even after all this time. Any other person would have thrown in the towel, but not Emma. She fought and dug, and fought some more until she got what she wanted. And she didn't even realize what she was in for. Emma had thrown herself into a dangerous situation without a safety net and Crawford was going to capitalize on that blind bravery and use it to his advantage. Landon got the whole "protect the nation—the masses—at all costs," but Emma's life was a casualty he wasn't willing to simply sit back and accept. After everything she'd told him, he couldn't help but feel as though he'd failed her six years ago by letting her father take the fall for a crime he hadn't committed. He refused to fail her again.

Landon's eyes drifted shut and he let the gentle sounds of Emma's breathing lull him. He just needed to sleep. A little rest would bring him some much-needed clarity and focus. Tomorrow was a new day and he'd be ready to face it like a professional. No matter the personal cost. Even if that cost was a chance with the one woman he wanted more than anything.

Chapter Thirteen

Everyone I know—even my best friend—thinks I'm dead.

Emma inhaled a deep breath and brought her arms high above her head, chin tilted toward the ceiling as she paused in the Sun Salute position. Her palms came together and she brought them down to heart level as she exhaled and shifted into Warrior's Pose. There wasn't enough yoga on the planet to bring her the level of calm she needed, but at this point she'd take what she could get.

The events of the previous night took up way too much space in the forefront of her mind, and no matter how many times she tried to forget them—to clear her thoughts and focus on the meditation techniques—she couldn't banish the sound of Landon's voice from her ears when he said, *"Do you have any idea how hard it is to be this close to you? The things I want to do to you right now?"* Emma's stomach clenched tight as she remembered the way his lips had felt on hers. His teeth nipping at her bottom lip . . . and the sting of his rejection when he'd finally come to his senses and opted to sleep curled up in a ball on the armchair rather than in the bed with her.

Ugh.

She looked to her right, her eyes roaming freely over Landon's contorted form. A self-satisfied smirk grew on her face as she thought of the tight knots and stiffness he'd suffer today from sleeping that way. Not that his mild discomfort could even compare to the hurt she felt at his rebuff, but still. At this point, she'd take what little retribution she could get.

Emma plopped down on the bed—yoga wasn't doing anything to calm her—and snatched the TV remote from the nightstand. She flipped through the channels, unconcerned that the noise might rouse the hotshot deputy marshal camped out on the chair, and searched until she found ESPN. If she couldn't find a state of Zen through meditation, *SportsCenter* was bound to do the trick.

"What are you watching?"

Landon sounded a little better than death warmed over, his voice heavy with exhaustion and carrying the slightest rasp. Which did absolutely *nothing* for Emma. Not sexy. Like, at all. Rather, she attributed the glow of warmth that radiated over her skin to Gilberto Silva recapping the Sounders game last night. Yep. That was it. Nothing turned her on like listening to the witty banter of a sports anchor walking her through the highlights as she watched the replay of Clint Dempsey evading the Galaxy's defenders to score the winning goal. In fact, maybe when this was all said and done, Emma would see if Tyson could hook her up with one of the guys from the team. They were all pretty good friends and it was time she got out there and started dating again.

"*SportsCenter*," she finally replied. As though on their own, her eyes wandered to where Landon was stretched out on the chair, his usually tidy hair rumpled with sleep and his bright blue eyes still a little bleary. It was totally unfair that he would look so cute disheveled like that when she looked like Godzilla for about an hour after she woke up. "I'm catching up on the scores."

When you grew up not only playing sports but also hanging out with guys who ate, drank, and breathed sports, there wasn't much more that interested Emma. Except for maybe a beautifully designed website, well-constructed code, or the satisfaction of stealing millions of dollars from criminals who prided themselves on their ability to hide their laundered money. Okay, so maybe she'd be retiring that particular interest now. . . .

From the corner of her eye, Emma couldn't help but notice that Landon had sort of zoned out, his glassy-eyed expression dazed and blank as he stared at the TV. She wondered if it was *SportsCenter* in general that he found mind-numbing or if he was simply still tired. What did Landon McCabe like? Was he a football guy or was basketball more his style? Maybe he favored European sports like rugby or cricket. She found herself wanting to ask him, to dig around in his brain and learn as much as she could about him. Then, she reminded herself that he'd dismissed her with a verbal pat to the head last night, seemingly unaffected yet again by the moment they'd shared. What was it about McCabe that made him so damned unreadable? Emma could usually get a pretty good bead on people, men especially. One of the benefits of hanging with a testosterone-fueled posse. But Landon was a complete mystery. He ran hot and cold, his gaze fiery and full of passion one moment, icy and detached the next. She'd never met a guy who turned on and off as quickly as he did. Did he really want her in the way he'd said last night? Or had his words been nothing more than lip service?

Though, she hadn't been disappointed in anything his lips had done to her last night. Those kisses made Emma breathless just thinking about them. There was no point in continuing to figure him out, she supposed. He'd made his feelings pretty clear. She had to accept that distance was the safer option at this point. No need to learn any more about Landon than she already knew. Because that was almost too much as it was. Like, for instance, the fact that he kissed like LeBron James dunked—transforming the simple act into a work of art, a display of skill and precision that boggled the mind.

Landon rubbed at one eye with the heel of his palm, a slow, tired motion that made him look more like a kid than a grown man. Emma's heart clenched as she watched him and she forced her gaze back to the TV. "It didn't really hit me until this morning that, as of right now, everyone thinks I'm dead. Is there any way I can call my friend Jeremy, and maybe Tyson, to let them know that I'm okay?"

Landon snapped to attention at her words, a deep crease digging into his forehead. "No."

"No?" Emma repeated. "Just . . . no. This isn't even open for discussion?"

"Nope," Landon said.

He threw the blanket off his body and levered himself out of the chair with some effort. Good. He deserved every bit of discomfort he was feeling and then some. "That's not fair, Landon. It's cruel to put people through something like that when I don't have to."

"You should have thought about that before you stole millions of dollars from a bunch of ruthless arms dealers," he quipped. "Now you have no choice but to see this through to the end."

"I wouldn't have had to steal anything if you'd done your job in the first place." It was a low blow, but Emma didn't care. Landon had hurt her with his casual dismissal, and she wanted him to hurt right back.

Landon's eyes narrowed and his jaw clenched. "I hate to break it to you, Emma, but there's no need for further investigation when a suspect confesses. Which your dad did willingly without coercion. I did my job. To the letter. Maybe you ought to remind yourself of that the next time you're looking for someone to blame for your own rash behavior."

Rash? *Rash?* If steam could have billowed from her ears, Emma would have been Old Faithful by now. There was nothing rash about six years' worth of digging. And likewise, nothing rash about the failsafes she'd constructed to bury that money so deep that Sousa would never get his hands on it. She'd practically put her life on hold to exonerate her dad. Oh, Emma knew that the pictures of her scattered all over the Internet told a different story, but it wasn't her fault if Landon was too damned blind to see past the paparazzi's interpretation of her life for what it really was.

Lonely.

"Or maybe you're using my rash behavior to assuage your own guilt over putting an innocent man in prison." It was easier to be mad at Landon than sit around and wallow in self-pity. She could use anger. Sadness and hurt didn't do anyone any good.

"Go ahead and think that if it'll help you to sleep at night."

Of all the lousy, jackassed—

A loud knock interrupted Emma's train of thought, and Landon put a finger up to his lips, commanding her to silence. Her heart thundered in her ears and she held her breath as though the simple intake of air would give her away. Landon crept to the door and gently eased his gun from the holster that hung from his left shoulder. He reminded Emma of a hunting cat, all sleek lines and quiet grace. Slowly, he flipped the latch across the door before opening it a crack and peeking at whoever was on the other side.

Emma let out a breath when Landon's stance relaxed and he swung open the lock to let Bill Crawford inside. "Good, you're both up." Crawford didn't waste time with pleasantries as he took a place at the front of the room, effectively blocking out Gilberto Silva and the highlights from yesterday's soccer game. Damn it. "We've come up with what we're hoping is a passable cover story that will justify your presence, McCabe, and keep Emma in the game."

"All right," Landon replied. "What are we looking at?"

"First off, don't be surprised to find out that an internal investigation into your actions and cases has been ongoing for the past several months. It took a bit to fabricate the records and evidence, but we managed to put something together. I have to say, you didn't make it easy for us. You're squeaky clean."

Emma cast a sidelong glance at Landon. His smirk spoke more of pride than arrogance. She'd always known that at his core, he was an honorable man. "What did I do?" Curiosity sparked in his blue eyes. "Steal evidence? Falsify records? Sexually harass a coworker or two?"

"Misappropriation of government funds. Shaking down witnesses and suspects for money. Accepting a bribe or two. Oh, and a couple of instances of recovered cash going missing from evidence. We needed you to come across as a greedy son of a bitch."

"Sorry to break it to you, Crawford," Landon remarked. "But if these guys do any sort of digging, they'll find out that I don't really need to steal to get my hands on money."

Emma didn't miss the hint of embarrassment in his words. As though he hated to admit that he had more than enough cash to set him up comfortably.

"I'm aware," Crawford said, unconcerned. "And I've taken care of that as well. Sorry to break it to you, but your bank account is going to be a little light for the next week or so. You might want to consider operating under a tight budget."

Landon leaned a shoulder against the wall and folded his arms across his chest. The look of amusement on his face piqued Emma's curiosity. Any other person would've blown a gasket at the prospect of having his bank accounts wiped out. Temporarily or not.

"Okay, you've established that I'm dirty," Landon

said. "What about Emma? How do we fit together in this scenario?"

"We've covered that angle as well," Crawford replied. "Cesar was skeptical at first, but if you two can play your parts, we shouldn't have any problem convincing him that you and Emma are lovers."

With those last words, Emma put on the brakes as her brain came to a screeching halt and spun out. Was Crawford out of his mind? *Lovers?*

She didn't dare look at Landon as Crawford continued to talk as though he hadn't dropped the mother of all bombs on her. Cesar wasn't an idiot. If he'd been fed a story that Landon and Emma were sleeping together, he'd settle for nothing short of watching them do the deed himself before he trusted them. This plan had disaster written all over it.

"Cesar has already been told," Emma said rather than asked. "I mean, how did your undercover guy even work something like that into a conversation?" *Oh, by the way, Cesar, I wanted to let you know that after I faked Emma's death, I discovered that Deputy U.S. Marshal McCabe will be sticking around a while because not only is he a dirty cop, but he and Emma are getting busy if you know what I mean.* "Are you guys out of your minds? There's no way he bought that story, no matter what he told your guy to the contrary."

Crawford stared at her as though she were speaking a foreign language. Apparently these SOG guys didn't spook easily, because from the way he was acting, Crawford wasn't quite sure what all of the fuss was about. Then again, Crawford hadn't had Landon's tongue in his mouth last night, either. It was humiliating enough to have struck out not once, but twice, with McCabe. Now she had to pretend like they were a cozy couple?

They might as well shoot her now and call it a day.

Landon didn't even blink an eye at Crawford's cover story that he was on the take, but he broke out into a full-body sweat at the suggestion that he and Emma were sleeping together. Holy fucking shit. *Lovers?* He'd spent most of the past sleepless night convincing himself of all the reasons why keeping his distance from Emma was important. Hell, the hours between 4 and 5 AM had been spent coaching himself not to stand too close to her, not to touch her, not to inhale her sweet scent or find an excuse even to pick a piece of damned lint off of her shirt. Exhaustion had finally won out after that, and then he'd had to start all over again at six when he woke up to find Emma stretched out and bent over, her tight, pert ass mere feet from where he sat while she assumed pose after torturous pose. Who knew yoga could be so damned erotic?

And after he'd talked himself down from a raging hard-on—so he wouldn't be humiliated when he walked across the room flashing his arousal like a neon sign—Crawford had the nerve to stroll in and tell him this? No. Fucking. Way.

"I'm with Emma on this one." She turned to look at him, her expression pinched, but he didn't acknowledge it. Couldn't. "There simply isn't enough time to establish that sort of cover. This isn't something you can create a bogus paper trail for. I've only been in the city for a couple of weeks and this Cesar has been keeping an eye on Emma for at least that long. If he acted like he bought the explanation, I have to assume that he's playing you."

There was no way he could keep his relationship with Emma platonic if he was forced to demonstrate his affection just so some pervert would buy the story that they were sleeping together. He might as well haul his ass back to Portland and hand his badge in to Monroe right now.

"Sousa and his men have no idea what Emma was up to prior to her coming out of the woodwork to claim responsibility for the stolen money, which leaves plenty of unaccounted-for time in which you began your relationship. The official story is that you've been working together for months. You have history with Emma since you were the arresting deputy on Javier's case. Who better to help Emma exonerate her dad while ripping off the criminals who put him in jail in the first place? It's a totally believable angle, and actually, I can't believe how well it fit into our plans. I sort of wish we'd thought of it in the first place. At this point, Teyo Sousa is interested in one thing and one thing only: getting his hands on his money so he can buy his bomb," Crawford continued. "The only thing keeping Emma alive at this point is the fact that she's the only way that can happen. If Sousa didn't need her, she'd be dead. End of story."

A hot lick of apprehension traveled the length of Landon's spine, a reflection of the fear in Emma's gaze and the nervous energy she was throwing off from Crawford's unfiltered assertions. But if he tried to butt in and downplay this for her, shrug it off like it was no big deal, he wouldn't be helping her. "I agree with you there. Until Emma returns his millions, she's safe. It's after the exchange that worries me. That's when the situation is going to get messy." It was important that she understood what was at stake here. Namely, her life. She'd thrown her hat in the ring with some serious players, and now she had no choice but to follow through with the game.

"I'm not saying Cesar isn't skeptical," Crawford continued. "Which means that Sousa is nervous. Your presence is going to complicate things, but it's not going to affect our time line. This will be wrapped up before the end of the week. Period. And as far as afterward goes, that's why we've got a man on the inside."

Minimal? Not if he had anything to say about it. He'd get Emma out of this situation completely unscathed even if it killed him. True, his presence had complicated an already touchy situation, but Landon refused to let Crawford make him feel guilty over inserting himself in this operation. No matter what he did or didn't feel for Emma, she needed protection and someone needed to step up and take care of that. Whatever was happening on his end of the investigation fell on Crawford and his people.

"Okay, fine. Let's say for the sake of argument that Cesar buys that Emma and I have something going on the side and gives his boss the thumbs-up to move forward. Then what? What's her part in all of this and how quickly can we get her out of it?"

"We'll be flying blind from here on out," Crawford explained. "The problem is that this situation escalated too quickly for us to do any sort of reasonable damage control. My guy has been working this case for a year, and I'm not going to compromise him by trying to make any more contact than what's absolutely necessary. Emma's interference put a monkey wrench in an undercover op that's taken us a goddamned long time to set up."

"Maybe I wouldn't have interfered if I'd known what was going on." Emma's cold tone chilled Landon to the bone, but Crawford merely quirked a brow. "It's not my fault you guys didn't cover all of your bases."

"You're lucky you're not in jail right now, Emma. Or worse." Crawford fished two cell phones out of his jacket pocket and tossed them on the bed. "Your phones. I've made sure they're clean. No taps, no GPS tracking. Cesar should be calling to arrange a meet in the next couple of hours."

"So that's it?" Emma didn't sound quite as accusing, but her tone hadn't warmed in the slightest. "We meet with Cesar, make the transfer, and he lets my dad go. And then I'm out of this. Right?"

Crawford gave a noncommittal shrug that caused Landon's gut to burn with anger. "That's up to Cesar and his employer, isn't it? Like I said, none of this is running according to plan so we're going to have to wing it. I suppose it's fortunate we have McCabe to keep an eye on you, because if Cesar gets even a whiff of something dirty, Sousa won't hesitate to kill your father—or torture you—just to teach you a lesson."

"What are the chances we'll come into contact with your man?" Landon asked. If they got into anything sketchy, he'd like to know who he could shoot at and who he should leave alone. "I think it's best at this point to plan for the worst possible scenario."

"Worst possible scenario?" Emma drew her knees up, hugging them tight to her body. She looked like a scared child, more like that girl Landon had met six years ago than the woman he knew now. "What do you think could happen, Landon? And don't bullshit me. Give it to me straight."

Crawford gave him a look that said, *Well, she asked for it.* Landon let out a slow sigh and raked his fingers through the short strands of his hair. "You pissed off a very dangerous man, Emma." He leveled his gaze on her and she gave him look for look. Bravado? No, Emma was too ballsy to fake it. "First, he's going to make sure you give him his money back. Then—"

"Just say it, Landon. I can take it."

"Then he's going to make an example out of you to make sure no one ever tries to fuck him over again."

Emma swallowed visibly and let out a shuddering breath. A less stalwart soul would have crumpled into a useless heap of nerves by now, but not her. She was made of steel. "Well, I guess we'd better make sure to keep the upper hand, then."

Landon gave her a wan smile. "Yep. That's pretty much it."

Crawford checked his watch and headed for the door. "I've got a meeting in thirty minutes, but don't worry. We'll know what's going on. If anything changes, I'll be in touch later tonight." He gave Emma a nod in parting and then stepped out into the hall. He said, "Good luck," to Landon as he closed the door behind him.

The quiet that descended with Crawford's exit was deafening. Landon didn't know what to say. How to proceed from here. He didn't take undercover assignments for a reason. No matter how he tried, he was always uncomfortable with the level of dedication it took to make someone truly believe the line of bullshit you were feeding them. Landon preferred assignments that allowed him to be straight. The less deception, the better.

Emma stared at some faraway spot on the wall, her expression blank. She was a million miles away. Landon rubbed the back of his neck in an attempt to work out the knot from sleeping in that lumpy, uncomfortable-as-fuck chair. No doubt Emma had whiplash from how quickly he'd changed gears with her last night. And now, they had to pretend as though there was much more between them than a few kisses. Admittedly, they had been hard-core. Even better than the first time he'd kissed her on the roof. Landon doubted he'd ever forget the softness of Emma's lips or the way her breath in his ear had turned him into a single-minded asshole hell-bent on getting her clothes off as quickly as possible.

"Tell me what to do."

He almost couldn't hear her words over the TV, and she was still staring blindly at the far wall. If she hadn't tried to play the vigilante, Emma wouldn't be in this mess right now. But Landon was through chastising her for decisions she couldn't undo. He needed her focused and on task if they were going to survive Crawford's mission. Because he had a feeling that if things went south, no one, not even the SOG, would get them out of it.

"We can do this, Emma. I'm not going to let anything happen to you or your dad. I promise."

Chapter Fourteen

"What if he asks for proof?"

Landon quirked a brow, wondering exactly what sort of proof they'd be asked to provide. A hot shower had managed to work loose some of the knots in his back and shoulders. His mind was clearer, too, as he'd used the time alone to form a game plan and prepare himself for the task at hand. "First of all, I doubt he'll ask for proof, Emma. You have to remember, this is about one thing for them: getting their money back. You have to think like them, put yourself in their shoes. They respect strength and ruthlessness and little else. Don't give them a reason to doubt you and they won't. Understand?"

"Have you ever done this before? The undercover thing, I mean?"

The insecurity in her tone was going to be a problem if he couldn't do something to bolster her confidence. So far, Emma hadn't even made an effort to get cleaned up and dressed. And while Landon didn't object to her tight spandex lounge pants, he wanted her to look like she had her shit together when they met with Cesar.

"I'm not going to lie to you, Emma. I've never taken an undercover assignment before. But that doesn't mean we can't do this convincingly. And no matter what you think to the contrary, I'm damned good at my job. I've been in stickier situations than this. It's going to be okay. You have to trust me."

"What do we do?" For the first time in an hour, she made eye contact with him and the intensity of her gaze made Landon's lungs seize up. She was the most beautiful woman he'd ever laid eyes on and the truth of the matter was, it wouldn't be hard for him to pretend that he was completely head-over-heels in love with her. "I mean, do I throw myself all over you, kiss you in front of Cesar, stick my hand in your back pocket?" She gave a sad laugh. "I'm not sure how couples behave when conducting a business transaction with arms dealers."

"The same way non-couples do, Emma." Landon rifled through the dresser drawers for something suitable to wear. He wanted to be sure he looked the part, a cop who liked money and wasn't opposed to bending the law to get what he wanted. If Cesar had done his homework—and Landon suspected he had—his part in all of this would be the toughest sell. "You have to get into the right mind-set. You're a badass who stole millions of dollars from hardened criminals. They have something you want and you're playing hardball to get it back. That doesn't make you weak, Emma. You still have the upper hand and they know it. Without that money, Sousa can't get what he wants. You have all of the control for now.

It's important that you go into this situation believing that. Do you understand me?"

Emma nodded, but he knew none of what he'd said had registered. Damn it. He strode to the bed and sat down on the edge, catching her by the shoulders and forcing her to look at him. "This isn't the time to lose focus. I know that this turned out to be a hell of a lot more difficult than you imagined, but this isn't only about clearing your dad's name anymore. This is about saving his life and yours as well. This is about making sure that the Special Operations Group can do their job and stop this asshole from getting his hands on that dirty bomb. We have the opportunity to do something good here. Let's not waste it."

"I can do this." Her dark eyes were fathomless as she looked at him. And dead serious. Landon respected her resolve and the fact that when it was gut-check time, Emma could step up and do what needed to be done. "I'm okay, Landon, really. It's just been . . . a lot to take in so quickly. I won't disappoint you. Or anyone else. I'm ready."

"Okay. Good." He gave her a reassuring smile and pushed himself off the bed. "Now, get in the shower and get ready to go. Cesar could call any time."

Emma propelled herself off the bed without another word, snatching up the bag of clothes Crawford's guys had bought her the night before, and headed for the bathroom. Landon powered on his phone while trying to distract himself from the thought that Emma was right on the other side of the door, taking off her clothes. He'd known guys who worked undercover who had to undergo extensive therapy after an assignment. The lines between reality and fantasy blurred to the point that it became tough to leave that contrived life behind and return to the real world.

After spending time close to Emma, pretending that there was so much more to their relationship than there really was, would he be able to put the fantasy back on the shelf where it belonged when it was all said and done? Somehow, Landon didn't think it would be any small feat to walk away from Emma Ruiz.

Landon heard the spray of the shower come on in the bathroom and he dialed Galen. He needed Emma to be confident and he couldn't let her see— or hear—him express his own worries. After a few rings, Galen answered. "Before you say anything, you better know you've reached your quota for favors for the rest of the year."

Oh, he was *well* aware of it. In fact, Landon had a feeling he'd be paying Galen back for the rest of his natural life.

"You trained for undercover ops with SOG, right?"

Galen was a part of the U.S. Marshals' elite team of specially trained marshals. They handled high-profile and dangerous cases and had to be ready to move sometimes at a moment's notice. He'd always given Galen shit for his glory-hound ways, but now Landon was wishing he'd applied for the program as well. At any rate, he'd be more prepared for the situation he'd thrown himself into.

"Sure," Galen replied. "We had to undergo all of this psych-eval bullshit to make sure we could handle it."

"Got any pointers you'd care to offer?" Landon

couldn't do much about his rueful tone. It rankled him to think that he needed advice at all. He should've been able to handle the situation on his own.

"What's the story?"

So far, Galen had asked very few questions and Landon liked it that way. But there wasn't anything about him that Galen didn't know, so there was no point in holding back now. "In a nutshell? Emma Ruiz stole several million from a nasty arms dealer who is now holding her dad hostage to get it back. The SOG is working with DHS and the FBI to take the bad guys down, and they need her to give all of the money back so they can bust the asshole in the process of trying to buy a dirty bomb. I'm playing the part of her greedy, crooked-cop boyfriend until we can wrap this up."

Galen was silent for a moment before busting out into a round of laughter that made Landon wish his friend were here so he could pop him in the nose. "Is that all?" Galen's facetious tone was doing little for Landon's mood. "Jesus Christ, Landon. You sure stepped in it."

"Fuck off," he growled into the receiver. "Like you've never gotten in over your head."

"True," Galen conceded. "But after today you're not allowed to give me a single ounce of shit about Harper."

Giving Galen shit about his relationship with Harper was the least of Landon's concerns right now. "How did you keep it separate?" he asked. "How did you keep your head on straight when you were with her so you could focus on the job?" It wasn't like he had anything to worry about opening up to Galen. They were closer than brothers. But it was hard for him to admit—even to himself—that his feelings for Emma might be a little more than just professional.

"I didn't, obviously," Galen said with a snort. "You've got this weird, hostile history with Emma that's gotta be complicating the shit out of things. But, ultimately, you're going to do your job because you're a professional and damned good at it. Just remember, with undercover the trick is to keep the lie believable. Don't go over the top because they'll know you're full of shit. Don't downplay anything either because that'll throw up a red flag, too."

Landon gave a rueful laugh. If only a shared hostility was all he and Emma had between them. "So basically what you're saying is I'm screwed either way."

"The catch with working undercover is that *you* have to believe the story you're selling. That's more important than anything. If you buy it, they'll buy it."

"I guess I know what I need to work on, then. In the meantime, can you do some recon on the down low? I don't want to have to rely on Crawford for all of my intel. I'm pretty sure I'm on a need-to-know basis at this point."

"What do you need?" Landon asked.

"See what you can dig up on a guy named Cesar Molina. Also, his boss, Teyo Sousa. And between you and me, I'm pretty sure there are some guards over at the federal prison in Sheridan on their payroll. I want to take those bastards down."

"I'll get something going on my end, but we'll keep it quiet until you're out of there. In the meantime, I'll see what I can dig up on your guys. You want me to call you if I find anything?"

"No. Leave a message at the hotel. I'll call you when I can talk."

"Got it," Galen said. "Take care of yourself, man."

"Please." Landon refused to let the moment get too heavy. "I've got this locked down. I'll be the one doing TV interviews when it's all done."

"And I'll gladly let you," Galen replied. "That shit is exhausting. Later."

"Later." Landon ended the call and his gaze wandered to the closed bathroom door. All he had to do was believe the lie that he was in love with Emma Ruiz.

Emma lingered in the shower longer than she should have. She'd spent most of the night tossing and turning, plagued by dreams that glazed her skin with a sheen of sweat and caused her body to ache with want. It was stupid to lust after someone who couldn't make up his damned mind. Who knew McCabe was so fickle? He'd turned her on and off so many times over the past couple of days, Emma was beginning to feel a little like a light switch. And now, not only was she going to have to get cozy with him, she was being forced to pretend that she and Landon were sleeping together.

Talk about torture . . .

When she'd set her plan to clear her father's name in motion, she'd had no idea whom—or what—she was up against. It was foolish to think she'd ever had the upper hand. And now that she knew what sorts of criminals Cesar and his boss were, it made her more nervous than ever to think about what she had to do. If she'd known they were arms dealers and terrorists, Emma never would have behaved so flippantly.

Too late now, though. Her bed was made. Time to lie in it.

Though it pained her to leave the warmth of the shower behind, Emma toweled off and dug through the bag of clothes Crawford's men had supplied her with. Those elite marshals must've had a personal shopper on the payroll, because she doubted any of the guys she'd met could have picked out the clothes in the bag. Black, skinny slacks, a yellow tunic-style shirt with a deep V-neck, and a pair of black stilettos. Granted, Emma would rather wear a pair of ballet flats than heels, but she assumed that Crawford wanted her to look well put together. Dress to impress and all that. At the bottom of the bag she found a tube of mascara, eye shadow, and dark red lipstick. Well, she'd put the shadow and mascara to use, but that lipstick was staying in the bag. She looked in the mirror, still a little foggy with steam, and assessed her dripping hair. No way would the tiny blow-dryer affixed to the wall have the power to tackle her unruly, heavy curls and without a flat iron, she'd be left with a frizzy curltastrophy. Then again, since she was officially dead, she'd better play it safe and wear the atrocious blond wig when they met Cesar. In which case, Emma had one more reason to dread leaving the hotel today.

Yay.

Despite the setbacks, she tried to focus on what really mattered: getting her dad back. She tried to remain detached, refused to think about what they might be doing to him or what sort of shape he was in. If she worried about those things, she'd crack for sure, and everyone, including Landon, deserved to have her operating at one hundred percent.

She felt a little more human now that she was showered, but truth be told, she would have rather stayed in her leggings and T-shirt. The best part of working out of her home was the fact that she didn't have to get dressed up and spend an hour to make herself presentable before going in to the office. She just rolled out of bed and into her desk chair.

Even when she was a teenager, Emma had found the whole girl routine a bit daunting. And the fact of the matter was women wore makeup for the benefit of other women. Guys didn't care about makeup, and most of the ones she hung out with hated it when the women they dated wore too much of it. Makeup was little more than armor women wore as they rode into battle. Emma's was a mask of protection, of confidence, something she could hide behind so people wouldn't see the vulnerability underneath. She painted it on for the picture takers, the onlookers, for the people who thought they knew her. But the truth was that there were very few people Emma trusted. And even fewer who got a glimpse behind the mask, those who really, truly knew her. She wondered, as she hung her towel up on a hook to dry, if she could trust Landon or if he was someone she'd need to protect herself from. She didn't think she would survive it if she allowed him to hurt her. She'd take loneliness over heartbreak any day.

When she emerged from the bathroom, Landon was dressed and ready to go. Emma bit down on her bottom lip, more to keep her jaw from hanging open than anything. Damn, could that man wear a

pair of jeans. Apparently, someone didn't need any
help in the wardrobe department. Outfitted in designer everything from head to toe, Emma had to
assume that three-quarters of McCabe's salary went
to this clothes budget. Not that she was complaining.
He looked good enough to eat. Like a gourmet meal
that had to be savored to be truly appreciated.

Pretending to be his girlfriend was going to be the
hardest thing she ever had to do and not because
the idea was unbearable. On the contrary, Emma
worried that she'd become too involved in the game
they were playing. It was all too easy to remember
how good it felt to be in his arms. The way his mouth
slanted across hers, hungry and demanding.

"Looks like Crawford's boys did okay in the shop-
ping department."

Emma shook herself from her thoughts to find
Landon staring at her with a hungry expression
that turned her insides to mush. Once again, he'd
managed to flip her like a switch with no effort
whatsoever. How could she be expected to walk a
straight line, let alone stand on her own two feet,
when his gaze devoured her like that?

"You don't look too bad yourself," she remarked
as she retrieved her cell from the bed and checked
her e-mail. Not that a dead woman would be able to
respond to any of the messages. She just needed a
distraction so she wouldn't be tempted to stare. "Do
we look like a couple of amateur criminals? Because it sort of looks like we're dressed for a night
on the town."

Emma bit back a smile as she imagined going out
with Landon on a real, honest-to-God date. Where
would he take her? What would they talk about? And

if she suggested they go back to her place at the end of the night, would he accept her invitation or let her down gently like he'd tried to do last night? *Ugh. Snap out of it, you idiot!* Acting like a doe-eyed little girl with a crush wasn't going to help her remain detached. If she was going to go forward with this ruse—and she was—she needed to guard her heart first and foremost.

"We've got to dress the part, Emma. Sousa is going to assume that we want more than only your dad's release. You know things about him and his organization now. Things that could cause you both a lot of problems down the road. This won't be a simple exchange—money for your dad. There'll be negotiations, a back-and-forth that might take more than a couple of days to arrange. I need you to be prepared for that and ready to bring your A game."

"We're going to need an insurance policy." She'd never considered it—another knock against her— but Landon was right. Cesar wouldn't simply hand over her dad in exchange for a funds transfer and call it a day. Once his boss got what he wanted they were all as good as dead unless she could give them a reason to reconsider burying them all in unmarked graves. "Otherwise, there's no reason for them not to kill us once Sousa gets his money back."

"Pretty much," Landon agreed. "I've been mulling it over, and blackmail seems too easy. They'll expect it. I think our best bet at this point is to make them believe that you could be an asset to their organization. That we *both* could be."

"Are you suggesting I ask them for a job?" That was the last thing she would have expected. "Landon, negotiating those sorts of terms could drag this out for a week or longer."

His expression changed when she said his name and she couldn't help but remember the intensity in his voice when he'd demanded that she call him by his first name. Her stomach kicked up into her throat before floating down on a blissful cloud that sent pleasant shivers over her skin. *Detach, damn it. Do not think about last night.*

"It can't take a week because Sousa doesn't have that kind of time. Crawford said the buy is going down within a week. Suggesting they bring you into their fold is the best play at this point. Sorry, Emma, but you're going to have to give up the reins and have a little faith on this one."

"But what reason would I have to work for them? I mean, my God, I was trying to put them all in jail two weeks ago."

Landon canted his head to the side and said, "Money. Money is your one and only reason. Money to pay for your dad's medical expenses. Money to keep you both comfortable. Guys like this, they'll understand that sort of logic, Emma. Money is power and they worship that above all else. They'll respect you more for your greed than your selflessness."

Nothing like lowering yourself to the level of pond scum . . . "Okay. I can do that." Emma had spent enough time in the company of a few entitled rich assholes to know how to behave like one. Or rather, like she wanted to be one. Her phone rang and she looked at the caller ID—Cesar—before lifting her gaze up to meet Landon's.

He flashed her a reassuring smile and said. "Show time. Let's do this."

Emma swiped her finger across the screen and brought the phone up to her ear. "Hello?"

"You sound pretty good for a dead girl, *chica*," Cesar crooned. "My employer wants to meet you. Listen closely and follow my directions to the letter. Otherwise, I gut your *padre* like a fish. Understand?"

I can do this. I can do this. I can do this. Emma swallowed down the lump of fear that rose in her throat, steeling herself for what had to be done. "I understand. Tell me what to do."

Chapter Fifteen

This was the part of the job that Landon lived for. The high.

Anticipation coiled in his stomach like a snake about to strike and a pleasant rush of adrenaline trickled into his system the closer they got to their destination. Riding in the backseat of one of Sousa's tricked-out Range Rovers didn't even faze him, despite the fact he'd been patted down and relieved of his Glock. He knew what to expect and only an idiot would have let him ride to their destination armed. Likewise, they would have been suspicious if he hadn't come with at least one weapon strapped to his body. Landon relaxed into the plush leather seat as though this were nothing more than a pleasant drive through the country and rested his palm high on Emma's left thigh. No time like the present to establish proof of intimacy for their hosts. A tingle of electricity sparked from the contact, traveling the length of his arm, intensifying the rush he already felt.

Don't get distracted. Focus on the job.

Focus was usually the one thing Landon had a good grip on. Laser precise, his colleagues at the Portland office joked that he was unshakable when he set his mind on a task. If any of them could see him now, barely able to restrain himself in Emma's presence, his reputation might take a hit. He gently squeezed her cotton-clad thigh, an action that he hoped came across as reassuring. All it did for him, however, was invoke fantasies of tearing her damned pants off so he could feel her naked flesh as he massaged her in his palm.

So professional.

Emma stiffened beside him—definitely *not* reassured—and he reached over, tucking a finger beneath her chin and guiding her face until she turned to look at him. He leaned in toward her, and she mirrored his action until his mouth hovered near her ear as though he were simply kissing her cheek. "I've got you, Emma," he murmured low so none of Sousa's lackeys could hear. "I'm not going to let anything happen to you."

She put her hand over his and squeezed. Landon reveled in that warmth, the skin-on-skin contact. "I won't be a liability," she whispered back. "I can do this, Landon." She pulled back and their eyes met. A corner of her mouth hinted at a smile before she closed the distance between them and put her lips to his.

An easy, slow kiss. Petal-soft and warm. Landon's brain buzzed and his body flooded with heat, better than tossing back a couple of shots of top-shelf tequila. When she pulled away, her dark brown eyes were heavily lidded and a lazy, satisfied smile curved her full lips. He swore if those goons weren't in the front seat right now, there wouldn't be anything stopping him from getting her naked and on his cock by the next stoplight. So much for his vow to keep this professional. Jesus Christ, she tied him into knots.

And it felt damned good.

Though it would have been better to err on the side of caution, Landon captured her mouth for one more kiss. Screw the job—the adrenaline rush he got from kissing her was supercharged, racing through his veins like quicksilver. He was hopelessly addicted, and if Landon thought that this mindless want of her would go away simply because he had a job to do, he was kidding himself. Nothing short of a lobotomy was going to get Emma out of his head any time soon.

The sound of snickering from the front seat caused Emma to pull away, and she averted her gaze, turning toward the window as though embarrassed. Though PDA was sort of necessary to sell the hot-'n'-heavy lovers angle, Landon supposed a full-on peep show wasn't what Emma had in mind. He looked up to find the driver smirking at him through the rearview mirror and Landon promised himself that if shit went sour, that son of a bitch was going to be the first man down. *Let's see your expression when I break your femur, you smug fucker.*

Rather than heading out of downtown as he'd expected, they turned toward the city proper. Did the arms dealer rent an office in a swanky skyscraper or some shit?

"Hey, I don't suppose you'd mind telling us where we're headed?"

"As a matter of fact, I do mind," the driver quipped.

"The only thing you need to know is that you're damned lucky to be alive right now. Other than that . . . you don't know shit, so shut your fucking mouth and sit there."

Oh yeah, that asshole was going to be the first one to get his face smashed into the next available sidewalk. Landon hadn't been exaggerating when he'd told Emma that guys like these respected ruthlessness. And though it was a dangerous tightrope to walk, he knew that he'd have to play the part of a dirty cop and push his luck as far as it would go.

But pushing his luck only went so far with Emma sitting right beside him.

No need to invite any undue wrath quite yet. These guys were nothing more than low-level henchmen. Expendable. He suspected that Sousa wouldn't bat a lash if Landon took one of them out. The most important thing at this point was to get Emma a meet with the head honcho himself. After that, he could form a more solid game plan.

"Where do you think they're taking us?" Emma leaned in to whisper the words and Landon brushed his thumb across her jaw. He loved the way her eyes became hooded every time he touched her. As though even the slightest contact had a deep, resonant impact.

"They won't be dragging us off to some remote location or empty warehouse quite yet." Though he meant it playfully, Emma's brow creased and her dark eyes shimmered with concern. "It'll be okay, Emma," he reassured her. "I just mean that you're an asset to Sousa and his organization right now. He's not going to do anything to jeopardize your safety."

"Right," she said on an exhale. "Okay, good."

Emma settled back into her seat, but she reached out and threaded her fingers with Landon's as she did. It felt so natural to sit here like this, her hand resting in his. And why did that scare him more than the guys in the front seat armed to the teeth and ready to put a bullet in his head the second he stepped out of line?

The rest of the drive was quiet and Emma turned away to stare out the window at the traffic clogging the downtown streets. Landon forced his focus from the woman sitting next to him, instead listening carefully to the words of the men speaking Spanish in hushed tones from the front seats. Which did him little good since the minimal grasp of Spanish that Landon possessed was barely enough to order a burrito. He probably shouldn't have mocked Galen so much for his fancy French talk. It might've been a good idea to learn a foreign language or three in case he wound up in a situation like this.

"Get out."

Landon looked up to find they'd pulled up in front of the Metropolitan Grill. Wow, when he'd assured Emma they'd more than likely meet Sousa in a public place, he never would have assumed they'd be sitting down for a quiet lunch. Especially now that Emma was assumed dead. Totally ballsy. Thank God they'd dressed the part, because it would have been embarrassing as hell for Emma to show up in her curve-hugging workout pants. Not that Landon would have minded . . .

Emma turned, apprehension pinching the delicate lines of her face. He gave her hand a reassuring squeeze. "Ready?"

"Ready," she said with a nod.

Once inside, the hostess took them to their seats, sans armed escort. Maybe none of Sousa's goons were housebroken yet. Not that it mattered. Landon had enough on his mind as he surveyed their surroundings, making note of exits, obstacles, and anything that could be used as a potential weapon. A butter knife wasn't exactly deadly, but it'd do in a pinch.

Emma's grip on his hand tightened the closer they got to the table, and Landon noticed the guy from the club—whom he now knew as Cesar Molina—sitting next to his boss. Cesar was Sousa's right-hand man, it would seem. Landon thought of how he'd grabbed Emma's arm roughly that night and practically pushed her to the rear of the club. Anger burned a path from his gut all the way up his throat, so hot that Landon thought he might breathe fire and burn the asshole to a crisp.

That would be awesome.

"Emma, please have a seat." Teyo Sousa's familiarity with her did little to cool Landon's jets. Rather, it put him even more on edge until he felt uncomfortable in his own skin, itching for a fight. He fixed a pleasant smile on his face and tried to keep his teeth from grinding right down to the gums. *Play it cool, man. Just settle your ass down.*

"You too, Deputy." The invite came across as an afterthought, and the insult wasn't lost on Landon. He was an unfortunate complication that would need to be dealt with. And wasn't that too damned bad.

Instead of sitting down, Landon pulled out Emma's chair. He waited for her to sit and then scooted her closer to the table, planting a kiss right below her ear as he did so. Sousa's dark, fathomless eyes settled on him and the other man's lips quirked into a half smile that didn't quite reach his eyes. The obvious size-up didn't intimidate Landon in the slightest. *Bring it on, asshole.*

After Landon took his seat, Emma placed her elbows on the table and rested her chin on her fingertips as she regarded the man who'd kidnapped her father. Landon had to give her credit—she was cold as ice, and totally in control of her emotions. Steel. "All right," she said. "Now that we're all here, let's get down to business."

On the outside, Emma projected serenity. On the inside, fear gnawed at her stomach and clawed at her mind, urging her to bolt, and yet she was angry enough to scream at the same time. She fiddled with her wig—her head was sweating like she'd recently run a marathon—and kept her face tilted downward, careful not to make direct eye contact with any of the patrons. It was a long shot that anyone would recognize her, but her luck hadn't been stellar up to this point and she wasn't taking any chances. Rather than worry about her appearance, Emma tried to focus on the man she'd been brought to meet—the once childhood friend of her dad—and not the fact that Teyo Sousa had taken him right out of that prison van as though it were nothing, just so he could use a sick old man as leverage. Then again, wasn't Emma using his money in the exact same way? Maybe they were more alike than she wanted to admit.

Sitting across from her was a man who wasn't

a stranger to decadence. Sousa was the healthy, vibrant middle-aged man her father should have been. He didn't give off an arms dealer vibe, but rather blended in perfectly with the high-brow crowd eating lunch around them. His tailored suit had likely cost more than most people made in a month, and he held himself with a certain regality that told Emma a lot about how he thought of himself. A king among paupers who possessed the power to decimate his enemies with nothing more than a snap of his fingers. Power-player. Charismatic. Ego-maniac. And presumably a few eggs short of a dozen. Wouldn't you have to be to peddle weapons of mass destruction without even a twinge of conscience?

Beside her, Landon leaned back in his chair, the epitome of calm. She wondered if he felt even a little rattled, but then, he probably threw himself into dangerous situations like this on a daily basis. Which made her even more determined than ever to put on a good show. No way would she let Landon upstage her. She wanted him to know that, despite the fact that none of this had gone according to her plan, she was still capable of getting herself—and her father—out of this mess.

Emma didn't need anyone to come to her rescue.

"I have to say, you're not quite what I expected," Sousa addressed her head-on as though Landon weren't even there. "Though you do have your father's stubborn streak. Even as a boy, he was like a badger. Once he sunk his teeth into something, he wouldn't let go. Had you been anyone else, I would have simply killed your father and then come after you. But we have a history, your father and I. And even thieving little *putas* like you can be afforded leniency."

Did he kiss his mother with that mouth? Landon's body went rigid beside her, and Emma sensed the angry tension rolling off of him in waves. No matter what the language barrier between them, Landon must have sensed the innuendo in Sousa's tone. He might have looked civilized and respectable, but the arms dealer was nothing more than an animal. And though it warmed her to think that Landon was enraged on her behalf, she needed him to keep a level head. Not that Emma was happy with being called a bitch.

She leaned in as if sharing a secret and let her gaze wander leisurely from Cesar to his boss. "I can appreciate the fact that you might be a little upset over being played by a . . . little *puta* like me. But don't you think your anger is a bit misplaced? I mean, sure, I stole your money, but aren't you even a little interested in how I managed to circumvent your security? I mean, your tech, whoever he is, must not be very good at his job because it took me less than a minute to get through your protocols and take that money right out from under your nose."

Sousa sat back and folded his arms across his chest as he regarded her. A long moment of silence stretched out between them, and Emma fought the urge to squirm under his intense scrutiny. She just had to keep it together.

"So you're clever. So what? There's always a bigger fish waiting in the shadows to eat the smaller ones. You're not the biggest fish in the ocean, *pequeña*. I'm sure I could find one to swallow you up."

"Maybe," Emma said with a shrug. "But I'm not as

small as you think I am. You can go fishing all you'd like, Señor Sousa. That still isn't going to change the fact that I have your money and you don't."

"Good afternoon, everyone. Welcome to the Metropolitan Grill." A tight smile settled on Sousa's face as a perky waitress filled their water glasses. "My name is Janelle and I'll be your server today. Our specials include a fresh artichoke appetizer that's tossed in olive oil and lemon juice and grilled over live mesquite. We also have a chicken Waldorf salad, and our soup of the day is a seafood stew that, I have to tell you, is my absolute favorite menu item. Would anyone be interested in—"

"We'll let you know," Cesar cut her off with one of his trademark scowls and Emma was surprised their waitress didn't melt from the heat in his glare. "Now get the fuck out of here and don't come back unless we call you over. This is a private conversation."

"Cesar," Sousa snapped. What followed was a string of angry Spanish that made Emma's ears burn. A slew of threats and curses and a brief chastisement on social graces that shut Cesar up in a heartbeat. He might have been a lowlife criminal, but keeping up appearances was apparently important to Teyo Sousa.

"You'll have to excuse my associate's bad manners," Sousa said to Janelle. "Perhaps you'll give us a few more minutes while we conduct our business?" He motioned for her to come closer, and when she rounded the table to stand by his side, he slipped a folded-up bill into the pocket of her apron. "My apologies."

Emma wanted to gag at his mock show of gallantry. To shoot up out of her chair and scream,

"He's an arms dealer and human trafficker for Christ's sake! He probably trips grandmas and steals candy from babies in his free time, too!" But no. She had to sit there and watch as Janelle flashed him a smile brighter than the sun before heading back to wherever she'd come from as though Cesar hadn't snapped at her like a rabid pit bull.

"Now, before we're interrupted again, let's get back to business. I want my money. You want your father returned to you. If you can guarantee that my funds will be safely deposited into the account from which you stole them, I can guarantee that you and your father will be reunited by tomorrow."

Emma knew he was lying through his teeth, but that didn't do much to quell the hope that swelled in her chest. She wanted to agree right then and there, give him whatever the hell he wanted. Landon cleared his throat beside her, as though gently urging her to use caution. Emma reminded herself who Sousa was and what they were here for. The only way she'd be reunited with her dad that way was in the morgue.

"It could be that easy," Emma mused. "But I doubt it. First of all, who's to say my father is even still alive? The last proof I received was a picture that, to be honest, didn't exactly elevate my hopes that you were taking decent care of him. And secondly, do you think I'm so foolish, Señor Sousa"—she addressed him with respect despite her disrespectful tone—"that I'd just give you your money back and trust that you'll deliver my dad to me, safe and sound?"

Emma looked askance at Cesar, and he gave her an arrogant smirk. What a jerk. He slung one arm over the back of his chair and chuckled before turning his attention to his employer. "Told you."

Told him what? That she was a raging pain in the ass? Stubborn? Arrogant? Difficult and not a team player? "You can think whatever you want, but you're the one who started this. Not me. If you hadn't threatened and blackmailed my father and sent him to prison, you wouldn't have to be dealing with me right now."

Sousa ignored her words and shifted his focus to Landon instead. "And how do you fit into all of this, Deputy? It's not often that I entertain federal law enforcement, but I have to admit you've piqued my curiosity. We did a little checking into your history with the Marshals Service. You've managed to rack up quite the list of allegations, haven't you?"

Emma glanced at Landon from the corner of her eye. He answered Sousa with an arrogant smirk and a casual shrug of one shoulder. "Allegations, yes," he said. "But nothing that'll stick."

"Tell me, what does your agency believe about our dear Emma's death?"

"Whatever I tell them," Landon remarked. "We loaded her up into an ambulance, took her to the hospital, and as far as they know, she died en route. Don't you watch the news? They held a press conference and everything."

"I saw it," Sousa said. "But don't think for a second that your sitting with me here now is indicative of trust. Your greed"—his eyes slid to Emma—"in addition to other things, might be motivating your actions, but I won't hesitate to have one of my men take care of you the second you walk out this door if I feel like you're a threat to the business I'm trying to conduct."

"You don't have to trust me," Landon replied in a cool tone that gave Emma chills. "As long as she trusts me. Emma's in charge here, not me. I'm here to protect my own interests and to make sure nothing happens to her."

"Your own interests?" Sousa muttered. "Such as lining your own pockets if the occasion arises?"

Another casual hike of his shoulder.

Sousa said something to Cesar in Spanish, a derogatory comment that suggested Landon might be a little "pussy whipped," and they both had a nice little chuckle at the aside. Landon's eyes narrowed and his fists clenched so tight that his knuckles turned white. Emma doubted he spoke a word of Spanish, but you didn't have to know the language to pick up on the innuendo.

"You said that I'm a small fish in a big pond." Emma reached over and cupped the back of Landon's neck, massaging gently before passing her palm across one tense, heavily muscled shoulder and down his right forearm. He relaxed into her caress and the nervous butterflies in Emma's stomach swirled in a riot. Touching Landon affected her more intensely than sitting face-to-face with a terrorist. She didn't know if that should make her feel brave or just plain foolish. "Who's to say the CIA or DOJ doesn't have a bigger fish than me?"

"What are you getting at?"

Cesar looked as though he might throttle her, and it gave Emma a perverse sense of satisfaction to have rattled his chain. He was quite the guard dog, wasn't he? Looking out for his master like that. "I'm suggesting that maybe you have the wrong people on your payroll."

Sousa burst out into a round of raucous laughter that drew the attention of the diners around them. "And you think you're the right person?"

Emma shrugged. "I might be."

"And what would you be interested in getting out of a business relationship with me, Emma?"

"Money," Emma said. "What else would I want? You managed to get my dad out of jail and I don't plan on sending him back there once you let him go. He's sick and needs taking care of. When this is all said and done, I'll need to get him—as well as myself and Landon—out of the country as soon as possible. I'm offering you a trade. Our services for your help. I have skills you can use. Landon, for the time being, can make sure that federal law enforcement steers clear of your operation while you conduct business. You have the cash and connections to set us up. I think that's a reasonable offer, don't you?"

Sousa gave her an appraising look. "I've done pretty well for quite a while without your particular set of skills, Emma. And as far as the marshal goes, who's to say I don't already own a dozen exactly like him. What makes you think I need you at all?"

Emma smiled. "This is the technology age. Pretty soon, operations like yours are going to be run by people like me at twice the efficiency with triple the secrecy. As far as Landon goes, we're a package deal. No negotiation on that front. And I can be a pretty big pain in the ass when I don't get what I want."

"Really? Because I see you as nothing more than a minor inconvenience at this point."

Emma leaned in as though sharing a secret. "Oh, but I took your money *so* easily. Aren't you even a little worried about what other information I could already have my hands on?"

Any good humor at their table quickly evaporated with Emma's words. "You know *nothing*."

Emma took a sip from her water glass. Sousa's accent became thicker, more defined when he was agitated. A nice little tell to let her know that she'd gotten under his skin. All she needed now was to plant a seed of doubt and let his imagination do the rest. If Crawford's intel was correct, Sousa needed to get his hands on his money ASAP. If he was worried about who else might be digging around in his business, he might be tempted to keep Emma around for a while. At least long enough for him to get his hands on the bomb. And in doing that, she hoped to ensure her dad's safety as well.

"I know more than you think," she said.

Sousa leaned over and whispered something to Cesar. The other man pulled his phone out of his pocket and hit the speed dial, barking orders in Spanish to someone on the other end. Emma only caught half of it, but it sounded as though Cesar was making arrangements for another field trip. *Great.* In what felt like seconds, they were surrounded, four of Sousa's men standing behind them and drawing curious stares from the other diners. Not exactly the way to deflect attention. Blond wig or not, Emma could easily be recognized if the right person was curious enough to give her a good look.

"This meeting is over," he said. "Good afternoon, Miss Ruiz. Deputy."

Chapter Sixteen

Their prompt dismissal didn't leave any room for continued discussion. Landon sensed Emma's panic mounting as her eyes grew wide, her expression full of worry. If she let her emotions get the better of her now, they were as good as screwed.

"What about my dad?" Emma asked, her voice little more than a controlled burn. One of Sousa's guys grabbed her by the arm and she jerked free, causing curious murmurs to erupt around them.

"It's time to go," Landon said softly as he urged her away from the table. He threw a pointed look Sousa's way and added, "I'm sure this isn't over."

Sousa didn't respond, simply returned Landon's stare with one of his own. Cold. Calculating. Emotionless. Whether he decided to use Emma or not, it was clear that they were as good as dead once she was no longer useful. She knew too much for her own good. Her bravado had touched a nerve, and though Emma had played her part exactly as Crawford had expected her to, Landon doubted their

situation would have any other outcome regardless
of her behavior.

And Crawford probably knew it.

As they turned and headed out of the restaurant,
his skin crawled with the sensation of being watched.
A burst of adrenaline dumped into Landon's gut,
spreading through his limbs as they walked, and he
held his arms tight at his sides to keep from swinging at the first available body. He was painfully aware
of the fact that he had no weapon and they were
outnumbered. That wasn't to say he couldn't be a
scrappy son of a bitch when he needed to be, and if
push came to shove, Landon was going to be sure to
take some of Sousa's men with him.

The same dark blue Range Rover was parked outside of the restaurant waiting for them. Landon had
to give these guys credit: they'd stepped out of the
box with their vehicle color. No stereotypical black
rigs for these criminals. They were met by three
more escorts, two of whom weren't any of the guys
who'd dropped them off. Just how many people did
Teyo Sousa have on the payroll, anyway? And how
many of them did it take to guard one crooked marshal and one agitated hacker? If anything, Sousa was
showing how big a coward he was if he had to hide
behind so many to see his dirty deeds carried out.

Either that or Emma was way more intimidating
than Landon gave her credit for.

"Get in the car."

The new guy was rougher around the edges than
the rest of Sousa's employees. Though most of them
sported ink of some kind, this guy sported tattoos on
his forearms as well as on each of his fingers right
above the knuckles. He was tall, corded with bulky

muscle, and wearing ragged jeans and a T-shirt rather than the more expensive clothes the other guys favored. And whereas most of Sousa's guys were Latino, he'd be surprised if this MMA-looking dude spoke a lick of Spanish. It wasn't only his clothes or tats—or his white-bread appearance— that had Landon on edge, though. This guy had a hardness to him, a bone-deep iciness, void of emotion, that went beyond a bunch of thugs who peddled weapons and women to the highest bidder. Even hardened criminals had a tendency to wear their negative emotions on their sleeves. They were brash, impulsive. But not this guy. One look at him and Landon knew that he'd checked his emotions at the door a long time ago. All of them. *One of these things is not like the others. . . .*

Emma paused at the open car door and gave their escort a wary glance. He returned the gesture with one of his own—a snarky grin that showcased a set of deep dimples and banished his hard edge for a brief moment. Then, he winked at her. *What the fuck?*

Ordinarily, Landon's first thought would be to get up in the guy's business. Especially since, for all intents and purposes, Emma was supposed to be his girlfriend in this scenario. Whether or not it was true was inconsequential. He should bust the SOB straight in the face for even giving her a sideways glance. But there was something about his expression. The guy wasn't coming on to Emma. He wasn't even remotely hostile. Which meant that he had to be Crawford's inside guy. It would explain his look, anyway. Most undercover guys lived the part. And it looked as though he'd been undercover for a while.

"Where are you taking us?" Emma asked. Landon

appreciated the way she asked their escort at large, though he doubted she had any clue that one of these guys could be undercover SOG. "I want to see my dad."

The driver and front-seat passenger exchanged a knowing look. Crawford's easy-peasy plan was turning into one big clusterfuck. "Get in the car, Emma," Landon murmured. He urged her up into the backseat and took a quick look around before he climbed in behind her. A second vehicle parked behind them carried three or four more guys, all of them presumably Sousa's. Their entourage was bigger than he'd thought. Closer to seven or eight guys than just a few. He suspected they weren't heading back to the hotel any time soon, which meant their meeting with Sousa had been nothing more than a chance for the arms dealer to size up his opponent.

The question was, had he found Emma worthy?

She sat ramrod straight in her seat, hands folded in her lap. He needed her to relax. These guys scented fear like a pack of hungry wolves and they wouldn't waste an opportunity to exploit any weakness. "I was sort of looking forward to lunch," Landon remarked. "I've wanted to eat there ever since I got to town. I feel cheated." He smiled at her and leaned in, knocking his shoulder against hers. "Did you see the porterhouse the dude at the next table was eating? I seriously wanted to jack it right off his plate."

Emma's shoulders relaxed with his words, no longer creeping up toward her ears with tension. "The food is really good there," she said with a wan smile. "Jeremy took me there for dinner once and they have the best crème brulee I've ever eaten."

He might have coaxed her into relaxing, but at the mention of Jeremy's name, Landon's tension level jacked up into the stratosphere. Screw their life-or-death situation, the fact that they were surrounded by hardened criminals who wouldn't hesitate to kill them in the blink of an eye. Nope, what really, *really* got under his skin was the thought of Emma with another man.

Son. Of. A. *Bitch*.

Landon's jaw clamped down and he had to force it open as he asked, his voice tight, "So, remind me, who's Jeremy again?"

One of Sousa's guys snickered from the front seat and it took every ounce of control he had not to lean forward and punch the asshole in the back of the head. Emma quirked a curious brow and her luscious lips curved into a half smile. She leaned in close until her mouth hovered near his ear and whispered, "What's the matter, McCabe, jealous?"

A shock of heat bolted down Landon's spine and settled in the region right below his hips. It was absolutely perverse that he could be so turned on given their situation, but his body didn't seem to give a single shit. His hand acted of its own volition, snaking around Emma's waist. His own voice was thick when he replied, "You have no idea."

Just like any hopeless addict, Landon reveled in the rush of excitement that filtered through him and welcomed the threat of the unknown looming before him. It was the reason why he jumped out of airplanes, climbed cliff faces without safety rigging, dove off of bridges with nothing more than a tiny parachute to save his ass. And it was why, when he had no idea if their next few moments would be their last, all he could think of was kissing Emma Ruiz one more time.

He unbuckled her seat belt with his left hand and pulled her close to him with his right. He couldn't be bothered with trivialities like the buckle-up law when his body urged him to hold Emma as close to him as possible. The other passengers melted away into the background of Landon's mind until there was nothing left but the two of them. Whoever this Jeremy was, Landon was going to make damned sure that Emma never had a reason to think about him again.

"Unless you plan on sharing, I'd reconsider what you're about to do."

Landon didn't have to turn around to know the voice speaking low from behind him belonged to Crawford's guy. Common sense was nonexistent when all he could think of was touching Emma, kissing her, inhaling her scent. His heart beat triple time and he was so damned wired all he could think about was fighting or fucking, and it would take one or the other to calm him the hell down. *Get a grip and keep your head straight.* He inclined his head to let the other man know that he understood the gentle warning. Sousa's guys were still ruthless scumbags after all. If they didn't have any problem peddling innocent women in the sex trade, they certainly wouldn't have any qualms about hassling Emma given the chance. And Landon's overzealous behavior would be nothing more than a green light for these bastards. If he didn't respect Emma enough to keep his hands off of her in the presence of an audience, why should they do the same?

He eased Emma away from him and reached over her to secure the seat belt across her torso. Her brow knitted in a strange mixture of hurt and confusion, and her expression sliced through Landon's chest like an old, rusty blade. *Ouch.*

A heavy sigh deflated his lungs completely, though it did nothing to calm him down. Landon eased his head back on the rest and closed his eyes in an effort to shut out his surroundings so he could gain even a small glint of clarity. How much worse could he fuck things up with Emma before this was all said and done?

Did he even want to know?

Landon switched gears faster than a safety running in a touchdown from an interception. Whatever the guy sitting behind him had whispered in his ear, it had been enough to cause Landon to put on the brakes. Emma's emotions were already raw and close to the surface; she didn't need the added stress of Landon's hot/cold treatment. If he was merely playing the part of the overzealous lover, fine. But how about a little follow-through? Why put on a show and make her feel like a meal that's about to be devoured only to be put back in the fridge and allowed to cool? And why was she more pissed off about the words putting an end to their play than the fact that she was being carted off to God knew where for whatever reason? Her infatuation with Landon had officially become a sickness. Or, more accurately, an unhealthy addiction.

The rest of the drive passed in stoic silence. Sousa's henchmen weren't big on small talk, and even if they were, Emma wasn't interested in shooting the bull. If anything, she spent the drive contemplating how much she was going to enjoy seeing them all arrested and thrown in some hole to rot for the rest of their lives. The accumulated acts of atrocity carried out by Sousa and his people probably went way beyond anything Emma could imagine. If she could help, even a little, to put these guys away, she'd do whatever she could.

It's what her dad would want her to do.

Emma folded her hands in her lap and tried not to think about the man sitting beside her, or the others to the rear and front of her. If she did, she'd lose her cool, though for two completely different reasons. Though she'd promised Landon she could play her part, Emma was starting to think that the sooner this was all over, the better. With every passing minute, Landon became more to her than simply the embodiment of a young girl's fantasy. And the real live Landon McCabe might be harder for her to get over than any crush she'd ever had. After they arrested Sousa and dealt with the issue of her dad—hopefully his unconditional release— he'd go back to Portland and whatever life he had there. And Emma would go back to hers. The problem was, she wasn't sure she wanted to go back to that life.

Emma rested her head on Landon's shoulder. Angling her mouth near his ear, she murmured, "How long will I have to be dead?" without really realizing the impact the words would have on her. As though she'd taken a full-body tackle, the air left

Emma's lungs and her chest ached. Did it really matter how long she remained in this purgatory of nonexistence? Her life had been empty and hollow for a long damned time before all of this started.

The look that Landon gave her conveyed the sort of sadness and regret that accompanied a death. He turned so that his mouth rested high on her cheek. As he cupped her face in his warm palm, his lips brushed the shell of her ear. "I wish I could answer that for you, Emma, but you know that's not possible." He kissed her cheek and down her jaw as though to mask their private conversation and whispered words. "We can't be having this conversation in mixed company. No red flags, got it? Try not to worry about it, though, okay? We'll work it out, I promise."

McCabe probably shouldn't have made promises he couldn't keep. There was more to it than the issue of her faked death, and she knew it. She'd committed crimes. Hacked a bank account. Stolen money. Did it matter that the crimes had been committed against criminals? If anyone found out what she'd done, her professional life would be over. Clients wouldn't trust her and her reputation would be forever marred. Too late for that sort of regret now. Maybe Jeremy could help get her a job at CenturyLink Field selling corn dogs or something.

The car slowed to a stop and Emma took in their surroundings. They'd left the city behind and the Industrial District stretched out before them, almost a city in itself comprised of myriad warehouses and storage yards, with Puget Sound beyond. It occurred to Emma that worrying about her future might be a moot point. She'd taunted Sousa, dangled his stolen money in front of his face, and she doubted he'd let her go with nothing more than a slap to the wrist.

"All right, princess, time to get moving."

At their tattooed escort's words, Emma climbed out of the car behind Landon, only to find herself flanked on all sides by Sousa's men. What did they think? That she'd bolt the first chance she got? They were all heavily armed, and she wasn't about to try and outrun a bullet anytime soon. Landon walked beside her, his gaze roaming over their surroundings as though cataloging every detail to memory. A large warehouse loomed before them, and Emma took a cleansing breath as one of Sousa's men knocked three times in succession, twice quickly, and then three times again. The door swung open and their small entourage parted to allow them passage inside.

Well, everyone but one guy. His smarmy expression left little to the imagination, and he looked Emma up and down like she was a tree he'd like to climb. An anxious knot coiled tight in her stomach as she walked through the doorway, partially obstructed by his large frame. He crowded her on purpose, pushing his body into hers, and whispered something in Spanish about how he wanted to sink his teeth into her ass. *Eww.* The thought of having any part of him in contact with any part of her made Emma's stomach turn. Her skin crawled as he bent over her and his breath fanned across her face. He took up the entire doorway, forcing Emma to turn to the side in order to sidle past him. His body touched hers in more places than was appropriate, and Emma stifled a gag. The dude reeked of cheap cologne and cigarette smoke. She'd rather lick a spoon she found on the street than get up close and personal with one of Sousa's lowlife employees.

So far, she'd engaged in thievery, experienced life-threatening situations, gone nose-to-nose with an arms dealer, and become a spy and coconspirator. And none of it got under her skin the way this skeevy walking cliché did. *Blech.*

In her haste to get past the olfactory nightmare invading her space, Emma didn't notice the storm brewing to her left. From the corner of her eye, she caught Landon staring in her direction. Brows pinched, his mouth a hard line, the expression on his face spoke of barely contained rage. If looks could kill, Sousa's guys would have melted into puddles of goo, like those Nazis in *Raiders of the Lost Ark*. His teeth were clenched so tight it almost distorted his features, squaring his jaw. He bent at the knees, his powerful thighs bunching under the denim as though he was preparing to launch himself at the guy, who still hadn't bothered to get out of Emma's way and let her through the door.

"Luis!" the tattooed guy barked from behind Landon. "Knock it the fuck off and let her by. She's not here for you to play with."

Emma met Luis's gaze and smirked. His lip curled as he stared down at her, the cold depths of his nearly black eyes promising retribution. The knot in her stomach tightened to the size of a tennis ball. Okay, so maybe it wasn't a good idea to get cocky. Tattoo guy jumped in to save the day, but from the concerned glance he shot the deputy's way, she had a feeling it had more to do with keeping Landon in one piece than protecting her. Which was weird to say the least. *Ugh.* Emma had officially had her fill of testosterone for the day.

"This way."

Tattoo guy jerked his chin and Emma rushed to catch up, pushing herself past the asshole, who'd moved barely enough to let her past without any skin-to-skin contact. Landon didn't budge from where he stood, just stared the guy down until an uncomfortable silence descended. You could have heard a freaking pin drop in that warehouse and the tension made the hair stand up on the back of Emma's neck.

Would it kill Sousa to add a few girls to the payroll?

"Landon?"

He broke the stare-off with Luis and seemed almost surprised to find her pulling him through the doorway. Emma tilted her head to the side and rose up on her tiptoes to plant a light kiss on his lips. After all, they were supposed to be lovers and it seemed like the natural thing to do. The innocent kiss she'd planned turned onto a sinful path when Landon cupped the back of her neck and held her tight against his chest. He slanted his mouth across hers, the kiss almost bruising in its intensity as he thrust his tongue in her mouth. Emma started as his free hand slid down her side and over her hips to cup her ass.

Whoa. The boy ran so hot and cold Emma didn't know if she should take off her clothes or put on a parka. And why was he so enthusiastic right now when he'd all but rejected her in the car earlier? Was he trying to make a point? Assert ownership?

Because if that was the case, maybe he should pee on her leg and get it over with.

With a gentle shove at his chest, Emma broke the kiss. Her fingertips moved to her lips of their own accord and her breath shuddered in her chest. "*Tus besos me hacen loco.*" It spoke to the degree that Landon rattled her that Emma would revert to Spanish. The words left her mouth in a rush, so fast, her mind barely had a chance to catch up, but it didn't make them any less true: his kisses drove her absolutely crazy.

Landon smiled wide, his eyes no longer hard, but shining with a heat that turned the anxious knot in Emma's stomach into a ball of fire. She wobbled on unsteady legs, still light-headed from the effect of his mouth slanting across hers. The kiss had been meant to distract him. To break the tension of the moment. Like with their first kiss, on the roof, she'd never expected him to respond with the level of enthusiasm he'd displayed.

"As much as I'd love to put on a show for our friends here, don't you think we should get moving, McCabe?" If he'd been playing the part of the possessive boyfriend, he deserved an Oscar for his performance. "*Dios mio. No puedo entenderte.*" She couldn't figure him out. "Let's go."

Emma swore he was going to drive her to drink by the time this was all over.

Chapter Seventeen

Landon could finally say he knew exactly how a bottle of soda felt when someone shook it too hard. If he ever managed to twist the cap off and release the stores of energy pent up in his body, he was going to blow. And it was guaranteed to be messy. Already he found it hard to get a grip. One second all he could think about was tearing the arms off of the asshole crowding Emma, and the next he'd latched on to her like a leech, all but sucking her face off.

Classy, dude.

She gave him a look like he'd lost his damned mind, and that wasn't too far from the truth. For the past couple of days, he'd straddled the line between desire and duty, never willing to cross either and take a side. Emma had to find it annoying because it was driving Landon out of his fucking mind. He was sure he'd pay for his fickle behavior later. Considering her feisty nature, Landon was more wary of the petite brunette than all of Sousa's men combined. He was *so* fucked.

"Emmalina?"

A voice echoed from a dark corner of the warehouse, and Emma let out a strained sob before taking off at a run. Landon hurried to catch up, brushing past several armed guards to find Emma going to her knees near a mattress on the concrete floor. And seated on that mattress was a very thin and ragged Javier Ruiz.

"Dad!" Emma cried as Javier folded his daughter into his arms. Landon's chest grew uncomfortably tight as he watched her cry like a little girl, holding on to her dad, who appeared almost too frail to put his arms around her. "Oh, Dad. I'm so sorry. I was only trying to help you. I had no idea this was going to happen."

"Shh, *mija*. It's all right. Just calm down." His eyes met Landon's, and they crinkled at the corners with amusement. Yeah, he supposed Javier might find it amusing that the guy who'd arrested him and taken his confession in the first place was standing here with his daughter now. "Deputy McCabe, nice to see you again."

He might have looked as though he were knocking on death's door, but Javier's voice carried a strength of character that belied his ailing body. Landon would have laughed at how proper and civil this all was if they weren't about to be dumped in a shallow grave somewhere. He knelt down and said, low, "Sir, are you all right? Have you been hurt?"

In his answering smile, Landon saw a little of Emma's feistiness. "Not that it would matter at this point, but no. I have not."

"All right, you've seen your dad and know he's

alive. Now, it's time for you to do something for Teyo."

Emma turned a tear-streaked face toward Crawford's inside man. "What are you talking about?"

"If you want to play with the big boys, you've got to prove yourself."

She swiped at her cheek and slowly pushed herself to stand. "And if I do this . . . we can go?"

"You can. Your boyfriend, too. But we're keeping your father for insurance."

"What?" Emma's voice escalated, resonating throughout the warehouse space. "What am I supposed to be doing for you? I assumed Teyo wanted his money back right now. That was our original arrangement."

"It was. But now you have a new one. Or do you not remember asking him for a job an hour or so ago? If you think he's going to put you on the payroll without an interview first, you're crazy. He's not sure if he trusts you"—his gaze slid to McCabe—"or your boyfriend yet. It's not my problem if you don't like the terms of this new agreement. I suggest you suck it up and deal with it, princess."

Emma marched up to Crawford's man. She pulled back her right hand and slapped him hard enough to ring anyone's bell. Aside from a quiet grunt, he took the full brunt of Emma's rage without even blinking. "Better watch out, Damien," some asshole snickered from the shadows. "She looks like the type who'd go for the nuts next."

The comment was answered with a bout of laughter from the warehouse at large, and though Landon didn't think the snide remark was half as funny as everyone else seemed to, Emma was *totally* the type who'd go for the nuts next. It might not have been a bad idea for Damien to take his cronies' advice and back up a step or two.

But the undercover SOG marshal stood his ground, leveling an unwavering glare on Emma that forced her back a step. Landon didn't appreciate the other man's intimidation tactics, but he supposed that he was here to play a part and it wouldn't look good if he went easy on her. Whether or not Landon was happy about their situation, they were in it and there was nothing he could do but go along for the ride.

Emma looked back at her dad, all five feet, four inches of her body shaking with emotion. Landon stepped up to Damien. If he didn't do something to intercept her before Emma lost her cool completely, this could all go south pretty damned fast. Leaving Javier behind wasn't ideal, but if Sousa had laid out a task for Emma—a test of loyalty, perhaps—there was a pretty good chance they'd all make it out alive.

Alive was good.

"Personally, I think this is all a load of bullshit." Landon grabbed Emma's hand and guided her behind him. "We wouldn't have gone through all of this trouble just to screw Sousa over. How many hoops are we going to be expected to jump through? I doubt any of us has the time for these sorts of games."

"You're not jumping through anything, asshole." Luis, the bastard Landon was itching to coldcock, stepped up next to Damien and folded his arms across his chest. "Your girl here is the one who's got to prove herself. So shut the fuck up, yeah?"

Landon bit the inside of his cheek to keep from saying something he'd regret. Before this was all said and done, he was going to show that asshole how much he appreciated dickish attitudes like his. With his fists. He reached behind his back and Emma took his hand. As though she'd read his mind, she pressed up against him and wrapped her free hand around his torso to settle on his chest. Her breasts rubbed against his back, a delicious torture, and Landon shoved that particular distraction to the back of his mind. Goddamn, her hand felt good splayed out on his chest. . . . "She doesn't do anything unless I give the green light. You got that, asshole?" He reached up to stroke Emma's fingers and she shuddered against him. A satisfied smirk that had nothing to do with their current situation—and *everything* to do with his effect on Emma—settled on Landon's lips.

"You're wasting time," Damien responded. His words were obviously directed at Landon. A warning not to press his luck. "Right now, we hold all of the cards, so I suggest you get to work, Emma."

True enough. At this point, resistance would get them nothing but bullets to their heads. Emma had no choice but to do as they instructed, and it was Landon's job to give her the support she needed to see this through. "Okay, baby." He patted her hand, which was still resting on his chest. "Let's do this."

Damien led the way past Javier's makeshift bed, to a small office furnished with nothing more than a desk, a few chairs, and a single laptop. Emma cast a fleeting glance at her dad before squaring her shoulders and walking through the door. She made a beeline for the desk and sat down, pulling the laptop close. Landon admired her strength. He'd never known any woman as tough as Emma. He only hoped that maintaining that resolve wouldn't break her completely.

"What do you want me to do?" Emma asked as she positioned her wrists above the flat surface of the computer, her fingers hovering over the keyboard.

"Mendelson." The disgust in Damien's voice didn't go unnoticed. Landon was pretty sure Emma shared the sentiment. "Mister big-shot CEO Shanahan has been running off at the mouth, and Teyo wants him kept quiet. All we need you to do is work your magic. Shift some numbers around, plant a file or two in their primary server. Cesar says you like to brag about the information you gathered on Teyo and Shanahan. It should be an easy task for you to put some of it to good use, no?"

Emma canted her head to the side as she regarded Damien. "I can do it. Easily. But if I do, I'd like some assurances."

"Didn't you hear me earlier?" Luis piped in from behind Damien. "You got no say."

Damien held up his hand. "Jesus, can't you keep your trap shut for even a second, Luis?" He glanced pointedly at his comrade and said, "He's a loud-mouthed bastard, but Luis is right. I don't have to offer you any assurances."

"I just want you to promise that you won't hurt my dad," Emma said. "That's all."

"You have Teyo's money," Damien replied with a shrug. "Your daddy's nothing but insurance, princess. Nothing's going to happen to him as long as Teyo gets his money back."

"Fair enough," Emma said with a nod. She didn't

make eye contact with anyone, merely cast a sad glance at the doorway, and it tore Landon up that she might be ashamed of what she'd done. It had been stupid, sure. But also damned brave. "I'll need a high-speed connection. Are you all set up?"

Damien nodded.

"Okay, then. Here we go."

Landon watched in awe as Emma went to work. Her fingers flew on the keyboard, pulling up window after window, the code that appeared on the screen looking more like some alien script than anything legible. He marveled at her unbreakable concentration, her brow furrowed as she worked her bottom lip between her teeth. No one could say Emma Ruiz wasn't a force to be reckoned with. Already, Landon knew he was powerless to fight it.

After a half hour of uncomfortable silence, Landon wandered toward the door. "And where in the hell do you think you're going?" Damien barked.

"I thought I'd check on the old man, if that's all right," Landon said. "You know, to keep my girl from worrying while she's trying to work."

Damien grunted his consent and jerked his chin toward the doorway. "You got five minutes. Take any longer than that, and I'll send Luis after you."

Landon gave a crisp nod and strode from the office where Emma worked to check on Javier. He sat on the mattress with his back to the wall, eyes closed. Without opening them, he said, "You keep her safe, Deputy. Do you understand me?"

Landon sat down next to Javier on the mattress. "I swear to you, I won't let anything happen to her. To either of you."

Javier let out a derisive snort. "It's the folly of

youth that you all think you can take on the world. Bravery can indeed be a foolish thing."

Landon laughed. "I suppose so. But that doesn't change the fact that your daughter is prepared to do whatever it takes to put things right. You raised a child who isn't afraid to fight for the people she loves. She stands by her decisions and her convictions. I think any father would be proud of a daughter like that."

"Oh, believe me, pride in my child isn't the problem, Deputy," Javier mused. "It's the worry over what will happen to her when those convictions get her into a mess she can't get herself out of."

Like right now? "That's why I'm here," Landon said. "To make sure that doesn't happen."

"Be sure that it doesn't." Javier peeked at Landon through the slit of one eye. "Or you'll have me to deal with."

Javier might have been ill, but he was far from weak. "Believe me, I'm not looking for a fight. I know better than to go up against you—or your daughter—again."

"Good boy. Now, go check on her, will you? It's far too quiet over there."

Javier resumed his inert state: eyes closed, expression relaxed, effectively dismissing Landon to more important tasks. *Okay, then. Glad we could have this talk. . . .* He meant what he'd said, though. Landon would die before he *ever* let anything happen to Emma.

By the time Emma finished up planting enough evidence in Mendelson's corporate server to send the CEO to prison for the rest of his natural-born life, she was exhausted. Mentally. Physically. Emotionally. You name it, she felt it. Right down to her bone marrow. Totally and completely spent.

"Done." She pushed out her chair and stood to face Damien. "There's enough buried in Mendelson's system to bring Shanahan in line. A call to the FBI is all it would take to put him away for a good long time. Sousa shouldn't have anything to worry about from here on out."

"Good." Damien smiled and though the expression was cold, his eyes expressed something else. Reassurance, perhaps? "I'll relay this information to Teyo. Once it's confirmed that we have Shanahan by the balls, we'll negotiate the transfer of Teyo's money as well as the terms for your continuing employment."

"And my father's release?"

Damien leveled a cold, emotionless stare on her and Emma shivered. "Yeah. Your father's release, too."

"All right. What now?"

"Now? It's time for you to get the hell out of here, princess. I've got work to do, and where Teyo might be willing to put a little cautious trust in you, I'm not." Damien barked a couple of orders to his guys, one of which was to bring the car around so they could leave.

"Can I say good-bye to my dad first?" She didn't want to leave. Couldn't stand the thought of leaving him here with these people, but Emma knew if she pressed her luck they'd all pay the price. Tears stung at her eyes, but she kept her emotions in check as she remembered Landon's words. Guys like this respected ruthlessness above all else. Crying in front of them would only exploit her weakness.

"Make it quick," Damien said as he headed for the front of the warehouse and the group of guys loitering near the doors. "I haven't got all fucking day to wait around on you."

Emma went to her dad and wrapped her arms around him. He was so thin. Almost a shell of the man he'd been six years ago. He held her tight before letting her go and guiding her into Landon's arms. Her brow furrowed. The symbolism wasn't lost on her. Had Landon picked up on it as well? Because by accepting her into his arms the way he had, a silent vow had been made to her father. A promise that he'd keep an eye on her. Keep her safe.

Somehow Emma doubted that Landon would be thrilled at the prospect of being saddled with her.

"I'll be back soon," Emma promised. "Try to get some rest, okay, Dad?"

"I will, *mija*. Don't worry about me. Everything will be fine, you'll see."

She let Landon lead her away, but she looked back, worry eating away at her stomach like acid. There were still too many variables, too much unaccounted for. It was totally possible that all of this would get them nowhere. That once everything was said and done, Teyo Sousa would kill them to cover his bases. And Emma would be responsible for it all.

Her spine straightened and she pulled away from Landon as panic built to a deafening crescendo that pulsed in her ears. Her head was like an overinflated balloon atop her head. Blood rushed to her brain and her heart pounded in her chest like a bass drum as she tried to control her rapid breathing. When she'd tried to exonerate her dad, he'd been kidnapped. And in dragging Landon into all of it, she'd made him an accomplice to her crimes. Now, she was trapped. At the mercy of a sadistic asshole who bought and sold people and weapons of mass destruction like they were boxes of crackers at the grocery store. Oh, and then there was the icing on the cake: she was technically dead. No one—not a single one of her friends—knew she was alive. How had this become her life?

As though her current predicament wasn't stressful enough, Luis apparently thought his single duty was to stand in the doorway. She'd already run that gauntlet once; doing it again didn't exactly fill her heart with joy. Especially since she was already on the verge of a full-blown panic attack. *Ugh.*

Landon grabbed her by the elbow and Emma paused, her brow arched. "Let me go out ahead of you," he said. "Just to be safe."

Safe? As in, *Let me be the first one out in case there's a firing squad waiting for us outside.* That sort of safe? Her mind was too unfocused to voice a reasonable protest and it wasn't as though she'd be able to change Landon's mind anyway. Luis stepped out of the way, letting Landon through the door, and Emma let out a sigh of relief. Maybe he was through with acting like a dick.

Nope. The second Landon was through the doorway, Luis reoccupied the space. He looked Emma over from head to toe, the sensation similar to being coated with a thick layer of slime. *Gross.* Emma steeled herself and headed for the doorway, head held high and shoulders back. She refused to let him intimidate her. He didn't deserve the satisfaction.

As she eased through the doorway, his body hunched over hers and he put his face close to her head, inhaling a deep breath. The whisper of contact made Emma's skin crawl and when she tried to rush past him, he thrust out one bulky arm, blocking her path. "I wonder if you taste as good as you smell." His hot breath in her ear caused Emma to shudder. "I bet you're tight as a fist, too."

Emma pushed at his arm, but she might as well have been pushing against an oak. Her face grew hot and adrenaline dumped into her system, making her legs weak and shaky. "Move." She infused the one word with every ounce of bravado left in her stores.

Luis answered her with a leering grin that made her stomach bottom out. Her mouth went dry, and she tried to force something, anything, out. But before she could utter even a squeak of protest, Luis's arm was knocked away and Landon wrapped his hand around her wrist, hauling her out of the way. Emma took a stumbling step through the doorway only to have Damien catch her before she fell flat on her face.

"Landon—"

Whatever she'd planned to say died on her tongue as Landon's fist swung out at Luis's face. The contact was solid. A sickening crunch that Emma almost felt in her own jaw. Caught off guard, Luis stumbled back, but Landon didn't let off. He came at the taller man with a ferocity that startled Emma, his fist connecting with the other man's face once

again before Luis finally had the common sense to
fight back.

He shoved Landon away, but it didn't deter him.
He came at Luis, body hunched as though he intended to lay into him with a full-body check. Luis
reached for his waistband and produced a weapon
almost too large to be considered a handgun and
swung it up into Landon's face.

"Come at me," Luis goaded, regaining his cocky
attitude once he had the upper hand. His tongue
flicked out as his bottom lip, lapping at the blood
that dripped from the split. "Come on!" His voice escalated, taunting Landon, who stood stock still, his
expression seething with rage. "Do it, *hijo de puta*!"

Never once had Emma thought of Landon as
threatening. Sure he had the tough-guy cop routine
down, but beyond that there was an easygoing openness to him that she couldn't help but find attractive. Now, though, she was seeing a totally different
side to Landon McCabe. One with rough edges and
violent tendencies, and yeah, he was sort of scary.

And *oh-my-God sexy*.

She shouldn't be turned on by the dark look in
his eyes, the hardness of his expression, or the fact
that his body was tense and practically vibrating
with restraint. His broad chest heaved with labored
breath and his nostrils flared. Emma couldn't
breathe. Couldn't speak. Her eyes didn't even want
to blink. And forget about a heartbeat at this point.
As the reality of the situation hit her, every particle
of Emma's body froze, fear settling over her like a
heavy mantle as she watched Luis shove the barrel
of his gun into Landon's face. *Oh my God. This is my*

fault. He's going to shoot Landon in the face and it's my *fault.*

"Stop!" The word exploded from Emma like a shot and she rushed forward, inserting herself between Landon and the barrel of Luis's gun. Stupidity was obviously the better part of valor in this case, because Emma had no freaking idea what she was doing.

Luis's expression went from stunned incredulity to amused hilarity in a second flat. He busted out into a round of raucous laughter. "Good thing you have your girl here to fight your battles for you, asshole." He thrust his chin in Damien's direction and said, "Can you believe this shit, *hermano*? His woman has bigger *cajones* than he does."

Behind her, anger radiated from Landon in palpable waves. His chest brushed up against Emma's back with every breath he took, stirring the hairs on the back of her neck. Damien cursed under his breath, the sounds of his footsteps brushing against Emma's consciousness as he approached them. "McCabe, get in the car. Emma, unless you want your father's stay here to be even less accommodating than it already is, I suggest you follow him."

In front of her, Luis's eyes narrowed, and she suspected that this hiccup was about to cause more than a little trouble between Damien and the other man. Great. All the past few weeks had managed to prove to Emma was that the more she tried to fix things, the more broken they became.

The heat of Landon's body disappeared and he sidestepped her. Talk about stubborn stupidity. It wasn't enough that Landon had been about to get his face shot off—he wanted *another* go at Luis?

Damien intervened, grabbing him by the collar of his shirt as he gave him a solid shake, like a wolf bringing one of its pack members into line. Landon seemed to get the hint and threw Damien's grip off before heading toward their ride, the sounds of his departing footsteps like ominous thunder in Emma's ears. She closed her eyes for a fleeting moment and let out a weary sigh before turning on the balls of her feet and following Damien and Landon out the door toward the awaiting car.

Great. Who else could she manage to piss off today?

Wait. Maybe she shouldn't ask.

Chapter Eighteen

"Crawford said you were going to be a handful, McCabe," Damien remarked as he pulled out of the warehouse lot. "But I didn't think you had a death wish."

Emma wondered how they'd managed to leave without a full escort. Though it stood to reason that, once her task was done and they figured she could be trusted to a certain degree, Sousa's guard dogs would back off. It was nice to know that her suspicions were confirmed that Damien was in fact the SOG marshal working undercover. It made the wink he'd given her after lunch a lot less unsettling, anyway.

Landon sat at Emma's side, stoic. He stared straight ahead, his eyes focused on some unknown point. A muscle ticked in Landon's cheek, his jaw sawing back and forth as if he were making a meal of his own teeth. Nervous energy skittered up Emma's spine. He was pissed—there was no doubt about that. But now that they'd left the warehouse behind she figured he'd take the opportunity to cool off.

Maybe McCabe wasn't the sort who bounced back quickly.

Rather than respond to Damien's ribbing, Landon remained silent. He looked like he might blow at any second and Emma was afraid of making even the smallest misstep to set him off. "I know it's not your responsibility, but have you been looking after my dad?" Emma was pretty sure the last thing on Damien's list was watching out for an ailing old man, but she had to ask. "I mean, he's holding up all right, isn't he?"

"I'm doing what I can," Damien said. "I'm not around a lot, but when I am I check in on him. He seems to be holding up fine. Sousa won't let anything happen to him until he gets his money back, Emma. They won't be giving him the gold-star treatment or anything, but at least he won't be intentionally hurt."

Intentionally. That one word tied Emma's stomach into an unyielding knot. "I never should have taken the money," she said more to herself than Damien.

"No," Damien said. "You shouldn't have. But it's too late to worry about that now. Focus on damage control, on convincing Sousa that you want on his payroll. You did a good job today. You proved not only your worth but that you're willing to do what he asks of you. With any luck, we'll have this wrapped up soon."

"But that depends on how quickly I give Sousa back his money, right?"

"More or less." Damien shrugged. "He's calling the shots now. Your job is to sit tight and play your part. Do that and this will all turn out fine."

She wished she could be so optimistic.

The rest of the drive passed in silence. Beside her, Landon sat like a statue, anger radiating from every pore. For the first time all day, Emma almost wished she was back in the warehouse with Sousa's men rather than about to be dumped off to spend the rest of her evening cooped up in a hotel room with one super-cranky deputy U.S. marshal. With any luck, the hotel cable carried the beIN SPORTS network. A good soccer game was the distraction she needed to take her mind off of her growing list of worries.

Or maybe not . . .

Damien pulled up to the rear entrance of the hotel, and Landon jumped out of the backseat, slamming the door behind him. The SOG marshal returned Landon's gun to him, and he waited with his back turned to Emma, arms folded at his chest. "I'll be in touch. I suggest staying close to your phone." He rolled up his window and pulled out of the parking lot, leaving a car's width of distance between Emma and Landon. Those few feet that separated them might as well have been miles.

Landon didn't take a single step until Emma caught up to him. Even then, he waited for her to take the lead, staying close behind her right shoulder, almost crowding her but not quite.

"Are you going to say anything?" Emma hustled through the back entrance and made a beeline for the elevator. Urgency took on a new meaning with her head sweating like someone had encased it with a layer of heated plastic. Which wasn't half as annoying as her itchy scalp. When all of this was said and done, she was ceremoniously burning the damned wig. She doubted it did much of anything to change her appearance anyway. The only thing it was good for was pure, unmitigated torture.

Landon refused to speak, all but ignoring her as they stepped inside the elevator. He punched the button for their floor with so much force, she'd be surprised if the button ever worked properly again. Why was he behaving like a spoiled teenager who'd lost his Internet privileges? Was he pissed off that Damien had pulled him out of the warehouse before Luis could blow his fool head off? Or maybe it was Emma's own interference that had him so bent out of shape. She cringed as she took a tentative step back. Now that she thought about it, she could see how that might have dinged his ego.

Great. Was there anything she hadn't managed to screw up yet?

The elevator doors slid open on the second floor to a couple waiting to jump on board. Emma reached up and pulled the blond locks of her wig down around her temples, averting her gaze as she maneuvered to the rear of the elevator. One floor passed and then another. Though it was unlikely anyone would recognize her out of the blue, she couldn't help but feel nervous. She'd really crossed the point of no return, hadn't she? Criminal. Thief. Extortionist. And dead.

Being dead was the worst part.

When the doors opened to their floor, Emma politely excused herself as she slid past the other passengers. Landon stomped out behind her, each step pounding on the carpet as he followed her to their room. Crap. They hadn't had time to get a different room. Or adjoining rooms as Landon suggested the night before. Well, tonight was going to be an absolute *blast*. He shoved the key card in the slot and cranked the doorknob so hard it was a wonder he didn't break it off. Emma walked in behind him, closing the door and swinging the latch into place. Without a glance backward, he strode past the bed, jerked open the sliding glass door, and stepped out onto the terrace, slamming it shut behind him.

Emma slouched down on the bed and grabbed the remote and a room service menu from the bedside table. She hoped the hotel bar delivered because she needed a drink.

Landon filled his lungs with cool air and held it there for a few moments before releasing it. Roiling thunderheads darkened the sky, making it seem much later than it really was. Closer to evening than only late afternoon. He took another deep breath and one more. No amount of fresh air was going to calm him down, though. He was about to climb right out of his fucking skin.

He'd never lost his grip like that before. Hell, he wasn't even close to leveling out now. A cool breeze washed over him, and Landon gripped the wrought-iron railing and let his head hang between his shoulders. His nostrils flared as he took another deep breath in an effort to cleanse the anger from his system. Jesus, what in the hell was wrong with him?

"Landon?"

Emma's voice slithered over his skin in a warm caress. It was like silk, smooth and soft and decadent. His gut burned as he thought of that piece of shit Luis blocking Emma's path out of the warehouse, burying his face in that ridiculous wig and eyeing her like his next meal. Anger flared hot and fresh at the memory. Before this was over, he was going to beat that fucker's smug face into a pulp.

"Yeah." He couldn't force out more than just the one word. And that even seemed like too much. It choked him on the way up, a harsh sound that caught on the knot that had formed in his chest.

"I . . . I um, haven't eaten anything yet today and I'm starving. Is it okay to order room service?"

Landon locked his elbows and stretched out his back. *Can you be more of a dickhead?* "Go ahead and order whatever you want. But don't answer the door when the food shows up. I'll take care of it."

"Do you want anything?"

Her sheepish tone cut straight through him, slicing every major organ to leave a path of bloody destruction. It was damned tough to hold on to his anger when she spoke to him like that. And really, who exactly was he pissed off at? Her for stepping in and virtually emasculating him in front of Sousa's men? Damien for pulling him away from Luis before he took a .45-caliber bullet to the temple? Or himself for his own unchecked jealousy the second another man laid eyes on Emma? What. A. Loser.

"Just get whatever sounds good." He was too wound up, too damned embarrassed by his childish, macho bullshit behavior to turn and look at her. He simply braced his arms against the railing like an idiot, head bowed. "And order as much as you want." Because, since they'd emptied his bank accounts, you could bet that Crawford and the SOG were going to be covering his tab from here on out.

"All right." Emma paused, and even though he

couldn't see her, he knew she'd taken a step closer. Could almost feel her at his back. "It looks like it might rain. Do you want me to bring you a coat?"

He snorted. Was it that she felt bad about stepping in between him and Luis and was trying to make amends for the virtual castration? If so, further coddling wasn't going to improve his sour mood. "I'll be fine. Remember, don't answer the door. Got it?"

"Yeah." Emma's tone chilled from his curt response, proving that no matter how big of an asshole he could be, there was always room for him to sink lower. "Got it."

The sliding glass door whispered shut, leaving Landon alone on the terrace with nothing but the sound of the rushing wind for company. Even in his humiliation, his anger, his damned stubbornness, he wanted Emma so bad that it hurt. A bone-deep ache that ate at his marrow and left him completely hollow.

He might as well be that stupid rookie kid again, lusting after the pretty girl. And what's worse, she had so little faith in his ability to take care of himself, of them *both*, that she'd stepped in when she'd thought he was in over his head. With a vote of confidence like that, maybe he should turn in his badge and call it a day. After all, he could always ask dear old Dad for a job and make his family happy. Yeah, right. He'd rather gnaw his own arm off.

With a groan of frustration, Landon pushed himself away from the railing and spun around, leaning his ass against it so he could see inside the room. The drapes partially obscured his view, but it wasn't like he wanted Emma to notice him watching her like some sort of creepy jerk. Still, the cityscape beyond, Puget Sound in the distance, not even the majesty and violence of the building thunderstorm held his interest the way the woman inside that room did. He could watch her for hours, even if she did nothing more entertaining than fold laundry.

She'd removed the blond wig, thank God, and let the dark curls of her hair fall down over her shoulders in a wild tangle. Her expression thoughtful, she puttered around the room as though looking for something to distract her. After a few moments, she settled on the bed, remote control in hand. She leaned against the headboard, legs crossed at the ankles, and her eyes drifted shut. Landon leaned forward as her lips parted, as though he could reach right through the glass and touch her. A raindrop smacked his shoulder. Another bounced off the top of his head. *Tap, tap, tap.* He couldn't be bothered to notice when the rain picked up in earnest, pelting him with cold, wet drops. His attention was focused on Emma, her fierce beauty and commanding presence. How could he possibly go back to his life after this? After having kissed her, touched her. Each moment with Emma made Landon crave more. And despite his self-coached detachment, he was forced to admit to himself that distance was the last thing he wanted when it came to her.

Landon closed his eyes and expelled a gust of breath. The din of the rain drowned out everything, even his own ridiculous thoughts. He welcomed the void and simply listened as the pitter-patter of a light shower transformed into the deafening rush of a deluge.

"What are you doing?"

His thoughts exactly. What in the hell was he doing? It was ridiculous to want a woman he barely knew, or even think about pursuing a relationship with someone who was involved in not only a past case but a current one. Jesus.

"Landon. Get out of the rain. Are you crazy?"

Yes. He was abso-fucking-lutely crazy. He had to be, right? Was there any other explanation for his behavior over the past week?

"Landon!"

Warm hands cupped his face, and he opened his eyes to find Emma staring at him, her brow furrowed, expression pinched. Had she been trying to get his attention? Shit, he was so lost in his own thoughts he barely noticed. Droplets of water clung to Emma's dark lashes, trickled down her face, and soaked her clothes through. When had it started to rain so damned hard? And what was she doing out here in this weather? She was probably freezing.

"Landon, what's the matter with you?" Emma searched his face, her thumbs brushing his cheeks. "Come inside. You're going to catch pneumonia."

His emotions were still too close to the surface. The storm blowing around them was nothing compared to the one raging inside of him. With his control hanging on by a thread, even the slightest touch sent him reeling. He wanted her. Needed her more than air. And damn it, he was tired of suffocating.

Landon took Emma in his arms and crushed her to him. His mouth descended on hers, hungry, demanding, desperate in his ferocity. She melted against him, the cold of the rain dissolving under

Emma's heat. Her mouth slanted open on his, and he deepened the kiss, his tongue sliding against hers in a firm caress that only made him hungry for more.

The rain didn't bother him, nor did the violent rush of wind that whipped at Emma's drenched hair, sending the heavy curls this way and that. Landon's brain short-circuited, along with any decent decision-making skills. His lust overtook everything else, and he released his grip on Emma for as long as it took to peel her wet shirt off of her body. The momentary separation was brief as their mouths found each other again and a gust of wind stole the garment from Landon's grip. Where it went from there, he didn't really care.

Emma's enthusiasm matched his own as her fingers fumbled with the buttons on his shirt. She popped the last two in her impatience, and the urgency of her actions made Landon's cock throb almost painfully. He wanted to be inside of her so badly he couldn't think of anything else. She shoved his shirt down over his shoulders and he shrugged it the rest of the way off. Not wasting a second, she went for the button on his jeans, working it free with one hand while she pulled his zipper down with the other.

Her kisses were a drug, sweet, intoxicating, and instantly addictive. Landon couldn't bring himself to stop even long enough to take a breath. She matched his fervor as their lips met again and again, tongues intertwined in a sensuous dance. His impatience mounted and Landon grabbed the cup of her bra, dragging it down to reveal one full, perfect breast. He cupped the weight in his hand, massaging as he brushed the pearled peak with his thumb. Emma arched into him, a low moan vibrating through him as they kissed.

Emma's arms went around him, her palms traveling down his lower back and into his jeans to cup his ass. Her touch was electric, sending a rush of adrenaline through Landon's system that reminded him of skydiving. An exhilarating free fall that made him feel so alive he wanted to shout his elation. She cupped his ass, her nails biting into his skin. He thrust his hips into her, his erection barely restrained by his open jeans and pressing against the thin fabric of his boxer briefs. One hand snaked around and palmed the bulge there and Landon's breath caught in his chest. She stroked him through the fabric, and he thought he'd come right then and there, it felt so damned good.

She shivered as a gust of wind swept over them, and Landon came to his senses, albeit a little. As much as he wanted her right here and now, he needed to get her inside, where it was warm. Words were an inconvenience at this point, especially if it meant he had to stop kissing her for even a second. He wrapped his arms around Emma to steady her and slowly maneuvered them closer to the glass door. When it stayed their progress, Landon reached behind her to slide it open and eased them into the room, turning to slide the door closed behind them.

"Wow, that took some serious skill," Emma murmured against his mouth. Her warm laughter traveled the length of Landon's spine, and he took her bottom lip between his teeth before sucking gently.

"You haven't seen anything yet." He abandoned

her mouth for her throat, and Emma tilted her head back to expose her neck to him.

"So far, you're pretty impressive." A slow moan followed on the heels of Emma's words, and it was all he could do to keep from tossing her down on the bed and fucking her senseless. He nipped at the sensitive skin at the base of her ear, and she shuddered against him. A slow smile spread on his lips, and he repeated the action, this time dragging his teeth against her flesh slowly.

A loud knock interrupted the moment followed by a call of, "Room service."

Landon cursed under his breath. *Of all the shitty timing* . . . "Be right there!" he called back, surprised at the thickness of his own voice.

"I forgot about the food," Emma said with a laugh.

"I thought you were starving?"

Emma's eyes were heavily lidded as a seductive smile spread across her lips. "I am. But not for food. Not anymore."

Ho-ly shit.

Chapter Nineteen

"Stay out of sight, okay?"

Landon's gaze raked over her in a way that warmed Emma from the inside out. She was dripping wet, wearing nothing more than her pants and a bra. He didn't need to worry about her jumping out to say hello.

He waited by the door until she slipped into the bathroom. Once she was tucked out of sight, he opened the door and exchanged a pleasant hello with the hotel employee. As Emma waited, she touched her fingertips to her lips, skimmed the skin at her throat and trailed down lower between her breasts. From day one, Landon had been sending her mixed signals and it seemed as though interruptions like this one always sullied the moment and urged him to rethink his actions. Well, she wasn't going to let that happen again.

Emma quickly unfastened her button and peeled the stretchy skinny-legged pants from her body. Holy crap, a cotton/denim blend was like superglue once it got wet and made contact with skin. After a brief struggle that sent her stumbling more than once, she managed to get her pants off and checked her reflection in the mirror. God, she looked like a drowned rat.

From the rack beside the shower, Emma grabbed a towel and dried her hair as best she could. If anything, it looked more wild and unkempt than before, but she wasn't about to worry about it when there was a half-naked Landon McCabe waiting on the other side of the door. She was in the red zone and this was her Hail Mary. If she didn't take a chance and drive in for the touchdown, she might as well call the game. It was now or never.

Emma waited for the sound of the door closing before she emerged from the bathroom. Her heartbeat sped like hummingbird wings as she tiptoed out into the room almost completely naked. Would Landon reject her yet again? Oh boy. She thought she could do this . . . but really, Emma wasn't sure she could take another one of Landon's cool dismissals. His back was turned to her as he arranged the plates of food on a small table in the far corner of the room.

"You ordered quite a spread," he said with a laugh. "I had no idea that room service delivered . . ."

The words died on Landon's tongue as he turned to face her. Emma's heart jumped up into her throat as every ounce of blood in her body rushed to her head. What was he thinking? His jaw went slack and his eyes widened a fraction of an inch. She'd never felt so exposed. And though she wasn't completely naked, she might as well be. Her heart was bare as she offered herself to Landon, and what happened from here on out was entirely up to him.

"Jesus Christ, Emma," he breathed as he scrubbed a hand over his face.

She folded her arms across her chest to shield her body, suddenly self-conscious. So much for the Hail Mary. Her fourth-down drive had ended in an epic failure. She was done. *So done.* She couldn't keep getting to this point with Landon only for him to put her at arm's length. Spinning on a heel, Emma couldn't get to the bathroom fast enough. She was locking herself in and not coming out until Landon was nowhere to be found.

"Where are you going?"

Landon's hand gripped her wrist as he hauled her against his chest. His bright blue eyes shone with a heat that weakened her knees and quickened her breath. "To go put some clothes on?"

She hadn't meant it as a question, but she couldn't help the way her voice squeaked at the end. How sexy was she? *Ugh.* Landon's lips spread into a wicked grin and her stomach did a backflip. Words couldn't even begin to describe how that smile affected her. "No, you're not." His voice was a sensual growl that caused a warm rush between Emma's thighs. He could make her wet with nothing more than his voice. "In fact," he reached behind her to unfasten the clasp on her bra, "you're not nearly bare enough for what I want to do to you."

"Oh." The word left Emma's lips in an almost silent whisper as Landon eased the straps down her arms and removed her bra.

"I know I've been a crazy, fucking asshole for the past few days, but ever since that night on the roof"—he leaned down and placed a kiss at the swell of one breast—"I haven't been able to get you out of my head."

Emma arched into his touch, a sigh slipping from between her lips. "Landon . . ." The words she wanted to say wouldn't budge. That she'd wanted him for so long. Thought about him for years. That she beat herself up for wanting the man who'd arrested her dad. That she blamed him for the loneliness she'd felt over the past six years and yet she wanted him still. Needed him. The past week had been like a dream come true despite the nightmare she'd drawn everyone into.

She gasped as he took one stiff nipple into his mouth and sucked. Emma gripped onto his shoulders, bending back in his arms as he suckled her. His mouth was a brand on her skin, the sensation throbbing low between her thighs. When he pulled away to look at her, the cool air puckered her nipples even tighter. He took a few steps backward and eased down onto the armchair, pulling Emma down on top of him. She straddled his waist, the hard length of his erection brushing against her core through her underwear, and she kissed him, rocking her hips in a gentle rhythm.

Landon bucked his hips in the air, shoving his jeans down his thighs as he shimmied them off completely. There was something about his *almost* bare state that Emma found incredibly erotic. A couple of scraps of cotton fabric were all that kept their bodies from joining and it was a sweet torture she enjoyed.

"I could kiss you for hours," Landon said against her mouth. "Just sit here and taste you for days." His tongue darted out at the seam of her lips and Emma opened to him, kissing him deeply. She slanted her mouth across his and he cupped the back of her neck, holding her tight as he ground his hips hard against her core. A pleasant jolt shot through Emma's body and she moaned into his mouth as she rubbed her palms over the sculpted marble bulge of his pecs. How many times had she fantasized about making out with Landon McCabe? And *O-M-G*, round three only confirmed that the real thing was *way* better than any of her girlish imaginings.

Touchdown!

His words warmed her heart, but his wandering hands did wicked things to her body that overheated Emma to the point of combustion. His fingers glided over her skin, down her shoulders and arms, across her collarbone and the swell of her breasts. Emma trembled as his fingertips feathered over her nipples, a pleasant tingle that resonated deep inside of her and made her already aching clit throb with the need for release. Landon took his time with her. He kissed her the way that some people ate a decadent dessert, as though reveling in every spoonful.

If Landon were a dessert, he'd be a flourless chocolate cake: rich, indulgent, and sinful, with a hint of bite to the sweetness. *So good.*

He wrapped his arms around her waist and kissed her hard before standing up straight, giving Emma no choice but to wrap her legs around his waist. With a quick spin, he deposited her in the chair, scooting her ass to the edge as he went down to his knees before her. Their eyes met and Emma's breath caught at the intensity of his crystalline blue gaze.

He didn't look away, kept his eyes locked on hers as he hooked his fingers in the waistband of her underwear and pulled them down over her thighs. Landon dragged the garment slowly down, past her knees, then her calves and Emma lifted her feet so he could remove them completely. Chills chased across Emma's skin as he dragged his palms up the insides of her thighs. He eased her legs apart and his eyes dipped down to her sex and stayed there as he hissed in a breath.

Anticipation coiled into a tight knot deep in Emma's stomach. The moment stretched out as Landon simply looked at her. "Beautiful," he murmured under his breath before reaching out to pet her. Emma whimpered as the pad of his finger swept over her clit, already swollen and so sensitive to his touch.

Landon came up on his knees and kissed her, a slow, soft kiss that made Emma's toes curl. "You feel so good." He worked his fingers over her slick flesh and let out a deep, contented sigh. "I can't wait to see if you taste as good."

Emma's brain went blank. The thought of having Landon's mouth on her in that way, licking and tasting her, short-circuited her thought process until all that was left in her mind was a pleasant buzz. Who needed a beer to relax when she had Landon McCabe whispering naughty things in her ear? She might melt right into the upholstery if he said one more thing.

"Oh, God, Landon. Do it." It might have been brazen, but Emma couldn't be bothered with whether or not she sounded a little too desperate and wanton. If that's what it took to spur him into action, she'd say any dirty thing he wanted her to. "Put your mouth on me."

* * *

Landon knelt before Emma as though in prayer to some sacred deity. And make no mistake, she was every bit a goddess laid out in front of him, her thighs spread and inviting, her glistening pussy begging for his touch. He could worship her for days, until he was too weak to move and dehydrated to a mound of dust. Landon could think of worse ways to go. Who needed food or water, anyway? As long as he had Emma, he didn't need anything else.

Sure, but you don't really have *her. She's isn't yours.*

Landon pushed the annoying voice of insecurity to the back of his mind. He'd take whatever he could get at this point. Even if it was only for tonight.

Emma's lips curved into a soft smile that went straight through his chest like an armor-piercing round. Would it be creepy to admit that he wanted to stare at her for a while, devour every inch of her flawless, oiled-bronze skin with his eyes? He let his gaze wander, down the slim column of her throat, over the swell of her high, pert breasts and the erect dusky nipples he ached to reach out and touch. His gaze ventured lower and he took in Emma's slim waist, which flared out at the delicious curve of her hips, over her thighs and dipped once again to her sex, dripping with her arousal. Sweet Jesus, she was perfection.

Emma's brow furrowed and she worried her bottom lip between her teeth as though unsure. She sat a little straighter in the chair and said, "It's okay, Landon. You don't have to . . ."

Fucking hell. He'd sat there too long, staring like some stupid kid who'd never seen a naked woman before, and now she thought he wasn't into her. How could she not understand the effect she had on him?

"Emma." Landon shook his head and gave her a rueful grin as he once again positioned her on the edge of the chair. He guided one leg up and kissed her calf, the inside of her knee, her thigh. "You have no idea how badly I want to." His eyes never left hers as he kissed his way to the juncture between her legs. "I wanted to see you first, take in every inch of your body and enjoy the sight of it."

"Oh."

The husky tenor of that one word made Landon's balls draw up tight. Her brown eyes shimmered, her lids heavy as he ran his palms up her thighs and urged her to open for him once again. He dipped his head to that sweet spot he'd been dying to taste and flicked out with his tongue over her stiff and swollen bud.

"Oh my *God*."

Emma's breathy gasp on the heels of her passion-infused words pinged around inside Landon's head, and all logical thought took a temporary leave of absence. He buried his face between her legs, lapping at her, sucking as a rush of adrenaline so intense it made him dizzy coursed through his veins.

Emma was the high Landon had been searching for his entire life.

What started out as a gasp transformed into a desperate whimper as Landon dragged the flat of his tongue against her soft flesh. He drew her swollen bud into his mouth and sucked. Emma's back arched off the chair, and she dug her nails into the armrests as she thrust her hips, pressing against

Landon's mouth. He'd said he could kiss her all night, but he'd rather his mouth was buried between her thighs.

"*Uhng . . .*" Emma's low, desperate moan spurred Landon on. Her scent, the evidence of her arousal sweet on his tongue, drove him wild. With one hand, he cupped her ass, tilting her up toward his mouth, and with his other, he eased one finger, and then another inside of her.

Emma lunged forward as he worked his fingers inside of her tight channel, his tongue swirling over her clit. She cried out as her hands dove into his hair, fisting the short strands as she held him tight against her. Landon had her on the edge; it wouldn't take much to send her over completely. His cock throbbed, jutting out from between his legs, so hard he felt the slightest bit of discomfort.

Damn, this was without a doubt the best adrenaline high of his life.

In an impulsive rush, Landon propelled himself to stand, pulling Emma up with him. Her surprised *yip* brought a smile to his face, and he spun them around until he was sitting in the chair again and she was standing before him gloriously naked.

"You're fucking beautiful, Emma."

She smiled, an expression so open and radiant that it stole Landon's breath. Her gaze slid down the length of his body and settled at his cock, barely restrained by his underwear, where it remained for a few moments before she looked up at his face. "I'm sort of at a disadvantage here, don't you think?"

Good God, her voice, so husky and thick with passion, caused his gut to clench tight with lust. He answered her with a smile of his own and kept his gaze locked on hers. He eased off his boxer briefs in a clumsy tangle of fabric, kicking them to the far side of the room. Emma laughed, and the sound rippled over Landon's skin like cool lake water on a too-hot day.

She was every bit the seductress when she said, "That's better. Impressive, Deputy."

Her hungry expression sparked a fire in Landon's blood, and he reached out, capturing her hand in his. He pulled her to him and she climbed up on his lap, once again straddling his hips. Emma went up high on her knees and bent at the neck to kiss him. Landon had to tilt his head up to meet her, and the damp curling tendrils of her hair formed a dark, fragrant curtain around them. Her lips caressed his, slowly, deliberately. Almost a tease. The contact merely a ghost of what Landon wanted. "Kiss me like you mean it, Emma."

"Oh, I am," she whispered. "I can taste myself on your lips, Landon. You made me feel so good."

A few years back, Landon's chute had failed to open properly during a routine skydive. His brain had gone completely blank before it rebooted and he'd had the good sense to throw his backup. Right now, hearing those heated words from Emma, he was totally in reboot mode.

"Jesus Christ, you're going to make me come if you keep talking like that." Her soft, low laughter threw yet another wrench in the cogs of his thought process. Emma exuded raw, natural sensuality without even trying. The woman was made to love and be loved. And Landon was going to love the shit out of her tonight. He kissed her once, slow. "You taste so sweet. Next time, I want you to come with my mouth on you."

"Next time?" Emma raised a brow and slid down a couple of inches, just enough to brush her slick heat against the engorged head of his cock. Landon let out a tortured groan. "We're not even finished with this time and you're already making plans for next time?"

Landon shrugged a shoulder. "What can I say? I'm a planner."

Conversation dwindled in lieu of kisses and that was fine by Landon. There was plenty of time to explore the merits of dirty talk later. Right now, though, he wanted more of her mouth on his mouth. As they made out like a couple of teenagers, Emma took the initiative to push their play way past that of a couple of innocent kids. She continued to tease Landon, sliding her pussy against his cock without allowing him to enter her.

As his sensitive head brushed her clit, Emma grabbed Landon's face and kissed him fiercely. She nipped at his bottom lip as she continued to rock her hips against him, the sting of her teeth the perfect complement to the intensity of sensation as she pleasured herself against his erection. Landon gripped Emma's hips, his fingers biting into her flesh, and she stilled, the heat of her body hovering above his hypersensitive head.

"Landon," Emma said between desperate pants of breath. "Unless you came prepared to play, this is as far as we can go."

Her words were nothing more than *blargh, urgh, spltfft,* in the back of his mind. He knew she was trying to tell him something important, but for the life of him he couldn't translate the sounds. Like some sort of deranged caveman he grunted as he thrust up, desperately seeking her heat.

Emma rose up higher on her knees, a gentle laugh vibrating in her chest. "Landon. Did you hear me?"

"Later." He buried his face in her throat, kissing, biting, sucking. Somewhere in his subconscious he recalled her saying something about coming prepared to play? What did she mean? He was dying to play. Little toddlers hopped up on sugar and waiting in line at Chuck E. Cheese had nothing on his eagerness. Emma pulled away and cut him a stern look.

Wait. Did she mean . . . ?

"Not later, Landon. Now."

Condoms. She wanted to know if he had any condoms.

"Wallet," he groaned, still in caveman mode. "Pretty sure. Yeah. Wallet."

Emma laughed, her brown eyes sparkling with mischief. "Okay, then. Don't move."

Move? He wasn't going *anywhere.*

Chapter Twenty

Though Emma didn't want to admit it, she'd been sweating there for a second. Because, honestly, the idea of stopping now barely registered. Already, it took an act of sheer will not to throw caution to the wind and go for it. For a long moment, she remained right where she was, her gaze locked with Landon's while she inched her hips toward his. Her clitoris was swollen and aching. In fact, her entire body was wound tight and her limbs shook with the need for release. The way Landon's eyes smoldered when he looked at her excited Emma beyond anything she'd ever felt before. It seemed as though she'd waited forever for this moment. And she wasn't going to waste another second.

She braced her arms on the chair and leaned in for a kiss before pushing herself away. Landon lurched forward, following her, as though unwilling to separate their joined mouths. "Don't go." The gently urged command caused Emma's stomach to tighten and twist. He moved his hips and his shaft passed through her folds, a teasing caress that made her body limp and her lids heavy. Landon's voice growled in her ear, "Don't move a muscle."

Okay. No problem. He could tempt her into anything with nothing more than his voice. Emma rocked against him, gasping at the jolt of pleasure that shuddered through her. His full-court press didn't stop there, though. Landon reached up to fondle her breasts, kneading her flesh and circling her nipples with his thumbs before pinching lightly. Emma threw her head back and a low moan reverberated through her. If she didn't move now, she never would.

"I'll be right back." She pushed herself away from the chair. Landon reached out to catch her, but she spun away from his grasp. Emma looked back as she crossed the room, taking in the sight of one very naked Landon McCabe sprawled out on the chair, all hard lines and defined muscle. His six-pack flexed as he relaxed in the chair and Emma raked his body with her eyes, pausing at the hard length of his erection jutting out proudly from between his legs. The man was built like a god.

Emma groped on the floor for his jeans, reluctant to tear her gaze away. Landon's mouth quirked into a sardonic half smile that melted her bones until she wondered how she managed to stand up straight. The moment should have been awkward, a break in the mood that might end things before they began. But this was different. Landon's playfulness, the way Emma felt so at ease with him. If anything, their stalled-out momentum made her want him even more. Who would have thought that the sense of rightness she felt with him could be such a turn-on?

When she finally found his jeans, Emma rifled

through the pockets until she found Landon's wallet and the single condom tucked inside. "Should I even ask why you carry this around?" She waved the little foil packet as she walked slowly back to the chair.

He tried to snatch it from her grasp, but she pulled it away with a sly smile. "I always leave my house prepared for anything," Landon said. "That one though, has a story behind it."

Emma quirked a brow. "Oh really?"

"Yeah, it has to do with my buddy Galen, a sting operation in Beaverton about a year and a half ago, and a waitress at an Applebee's."

"Waitress?" A pang of jealousy shot through Emma as she regarded him. Maybe this particular foil packet was a keepsake from a box he'd bought in order to bed the Applebee's waitress? The thought of Landon touching another woman, kissing her, putting his mouth on her and licking her senseless made Emma see red. Or was it green? Either way, she didn't like it.

Landon gave her a bemused grin. "It's not what you think. And I'll be more than happy to tell you the story later. But right now . . ." His gaze ignited a fire over Emma's skin as his eyes swept her from head to toe. "I have better things to do."

"You don't say? Like what?" Emma infused her voice with as much sensuality as she could muster. Did she sound sexy or more like she'd finished a five-mile run? *Crap.*

Landon moved his hand slowly down his chest, and Emma's breath caught while her attention was glued to what he was doing. He ventured down past his hips and fisted his erection, stroking himself slowly from the glossed, rosy crown down to the root of his shaft and back up again. "Like getting you back over here and on top of me for starters." He stroked himself again, and a sound that resembled a strangled croak lodged itself in Emma's throat. Holy crap, Landon was so hot she was surprised the room wasn't engulfed in flames.

Did it matter who he'd been with over a year ago? He was here with *her* right now. And if Emma had it her way, he'd never be with anyone else ever again. "Maybe I'll stand here for a while," Emma suggested. "And watch."

Landon hiked a well-muscled shoulder. "Suit yourself."

His gaze didn't waver as he stroked his fist down the length of his erection. Emma's lips parted with her quickened breath, and a low groan issued in Landon's throat as he pumped his hips up into his grasp, his own breathing growing more ragged by the second. Emma took a step toward him—God, he had her so wound up that her thighs were wet from her arousal. Another stroke and Landon's hips jacked up off the chair. As though she couldn't help herself, Emma took one more step closer.

"I thought you wanted to watch," Landon remarked, his voice a husky rumble as she closed the remaining distance between them.

"I'm really more of a full-contact player than a spectator," Emma murmured as she tore the foil packet open.

Landon paused as Emma bent over him to guide his hands away. He reached out to caress her—apparently, his hands needed something to do—and pleasant chills broke out over her skin as his fingers trickled from her shoulders, down her arms, and settled on her waist. Emma's thumb barely met her fingers as she stroked him, rolling the condom over the impressive length of his erection. "You've only got one of these. Better make it count."

Landon grabbed her tight around the waist and lifted her until she was where they'd begun— straddling his hips. He wound his fists in the length of her hair and hauled her against him, kissing her as though starved for the contact. No longer playful or teasing, through with taking his time, Landon got right down to business, and this more aggressive side of him drove Emma crazy with desire. She had to have him inside of her. Now.

Rising up on her knees, she positioned herself, but not before she rubbed her clit against his swollen head once, and again. And then again. It felt so good, the sensation so intense that Emma moaned as she buried her face in Landon's hair, inhaling his clean, outdoorsy scent and holding it in her lungs.

"Oh, God, Emma, I need to fuck you." Landon's desperate tone spurred her on, and Emma slid down, taking him inside of her slowly to allow her body to accommodate his girth.

His arms shook as he held her, his thighs trembled with each tentative inch. She knew he was holding back, allowing her to control his penetration, and likewise, Emma's body vibrated with restraint. Slow simply wasn't going to cut it.

In one last quick thrust, Emma took him as deep as she could. Their sounds of passion melded into a single desperate sound, her cry and Landon's guttural shout, muffled as he buried his face in the crook of her neck. It took a moment for her body to adjust, and Emma panted through the sensation as she gently rocked against him. Landon held her tight, one hand still in her hair while the other wandered to her waist. He urged her on, guiding her hips in a gentle rhythm as his mouth ventured past the column of her throat, over her collarbone to her breast. She inhaled a sharp breath as he captured her nipple in his mouth, sucking greedily as he nipped at the hardened peak.

"Landon . . ." Emma breathed. "That feels so good."

He bucked his hips up and the sharp sting of his deep penetration was only momentary as a warm glow radiated in Emma's core. She rose up on her knees and plunged back down, evoking a tortured groan from Landon that filled her with a heady sense of power. She'd fantasized about this moment, what it would feel like to have Landon want her. And now she knew that nothing she'd imagined could compare to the reality. He lapped at her breast with vigor before switching to the unattended side. The cold air teased her nipple when Landon drew away, and Emma gasped as she ground her hips into his. His rock-hard shaft slid against her sensitive clit, and she pressed into him as her body coiled tight. *Oh, God, a little bit more* . . . A thrust, maybe two, and she'd be there.

"Oh . . . Landon . . ." Emma whispered into his hair. "You're going to make me come."

Damn it, not yet.

As much as it boosted his ego to know that he could pleasure Emma so easily, Landon wasn't ready for this to be over. Especially since this was his one and only shot tonight to feel her tight, slick heat hugging his cock.

Landon took her hips in both of his hands so he could control her motions. "Not yet," he murmured close to her ear. "Hold on, Emma. I want this to last."

She tried to take him deep, but Landon held her steady, allowing only for a shallow penetration. Her frustrated sounds made his balls draw up tight and, yeah, he wanted to come so bad it hurt. But he refused to give in to that urge, and it took every ounce of self-control he had to maintain.

He held her still, thrusting slowly up into her, and Emma's head rolled back on her shoulders as she let out a low moan. She dug her nails into his shoulders and her thighs quivered against his with the contraction of each individual muscle. He pulled out every bit as slowly, and Emma sighed, only to inhale a sharp gasp when he thrust quickly and so deep that he felt it in every nerve. For long, torturous minutes he kept the unrelenting pace. In. Out. In. A slow caress of their joining bodies until Emma quit trying to rush him and mirrored his unhurried motions.

Landon released his grip on her hips so he could take her heavy breasts in his hands. Supple, her skin like satin in his palms. He tugged at the pearled peaks of her nipples, loving the sweet mewling sounds she made when he teased her that way. Over the years, he'd had his fair share of flings. Even a few girlfriends. But no other woman had been as responsive as Emma, so in touch with her own body and her pleasure. Her confidence turned him on like no other, her openness and lack of embarrassment or shame. She displayed her glorious body proudly to him, teased him with it, even. Emma was fire and steel. Perfect. No other woman would ever measure up after this.

Afternoon gave way to evening and the room darkened to a smoky gray. Landon's eyes met Emma's, and they locked, frozen on each other as their bodies met and parted. Met and parted. They were so in sync that it felt more like a sensual dance. Not clumsy or bumbling. But unhurried. Erotic. Tantalizingly slow. They held on to one another as though afraid they'd be separated, a cleaving of limbs and torsos. With each slow thrust, Emma cried out, her lids heavy and her mouth parted and inviting. Landon smoothed back her hair and cupped her cheek before their lips met in a kiss. Slow, exactly like he was fucking her, his tongue easing past her lips to play with hers, enticing and sweet.

Minutes sped by, as evidenced by the darkening room, but to Landon, time stood still. Rain pelted the window and the wind howled outside, but it was nothing compared to the storm that raged between him and Emma. A deep connection was being forged between them, solid and unmovable. Permanent. Something that Landon was helpless to fight and yet the prospect of surrender scared the shit out of him.

The thought awakened a primal urge deep inside of him. A need that demanded satiation. He pushed up from the chair and cupped Emma's ass in his palms, urging her up and down over his shaft. On wobbly legs, he moved them to the bed and gingerly deposited her on top of the mattress. Her expression was bemused, a half smile curving her mouth. "What happened to slow and steady?" she purred.

Ah, hell. "Slow and steady is good," he responded. "But I need to have you hard and deep. Right fucking now."

Emma moaned her approval, her back arching off the mattress as she raised her hips up to meet him. Landon drove home in a single forceful thrust, and they both cried out as he pulled out and thrust again. Hard.

"Oh God, Landon. Yes. Just like that. Don't stop. It feels so good." Emma's words were spoken through gasps of breath, and Landon's own were puffing in his chest as he fucked into her.

Need drove him as Landon buried himself to the hilt in her tight warmth. He pounded into her again and again, the sound of their bodies coming together only spurring him on. His sac ached for release, his cock head throbbing as Emma's inner walls clenched around him. As though she were holding him in, the constrictions grew tighter, and Landon gnashed his teeth as a desperate growl built in his chest.

Words, sweet and soft, then frenzied and intense, buffeted his ears with each thrust. *More. Harder. Don't stop. Again, just like that. You're so hard. I need to come. Please, Landon.*

Yes! To all of it, yes. Landon couldn't form a single syllable to save his life, and yet he absorbed every word from Emma's mouth into his skin, his very soul, as though he needed those words as much as he needed her body.

Beneath him, Emma went rigid, her legs tightening around his waist. Her head came up off the bed and she buried her face in his neck, kissing, licking, nipping as she muttered unintelligible words that ended on sobbing cries of pleasure, igniting over

Landon's body like wildfire. His name exploded from her lips as she came, and her body went limp beneath him as her sex clenched him tight, pulsing and drawing him deeper, squeezing his swollen head until Landon's own need for release overtook him.

With a loud, forceful shout, he came, pumping his hips in a disjointed rhythm as the orgasm rocked through him, drawing up from his balls through his shaft and exploding from his head in a series of spasms that left him gasping and limp on top of her. Emma's deep, throaty laughter awakened him from his stupor, and for a second there, Landon thought he might have blacked out. Holy shit, he'd never felt anything like it. So intense. A full body and mind experience that left him rattled and spent.

"Emma," he breathed against her hair. Their chests met and parted with their labored breath, and Landon shuddered as an aftershock passed through him. He tried to pull out, but the sensation was still too intense and so he stayed right where he was, cradling Emma in his arms with his cock still buried inside of her. "Emma."

"Don't move." Her voice was small in his ears, not the fiery, passionate tenor that had sparked him to life. Now her words were laced with emotion that burrowed into Landon's chest and held on with sharp teeth that refused to let go. "Lie here with me for a while. Okay?"

No problem. Landon's limbs weighed him down. Content and sated, there wasn't a chance he was going anywhere anytime soon.

Words failed him. Always the guy with a quick comeback, a smart-assed quip, Landon found himself unable to articulate the feelings that tightened his chest as he held this woman in his arms and rested his head against her chest, taking comfort in her warmth against him and the steady beat of her heart. *Jesus.* What was happening to him?

Landon rolled to his side, worried that he was too heavy. He didn't want to squish Emma and his muscles were twitching from the effort it took to keep the bulk of his weight off of her. He withdrew from her and missed her heat the second their bodies parted. He wondered if Emma felt the same way, or hell, maybe she was happy to have him off her so she could take a decent breath again.

"Where are you going?"

Or . . . maybe she *wasn't* waiting for him to get off of her. "I . . . uh . . ." Jesus, no other woman on the planet affected him the way Emma did. He was seriously stammering like a stupid teenager. "I didn't want to squish you." Oh. Nice. Landon wanted to smack himself in the forehead. *Way to articulate, dickhead.* Romance and pretty words didn't come easily to him. But when you had grown up in a family that discouraged outward shows of emotion like Landon had, you learned to use sarcasm and humor as a shield pretty damned quick.

"You weren't squishing me." Emma's bright smile was as radiant as the sun, and it banished every shadow that had settled in the room. "I liked it. You. On top of me. Um . . . I mean . . ."

Looked like he wasn't the only one who had trouble saying what was on his mind. He smoothed the hair away from her face—he couldn't help himself—and hoped his smile wasn't as goofy as he knew it was. Emma obviously had some sort of superpower over him because he couldn't help but feel like a love-struck puppy every time he looked at her.

"Yeah, me too." Weren't they a pair? They rocked the dirty talk, but pillow talk was like trying to tackle the intricacies of astrophysics or some shit. "I liked it."

Landon tucked Emma against his body and let the silence that descended lull him. Outside, the rain continued to rail against the world, and he listened to the violent rhythm, the white noise that quelled any pesky thoughts that might interrupt the quiet moment. It felt so right to lie here with Emma wrapped in his arms, her naked body warm and soft against his.

What if this was the one and only time he got to have her this way?

The thought made it past his well-constructed barrier and dug in like a tick. A parasitic worry that threatened to suck the happy post-sex glow right out of him. He pushed the notion from his mind and forbade himself from thinking it again. Because Landon had no doubt that once would never be enough.

Chapter Twenty-One

Emma felt as though she'd won the World Cup, the Super Bowl, and the NBA championship all at once. She might've been a little tongue-tied, but who wouldn't be after experiencing the most awe-inspiring orgasm of her life? Landon McCabe was a bona fide *master* of sex. Every sensual, well-built, hard plane of him was made for pleasing a woman.

And *wow*, had he ever pleased her.

Emma wondered if she'd ever walk again after tonight. One night with Landon was enough to turn her legs to Jell-O. Permanently. She'd never felt so relaxed, so utterly spent. She could fall asleep right now and spend a good ten hours in dreamland without waking even once. Who needed a sleep aid? Find yourself a sex god and you'll never suffer from insomnia again!

Her stomach rumbled, a not-so-gentle reminder that she hadn't eaten in over twenty-four hours. Though the rest of her was good and sated, apparently her stomach wasn't. One could not live by great sex alone, she supposed.

"Was that your stomach?"

Landon's teasing tone should have made Emma cringe. After all, postcoital bodily noises didn't exactly rank high on the oh-my-God-sexy scale. But she knew it wasn't malicious teasing, and he was by no means appalled. He sounded more amused. Or maybe even . . . appreciative. "I told you I was hungry." She pulled back so she could look up into his face and flashed him a sheepish smile. "I'm pretty sure I burned all of my calorie stores in the past hour or so. I need to refuel."

"Do you want me to call room service? See if they'll reheat the food for us?"

No doubt it was all cold, and it was sweet that he'd offer. "There's a microwave over in that corner," Emma remarked. "I think between the two of us, we can figure out how to reheat it on our own."

Landon lifted his head off the pillow and looked around as though he'd never bothered to acquaint himself with the room. "Huh. We do have a microwave." His amazement made Emma giggle. "And a fridge. When did we get those?"

She tried not to pay attention to the way he said "we" or the warm fuzzy glow it caused. They weren't a "we" by any stretch of the imagination, no matter how right it sounded. "I think they've been here awhile." Emma disentangled herself from Landon's embrace. And though what she really wanted was to stay in his arms for the next day or so, her stomach wasn't going to let her get away with it. "Are you hungry? I ordered more than enough for two."

"Are you kidding?" He pushed himself up on the bed so he lounged against the headboard. Emma had to clamp her jaw tight to keep it from falling open as she took in his bare, muscled torso. *Sex. God.* "I'm starving."

As she rounded the bed and headed for the table, Emma felt Landon's eyes on her and it warmed her from the inside out. And though the thought that she could tempt him with her body filled her with a heady sense of power, there was one thing Emma didn't combine and that was nakedness and cooking.

Near the chair—would the hotel let her take that chair home?—where their erotic play had begun, Emma found her underwear. She looked around for her shirt until she remembered that she'd lost it somewhere on the balcony along with Landon's. Dang it.

"Top drawer on the right. I've got a few T-shirts, though if you want to eat like you are, I'm *totally* okay with that."

She looked over to see Landon staring at her, his eyes drinking her in, his expression heated. A quick assessment down the length of his body revealed that he was aroused, as evidenced by the impressive length of his erection tenting the sheet. What was she doing again? Emma gave herself a mental shake. Right. Yeah. Food.

"Hot plates and exposed skin are never a good combination," Emma remarked as she rifled through the drawer. She found a plain white T-shirt and slipped it over her head, inhaling deeply as she did, holding Landon's scent in her lungs. It was hard to concentrate on anything with him swirling around in her head like that and knowing that he was hard and ready to go again. Damn it, why didn't hotels come stocked with condoms in every drawer? Sometimes being responsible just sucked.

She busied her mind with food preparation rather than focusing on the distraction of a naked Landon stretched on the bed not five feet from where she stood. "I must have been really hungry." Emma laughed as she took the plastic covers from the plates. "And thirsty." In one hand she scooped up a couple of bottles, one soda and one beer. "Want one?"

"I had no idea that room service delivered beer to your room." Landon's eyes sparked with humor as he held out a hand. Emma handed him both bottles, she'd ordered several. "If I'd known that I would have been ordering in a long time ago."

"Right?" Emma grabbed a plate and crossed the room to pop it in the microwave. She set the timer and turned around to face him. "When we got back this afternoon, it definitely felt like a two-Corona day."

"And now?" The deep rumble of his voice was a sensual caress that made Emma's knees weak. Totally Jell-O.

"Now, I'm thinking there are much more con-structive ways to take the edge off."

His answering grin caused a pleasant flush, and Emma had to turn away to keep from performing a full-on gymnastics-style vault that would land her right on top of his lap. Her cheeks warmed as she remembered their passionate moments together, and her stomach tightened once again, though this time with a completely different hunger. The bell on the microwave dinged, giving Emma a start. Talk about letting reality go . . . she'd been right back in that moment, writhing under Landon's skillful ministrations. How could she ever go back to her old, boring, Landonless life after this?

"Do you want egg rolls or boneless hot wings to start?" She'd ordered about a quarter of the menu, a few appetizers, three entrees, and four desserts. Not to mention the soda and beer. They'd be lucky to get through it all.

"Egg rolls."

"Good," Emma said with a grin. "Because I really wanted the hot wings." She pulled both plates from the microwave and set them on the bed before grabbing a little plastic container of blue cheese dressing and a couple of forks. She handed Landon a fork and stabbed one of the spicy chicken nuggets, plunging it into the dressing before popping it into her mouth.

"You know, those really don't qualify as buffalo wings." He indicated the chicken with his fork. "They're more like buffalo nuggets."

"These are way better," Emma claimed as she dipped another piece of chicken into the dressing. "I don't like the skin, and besides, there's hardly any meat at all on a real chicken wing."

"True."

Landon held out the bottles of beer and soda, and Emma grabbed the Coke. Though she'd needed something to take the edge off earlier in the afternoon, she meant what she'd said. A couple of hours of play with Landon and he'd managed to buff that sharp edge completely smooth.

Emma dunked another nugget and held it out to Landon. "Want one?"

He leaned forward, and slowly wrapped his mouth around the fork, taking the dressing-soaked nugget with him as he leaned back. Holy. Crap. She'd never considered food particularly erotic, but Landon's steamy exhibition totally changed her mind. *Rawr*.

"Hmmm. Not bad," he said as he chewed. "Egg roll?"

Emma didn't think she could pull off the same feat of raw sexuality wrestling with an egg roll. Landon was a tough act to follow. "No thanks. I'll fight you for the cheeseburger, though." Ugh. *Fight you for the cheeseburger?* That was about the least sexy thing she could have said. *Way to follow up strong, Emma, you king-sized dork!*

"I don't know. . . ." Landon sized her up and a shiver rippled across Emma's skin. "I'm a hard-core burger fan. And I think I could take you."

Oh, he could take her all right. "I don't even warrant a bite? I mean, I did save you from getting shot today."

The playful smile melted right off of Landon's face, and Emma instantly regretted her words. She'd failed to consider that the episode with Luis might still be touching a nerve. *Time out! Time out!* She needed a do-over. Or a time machine. His expression further darkened, and Emma had a feeling that it would take more than a cheeseburger to make peace with Landon now.

"First of all, you didn't save me from anything." *Shut up, Landon. Shut up now.* "You're the one who put yourself in danger by stepping in. See, that's why I get to carry a gun and chase bad guys for a living. Because I'm *trained* to. You? Not so much."

Who needed egg rolls and burgers when Landon's

mouth was too full of his own damned foot? Emma's expression fell, and if she didn't look like she was about to kick his ass, he might have done it himself. It was over. Done with. Why revisit any of it? Because she'd pointed out that she'd saved him? Oh yeah, that was it.

"He had a gun. Pointed at your forehead." Emma spoke slowly as though Landon might be having trouble comprehending. "I couldn't just stand there and do nothing."

"You do realize that's why you're in this situation to begin with, right? Because you jump in where you shouldn't and find yourself in way over your head."

"So basically you're saying I should've sat back and let Luis put a bullet in your brain?"

No. Of course not. That wasn't what he was getting at, at all. "Pretty much. Yeah."

"You know, that's what I don't get about men." Emma dunked another boneless wing into the dressing with so much force that blue cheese oozed over the rim of the container. "You're all so worried about being the top dog that you'll do any stupid thing to prove it."

"And you weren't trying to be top dog?" Landon had no doubt that with Emma's competitive nature, being top dog was one of her priorities. "Don't put this solely on me. Because there is no way you stole all of that money from Sousa without gloating at least *once* over the fact that you got one up on him."

Was this a glimpse into what having a relationship with Emma would be like? Bouts of arguments interrupted by breaks of mind-blowing sex, only to fuel up and start all over again?

"It was about helping my dad."

"And you never once felt any sort of smug satis-faction? No patting yourself on the back? I call bullshit on that."

Emma's eyes narrowed and her jaw took on a stubborn set. That ridiculous adrenaline rush that Landon craved like a drug dumped into his system, rolling through his veins like breakers at high tide. *Sick.* It was abso-fucking-lutely sick that igniting Emma's anger would turn him on. But yeah, right in front of him, sticking straight up like a goddamned flag, his dick was waving hello just to drive the point home. *Jesus.*

Emma glanced at the dressing-covered chicken bite affixed to her fork, pulled back her wrist, and let it fly forward with a catapult action that launched the deep-fried, hot-sauce-and-blue-cheese-covered lump of chicken straight at him. It hit his chest with a slimy *slap!* and slid down between his pecs, landing on top of the tented sheet that barely concealed his upright cock. *Fabulous.*

For a second, Emma sat there and stared at him, horrified. Then she broke out into a fit of laughter that sent her rocking backward as she dropped her fork on her plate. *Holy mother of God, the sound of her laughter* . . . If her anger was a turn-on then her joy was more akin to the ecstasy of going straight to heaven. The elation he felt built until it had nowhere else to go and the laughter bubbled up from Landon's chest. "I can't believe you just threw food at me!"

He leaned forward and dipped his finger into the blue cheese dressing, smearing it across Emma's cheek. She squealed in response, laughing even harder as she swiped at her cheek and then licked the dressing off of her fingers. Landon launched himself forward, taking her down to the mattress in a tackle. The plate of boneless bites bounced off the bed and landed on the floor, scattering to parts unknown.

"Goddamn it, I can't even fight with you without wanting to fuck you."

Emma's laughter dwindled and her expression, though still playful, brought a heat that made Landon break out into a sweat. Damn, she was sexy. Without even trying. Which made her even sexier. So did that make her sexier-er? Who the hell cared? He lowered his weight on top of her and nipped playfully at her bottom lip before kissing her. Fingers teased his hair, nails raked his scalp as she kissed him back. They'd barely finished and he was ready to have her again, his erection throbbing between his legs as he ground his hips into hers. How was he supposed to live a normal life after tonight? Especially when all he could think of was keeping Emma as naked as possible for as long as possible. At this rate, they'd never leave the hotel room again.

"What about dinner?" Emma murmured against his mouth.

Landon kissed her, those soft rosy lips all the sustenance he needed. He looked over at the table, and Emma craned her neck back to follow his gaze. "I could slather you in hot fudge and lick it off of you."

Her expression smoldered. "Or maybe, I could lick it off of you."

The thought of Emma licking anything off of him blinded Landon with lust. Hell, she could bathe him in blue cheese dressing if she wanted. A thin sheet separated their naked bodies, and Landon craved that skin-to-skin contact like he craved air. He supported himself on his forearm as he shimmied the sheet out from between them. He'd make quick work of Emma's clothes, too. Even if he had to tear them off of her.

"Hang on." Emma's brow furrowed as a teasing smile played on her lips. "We're, uh, out of supplies. You might want to slow your roll, Deputy."

"True," Landon said. He wrapped his arms around Emma and rolled them both until she was seated atop him. Leaning up, he peeled his T-shirt off of her and took one nipple into his mouth.

Emma gasped as he sucked, arching her back and pressing into the contact. "I suppose there are other things we could do," she all but purred as she gripped his shoulders.

He pulled away, drawing a disappointed whimper from Emma. "There are. I mean, off the top of my head there are least thirty or forty things I could do to you that we wouldn't need condoms for."

"Thirty or forty?" Emma's throaty response tingled across Landon's skin. "There is that hot fudge sauce you mentioned . . ." She pushed him down until he was laid out flat on his back and eased herself slowly down the length of his body, pausing to kiss along his ribs, down his stomach, and the junction where his hip met his thigh.

Landon sucked in a breath as he realized what she was about to do. Oh, hell, *yes.* Her tongue flicked out at the head of his cock, wet, warm, and so damned soft. He bucked his hips as he stifled a groan. Just the thought of Emma's mouth on him sent his heart rate into overdrive. The act itself might give him a full-on heart attack.

"I can't get enough of you, Landon." She took the glossy head into her mouth and sucked. Those gorgeous brown eyes zeroed in on his face and he thought he might come right then and there from the sight of her. His need was mindless, primal. Urgent.

It took more than simple self-restraint not to thrust hard and deep into her mouth. He wouldn't last thirty seconds if he watched as she worked her mouth over his cock. The solution was clear. He needed something to do as well. "Turn around." His voice was a ragged plea, but Emma didn't stop, just kept licking and sucking, taking him deeper into her mouth as she maneuvered her body until her ass jutted close to his face. Landon worked her underwear down her hips and she kicked them off onto the floor. Now that she was finally, gloriously naked once again, he lifted her easily, setting her on top of his chest. Her sex glistened, dripping and swollen. Perfect.

Landon sealed his mouth over her clit and Emma moaned around him, the sound vibrating down his shaft right into his balls. Pleasure pooled in his gut, building and spreading to his limbs with every lick, every deep suck and nip of Emma's teeth. Landon's own desire spurred him into a frenzied state and he plunged his tongue into her opening before dragging it over her clit. Emma's thighs tensed against his cheeks, and he kneaded the firm globes of her ass in his palms, spreading her wide so he could enjoy her more fully.

He held her fast as she broke contact, crying out in long drawn-out sobs as she came. He brought her down slowly with gentle flicks of his tongue until her body relaxed against him. She took him into her mouth once again, working his shaft with renewed vigor. Landon's own orgasm teetered on the brink and when she swirled her tongue over his engorged head it sent him over the edge. His entire body trembled as she continued to lap at him greedily. The orgasm stole his breath, flooded his body with a fiery heat, and damned near short-circuited his brain as it crashed over him, wave after earth-shattering wave.

He was wrecked. Ruined. Utterly destroyed. Emma Ruiz had single-handedly undone him. He'd never be the same after tonight. The life—the man—he'd known was gone.

Chapter Twenty-Two

Burgers and pasta weren't exactly breakfast food, but Emma didn't care. Besides, if you ate at four in the morning, could it even be considered breakfast yet or were they still in midnight-snack territory? Either way, she was *starving*.

The past several hours had been a test of endurance. Landon McCabe didn't only have the body of a god—he had the stamina to match. She didn't know about him, but she was absolutely exhausted and there was a pretty good chance that her legs wouldn't be able to support her weight for a good week or two. But, *Dios mio*, did she ever feel good.

Pleasure continued to radiate through her. Memories of the wicked things Landon had done warmed her skin. The man could dirty-talk her straight into an orgasm, and he'd spent a half hour telling her about all of the naughty, sinful things he wanted to do to her without laying a single finger on her. When he finally touched her . . . she came within seconds. He was playful, imaginative, and drop-dead sexy. They'd made good use of the desserts at around 2 AM, and Emma suspected that the housekeeping staff would shit a brick when they saw the fudge-smeared sheets in the morning.

Wait. It was already morning, wasn't it?

A dreamy smile curved Emma's lips. Few women got to live out their fantasies in such a grand fashion and Landon had *delivered.* Tonight was definitely one for the record books.

"Can you pass the ketchup?"

Emma reached across the bed and handed Landon the little mini bottle of Heinz. They'd spread out the rest of the food picnic style on the bed, sharing from each other's plates. Her emotions teetered toward silly. Drunk. Her eyes met Landon's across the spread of food and both of them smiled like idiots before averting their gazes. She wanted to laugh for no reason. Laugh until she couldn't breathe. Emma couldn't let her emotions get out of control, though. Not when Landon might breeze out of her life as easily as he'd breezed into it.

"Do you think Sousa will contact us?"

The light, silly air was sucked right out of the room, replaced with something dark and somber. It wasn't that she wanted to talk about all of this, but she felt as though they needed to. To form a game plan so they'd be ready to go.

"Yeah." Landon popped a ketchup-drenched fry into his mouth and chewed. "He thinks he's got the upper hand now. Before, he was wary of you, unwilling to make the wrong move. But you came through for him. He'll want his money back first of course, but after that I think he'll let your dad go."

There was something about the way Landon refused to make eye contact with her that sent an icy chill through Emma's extremities. He was keeping something from her. "So, I give him his money, he gives me my dad. But that won't be the end of it, will it? Not for me anyway."

He looked away. "Probably not."

"Okay." She tried not to dwell on Landon's dark tone. "So I might be in for a little longer than I hoped. Crawford's guy will still be there. And once Sousa buys his bomb, Damien and the rest of the feds will run in and save the day."

She didn't leave room for argument. Not because she didn't doubt her own words. Because she *did*. To the moon and back. But there was no point in letting Landon see her fall apart. She didn't want that. Wouldn't be able to live with herself if he caught a glimpse of that weakness in her.

"Emma, I meant what I said. I'll get you out of this. I promise." Landon finally looked her straight in the eye and he said the words with such conviction that it left her shaken. "I will not, *ever*, let anything happen to you."

It was the sort of reassuring, unkeepable promise spoken to someone who'd recently been handed a death sentence. Emma drew her knees up against her body and hugged her arms around them. Sousa didn't want to hire her. He wanted her to pay for taking something that belonged to him. He wanted her *dead*. And Landon knew it. Hell, he'd probably known it from the start.

"My dad went to prison to protect me. Or weren't you listening when I spilled my guts to Crawford at the hospital?" She picked at her burger, her appetite flagging. "Shanahan—under Sousa's orders, apparently—helped to frame him and then he had the nerve to have Cesar tell my dad that they'd kill me if he didn't confess. And that's what Sousa made me do yesterday. Frame Shanahan the way they'd framed my dad. I'm not sorry I did it, either. I wish I could have done worse to him for what he helped do to us."

"I was listening," Landon replied. "Even before you spilled your guts, I suspected your dad's confession had more to do with protecting you than anything else. Admittedly, not until a few days ago, but Crawford's—and your—insight was pretty eye-opening. Did you know about Shanahan and the business with Mendelson before he went to prison?"

"No," Emma admitted. "He never told me. Before he was arrested, he told me not to believe the things people would say about him, but he never looked me in the eye and said he was innocent. He didn't tell me why he was so willing to confess to a crime that I *knew* he didn't commit."

"So you decided to find out for yourself?"

His tone didn't chide or ridicule her. Rather, Emma heard pride in Landon's voice. Emotion bloomed in Emma's chest. Damn it, it shouldn't matter so much that Landon would be proud of her, but it did. "It wasn't fair. I was alone, Landon. After my mom died it was just me and Dad. And then, it was only me. I couldn't let it go. I had to know the truth."

"And now that you know?"

"Now I know that I was basically orphaned because some greedy corporate asshole and his immoral criminal of a partner wanted to keep on being greedy and immoral." Emma cringed at her words.

"Sorry. I'm sure not all corporate assholes are greedy. Or even assholes. Or immoral."

Landon's hawkish gaze settled on her as though he was trying to poke around in her brain. "Why apologize to me?"

"Um, well, you know." Oh crap. *Crap.* Emma hadn't exactly been forthright with Landon about some of the more questionable computer activities of her past. She doubted he'd be thrilled to know she'd basically cyber-stalked him all those years ago.

He gave her a lopsided grin. "No, actually. I don't know."

Heat rose to Emma's cheeks and her stomach did one of those twisting backflips that knocked into her ribs and left a bruise. "I uh, well . . ."

Landon quirked a brow. "Yes?"

"I mean, I might have, sort of gone online and . . . oh my God, Landon. It was six years ago." Jeez, could she stammer a little more? Maybe she should crawl under the bed and call it a day.

"I'm waiting, Emma."

Blargh. Fine. She could fess up. Spying on Landon wasn't half as bad as stealing millions of dollars from arms dealers. Right? "Okay, so I had a little crush on you. And I was curious about you so I dug around the Web—and a government database or two—and found out some stuff about you. Like about your family and where you grew up." Emma paused, swallowed. Took a deep breath. "And I found your home address and phone number and stuff. All right? That's it. That's what I did. So that's how I know that your dad is Hugh McCabe and your family is über rich and fancy and you're sort of the black sheep who parted from the corporate herd to become a U.S. marshal. There. I said it. And yes, I know that hacking a government database is a crime." Dang, she'd gotten that all out in one breath! She was a little light-headed now, but at least the confession had been made.

"Wait," Landon said. "You *had* a crush on me? Like, you don't anymore?"

That's what he was going to take away from what she'd said? Emma grabbed the nearest pillow and launched it at Landon's head. He caught it in one hand and tucked it behind him with a laugh. "I won't give your ego the satisfaction of answering that question." Emma twirled a pile of fettuccini noodles onto her fork and stuffed it in her mouth. If she was chewing, he couldn't expect her to keep talking.

"Black sheep of the corporate herd," Landon said with a snort. He took a huge bite of cheeseburger, maybe to keep from having to talk, too. He washed it down with a swig of soda. "That's an understatement. What your investigation didn't tell you was that I'm more or less disinherited. Aside from a monthly stipend that shows up in my bank account once a month, my family hasn't had anything to do with me since I graduated the academy."

He tried to come off as though it didn't bother him, but Emma knew better. Landon's words radiated sadness. Family was such a precious thing. Emma had never had much of it, no one but her mom and dad. The rest of her extended family lived in Mexico and didn't really keep in touch. The thought that Landon's had turned their backs on him broke her heart. "Why? I mean, what you do is so *important*, Landon. You're making a difference, protecting people. Taking out bad guys. What is so shameful about what you do that your family would disinherit you?"

His lips turned up in a tight, sad smile as he looked down at his plate. Emma hated the sorrow she saw in his clear blue eyes. She wanted to cross the distance between them and hold him, but she knew that her pity would only upset him. "The thing is, my dad isn't much better than Shanahan or his partners at Mendelson. I mean, I don't think he's ever laundered money, or blackmailed or framed anyone, but that simply could be because no one's ever asked him to. I definitely wouldn't put it past the son of a bitch. I didn't want any part of that. I didn't want my sole motivation for life to revolve around money and how much of it I could make. And in my family, a man is measured by the numbers in his bank account."

Emma had grown up well off, but she'd never considered herself privileged. The media painted her in that light because of the company she kept, but in reality, her own checking account looked like a pauper's in comparison to those of her friends. And likewise, Landon's family's money made even Emma's wealthiest friends look poor in comparison. And he'd walked away from all of it because he aspired to something more.

"I don't know if my opinion matters or not, but you're one of the best men I've ever known."

Landon's throat felt as if it were closing up. He wanted to blame it on some freak allergic reaction to his burger, but he knew better. Emotion choked him. Stole the air from his lungs until he thought his chest might collapse on itself. She didn't know if her opinion of him mattered? Fuck, her opinion was the *only* one that mattered.

He'd given Galen endless amounts of shit for his starry-eyed, lovesick routine with Harper. And now, here he was, camped out on the bed after what he could only describe as the best sexual encounter of his entire life, emotions backing up in his system like a clogged drain. The only way to clear the pipes would be to let it all out, tell Emma how she made him feel. But the words wouldn't push past the clog. And Landon wasn't equipped with the tools necessary to get it done. One more thing he could thank his tight-assed family for: his stunted emotional growth.

"Yeah, well, you might want to reserve judgment until all of this is over. There's a pretty good possibility I won't have a job when it's all said and done."

"What do you mean? Why would you lose your job over this?"

Emma's bemused expression only served to further warm his heart. She was so naïve sometimes, her outlook so optimistic that there wasn't room for a single dark thought. Time to come clean. She'd made a confession to him, after all. He might as well return the favor. "After Crawford hijacked us, he basically told me to pack my shit up and go. Instead, I called in a few favors and forced my way into the operation. My chief deputy isn't exactly happy with me, and I think we both know how Crawford feels about my intrusion."

Emma laughed and it was time for Landon to be bemused. "I told Crawford that I wouldn't do a damned thing for him unless they brought you in," she said. "It was my one and only deal breaker."

Landon's emotional pipes clogged up a little more, further proving that it didn't take much for Emma to get to him. Already she was under his skin, embedded to the point that he was unsure he'd ever get her out of his system. Uncharted territory for sure. And scary as hell. "We're quite a pair, aren't we?"

"We totally are."

Silence descended as they finished eating. It was a companionable quiet, but it left Landon too wrapped up in his own thoughts. His gut churned with the anxiety he felt. He didn't like variables. Complications. And Emma was both. A giant question mark planted right in the center of his life. He should have been too goddamned exhausted for this kind of stress. The hours he and Emma had spent together were unlike anything he'd ever experienced with another woman. To say he was sated—and not a little dehydrated—would be an understatement.

Beyond the panes of glass that led out to the balcony, Landon watched as the sky began to lighten. A post-storm breeze had managed to blow the clouds away, and sunrise wasn't too far off. Another day of variables. What-ifs. Another day of hoping to God he could protect Emma. That she'd be safe.

"I need to get out of here." The words erupted from his lips, unbidden. A familiar need pooled in his muscles, a craving for the endorphin rush he got when he climbed, parachuted, whatever. The same rush he felt when he touched Emma's naked flesh and swallowed her passionate cries as he kissed her. Jesus. He was a fucking wreck.

Emma's face fell. "Oh. Yeah, okay. If you need some space, I'll be fine here by myself for a while."

Way to make her feel like she's the one you need to get away from, dipshit. He really should work on connecting his brain to his mouth. "No. I mean, I get a little antsy when I'm cooped up. I need to climb or jump off of something tall." Emma's brow knitted, which made Landon feel even more like a caveman. *Me need dive out of plane. Fall to ground fast.*

"You mean like rock climbing?"

"Yeah." He cupped the back of his neck and shrugged. "Climbing, skydiving, BASE jumping. I do a lot of kayaking in the summer."

"So . . . you're an adrenaline junkie?"

More and more he was beginning to think he was becoming less of an adrenaline junkie and more of an Emma Ruiz junkie. "Pretty much. I like the rush." Free-falling from a couple hundred feet was nothing in comparison to the rush he felt with her, though.

"Most people go for a jog when they're feeling cooped up," Emma laughed.

"I grew up in the world's most boring family," he remarked. "The most exciting thing my family ever did was swim in the ocean on a trip to the Maldives. And even then my mom complained about what the salt water was doing to her hair."

"Salt water is a killer," Emma teased. "So, what, the first chance you got, you jumped off a bridge just to prove that you weren't a cookie-cutter version of your plain-as-white-bread family?"

Landon drew up a leg and rested his arm on his knee. He didn't miss the way Emma's eyes tracked the movement, or the way her gaze warmed as it traveled the length of his body. Nor could he ignore the way his own body responded to it. "When I was fifteen, we took a trip to Hawaii. My parents gave me a wad of cash and told me to find something to do while they did their spa shit or whatever it is that rich, self-involved people do on vacation. Anyway, I took off to see the sights and I found some guys who were cliff-diving. I watched them forever. The free fall, the way they looked so at ease before they slipped into the water . . . it spoke to me, you know? So I waited until everyone left and I climbed to the top of the cliff and stared down into the churning water for a while. And then I jumped."

"Oh my God, Landon. You do realize you could have been killed, right?" He enjoyed the concern in her voice. It stirred something inside of him that he'd never experienced—or repressed—before. She leaned forward, as though she couldn't wait to hear the rest of the story. A large lump of emotion rose to his throat once again. He wasn't used to another person—besides maybe Galen—caring about him beyond the superficial crap. "What happened after you jumped?"

He looked away. This was the most he'd ever shared with any woman. Shit, the only other person who knew this story was Galen, and he was more of a brother than a friend. "I felt alive. Free. All of the pressure and bullshit that my dad put on me went away. The drop only took seconds, but it felt like hours, and before I hit the water, I was addicted to the rush. I snuck away every day for the rest of our trip and jumped off that cliff again and again until I was exhausted. I haven't stopped jumping since."

"I think you're the only person I know who uses life-threatening activities as a stress reliever."

"It helps to remind me that sometimes it's okay to let go."

Emma scooted her plate aside and crawled over the sheets toward him. Her eyes were dark, limpid pools shrouded by hooded lids, and her tongue flicked out to lick her lips before she continued her trek up the length of his body. A delicious buzz settled on Landon's brain right about the time Emma settled in his lap. And just like that they were all over each other: groping hands, searching mouths, and long, drawn-out moans.

Landon grabbed a fistful of Emma's hair and urged her head back so he could taste the flesh at her throat. "You're better than a free fall," he said against her skin. "Better than that first jump when I was fifteen."

"Landon. Shut up and kiss me."

Gladly.

Chapter Twenty-Three

Well, they could add a couple of broken plates to the food-stained sheets and mess of clothes that littered the hotel room floor. At first glance, it appeared as though somebody had partied like a rock star last night, but as Emma snuck out of bed and headed for the shower, she didn't really care.

Being dead had its perks.

In any other circumstance, Emma would have been terrified at the prospect that someone on the housekeeping staff might take a few pics of the trashed room to splash all over social media. But now, she was merely some unknown, faceless girl. Totally uninteresting and not even worthy of a hashtag affixed to her name.

After round four of oh-my-God-amazing sexual play with Landon, they'd fallen asleep around six in the morning. Who knew you could do so much, feel so good, without any actual penetration? Emma had to give him credit, Landon sure knew how to use his imagination. Even though she only had four hours of sleep under her belt, Emma found that she was too restless for slumber. She let Landon sleep though—God knew he needed it—and turned on the spray, waiting for the water to heat up. Her limbs were deliciously heavy, her muscles warm as though she'd completed an all-day workout. A hot shower would do wonders to revitalize her. The only drawback was the prospect of washing Landon's scent from her skin. She wished she could hold on to it forever and breathe him in whenever she wanted. The past twelve hours had been the most intimate of Emma's entire life.

For the first time in years, she didn't feel so alone.

She reached out to test the water before stepping under the spray. An audible sigh accompanied each relaxed muscle as the heat soothed her, and Emma closed her eyes, braced her arms against the shower wall, letting the water sluice down her body. Was there anything in the world better than a hot shower?

Yeah, there was. For starters, how about having Landon McCabe's skillful tongue on her—

"Emma?"

She started at the sound of his voice calling from the other room, and heat rose to her cheeks as though she'd been caught looking at porn on the Internet or something. These dirty images were all in her mind, however. Burned into her memory—hell, her very skin. Whether he realized it, Landon had left a permanent mark, one that wasn't ever going to go away. "I'm in the shower!"

Seconds later, the curtain was brushed aside and Landon leaned against the wall in all of his naked glory. He was so tall he almost reached the rod that held the curtain up and Emma couldn't help but admire every muscled inch of him. Having spent her fair share of time with pro athletes, Emma wasn't exactly a stranger to great bodies. But there was something about Landon that made every other guy dim in her memory until they were nothing more than pale comparisons to the man standing before her. He still had that swimmer's build, but the years had matured his body, made his shoulders wider, his body bulkier. Her gaze wandered down his torso and the narrow taper of his waist to the junction of his hips. His erection jutted out from between his legs, and Emma dragged her eyes back up to his. Landon McCabe was insatiable. She quirked a brow, and her breath caught as he did a little admiring of his own before stepping into the shower behind her.

Maybe Sousa had killed her a few days ago and this was heaven.

"Give me the soap."

She'd give him *anything* he wanted when he spoke to her in that dark, smoky tone. The soap was a no-brainer. Emma handed him the sudsy bar and he massaged it in his hands before lathering her shoulders, his deft fingers working her skin with the perfect amount of pressure as he washed her.

"Oh. My *God.*" Emma's moan echoed off the shower walls. The man was an artist. A virtuoso in the art of bathing. "Can we stay in here? Like, forever?"

Amusement rumbled in Landon's chest as he spun her around and went to work on her back. Pleasant tingles chased over Emma's skin as his palms massaged her, his touch firm as he moved in slow circles over her shoulder blades and then down each individual vertebrae of her spine. Emma went completely limp—it was a wonder she didn't slip right down the drain with the sudsy water.

"You're pretty good at this," Emma said on a sigh. "Should I even ask where you acquired the skill necessary to bathe a woman so thoroughly?"

His slick, soapy hands traveled downward, over the small of her back, swirling over her butt and the tops of her thighs. It was a good thing her arms were braced on the shower wall. Because she was pretty sure it was the only thing keeping her upright. One of Landon's hands slipped between her thighs and Emma's breath hitched.

"Maybe I was looking for an excuse to touch you," he suggested. "And as far as my skills go, I'm just really, *really* concerned about your hygiene."

Emma laughed. "Liar."

"Okay, so your hygiene is already good. But I did want an excuse to touch you. Plus . . ."

Uh-oh. That "plus" sounded a little too ominous. "What?"

"My motives aren't entirely selfish. I want you to relax, okay?"

Definitely ominous. "Why, Landon? What's going on?"

"Damien called. The buy is on and Sousa wants his money."

"All right." The sound of water rushing around her drowned out the sound of her own voice. She had known this moment was coming and she was ready. So why were her nerves getting the best of her all of a sudden? Her heart spun in a perfect spiral as it plummeted into her stomach and her tongue was trying to adhere itself to the roof of her mouth. The thought of walking back into Sousa's camp made her feel sick, but the quicker this was all over, the better. She wanted her dad out of Sousa's custody. He needed to get to a doctor. Who knew what a few weeks of captivity had done to him. "When do we leave?"

"We're meeting Damien at Pine and Second in an hour. Apparently, Sousa wants his men to keep their distance from the hotel. I think he's still suspicious of me."

"What does that mean?" If his men did anything to Landon, Emma would never be able to live with herself.

Landon leaned in close, his bare chest brushing her back as he reached around to lather her stomach. Her muscles clenched at the intimate contact and her eyes drifted blissfully closed. "It doesn't mean anything yet. Don't worry. He's simply being cautious. I'd be more worried if he wasn't suspicious. All it means is you're going to have to sport that god-awful blond wig one more time since we'll be out in public. We'll meet Damien, you'll transfer Sousa's money back to him, and your part will be played until he decides whether or not to keep you on the payroll. You, me, and your father will walk out of there, and you'll be one step closer to being free of all of this."

He was lying to her. His doubt crept over her like an early autumn frost. "Landon . . ." His hands swept up her torso to cup her breasts and Emma melted against him. What if this was the last time she'd ever feel his touch? Hear the warm timbre of his voice in her ear? What if right now—this moment—was their last together before Sousa killed them all to protect his secrets? Steam billowed around them as Emma turned in Landon's embrace. She splayed her fingers across the hard planes of his chest, rubbed her palms over his flat nipples, and drank in every detail of his face. The straight line of his jaw, the arch of his brows, dark lashes that fringed his eyes, irises light blue as the Caribbean and run with gold. Full lips that spread into a sinful smile that said, *Come a little closer and I will do dirty, depraved things to you, and you will beg me for more.*

"What?" His eyes searched her face, his brow puckered.

The words hovered on the tip of her tongue. *I love you. I've loved you since I was eighteen, even though I didn't really know you. I can't live without you. I don't want to.* But she couldn't say it. She was too afraid. If they made it out of this alive—which was doubtful—he might leave anyway and her heart would be irreparably broken. By keeping her feelings unspoken, she *might* salvage a tiny piece of herself. Maybe.

"What, Emma?" Landon pulled her close and put his mouth close to her ear. "Are you okay? You're sort of freaking me out here."

Tears stung at Emma's eyes and it felt as though her heart were swelling inside of her chest, about to explode. She swallowed against the lump of emotion rising in her throat and said, "I just want you to know that I won't let you down. And . . ." She breathed through the tears, stuffed them right down to her toes. "And that I'm sorry I dragged you into this."

"Look at me." Landon put her at arm's length and the hot spray of water ran in rivulets down her back. Despite the heat, she shivered. "We're going to be okay. I *promise* you, Emma. Everything is going to be okay."

He was a pretty liar, that much was certain. "I think you missed a spot." She looked down at her arms.

He gave her a smile that didn't quite reach his eyes. "Far be it from me to slack off on the job."

"My hair next?" She'd make these moments count. After he shampooed her hair, she'd wash him slowly, explore his body one last time.

"Sure," he said. "But I'm next."

Emma plastered what she hoped was a carefree expression on her face. "Promise."

Sousa wasn't stupid, but the good criminals never were. This close to the buy, he'd grown overly cautious, so it wasn't really a surprise that he didn't want Damien picking Landon and Emma up at the hotel. For all Sousa knew, the Marshals Service could be planning to ambush him there. They might have vetted Emma with that stunt to blackmail Mike Shanahan, but Landon was still a variable. And if they believed he was simply along for the ride for a piece of ass, well, then they deserved to get caught.

Following their shower—which had ended with yet another out-of-this-world orgasm for each of them—Emma had become unusually quiet. Landon didn't know if her introspective attitude had more to do with worry, or simply preparation, but he didn't like it.

She walked beside him down the sidewalk in her blond wig with large, round, ultra-dark glasses that practically swallowed her face. Emma kept close to him, as though they were connected by a short piece of string. When he shifted, she shifted. When his pace increased, she matched it. If she didn't settle down, it would throw up all sorts of red flags.

"Emma?"

Landon's heart seized at the mention of her name, which had been choked out in sorrowful disbelief. *Keep walking. Just keep walking.* They couldn't risk her being recognized, and likewise Landon didn't want to bring any attention to themselves by stopping to see who had called out her name. *Fuck.* He clamped his jaw down and swallowed the string of curse words that threatened to escape. Of all the shitty timing . . .

"Emma!"

Goddamn it. Whoever this guy was, he wasn't about to let up. The sound of his voice was closer now, bouncing as though he was running to catch up. If he didn't shut the fuck up, he'd draw the attention of everyone on the street. Beside him, Emma's step faltered, and Landon grabbed on to her elbow to keep her moving along. "Don't look back. Don't engage."

She was spun right out of his grasp, and Landon reached for his Glock tucked into the holster concealed by his coat. Their meeting spot was in sight and no doubt Damien was waiting. And watching. They couldn't afford any trouble right now.

Emma looked shell-shocked as the guy Landon recognized as her friend from the club held on to her shoulders, hunched over to get a good look at her. He snatched the sunglasses off her face, and Landon reacted, pulling him away from her and forcing him bodily into an alley to their left. The guy was built like a freaking redwood—a good foot taller and forty or so pounds heavier than he was—causing Landon to pull his gun in an effort to convince him to cooperate and get the fuck off the sidewalk.

"Emma, run!"

Landon rolled his eyes. Wasn't he a gallant son of a bitch. Emma stood stock-still on the sidewalk, her mouth opening and closing like a fish out of water. "Emma, get off the street," Landon barked. If their plan went south now, there was no telling what Sousa would do to them. "Now."

She came out of her stupor and dove into the alley, eyes wide and fearful. "Don't hurt him, Landon!" Jesus, what did she think he was going to do? Pop a cap in her boyfriend's ass? Though to be honest, it didn't seem like such a bad idea. . . . "Landon." Her warning tone indicated that she might in fact be a mind reader. "This is my friend, Jeremy."

Jeremy? The one who took her out for the fancy lunch at the Metropolitan Grill? *That* Jeremy? Now, he really did want to shoot him.

"Emma, what in the hell is going on?" Jeremy looked from Landon to Emma, eyes bugged out of his head. "I thought you were dead! The news reports said you'd been shot. I've been killing myself the past few days trying to get something— anything—out of the cops, but no one would tell me a goddamned thing. And I see you walking down the street . . . Jesus. Why are you wearing a wig? What the fuck is happening right now? And who is this clown?"

Clown? Landon choked up on the grip of his Glock as he pointed it at Jeremy's face. "This *clown* is the man trying to keep her alive, while you, asshole, seem to be hell-bent on getting her killed. Shut your mouth, calm the hell down, and I'll let you go. Got it?"

Jeremy looked to Emma for confirmation, and she said, "It's true, Jeremy. Landon's a U.S. marshal. I'm in protective custody. Sort of. But you can't draw any attention to us, okay? Landon's right. We all need to settle down."

Protective custody? Was that all she wanted this guy to think he was to her? Just the chump responsible for keeping her ass safe until she got her dad clear of Sousa? Anger and jealousy flared as his fist tightened around Jeremy's jacket.

"Landon?" Emma sounded unsure as she rested a tentative hand on his shoulder. "Please. Let him go."

His common sense snapped back like a rubber band as he took a couple steps backward and holstered his gun. Filling his lungs with a few ragged breaths through his nose, he peeked out of the alley and cursed under his breath. *Fuck.* Looked like they weren't going to catch a break.

Landon ducked back into the alley seconds before Damien's van came to a screeching halt, the nose of the vehicle angled toward them. "This is bad, isn't it?" Emma's frightened tone tore at him. He wanted to reassure her that everything would be all right, but he couldn't. Right now, he doubted any of them would make it out of this alive. A crew of four spilled from the confines of the van while Damien regarded Landon from the driver's seat, a hardness accentuating his already ominous expression. He obviously wasn't happy about the way things were going down either. Or the extra passenger he was about to acquire.

"Get in the van."

Landon was relieved of his sidearm by one guy, while another jabbed him in the shoulder with the barrel of an AK-47 to move him along. Their armed escorts didn't leave much room for argument. "Emma, get in the van."

"Em—" Jeremy reached out to stop her, gallant idiot that he was, only to have a couple of semi-autos shoved into his face. His nostrils flared, but he made no other outward show of aggression. At least he was smart enough to know when he was at a disadvantage.

"You don't need him." Landon jerked his chin in Jeremy's direction. "He doesn't know anything. Harmless. Another horny dipshit trying to pick up on my girl."

"Bullshit," Goon Number One barked. "You think we're stupid? He knows who she is. Get in the van, *pendejo*."

"That would be you, *asshole*," Landon said to Jeremy with a smirk. It was vital to his cover that he play the part of a compromised U.S. marshal. Showing off his conscience wasn't going to do anyone a damned bit of good.

"Cesar will decide if he's harmless or not, *policía*. You get no say. You're just along for the ride."

"Fair enough," Landon replied with an unconcerned shrug. God-fucking-*damn* it. He ground his molars as Goon Number Two poked Jeremy with the barrel of his AK to get him moving. Landon fell into step directly behind him and murmured, "Keep your eyes down and mouth shut and you might make it out of this alive. Understand?" Jeremy inclined his head, his acquiescence almost imperceptible. "Good."

It was going to be sticky enough getting Emma and her dad out of this situation in one piece. Now he had this possible ex-boyfriend to worry about too? *Fucking awesome.* Landon shook his head as he climbed into the van beside Jeremy, irked that the other man had decided to park his ass right next to Emma. Where he wanted—needed—to be.

The goons loaded in behind them and the door slid closed with an echoing finality that made Landon's gut clench tight. Beside him, Jeremy bent over Emma, whispering low in her ear as he took her hands in his. Way to keep a low profile, dumb ass. Landon's assurances that they barely knew each other wouldn't mean shit now that Sousa's guys were getting a front-seat show.

This operation was going south fast. And Landon needed to be a hell of a lot quicker on his feet.

Chapter Twenty-Four

"Jesus, Em, I can't believe you're really alive."

Jeremy was still looking at her like he'd seen a ghost, and guilt welled up hot in Emma's throat. "I'm so sorry, Jeremy. Everything happened so suddenly, I didn't have a chance to give you a heads-up. I can't believe you recognized me." So much for her brilliant disguise. She felt curious eyes on her. Sousa's guys . . . and one very cranky deputy U.S. marshal. The air was thick with Landon's annoyance, and Emma worried that he wasn't about to cool down any time soon. Nothing was going according to plan so far, and Jeremy's presence added another very complicated layer. "Listen, I can't tell you much, but these guys are big-time dangerous. Try to stay invisible. And don't—*no matter what*—attempt to be a hero. Okay?"

"First of all, I'd recognize you even if you had a bag over your head, Em. Secondly, I'm not going to just sit around and—"

"Jeremy." Emma squeezed his hands. "*Promise* me."

"All right." He searched her face, brow furrowed. "I got your back, though."

Emma smiled, but on the inside she wanted to throw her arms up in frustration. *Men.* Why did they all have to be so damned stubborn and gallant? Well, the good ones, anyway. Too many promises had been made already. Emma's unspoken promise to exonerate her father, Landon's promise to keep her safe . . . and now Jeremy. How many promises could be kept? And which ones would put someone she cared about in danger?

Tension settled heavy in the air; Emma could almost reach out and run her finger through it like frosting on a cake. Too much testosterone in an enclosed space was never a good thing, and there was plenty to spare in Sousa's van. When all of this was over, and everyone she cared about was safe, Emma swore she was going on a long vacation. To a secluded beach. Where anyone with a penis wasn't allowed.

The familiar trek to the warehouse wasn't doing anything for Emma's anxiety. Instead, it gripped her with unrelenting claws, pulling at her skin until she was tight enough to snap. Damien didn't utter a word. Didn't even glance at her through the rearview mirror. Instead, he looked straight ahead, his fists gripping the steering wheel so tight, his knuckles began to turn white. It didn't take a genius to know she'd screwed up. He was tense enough to snap. If she didn't have Sousa's money, Emma was certain that Crawford would have thrown her in jail days ago. And after screwing up his plans yet again, she had no doubt that Damien would have helped him put her there. At this point, she felt like nothing more than a burden to them all.

Damien pulled into the warehouse lot several minutes later. Armed guards waited to open the chain-link fence to allow them entrance. Emma had never seen so many automatic weapons in her life, and it made her wonder, how did these guys not stick out like a sore thumb? Seriously, didn't anyone patrol out here? Or was the bulk of the Seattle PD on Sousa's payroll, too?

More of the same armed-to-the-teeth thugs waited at the warehouse doors. Rather than dump them off outside, Damien waited for a couple of guys to pull open the large garage doors. He drove straight into the building and Emma chanced a look back. *Holy crap.* A convoy of vans strung out behind them, waiting to pull in. At least six of them. Exactly what sort of cargo were they hauling? Because she doubted he had vehicles full of code writers and software engineers in case she couldn't get the job done.

Damien drove deeper into the warehouse and parked. "You guys help get those vans unloaded. I'll deal with this."

A few murmured grumbles came from the back-seat, but other than that, Sousa's guys didn't complain. The back doors of the van swung open and the henchmen jumped out, leaving Emma, Landon, and Jeremy alone with Damien.

"What the fuck, McCabe?" He didn't waste any time laying into Landon, swinging around in his seat and pinning him with an angry glare. Emma's heart jumped up into her throat. He might have been one of the good guys, but Damien still scared the crap out of her. "Sousa is on edge as it is. Now we've got one more complication. Do you know how Teyo Sousa deals with complications? He gets rid of them."

Jeremy glanced at Emma, and another wave of sickening guilt washed over her. "It's my fault. If Sousa is going to punish anyone, it should be me."

Landon and Jeremy spoke at once, both of them erupting into a string of protests that made Emma's stomach tie into knots.

"Both of you, shut your traps," Damien snapped. "It won't matter whose fault it is. What's done is done. We have no choice but to focus on damage control now."

"What do you have in the vans?" Landon asked.

"The vans don't have anything to do with you," Damien said. "Sousa decided to make the most of his time and he's taking care of some side business while he's here. With any luck"—he snorted at the idea—"they'll be out of here before anything else goes down. All we need is for Emma to transfer Sousa's money to him. That's. All. Keep your heads down and play your parts and we might walk out of this alive."

"What about my dad?" Emma knew she sounded like a broken record, but too damned bad.

"Just do what you're told, Emma," Damien warned. "Make Sousa happy and he might return the favor."

Might being the operative word. Was it too hopeful to think that they'd all get free of Sousa unscathed? Probably. Emma said a prayer under her breath, asking for the safety of Landon, Jeremy, and her dad above all others.

"Let's get moving," Damien said. "I'll take you back to the office."

They filed out of the van single file, and Emma paused halfway out to glance back at the other vehicles. Sousa's men were unloading large wooden crates and stacking them against a far wall. "Eyes to the front, Emma," Damien growled. "Keep moving."

Jeremy waited beside the van for her, and from the corner of her eye, she caught Landon scowling at them from several feet away, arms crossed over his wide chest. Emma could fit both of her hands in one of Jeremy's, and he towered over her more diminutive form, a sapling in the shade of an oak tree. But he didn't make her feel safe. He wasn't the one she wanted to go to. Hold in her arms and never let go. She needed Landon's strength right now if she was going to get through this ordeal. And his apparent anger only made her more anxious.

He waited for Emma and Jeremy to follow Damien and took up the rear. Though she liked having him at her back, Emma would have preferred to have Landon at her side. The distance between them had grown wider from the moment Jeremy had inserted himself into the situation. *Damn it, Landon. Stop being such a butthole. I need you.* Had he forgotten that he was supposed to be her boyfriend in this little scenario? The implication of a lovers' tiff wasn't going to gain them any ground with Sousa at this point.

Emma rubbed at her arms as they walked, the chill in the warehouse soaking right into her bones. She tried not to let fear get the best of her as she chanced a quick look around only to find no sign of her father. What had they done with him? Emma placed one foot in front of the other, operating on autopilot until she made it to the door that led to the interior office. A small sense of relief fluttered through Emma's body. So close. She was so close to putting all of this behind her.

Damien ushered them into the office and Emma froze in midstep. Landon pressed his chest into her back and Emma reached back for his hand. He wound his fingers with hers and gave a squeeze that was almost too tight, too full of tension. Her breathing increased with her heart rate, and a jolt of adrenaline dumped into her system leaving her shaky. How could Landon possibly crave that sort of sensation? The man was clearly insane.

"Hello, Emma. Deputy. And . . ." Teyo Sousa paused, eyeing Jeremy with a sneer. ". . . *guest.*"

Sousa hadn't been there last time, supposedly keeping his distance from his own dirty dealings in an effort to keep his nose clean. Now, here he was, relaxed in a chair with Cesar standing to his right like the good little minion he was. Emma had hoped—prayed—Sousa wouldn't be here today, but she guessed when you stole millions of dollars from someone they wanted to make damned sure you gave it back.

"This one was a surprise." Damien jerked his head toward Jeremy. "I didn't know what to do with him so we brought him along."

"I dislike complications." Sousa couldn't have sounded more deadly if he were the grim reaper himself. "Especially when I'm working with a timetable."

"He's a friend of mine," Emma blurted, desperate to diffuse the situation before it got out of hand.

"He recognized me on the street. He's not going to cause any trouble. I promise." She really needed to stop making promises. She found herself doubting her ability to keep them.

"Maybe you shouldn't make assurances for your friends, Emma." Sousa's dark gaze narrowed as he inspected Jeremy once again, lips pursed. "You look familiar." He let the statement drop, waiting for Jeremy to fill in the blank.

Jeremy looked around as though wondering if he should speak up. "Yeah, um, I play for the Seahawks."

Sousa snapped his fingers with recognition though his expression didn't show the least bit of amusement. "Jeremy Blakely," he purred in his smooth accent. "I had seats on the fifty-yard line for one of your games last year. You played like shit."

Oh boy. Nothing pissed an athlete off more than insulting his game. But Jeremy simply shrugged his shoulders and said, "Everyone has an off day once in a while."

Sousa snorted, a corner of his mouth hinting at amusement. "True."

Well, at least now Landon knew why Jeremy had seemed familiar the first time he'd seen him. That didn't mean he wasn't still crazy fucking jealous of the bastard, though.

"He's definitely a complication." Landon stepped up to the plate, ready to take control of the situation out of Emma's hands. "But nothing that can't be dealt with. Later. Right now, we have business to conduct, don't we?"

Sousa chuckled. The wry amusement made Landon want to put his fist through the other man's face. "Maybe you'd like to *deal* with him, Deputy McCabe?"

Landon shrugged an indifferent shoulder. "If I need to."

Emma's jaw hung as if the hinges were broken. If she didn't get it together, Sousa would be even more suspicious of them than he already was. He sauntered up behind her and wrapped his arms protectively around her waist, high enough to brush her breasts as he shouldered Jeremy out of the way. Emma bristled, which he hoped was more out of nerves than the fact that she didn't want him to touch her. Especially after what had happened last night. But he needed to assert himself in front of Sousa. And showing his ownership of Emma would help in that department.

Like he'd hoped, Sousa watched him with interest. A knowing smirk curved his full mouth. "I have no doubt you'd take care of the problem if one arises."

Though he didn't outwardly show it, relief melted right down into the soles of his feet. The rush of adrenaline made him a little twitchy and his brain buzzed as he assessed their situation, which seemed to fall more into the clusterfuck category by the second. He shared a brief moment of eye contact with Damien. Yup. *Fucked.*

"I'm a busy man and I don't have time for this telenovela *tonterías.* Emma?" Sousa stood and held out an arm, indicating the table littered with computer equipment. "My money, if you please."

"Sure." Emma exuded confidence as she pulled

away from Landon's embrace and headed for the computer. She pulled out the chair as though ready to plop down and paused. "First, though, my father. If *you* please."

Sousa's dark eyes narrowed and he gave Emma a tight smile. "Of course. After all, what sort of business relationship can we have without trust?"

Emma smiled back, pleasant. "Exactly."

"Cesar, go get Javier so his daughter's mind can be put at ease."

With a superior smirk, Cesar left the room to go fetch Emma's dad. A few tense moments followed, during which everyone stood around and eyed each other with interest, worry, and not a little suspicion. Somewhere in the back of Landon's mind, the theme to Final Jeopardy played. *Do, do, do, do, do, do, do . . .*

Cesar returned with Javier Ruiz, who, considering his situation, didn't look any worse for wear. *"Mija."* He went to Emma's side and took her into his arms. They embraced for a beat too long, which only served to further annoy Sousa.

"My money, Emma." His tone conveyed his impatience. The man had a bomb to buy, after all. "Now."

A teary-eyed Emma pulled away from her father, and Landon hoped to God she could keep it together for a little bit longer. He needed her to be strong and quick on her feet. Emotions would only get in the way.

"You all might as well have a seat," Emma remarked as she took hers. "This is going to take me a few minutes."

Landon gripped Javier's elbow, gently urging him away from his daughter. "Sir?" He indicated a chair at the rear of the office, next to one that Jeremy had already slumped into. Javier gave Landon a questioning look when he noticed the other man. Landon simply shrugged and spoke close to Javier's ear. "Your daughter's a popular girl, it would seem."

The older man chuckled. "That she is."

Landon remained standing and alert while everyone else took a seat. Cesar looked bored, while Damien excused himself—presumably to check on the guys and vans in the main warehouse. Looking very much the part of slimy criminal, Teyo Sousa watched Emma with interest from his perch in the corner of the room. His *Godfather* impersonation did little to inspire awe in Landon, however. If push came to shove, he was going to shove the fucker. Hard.

Hyperalert, Landon scanned their surroundings. One exit that led into a larger space full of hardened criminals. The office had no windows, leaving them zero chance of bypassing the main warehouse to get outside. Not great. But they were in a small, enclosed space, which would give him the upper hand in a tussle. That is, until Sousa called for reinforcements. In which case, they were as good as dead. Meanwhile, Emma went to work, her fingers flying on the keyboard as window after window popped up on the screen. Emma paused. Leaned on her elbow, her face screwed up as she read whatever was on the display. She worried her bottom lip between her teeth before sitting back.

"Problem, Emma?" Sousa's tone had escalated to a notch above threatening.

"No, no problem," Emma said. "It's just . . ."

"Yes?"

Emma gave a nervous laugh. "I designed a few more obstacles than I remembered. I've almost got it, though. Give me a couple more minutes and your money is all yours."

Sousa made a steeple with his fingers and rested his chin atop them. He didn't look pleased, but Landon bet that short of hand-delivering his dirty bomb, little would put a smile on the arms dealer's face. Cesar shifted nervously in his seat. So did Jeremy. Only Javier and Landon showed no outward emotion, and he was willing to bet that they were both more high-strung than anyone else in the room.

Everyone except Emma.

"Shit." The word slipped from her lips as she clicked away at the keys.

She glanced at Landon and he read the panic in her expression. Like the crafty little hacker she was, Emma had managed to out-hack herself. *So* not good. Sousa caught it as well, and jerked his chin at Cesar, who got up out of his chair and sauntered right up to Emma's back. He poked the barrel of a .45 into the back of her head. Emma froze. Her fingers hovered above the keyboard and her breathing grew quick and shallow with fear.

At which point, Landon's tightly reined control snapped.

Years of training and a lifetime of not giving a single fuck about consequences spurred him to act as Damien walked through the door. It only took a beat for him to kick Damien's legs out from under him, but not before Landon jerked the man's sidearm from the holster and aimed it at Sousa's forehead. "It's not easy to concentrate when there's a gun pointed at your head. Know what I mean?"

Sousa didn't look even a little ruffled. He merely lounged in his chair with that annoying-as-fuck smirk on his face. His eyes slid to the side, and Cesar pulled back the hammer with an audible *click* that made Emma jump in her seat. Landon shook his head. Why did assholes like this always press their luck? He kept his gaze locked on Sousa, the gun unwavering in his grip. Behind him, Damien swore. No doubt the undercover SOG deputy was pissed at Landon for going cowboy on him. Well, too damned bad. He wasn't putting Emma at risk for anyone or anything.

"Let her work. She'll come through for you, but not with the barrel of a gun digging into her skull."

"Cesar." The one word was enough to call him off and he took several cautious steps back, his attention now focused on Landon.

Fine. Whatever. At least he wasn't pointing a gun at Emma's head anymore. Sousa's eyes gleamed like obsidian, and Landon was well aware of the fact that he'd made an enemy as he sidestepped Cesar, gun still drawn, and went to Emma's side.

"You okay?" he asked.

"Yeah," she responded on a shuddering breath. "Just a little shaken up."

"Okay. Take a couple of deep breaths. You can do this, Emma. Don't think about your dad, or me, or anything else that's going on behind you. Focus. It's just another day at the office. Right?"

"R-right."

Several tense minutes passed. He'd essentially fucked them over with his rash behavior, but it was too late to worry about it now. He wasn't returning the gun to Damien, either. They could pry it out of his cold, dead hands.

"Done!" Emma pushed herself away from the

desk, her chest heaving with rushed breath. "It's done. Look for yourself. Every last penny is back in your account."

Sousa raised a questioning brow to Landon in lieu of asking for permission to approach. Landon backed away and gave a single nod of his head. The only sound in the room was the *tap, tap, tap* of Sousa's overpriced loafers on the concrete floor. He stopped at Emma's left shoulder and peered at the computer screen. "Cesar, call our people in Jalisco. Tell them we're ready to move forward."

Cesar went for the door and Landon said, "I think it might be a better idea for you to conduct whatever business you have right here." Cesar looked at his boss as if to say, *Can you believe the balls on this guy?*

Believe it, buddy. They're big. And brass.

"I allowed your macho display for the benefit of keeping Emma on task," Sousa said, "but we're done here. Cesar, *tener cuidado de ellos.*"

Landon didn't know what he'd said, but the shit-eating grin on Cesar's face didn't fill him with hope that they'd be allowed to walk out of there. He leveled the gun on Sousa only to hear the distinctive *click* of a hammer behind him. Damn it. He'd lost sight of Damien and the bastard wasn't ready to blow his cover yet.

"I'll take my piece back, if you don't mind." The menace in his tone sent a chill down Landon's spine. Undercover guys like Damien went above and beyond codes and morals to protect their covers and operations. Sousa was a big fish and Damien would do anything in his power to keep him on the hook.

Even if that meant putting a bullet in Landon's head.

Chapter Twenty-Five

Emma's blood turned to ice in her veins.

Landon stood ramrod straight, a gun leveled at Sousa's head. Behind him, Damien shoved the long barrel of a nasty-looking revolver into the top of Landon's neck, his eyes devoid of emotion and his lips thinned into a hard line. He was supposed to be on their side, damn it! Not helping the bad guys. What was going on? Why? Didn't Damien realize that they were all going to die?

Take care of them, Sousa had said to Cesar. Whether or not the undercover marshal could speak Spanish, he should have heard the threat inherent in Sousa's ominous tone. Because Emma was pretty damned sure Cesar wasn't about to escort them to a hospitality suite.

Emma didn't want to die. Not before she told Landon how she felt about him.

"What about our deal?" she asked in an effort to buy time. She knew that Sousa would kill her the first opportunity he got. No honor among thieves—or arms dealers—and all that. But if she could get the people she cared about out of the building alive, at least her death wouldn't be for nothing. "You're still going to need someone to help cover your tracks. Erase your financial and digital footprints. I can do that for you. You know I can get it done."

"Teyo." Emma's dad rose slowly from his chair, and it tore at her heart to see how much effort the simple act took. "Does the past mean nothing to you? *Usted no es un hombre malo.* Emma did what you asked of her and the boy is only trying to protect her. Let us go. Your secrets will be safe."

Not an evil man? Emma swallowed down a burst of hysterical laughter. She wanted to tell her dad he was wasting his breath trying to appeal to Sousa's softer sensibilities. The man had none.

"*Te equivocas.* I *am* this man. I can't afford the high price of your morals, Javier. Good-bye."

Javier's expression fell with disappointment at Sousa's words. *You're wrong.* With the words spoken solely for her dad's benefit, he'd made it quite apparent that there would be no redemption, and no quarter given. They were all going to die. He headed for the door and Emma lunged for him, grabbing onto the sleeve of his overpriced suit jacket. "Please, don't do this. Let my father and Jeremy leave here. They haven't done anything." He stared down at her, his eyes so cold and emotionless that she shivered from the chill. "Let Landon go. I'm the one who stole from you. I'm the one who disrespected you. Make an example of me and me alone. *Te lo suplico.*" Please.

Emma released her grip on his arm as fingers of dread speared her chest and tightened her lungs. Teyo Sousa had not one ounce of mercy to spare for

her or anyone. Without a word, he walked through
the door, shutting it soundlessly behind him. In
trying to help her father, she'd condemned him.
By simply being his friend, she'd signed Jeremy's
death warrant. And in cleaving to Landon—falling
hopelessly in love with him—she'd destroyed him.
Oh, God.

"Get them in the van." Damien instructed Cesar
with the same cruel indifference as the rest of
Sousa's band of murderers. "And grab a couple of
guys to help you." He jerked his chin toward Emma.
"I don't want them anywhere near this facility." He
tossed Cesar the gun he'd taken from Landon.
"When you're done, meet me at the buy location."

Emma's attention split, divided among the three
other hostages in the room. As Cesar holstered one
gun in exchange for the other, Damien leaned in
toward Landon's ear. Who knew what shitty senti-
ments that traitor was whispering? She hoped that
Crawford found him and nailed his ass to the wall.
Her father looked at her with resignation, sadness
pulling at his already gaunt features. And Jeremy . . .
shit. He bounced on the balls of his feet, his arms
loose as though getting ready to go in for a touchdown. He'd *promised* her, damn it! No hero crap.

Jeremy lunged for Cesar, his over six and a half
feet of height towering over the shorter man, and
one of Jeremy's hands almost big enough to
palm Cesar's head and twist it right off. Emma's
heart leapt into her throat, and her pulse raced
at the same time her lungs seized up. Jeremy had
the advantage size-wise, but would it be enough to
wrestle the gun from Cesar's hand? The report of
the shot rang out, too loud in the enclosed space.

Emma's ears rang and her head swam. Focus seemed impossible with the amount of blood pumping into her head and her vision blurred. Jeremy listed backward as though in slow motion and a scream lodged itself in Emma's chest.

"Jesus Christ, Cesar!" Damien growled from between clenched teeth. "We're trying to lay low, not bring every cop in the Industrial District down here. You fucking idiot."

Jeremy crashed down onto the floor like a felled tree. Blood welled from his right shoulder, a bright crimson bloom that made Emma's stomach turn. In a heartbeat, she was beside him, cradling his head against her shoulder as she tore open the buttons of his shirt to assess the damage. Good God, as if she even knew what she was looking for.

"Maybe I should have just given the *hijo de puta* my piece," Cesar spat. "You know, to keep things quiet?" He gave a derisive snort, waving the gun around as he barked out orders. "You. Help him up," he said to Landon. "And you, old man, give him a hand." He hauled Emma up by her arm, his fingers biting uncomfortably into her skin. "You're sticking close to me." His sour breath caressed her cheek as Cesar sneered close to her face. "Ain't no one gonna jump me if they think you might get shot in the process, eh, *chica*?"

Damien gave Landon a rough shove toward Jeremy, who was now sprawled out on the floor, his loud moan of pain slicing through Emma's chest. "I-is he going to be okay, Landon?" Emma spoke around the tears, willing herself to be strong.

Landon examined the bullet wound, his jaw set

with anger and the muscle there flexing. Fire sparked in his eyes, blue gas flames that wouldn't be quenched. Landon was the comeback king, the guy who had a response for everything, most of the time accented by his trademark snark. But the quiet that had settled over him since he'd pulled Damien's gun on Sousa rattled Emma. Yet another side of Landon she hadn't known existed. She could almost see the gears turning in his mind. The plans forming. Landon McCabe could be a dangerous man too, it seemed. And thank God for it.

"All right, get him up and get moving."

Emma shot a glare Damien's way, cursing him to a thousand tortures, none of which would leave him with a single limb still attached. Cesar held Emma close to his body, taking several steps back to let Landon and her father help Jeremy to walk through the doorway. Damien followed, his gun trained on the back of Landon's head, and Cesar dragged Emma out last with a sick whisper in her ear. "I'm going to gut your *pendejo* boyfriend while you watch."

Emma mustered every ounce of bravado she had and laughed. She looked Cesar straight in the eye and said, "*No si te destripa primero.*" *Not if he guts you first.*

The vans that had followed them into the warehouse were gone now, and an eerie silence settled as the only sound was their shuffling feet and Jeremy's labored breath. That nasty bastard Luis and another guy with an automatic weapon waited for them by the van, the sliding door open and ready to accept their prisoners. And not a scrap of morality between them.

Landon helped Jeremy into the long middle

bench seat so he could sprawl out, and Emma's dad climbed in beside him. Cesar and one of his pals hopped in the front seat, leaving Emma and Landon to squeeze into the shorter third-row seat with the remaining guard. *Nice and cozy.* Damien walked up to the driver's-side window and exchanged a few low words with Cesar that she couldn't quite make out. Damien gave Landon one last pointed look and then turned his back on them, heading for where, Emma had no idea.

As the van pulled out from the warehouse and to wherever it was Cesar was taking them, Emma realized that this might be her one chance to say good-bye to Landon. The only opportunity she might ever get to tell him how she felt. She leaned in close—it wasn't tough considering how tightly they were jammed into the seat—but the words wouldn't move past the knot that formed in her throat.

I love you. So much it hurts. So much that the thought of losing you now makes me want to scream and fight and hurt anyone who might try to keep us apart. I love you more than I thought I could love anyone or anything. And I know that our time together has been short, but I think I've loved you since the first time I saw you. And even that bitter, angry, spiteful eighteen-year-old girl knew that you were a good man. You are the love of my life, Landon McCabe.

Emma pressed her forehead into Landon's shoulder. He didn't reach out to take her hand. Didn't put his arm around her or whisper words of comfort in her ear. He simply stared straight ahead, every muscle in his body solid with tension. Landon didn't want to have anything to do with her and really, she couldn't blame him. She'd got him into this mess, after all. And whereas she craved any

physical contact she could get: the solid comfort of
his shoulder, even a glancing touch of his finger, he
seemed content to pretend she wasn't even there.
Not even dead and I'm already a ghost.

"Don't touch me."

Emma's head snapped up from Landon's shoulder, at first thinking she'd imagined the callousness
of his voice. His eyes settled on her, those blue
flames now nothing more than ice. "Landon?" She
knew he was angry with her, but . . .

"I saw how you looked at him." Landon's accusation stung her like a thousand needles, his voice
loud enough for everyone in the van to hear. "You
think you can sit here and put your head on my
shoulder after you played me like that? Jesus,
Emma, you went to *him*. Put your arms around him.
I should have known better than to trust you. I don't
want you to touch me again. Ever. Don't even look
at me. I can't stand the sight of you for another
second."

Landon watched as something inside of Emma
broke with his words. Tears welled in her deep
brown eyes, spilling in rivulets down her cheeks. The
raw hurt in her soft features cleaved him in two, his
own pain so intense that he felt the urge to wrap his
arms around himself to keep his halves intact.

He'd done what he had to.

He hoped she'd understand, that somehow she'd
remember what he'd told her a few days ago. That
men like these only respected ruthlessness. And
if he was going to get them all out of this alive,
he had to be every bit as heartless and uncaring as

the bastards preparing to kill them. He leaned forward in his seat as though trying to put distance between himself and Emma, careful not to draw too much attention. "Put pressure on the wound," he murmured to Javier. "As much as you can."

He didn't acknowledge Landon with so much as a twitch, but who could blame him? He'd just publicly humiliated the man's daughter and treated her with cruelty and indifference when he'd made a promise to take care of her. He watched, though, as Javier pushed the heel of his palm against Jeremy's shoulder, eliciting a grunt of pain from the football star as he did as Landon instructed.

Emma sat up straight, the gentle sound of her tears stoking the fire of Landon's rage. It was a necessary hurt, one that would buy him the distraction he needed to save their lives. He prayed that she'd understand when everything was said and done, because even now, Landon wasn't sure he could forgive himself for dealing such a low blow. A lover's rift was the distraction that he needed, however, to get to the gun that Damien had left for him under the middle bench seat.

The undercover marshal hadn't left him completely in the lurch, but Jesus Christ, he was one armed man against three. His chances of getting the upper hand weren't exactly stellar. Damien had his hands full, though, and with any luck, in a few short hours, the Department of Homeland Security and the FBI would be busting Sousa's ass and confiscating the dirty bomb he was about to buy before the son of a bitch could arrange to deliver it to his associates in Mexico.

That was a hell of a lot of loose ends to tie up.

The drive was one of the longest of Landon's life, the minutes stretching into years as the distance between him and Emma grew wider and wider with each passing mile. Unspent adrenaline pooled in his gut and his brain buzzed with anticipation. Every thought in his head was crystal clear, his senses heightened and sensitive to every shift of each individual body in the van. Beside him, that son of a bitch Luis said something in Spanish to his buddies in the front seats that elicited their mutual laughter and Landon vowed that he'd be the first one to go down.

Thirty minutes later, Cesar pulled off the highway onto a dirt road that led them farther away from the city and out into a secluded, wooded area. No doubt he planned to execute them and dump their bodies in the woods. Cesar must have assumed it would take a week or so before anyone stumbled upon the bodies out here. And by then, Sousa and his entire crew would be long gone.

Landon peeked over the seat to check on Jeremy, trying not to be too obvious about it. Javier was still applying pressure to the wound, and from the looks of Jeremy's bloodied back, the bullet had gone through his shoulder. A favorable wound as gunshots went, but it wasn't going to help Javier in his effort to slow the bleeding. Jeremy's brow knitted tight as the van jostled them over a bumpy backwoods road, and Landon took in their surroundings, which grew more remote by the second.

Another ten minutes passed before Cesar pulled the van off the main road and into a stand of trees. He cut the engine and looked back at his prisoners, a sick anticipation twisting his dark features. Landon took a deep breath, readied himself for what was going to be one hell of a feat. This was some serious cowboy shit he was about to pull. Galen would be so proud. *Yee-haw.*

"Get out." Cesar barked out the order before hopping out of the van along with his companion in the passenger seat. The side door growled open, letting in the chill afternoon air. The forest smelled of rain and evergreens. Clean. It helped to clear Landon's mind until it was as sharp as a freaking razor. His limbs shook with the energy he'd stored, waiting to explode in a rush. His muscles ached from remaining inert, but it wouldn't be much longer before he put them to good use.

Luis and his buddy exited the van next. It pained Landon to sit by and not react as Luis grabbed Emma by the arm and hauled her bodily from the van, jerking her body against his, his dark eyes sparking with lust. Bastard. Javier was next, and Landon breathed a sigh of relief. *So far, so good.*

While Cesar dealt with Emma and Javier, Landon launched himself over the bench seat onto Jeremy. He made a show of grabbing him by the shirt and hauling him up, shaking him roughly before rolling them both onto the floor of the van as though Jeremy had flipped him over, making sure the football star was positioned on top of him.

"You and Emma thought you could play me?" Landon shouted as Jeremy struggled to free himself from Landon's grasp. "You were sneaking around behind my back. Admit it, you motherfucker!"

Their quarters were close, but Landon managed to free his right hand. He reached under the seat, groping until his fist made contact with cold steel.

Grabbing the gun, Landon prayed the damned thing wouldn't go off accidentally, and he reached between them again, stuffing the weapon into his waistband at his hip. Jeremy let out a shout of pain as one of Sousa's men hauled him off of Landon, wrenching his injured shoulder in the process. Shit, he hoped it wouldn't fuck up his shoulder too bad. The last thing the guy needed was a bad throwing arm. If they lived, Landon could probably expect a hefty lawsuit out of this.

Eh, what the hell. He'd worry about that complication later.

"I'm gonna kill you, you son of a bitch!"

Once Jeremy was clear of the van, Cesar leaned in, leveling his weapon on Landon. "Maybe we ought to let the deputy here take care of *Sancho* for us, huh, Luis?"

Luis snickered in response, and Cesar waved the gun in front of Landon, urging him to get up and out of the van. "You want to off Sancho?" he sneered as Landon crept out of the van.

He made sure to appear winded, resting his palms on his knees once he was on solid ground. "What are you talking about?" he said between breaths. "Who the hell is Sancho?"

"It means the guy who's running around with your lady. *'Prendé?* You want a piece of him or not, cop?"

Cesar's bloodthirsty expression wasn't doing much for Landon. But he'd wanted a distraction and this was it. "You're goddamned right I do."

Their armed guards formed a triangle around the two men and the only person to look more shocked at the turn of events than Jeremy was Emma. Luis stood with his arm wrapped tight around her waist—the son of a bitch—and Landon had to avert his gaze from her puffy eyes, tear-streaked face, and slack jaw.

"Landon, are you out of your mind?" Emma finally spluttered. "Stop this!"

He bent at the knees, hunched over and arms out. The guy holding Jeremy shoved him at Landon and he stumbled toward him, his left arm up to defend while his right hung limp at his side. Sousa's men began to take bets on the victor, with Cesar throwing down a grand on Landon. He ran at Jeremy, shoulder down, and aimed for the softest part of the other man's gut. He was weak from blood loss, and probably in the beginning stages of shock so it wasn't too tough to take him down. With their captor's attention focused on Jeremy, they ridiculed him for his weakness, and Landon hated that this had to go down at Jeremy's expense.

Reaching across his hip, Landon grabbed the gun from his waistband and swung it around at Goon Number One. He aimed for the chest and squeezed the trigger. The report of the shot echoed all around them as adrenaline pumped through his veins in a mad rush.

"Landon, watch out!" Emma's terrified shriek drew his attention and he whipped his head around as Cesar squeezed off a couple of wild shots. *Bam! Bam!*

The scream that followed cleaved right through Landon's skull as white-hot pain shot through his torso. He felt himself falling before he actually realized that he was going down, and he gritted his teeth against the pain, twisting mid-flight as he aimed for Cesar's chest and squeezed the trigger. Though it took only a second, time seemed to slow as Cesar's body jerked from the impact, his head falling back as his arms went wide. Blood welled from the bullet wounds in the center of his chest and he lurched backward, eyes wide and unseeing as he landed with a crunch of dried leaves and twigs.

Two down, one to go.

Luis seemed to be in shock, holding on to Emma, his human shield. Landon's vision blurred though his pain no longer registered. He was too far gone, too lost to the high to feel anything. He pushed himself up from the ground and leveled the gun at Luis's face as his breath wheezed through his lungs. "Let her go."

"Right," Luis snorted. "You're dead, *cabrón*."

"No, asshole. You're dead." Landon pulled the trigger without a second thought. Luis had the nerve to look surprised when the bullet struck him in the center of his forehead. Emma gasped and lunged forward, falling to the ground as Luis landed beside her. Frantic, she clawed through the grass, crawling toward her father, who was already on the ground, tending to Jeremy.

Landon took one stuttering step, and then another. As the adrenaline drained out of his body, it was replaced with a pain so intense that stars twinkled at the periphery of his line of sight. *Well, shit.* He reached for his side, and his fingers made contact with something warm and sticky. There was too much of the sickening wetness soaking into his shirt for a simple flesh wound.

"I kept my promise," he said as he went to his knees. "You're safe. Everything's going to be okay, Emma." Black spots swam in his murky vision and he thought he saw her scrambling toward him. *I love you.* Did he say it out loud? He couldn't be sure, couldn't feel his lips—couldn't feel much of anything, really. *Damn it, I love you, Emma. So much.*

"Landon?" Her voice came to him as though down the length of a tunnel. A faint echo that he strained to hear. "Landon?" Again, frantic. "Landon? Can you hear me? Stay with me!"

I'm here, Emma. I'm not going anywhere. But that was a lie, wasn't it? The darkness settled around him, thick and sludgy. It pulled him deeper, farther away until he couldn't see her anymore. It was okay, though. As long as Emma was safe, nothing else mattered.

Chapter Twenty-Six

Being dead wasn't supposed to hurt like this.

Son of a bitch.

Landon cracked one lid, and the brightness invading the room drove into his skull like an iron spike. His ribs ached and his torso felt as if someone had thrown him into a meat grinder turned onto high. The silhouetted form of a body sat next to his bed, the dark outline framed in sunlight.

"Something tells me you're not God," he said to the shape. "Unless you're making me pay for asking Jodie Thompson *and* Beth Farmer to prom my senior year. But in my defense, they got along just fine."

"You must be feeling all right if you're capable of being a smart-ass," Bill Crawford said from his perch. "Though I've got to admit, I could've lived another day without hearing about your prom threesome."

"What can I say"—Landon grunted as he tried to sit up—"I was in high demand."

Crawford chuckled as he pushed himself out of

his chair and approached the bed. "You're a tough son of a bitch, McCabe, I'll give you that."

As the room came more into focus, one unmistakable absence made Landon's heart clench inside of his chest. Panic rose hot and thick in his throat and he lurched forward in the bed, pulling at the wound in his torso. "Mother *fuck*," he said through his teeth. "That hurts like a bitch."

"Yeah, I wouldn't advise any sudden movements for a while." Crawford's easygoing tone was doing nothing for Landon's mood. "Why don't you settle back and let me bring you up to speed before you pull something."

"Where's Emma? Is she okay?"

"She's fine," Crawford said. "Her father was released from the hospital two days ago along with Jeremy Blakely. Everyone is okay, though the football player won't be on the field for a while. You saved their lives with your stunt, you know."

Crawford must've pieced it together after getting statements from the others. He still regretted having to hurt Emma with his pretense, but given the chance, he'd do it all over again. "What about Damien? Was he able to stop the buy?"

"He was," Crawford said. "Sousa is in federal custody, and he's not going anywhere any time soon. I hope you know he was just doing his job, McCabe. Under any other circumstances, he wouldn't have left you like that."

"I know," Landon replied. "It's all good. We've gotta do what we've gotta do for the job."

"That we do," Crawford agreed.

"Can I see Emma?" He had to explain himself in person, apologize for what he'd put her through. He needed to look into those endless brown eyes of hers, touch her petal-soft lips and kiss away all of the hurt he'd caused until she was breathless and had no choice but to forgive him.

"I'm sorry, but that's not going to be possible."

"What? Why the hell not?"

Landon tried to sit up again, fighting against the stabbing pain. Crawford eased him back down on the bed with a palm to his shoulder. "Lie down, you idiot, or I'm going to have your ass sedated. Sousa's in custody, but you know that's not the end of it. We've got to make sure she's protected and like you said, we've gotta do what we've gotta do for the job."

Realization was a semi-truck slamming into his chest as the air deflated from Landon's lungs. "WITSEC?" The word was bitter on his tongue and he pressed his head back into the pillow. "She's in witness protection, am I right?"

"We're good at what we do," Crawford said by way of an answer. "You know that. I have no doubt she'll be well looked after. Get some rest, Deputy. You earned it."

Without another word, Crawford turned, and walked out of the room, leaving Landon alone, too damned awake, and his brain *way* too active. Witness protection. Jesus. The Seattle office—probably Ethan Morgan—would have arranged for a new identity for Emma and her father. She was no doubt already halfway across the country with a bank account full of money and a nice cover story to go with it. Landon's stomach turned in on itself, the bile rising in his throat.

Gone.

Emma was gone. He loved her more than he loved

anything in this godforsaken world and he'd never get to tell her. Never see her beautiful face again or feel the softness of her bare skin against his ever again. Landon reached beside him and jammed his thumb down on the call button repeatedly as he swallowed against the golf-ball-sized lump that formed in his throat. His heart beat out of control and the machines hooked up to his vitals beeped and whirred in time, echoing his distress.

Moments later, a nurse rushed into the room, her expression pinched with concern. "Is everything all right, Deputy McCabe?"

"No," Landon managed to choke out. "I'm in a lot of pain here. Can you please give me something? Something to knock me the hell out."

She laid a compassionate hand on his shoulder. "Sure, I can. You hold tight, okay? I'll be right back."

Landon squeezed his eyes shut in an effort to block out the world. The nurse returned with a syringe and vial of something guaranteed to end his suffering—temporarily anyway. She dosed the syringe and inserted the needle into his IV tube. "This oughta do it," she said with a wink. "You'll be out in no time."

Thank fucking God. Landon drifted as the drug took effect. The bullet wound in his side was nothing compared to what he felt stabbing through his chest right now. And he knew as blissful unconsciousness overtook him that there wasn't enough morphine in the world to dull the pain of losing Emma.

* * *

"I'm sorry I can't call you. I feel like I'm leaving you in the lurch."

"Nah." Jeremy sat back in his recliner, carefully adjusting a pillow under his injured shoulder. Luckily, the bullet had gone straight through and he hadn't suffered any permanent damage. He wouldn't be playing for a while, but there were much worse fates than missing a football game or two. "I'm glad you're going to be protected. But once all of this is over, you'd better promise that you'll get your ass back here to hang with me. Got it?"

"Got it," Emma said with a laugh. "Jeremy, I'm so, so sorry about all of this. I should have called you. I should have told you what was going on and—"

"I told you to quit apologizing. I was in the wrong place at the wrong time. That's all. It wasn't your fault."

"You could have been killed, though."

"But I wasn't," Jeremy said. "I might be quick on the field, but I had no idea how to handle that shit. I'm lucky your boy had his shit together. If he hadn't roughed me up a little, we'd all be dead right now."

No one could ever accuse Landon of being slow, that was for sure. At the time, his harsh words had broken her heart. It wasn't until she'd seen the smaller pieces of the puzzle coming together that she'd realized Landon's plan. And in hindsight, she probably shouldn't have cursed Damien like she had. He'd done what he could to help as well.

"He really did save the day, didn't he?"

Emma flinched as the memory of watching Cesar shoot Landon welled up fresh in her mind. Her heart still ached with sorrow when she thought of cradling him in her arms, begging him not to die. Not to leave her all alone. Her father had had the good sense to search Cesar for a cell phone and call an ambulance, but by the time the paramedics and police had shown up, Landon had lost consciousness and his breathing had become so shallow she'd thought for a moment that she'd lost him. She was no stranger to hurt or loss, but in that moment, when she thought Landon had died, Emma had wished for the barest moment that she could die right alongside of him. Because the thought of living one day without Landon McCabe was more than she could bear.

"From what everyone's been telling me, this witness protection won't be a permanent thing, but until all of Sousa's associates are accounted for this is the safest option. I think you got the better end of the deal in this situation."

Though Jeremy's involvement was minimal, he'd been assigned a protective detail by the Marshals Service to keep an eye on him. And as a supplement, he'd hired a private security firm for added backup. Apparently, he wasn't enough of a threat to warrant a new identity, and thank God for it. Emma wouldn't have been able to handle the burden of guilt if she'd ruined Jeremy's life—and career—with her foolishness.

"What about your marshal?" A teasing smile lit Jeremy's face. "You gonna go see him before you blow out of town?"

Deputy Morgan—with Bill Crawford at his side— had made it perfectly clear to Emma that making contact with Landon wasn't a good idea. That hadn't stopped her from sitting beside him in that hospital room, though. She'd alternated between his room and her dad's for two days, checking on both of them until she nearly passed out from exhaustion. She'd refused to sleep until she'd known both of them were going to be okay, and when she'd finally gone down, she'd slept for twelve hours straight.

"My babysitters don't think that's a good idea," Emma replied. "And since we're leaving this afternoon, I doubt there's any chance I'll be able to sneak away. Plus, they're turning a blind eye to my less-than-legal activities over the past couple of years so I figure that, for now anyway, I'd better not press my luck."

"For now?" Jeremy arched a curious brow.

"You know me, Jer. I can only go so long without causing a little trouble."

"That's for sure," he said with a chuckle. "Now get over here and give me a hug before you duck out for the duration."

Emma wrapped her arms around her friend and bestowed a kiss on his cheek. "Not forever," she reminded him. "Just a while."

"See you in a while, then." Jeremy said, hugging her back.

"See you in a while."

Outside of Jeremy's house, Deputy U.S. Marshal Ethan Morgan waited for her in his government-issue, dull-as-a-block-of-wood sedan. She took a deep breath as she settled into the passenger seat and turned to give her dad a smile of reassurance that she didn't particularly feel.

"Ready?" Deputy Morgan asked as he put the car in gear and headed down the long, winding driveway from Jeremy's house. "At least you don't have to worry about a crowded flight," he said as he drove. "No coach tickets for you two. Our jet is nice and private, not to mention spacious. Plus, you get the added benefit of having three marshals along for the ride. Top-notch security, if you ask me. You're lucky."

Lucky. Emma scoffed at the word. Lucky would have been having the good sense not to get in over her head in the first place. Lucky would have been keeping Jeremy out of danger. Lucky would have been guarding her heart and getting through this without falling hopelessly in love with Landon McCabe. And lucky would have been waltzing out of all of this unscathed and living happily ever after with the man of her dreams.

Right now Emma felt far from lucky.

As the car rolled down the freeway, Emma leaned back in her seat and let her eyes drift shut. Sometimes in life, you had to make your own luck and she was going to make sure that she did everything in her power to turn hers around.

Chapter Twenty-Seven

One month later

"Your cushy vacation is over, dude. Time to get your lazy ass back to work."

Landon stared down into his empty glass as though the answers to all of the mysteries of the world were written there. Most nights he would have won a verbal spar with Galen, but tonight—like every night for the past four weeks—he found he simply didn't have it in him. "If I have to get shot in order to get a vacation, then I'm good with not taking time off ever again."

Galen raised his bottle of Stella in a toast. "Amen to that."

It probably wasn't a great idea to go out drinking the night before he was supposed to go back to work. Galen had been a good boy—one beer, and he'd nursed that. But not Landon. He was on his fourth Jack and Coke and he wasn't planning on stopping quite yet. "When do you have to pick up Harper?" It was girls' night or some shit, and for the past half hour Galen had been checking his watch as if counting down the minutes until he could go get her. *Fucker.*

"In a few," Galen said as though he weren't busting out of his skin to get out of there and go to her. It wasn't that Landon was jealous of what he and Harper had . . . oh, who the hell was he kidding? He was *absolutely* jealous of what Galen and Harper had.

"Go," Landon grumbled. He needed another drink. "You're driving me insane with the way you keep checking your damned watch."

Galen's pitiful expression only made Landon want to pop his friend right in the gut. He knew he was a fucking train wreck, but did Galen have to look at him like that? "I can stay for a while longer," he said. "I'm sure Harper won't be ready to leave—"

"Please," Landon interrupted. "She's probably climbing the walls and driving her friends fucking nuts, too. Do me a favor and get out of here. I'll see you at work tomorrow."

"You sure?"

"If you don't leave, I'm going to pick your ass up and throw you out the door. That sure enough for you?"

Galen gave him a last appraising look before pushing himself from the table. He shrugged into his jacket and braced an arm on the table leaning in toward Landon. "I'm here if you need me. You know that, right?"

The last thing he needed right now was for Galen to get all touchy-feely with him. "I know," he said on a sigh. "Now get the fuck out of here before you're tempted to hug it out or some shit."

Galen chuckled and laid his palm on Landon's shoulder. "See you in the morning."

"Later."

With Galen gone, Landon was allowed to wallow in his misery, undisturbed. A cocktail waitress made her rounds and Landon raised his empty glass. She walked over, a smile plastered on her face. "Another Jack and Coke?"

"Yeah." He wanted to ask her to hold the Coke and bring the bottle, but that probably wouldn't paint a very pretty picture. Besides, he did have to go in to the office tomorrow. It would be a good idea not to be too hungover.

"My shift's over in a half hour." She leaned a hip on his table and flashed him a million-watt smile. "Maybe we could go get a coffee?"

He could do it. He could take the eager cocktail waitress back to his place. Let her try to make him forget the damned hollow ache that was eating him alive. She seemed up for it, giving him some serious fuck-me eyes. . . .

"I think I'm going to have to pass. Sorry."

Disappointment darkened her expression. "You sure?"

"I'm sure."

"I'll be back with your drink in a sec."

As Landon drained his glass in a few gulps, he regretted his decision not to ask for the bottle. The mellow buzz relaxed him, but it wasn't delivering the full-body numbness he was looking for. How was it possible to hurt this damned bad and not die from it? For a month he'd been a useless heap. A zombie simply going through the motions, pretending to be alive. Inside, he was as lifeless as a corpse.

Emma was ever present in his mind. The memory of her a sweet torture that he refused to let go of. He knew how witness protection worked. Emma Ruiz was dead. For good. The Marshals Service would keep her identity and whereabouts buried for as long as it took the feds to wrap up their case to take down Sousa's operation. For weeks, Landon had been calling in favors, skirting the rules, flirting with the line that, once crossed, would get him good and fired. All in an effort to find her.

Emma Ruiz truly was a ghost. . . .

"Is this seat taken?"

Landon froze, the voice too familiar to be real. He refused to look up, to suffer the disappointment of seeing his waitress standing above him while his mind played cruel tricks on him. And yet, his body betrayed him, shaking with the need to see her face, to confirm that he was once and for all losing his grip on reality.

His breath sped in his chest, the familiar adrenaline barreling through his veins like fire down a tunnel. Slowly, he turned his head, fearful to hope and at the same time praying for a miracle. He dragged his gaze from the floor up, tracing the curves of her hips, narrow waist, and petite frame. His eyes met the endless brown depths of hers, and he scrubbed a hand over his face as he stared in disbelief.

Standing before him—so close he could touch— was the most beautiful ghost Landon had ever laid eyes on.

"You look like you could use some company." Her lips curled into a sweet, mischievous smile, and she held out her hand. "I'm Alessandra Batista. Well, for at least a couple more days, anyway. But you can call me Alex."

She might have been "Alex" to the world now, but she'd only ever be Emma to him. God, how he'd missed that smile. It lit her entire face with a moonlight glow that held him helplessly in orbit. Landon pushed his chair out from the table, wobbling a little on his feet as he gained his balance. Without a word, he took her into his arms and kissed her for all he was worth. If this turned out to be some sort of drunken delusion, he wanted to be damned sure he got everything he could out of it before he sobered up and came to his senses.

"Well," Emma breathed as he pulled away, "I should go away more often if I'm going to get a greeting like that when I come back."

Landon cupped her face in his hands and drank in every beautiful detail, committing each to memory. Not that he wasn't fucking ecstatic to see her, but WITSEC wasn't exactly easy to break out of. Then again, he wouldn't put anything past Emma. She took determination to an entirely new level. Her wide smile didn't falter as she took Landon's hand in hers and slid into the booth. How she even managed to move was a mystery to him because his fucking legs had gone numb the second he'd laid eyes on her.

"I don't think I've ever seen you speechless, McCabe." He settled down beside her, his mouth still hanging open like the hinges of his jaw were broken. "I've got to say, I feel sort of powerful, having the upper hand on you."

Landon shook himself from the stupor that had settled on him. The whiskey probably wasn't helping his reaction time, either. "What are you doing here? How?"

"You should know me well enough by now to realize that when I want something, I go after it." She laughed. "Oh, Crawford says hi, by the way."

"He knows you're here?" Jesus, he couldn't articulate for shit. He had the urge to pinch himself— you know, to make sure he wasn't dreaming. Emma was here. Sitting beside him. *Jesus.*

She quirked a brow. "You must not pay very close attention at work. Does your supervisor know about your attention deficit disorder?"

He couldn't even wrap his head around what he was seeing, and she was making jokes. Talk about a role reversal. "I haven't been back to work yet," he replied. "Tomorrow's my first day."

Emma's brow furrowed and she reached out to lay a gentle hand on Landon's torso. The heat of her palm soaked through Landon's shirt over the place where he'd been shot. "I was so worried about you." Her words were nothing more than a whisper. "Are you okay?"

"I am now." His own voice caught in his throat. "But seriously, Emma. What are you doing here? It's not safe—"

"You marshals," she interrupted. "All so high-handed."

"Emma."

"Landon," she teased.

Now wasn't the time for jokes. If she was recognized, word could get back to Sousa's organization. The guy might be in a cell somewhere, but that didn't mean he couldn't still order someone to kill her. He gave her a look and she sighed. "Fine. But for the record, you're no fun when you're all growly and concerned."

No shit. His tension level had jacked up into the stratosphere. "What's going on?"

"I'm sure you'll get the whole story tomorrow, but in a nutshell, since the rest of Sousa's associates have been rounded up, the investigation is winding down. Crawford wanted me to stay in Witness Security for the duration of the trial, but I refused. I'm not going to hide and put my life on hold because of Sousa or whatever threat he might present. I'm not an innocent victim, I willingly inserted myself into this situation, and I'm not going to waste taxpayer money and hide out for the rest of my life. I'm not any safer as Alex Batista than I am as Emma Ruiz and the Marshals Service knows that. I could be recognized anywhere at any time. I'm not going to hide anymore, Landon. I won't. I want my life back."

Fire and steel. Those two words described Emma to a tee. "And you're not even a little worried?" As though he had to ask.

"Not in the slightest." She reached out and brushed her fingers across his jaw. "Besides, everyone knows that the best marshals work in Portland . . . which is where I've decided to settle down. I know one in particular who's earned a reputation for protecting stubborn women with a penchant for computer hacking."

Landon captured her hand in his and brought it to his lips. He'd kill any one of Sousa's buddies who thought to do Emma harm.

Her dark eyes became hooded when his lips touched her skin, and a thrill shot through Landon's veins. He'd never get enough of her. Ever.

"So," Emma said, her dark eyes sparkling. "Are you done drinking for the night so we can get out of here?"

She didn't have to ask him twice. "My place?"

"Perfect."

Emma smiled into the pillow as Landon placed featherlight kisses across her bare shoulder and down her spine. A month apart felt more like years, and Emma had made every threat possible—including refusing to cooperate and hacking into a few government servers—until the feds and the U.S. Marshals Service had agreed to relocate her from Connecticut to Portland while they transitioned her out of witness protection. It wasn't exactly a small feat to bring someone back from the dead. The feds had argued that until an official press conference could be held, it was best for her to stay off the radar, which was fine by her. She'd stay holed up in Landon's apartment for the next week if he'd let her. And once everything was set right, they promised to fly her dad to Portland as well. Finally, after so many weeks of heartache, Emma's world spun straight on its axis. Life couldn't get much better than this.

"I'm going to have you in the shower and lick the water off your breasts," Landon murmured against her skin. "And then I'll lay you out on my dining room table and feast on you like you're my last meal."

"Landon," Emma chided. "That's hardly sanitary."

"Shhh." His breath on her bare skin sent a thrill through Emma's body and goose bumps rose on her flesh. "After that, I'm going to set you on my lap right on my living room couch and fuck you so slow that it takes you hours to come."

"Well." Emma's breath stalled with his heated words. "That certainly sounds like a good use of our time."

"And when we're done there, I'll take you up against my bedroom wall. Hard."

His erection brushed her backside, as smooth and hard as polished marble. Emma arched her back, rocking into him and Landon hissed in a breath as his teeth grazed her shoulder. "And after that?" His erotic talk nearly had her out of her mind with desire. They'd been at it for hours already and it still wasn't enough to sate them. They were as bad as a couple of addicts, not knowing when to stop. That was the thing, though. Emma didn't think she'd *ever* get enough of Landon.

"After that . . ." His voice was a sensual growl that made Emma's abdomen clench tight as a warm rush spread between her thighs. "We'll start right back here, in this bed, and I'll tease you with my mouth and fingers until neither one of us can wait another second."

"So you can tell me the thirty or so ways you want to fuck me—in wonderful detail, I might add—but can you come up with a few words to tell me how you *feel* about me?"

Funny that *this* was the question she was almost too afraid to ask. There was no doubt that Landon wanted her. He'd made himself crystal clear on that front. But were his feelings for her only physical? An intense chemical reaction and nothing more? She'd fought so hard to get here, back to him. Emma needed to know that all of it had been worth the risk.

The heat of his body left her as Landon pushed himself up and away. Cold fingers of dread speared her heart as she prepared for the worst. *Damn it, Emma. It's too soon to ask him that question. You're going to scare him away.*

He gently rolled her onto her back and Emma averted her gaze, unable to look into his face while he said words she didn't think she could bear to hear. Her body betrayed her as Landon settled himself between her thighs, sliding into her slowly as he filled her completely.

"Emma, look at me."

She couldn't. The pain of loving someone who might not love you back was debilitating. And still she wanted him. Craved him. Needed him deep inside of her the way he was now. Landon urged his hips against hers, and a tortured moan escaped Emma's lips. It was heaven and hell all at once, a purgatory she'd gladly suffer for as long as he wanted her to.

"Emma. Look at me," he repeated.

She finally met his gaze only to find, shining in his blue eyes, a depth of emotion that was so intense it caused her heart to stutter in her chest. Landon braced his elbows on either side of her and smoothed her hair away from her face with both hands. "I love you. Whether you're Emma Ruiz or Alex Batista, or even Gertrude Flatzengraf. I love you so much that I don't think I can take another breath unless you're here to give me air to breathe. The past month without you almost destroyed me. I can't live without you, Emma. I love every stubborn, clever, protective, fiery, beautiful, *SportsCenter*-loving inch of you. And I'll tell you every minute of every day if I have to until you know without a doubt that *I love you* and I that won't ever love anyone else as long as I live. Is that descriptive enough for you?"

Moisture stung at Emma's eyes and there was nothing she could do to stop the happy flow. A tear spilled over and trickled down her face as she laughed quietly at her own sentimental foolishness. "I love you, Landon," she said. "In all the ways that you said and more. I've loved you since the first time I laid eyes on you and I hope you plan on living for a long damned time because you're not getting rid of me any time soon."

"It's the badge, isn't it?" he teased. "The ladies love the badge."

Emma leaned up to kiss him, the gentle rhythm of her hips matching his as he thrust inside of her again and again. With their bodies joined, and now their hearts as well, she knew that nothing would come between them ever again. Her life had changed for the better. She'd been reborn and this new life would be filled with love and hold none of the loneliness of her previous one.

"It might be about the badge. A little," she said against his mouth. "Now, about that shower . . ."

Keep reading for an excerpt from
the next installment of the
U.S. Marshals series,

ONE TOUCH MORE,

available in November 2015 from
Mandy Baxter
and
Kensington Books!

As usual, his give-and-take with Dr. Meyers had earned Damien a pat on the head and the privilege of being allowed to resume his undercover work. Unfortunately, if he'd known Bill Crawford—the SOG director for the Pacific Northwest—was going to ship him off to Boise, Idaho, he might have saved himself the trouble and just taken the desk job. As far as assignments went, he reminded himself, it could always be worse.

For the past year, the U.S. Marshals Service's Fugitive Task Force had been hunting Gerald Lightfoot, a heavy hitter who'd managed to slip federal custody before they could slap his ass in the nearest supermax. A veteran of the drug trade, Lightfoot had a finger in everything from weed to heroin, and word was that he was now operating his syndicate in the United States from somewhere in Russia. By using the waterways, he'd been smuggling product down into the port of Seattle and distributing throughout the Pacific Northwest and California. His most recent specialty was a synthetic that was going by the street name of Stardust because of its glittery physical properties and because its ability to give the user a quick high was likened to being shot up into space. It had shown up in Idaho a few months back. Sales were quickly gaining traction and had grabbed the attention of the USMS only after several teens had died. The Boise PD had assigned a special task force to stop the flow of Stardust into the city, but they couldn't keep up with the suppliers and dealers. Bastards got craftier every fucking month.

It was a revolving operation, never staying in the same place for more than a month or two. Seattle, Portland, Spokane, and now Boise. The task force figured that they only had a window of about four weeks to nail Lightfoot's contact here before he pulled his product and moved on to the next city. The distributor in Boise was the key to finding Lightfoot, and had become the Fugitive Task Force's number-one priority.

Damien had been brought in to work the chain from the bottom up. First, locate the dealers, then hook up with Lightfoot's distributor. With such a tight time frame, he didn't have long to lay the groundwork.

"Hi! Are you checking in tonight?"

Damien looked up at the sound of the chipper voice and his brain went abso-freaking-lutely blank. The woman behind the counter gave him a wide smile as she tucked a section of her short hair behind her ear. Wide, blue eyes the color of a deep mountain lake stared back at him, fringed with dark lashes that made the blue that much brighter. He towered over her, yet he sensed in her a confidence that was far larger than her petite frame. And that smile . . . holy shit. It was the sort of expression that skirted flirtatious and made his chest hitch.

"Yeah," he responded with a smile of his own. "I'm early though, so if you can't check me in yet, it's not a big deal."

"Oh, I don't think it'll be a problem. Can I get your name?"

"Damien Evans."

Her voice rippled over him, smooth and sweet as whipped cream. He checked her name tag—Tabitha—and noted that she was also the assistant manager. She might be helpful later down the line, especially if this place did in fact turn out to be one of the hotels that Lightfoot's man was dealing from. Managers spent more time at the hotel than anyone, plus they made it their business to know the regular guests.

"Okay . . ." Tabitha scanned the computer screen and puckered her lips in concentration. Damien found the act entirely too distracting, his gaze locked on the dark pink flesh that looked as soft as flower petals. "Looks like you requested a room on the top floor. Is that still okay?"

"Yep." A bird's-eye view would help him to notice anything out of the ordinary in the parking lot or street.

"And you also requested a room facing the parking lot?" She cocked a brow and gave him a wry smile. "I have to admit, that's a first."

He smiled back, couldn't help himself. Damien wasn't exactly a playful guy. Gruff described him to a tee. But he found that he wanted to try, for the first time in what felt like forever, to be a little flirtatious back. "Would you believe me if I told you I was a writer for *Parking Lot Monthly* and this place made my top ten list for spacious parking spaces?"

Her laughter was infectious and it tingled down Damien's spine in a warm rush. "You know, our guests comment all the time that our parking spaces are extra roomy."

"It's all in the lot design," Damien agreed.

"Totally." Their eyes met and Damien swore the air sizzled between them. "Okay, well, here are your keys." Tabitha tucked two plastic cards into an envelope and slid them across the counter to him. "And I need to swipe your credit card. You won't be charged until you check out."

"No problem." Damien pulled the Visa that he used for undercover operations from his wallet and handed it to her. She swiped the card in the machine and handed it back.

"I have you down for seven days and if you need to extend or shorten your stay, just let me know."

"Sounds good." Damien tucked the card back into his wallet and retrieved the large duffel with his clothes.

"Then you're all set. By the way, I'm Tabitha." She reached out her hand across the counter. "I'm here most evenings until ten if you need anything."

He took her hand in his and the contact was electric, sending a jolt of excitement through Damien's bloodstream. Of all the shitty timing . . . After months, he meets a woman that he's attracted to and he's on a goddamned job. "Damien," he said in return, his voice only a little strained.

"Have a good one, Damien." Damn, that smile was enough to bring him to his knees. "If you need anything, don't hesitate to ask."

"I won't. Thanks."

Was it his imagination that she seemed interested, too? She was definitely throwing off some sort of vibe, but Damien was clueless when it came to women. Maybe this was just Tabitha's usual customer service charm. Still, he had at least a week to test the waters, didn't he? Dr. Meyers said he needed to loosen up a little and try to live some sort of life. This week was as good a time as any for a trial run.

"Hey, um, I was wondering. You wouldn't happen to know what's hot downtown? Bars or clubs?" He didn't want her to think he was on the prowl or anything, but he wanted a local's take on the city's nightlife.

"Scouting out locations for *Parking Lot Monthly*?"

Damien's lips tugged in a reluctant smile. He'd never been funny, but he racked his brain for something—anything—comical to say, if only to make her laugh. That sound was like the sweetest music. A song he could listen to on repeat. "Even nightclubs deserve a chance at the top-ten lists."

"Totally," Tabitha agreed with a chuckle. "Parking lots downtown can be tricky. But if you're also including parking garages—"

"Garages are just parking lots on steroids. Bigger and beefier."

"Exactly!"

Damn the sound of her laughter. It had a calming effect on him that none of the drugs Dr. Meyers had prescribed could manage. "Okay, so if you use the parking garage on Eighth Street, you can hit several downtown clubs from there. Liquid on Eighth and there's Fatty's on West Idaho. I think a new place just opened up near there called Equilibrium that's supposed to be pretty hot, too."

"Thanks." Three locations were more than a decent jumping off point. From there, he could ask around, maybe find out where the bulk of the product was being moved. "I owe you one."

"I won't forget it, either. Have a good one, Damien."

He took a faltering step away from the front desk, wishing he could talk to her for another hour or so. "You, too, Tabitha."

"'Night," she called after him with a wave.

Maybe this assignment wouldn't be too bad after all.

"Check you out, getting your flirt on."

Tabitha turned to face Dave and shook her head at the conspiratorial grin affixed to his face. "It's called good customer service. You should try it some time."

"Uh-huh." He clucked his tongue at her as he approached the desk. "I don't blame you. If I'd gotten to work a few minutes sooner, you can bet I would've flirted my ass off. Did you see those tattoos? And oh my God, his arms." Dave mocked a swoon. "Tall, built, and inked. *Yum.*"

Tall—pushing six-two at least—with the body of an MMA ass-kicker and an expression that screamed, *Cross me and suffer the consequences,* Damien had dangerous bad boy written all over him. Three-quarter sleeve tattoos covered his corded forearms and ran up his wide, sculpted biceps to disappear under the sleeves of his T-shirt. And though he looked as if he frequented dive bars and back alleys often, Damien didn't have that nasty, grunge-coated look to him. In fact, when he'd smiled, the soft openness of the expression had stolen Tabitha's breath. Deep dimples pitted his cheeks, and they'd lent a youthful lightheartedness to him that she never would have known was there if he hadn't smiled at her.

Yep, tall, built, and tattooed hit everything on Tabitha's *yes please!* list, but those same qualities in a guy often came with their own sets of problems. "Oh, he's yummy," Tabitha agreed. And he seemed like a genuinely nice guy, too. "But yummy can be trouble."

"Yes, it can."

Tabitha laughed at Dave's suggestive tone. Sure, Damien's golden-brown eyes had been hypnotic and his messy thatch of light brown hair practically begged to be touched, but he was a guest at the hotel. "Good thing for us he's off-limits, then." She and Dave had the same taste in men, which was why they were both often in the dating doghouse. Bad boys had their allure, but they only broke your heart in the end.

"I don't know," Dave said on a sigh. "I might be willing to lose my job over a shot at that."

"I would have your head." Tabitha swatted at him and Dave sidestepped her mock assault. "It's too hard to find decent front desk people. You can't ever quit or get fired, which means no hitting on guests for you, mister."

"Not that it would matter," he replied as though hurt. "Because that tattooed god was obviously hot for your lady bits."

She didn't want to admit that she'd felt a spark of connection between them. Or that in the course of their banter, her stomach had begun to unfurl gradually until it felt as though someone had let a swarm of butterflies loose to fly around. "My lady bits aside, I'm swearing off guys like that."

"You mean drop-dead-gorgeous walking pieces of art?"

"I mean guys who look like trouble." And despite the soft brilliance of his smile, Tabitha had no doubt that Damien was just as dangerous as he looked. "It's tax accountants and guidance counselors for me from here on out."

"Great," Dave replied. "That means more bad boys for me."

"You say that now, but after your next breakup you'll be begging me to help you find a nice guy."

"True. But until then, I'm sowing my oats."

"As long as you don't reap from the company fields, I'm A-OK with that."

"Fine. But I'm telling you now, if mister MMA even blinks at me with so much as minimal interest, all bets are off."

Tabitha laughed. "Deal."

"Speaking of gorgeous bad boys, how's your brother?"

Dave had been crushing on Tabitha's brother, Seth, for as long they'd known each other. He also knew how much trouble Seth caused in her life. Since they were kids, Tabitha had been bailing her younger brother out of one bad situation after another. And it wasn't like she could have ever counted on her less-than-responsible parents to help him out. He was the king of making bad decisions for the right reasons. Somewhere under his rough, troublemaker exterior was a good guy. He just needed someone to give him a chance to show that good side off.

"He's all right. He's trying to get a job working construction. If I can keep him on track for the next six months, I think he'll be set to start school in the fall. I've got him talked into a junior college to start. I really think he might follow through this time."

"I love a man with a tool belt." Dave flashed her a grin.

Another wave of guests entered the lobby, breaking up any further conversation, which was totally fine by Tabitha. She let Dave take care of checking them in and returned to her office to complete the food order for next week.

Seth might have been trying to get his act together, but the fact of the matter was this was his last chance to make a change. Tabitha had saved his bacon for the last time. Getting him out of his latest bout of trouble had cost her dearly, and now she found herself an unwilling partner to her ex's less-than-legal business dealings. Joey had been Seth's friend first. Tabitha had hooked up with him because wherever Seth was, Joey wasn't too far behind, and he'd been truly charming in the beginning. Well, charming in that dangerous bad-boy way that inevitably curled Tabitha's toes.

If she could go back and do it all over again, she would have taken Seth and left Boise in their wake before either of them could fall prey to that bastard. Hindsight was certainly twenty/twenty, but no amount of coulda, woulda, shouldas would change the fact that she'd found herself in a situation that was becoming more inescapable by the day.

Tabitha settled in at her desk and opened a browser

window on her computer. Her fingers hovered over
the keyboard, the cursor flashing in the Google
search bar. The keys clicked as she typed: FBI, Boise,
Idaho. Her pinky paused before clicking Enter. Did
the FBI even deal with guys like Joey? She hit the
backspace and typed: Boise Police Department, narcotics,
and clicked the first search result, City of Boise,
BANDIT Narcotics Vice Unit.

How many times had she stared at this phone
number on her screen? Tabitha's hands began to
shake and she twined her fingers together to keep
them still. One phone call shouldn't have been so
hard to make—after all, she'd done it before in the
interest of protecting her brother—but it was Joey's
promise to bring Seth down with him that kept her
from dialing the phone. Empty threats weren't
Joey's style. No, the asshole had tremendous follow-
through. Both Seth and Tabitha knew that he had
enough evidence gathered against her brother to
put him in jail for a good decade at least. Joey was
one of those rare sleazeballs who actually had brains
enough to keep himself out of trouble.

By getting others to do his dirty work for him, he
reaped all of the benefits of being a slimy criminal
while keeping his hands marginally clean at the
same time. It was Seth's bad luck that he'd trusted
Joey, and Tabitha's own stupidity that she'd turned
a blind eye to what he was doing until it was too
late. Despite her kicking him to the curb, Joey was
a permanent fixture in her life. He wouldn't let
her quit her job, and unless she wanted to see her
brother thrown in prison, she had no choice but to
let him use the hotel as a front for his dealers to sell
their drugs.

Not exactly the life she'd imagined for herself.

Closing the browser window, Tabitha clicked the icon for the hotel's Nightvision property management software and typed in the name Damien Evans. His reservation information popped up and Tabitha scanned the information he'd provided. Well, he'd rented a single. No additional guests, so he was presumably unattached. She hadn't noticed a ring, anyway. He'd given a California address so definitely not local, and he hadn't used a company credit card so he probably wasn't traveling on business.

"Trouble," Tabitha reminded herself as she exited Nightvision to focus on the food order. Damien might have been the embodiment of her perfect man, but the trouble Joey had brought into her life was more than enough proof that she needed to lay off of bad boys for good. She let out a derisive snort. At the rate she was going, she wasn't going to be *laying* anyone anytime soon. The past year of celibacy hadn't been too bad. No man? No problem. One less complication in her life. She needed to focus on finishing school, anyway, and getting Seth on the straight and narrow for good. Tabitha didn't have time for a relationship right now.

"Tabs?" Dave poked his head into her office. "Do you have a sec? Night audit accidentally double-booked a room and neither of the guests is willing to take a double instead of the suite."

She'd take trauma victims and sick kids any day over angry hotel guests. Though if Joey got his way, it wouldn't matter if she was an RN or not, she'd never get the opportunity to put the degree to use. "Yeah, I'll be right there." No use worrying about something that she couldn't change. At least not yet, anyway.

Angry guests might not have been her idea of a pleasurable distraction, but at least she wouldn't be worrying about Joey. Or the tattooed bad boy she couldn't seem to get out of her head.